Richard Wright

Richard Wright was born near Natchez, Mississippi, in 1908. As a child he lived in Memphis, Tennessee, then in an orphanage, and with various relatives. He left home at fifteen and returned to Memphis for two years to work, and in 1934 went to Chicago, where in 1935 he began to work on the Federal Writers' Project. He published *Uncle Tom's Children* in 1938 and was awarded a Guggenheim Fellowship in the following year. His other titles include his autobiography, *Black Boy* (1945), and *The Outsider* (1953). After the war Richard Wright went to live in Paris with his wife and daughters, remaining there until his death in 1960.

RICHARD WRIGHT

Native Son
With an introduction
by the author

PICADOR *Classics*
Published by Pan Books

First published in Great Britain 1940 by
Victor Gollancz
This Picador Classics edition published 1990 by
Pan Books Ltd, Cavaye Place, London SW10 9PG
9 8 7 6 5 4 3 2 1
© The Estate of Richard Wright 1940
ISBN 0 330 31312 6
Printed and bound in Great Britain by
Richard Clay Ltd, Bungay, Suffolk

To My Mother

*who, when I was a child at her knee, taught
me to revere the fanciful and the imaginative*

CONTENTS

INTRODUCTION: How 'Bigger' Was Born,
by Richard Wright   9

BOOK ONE   41

BOOK TWO   135

BOOK THREE   311

INTRODUCTION

How 'Bigger' was born

By Richard Wright

I AM not so pretentious as to imagine that it is possible for me to account completely for my own book, *Native Son*. But I am going to try to account for as much of it as I can, the sources of it, the material that went into it, and my own years' long changing attitude toward that material.

In a fundamental sense, an imaginative novel represents the merging of two extremes; it is an intensively intimate expression on the part of a consciousness couched in terms of the most objective and commonly known events. It is at once something private and public by its very nature and texture. Confounding the author who is trying to lay his cards on the table is the dogging knowledge that his imagination is a kind of community medium of exchange: what he has read, felt, thought, seen, and remembered is translated into extensions as impersonal as a worn dollar bill.

The more closely the author thinks of why he wrote, the more he comes to regard his imagination as a kind of self-generating cement which glues his facts together, and his emotions as a kind of dark and obscure designer of those facts. Always there is something that is just beyond the tip of the tongue that could explain it all. Usually, he ends up by discussing something far afield, an act which incites skepticism and suspicion in those anxious for a straight-out explanation.

Yet the author is eager to explain. But the moment he makes the attempt his words falter, for he is confronted and defied by the inexplicable array of his own emotions. Emotions are subjective and he can communicate them only when he clothes them in objective guise; and how can he ever be so arrogant as to know when he is dressing up the right emotion in the right

9

Sunday suit? He is always left with the uneasy notion that maybe *any* objective drapery is as good as *any* other for any emotion.

And the moment he does dress up an emotion, his mind is confronted with the riddle of that 'dressed up' emotion, and he is left peering with eager dismay back into the dim reaches of his own incommunicable life. Reluctantly, he comes to the conclusion that to account for his book is to account for his life, and he knows that that is impossible. Yet, some curious, wayward motive urges him to supply the answer, for there is the feeling that his dignity as a living being is challenged by something within him that is not understood.

So, at the outset, I say frankly that there are phases of *Native Son* which I shall make no attempt to account for. There are meanings in my book of which I was not aware until they literally spilled out upon the paper. I shall sketch the outline of how I *consciously* came into possession of the materials that went into *Native Son*, but there will be many things I shall omit, not because I want to, but simply because I don't know them.

The birth of Bigger Thomas goes back to my childhood, and there was not just one Bigger, but many of them, more than I could count and more than you suspect. But let me start with the first Bigger, whom I shall call Bigger No. 1.

When I was a bareheaded, barefoot kid in Jackson, Mississippi, there was a boy who terrorized me and all of the boys I played with. If we were playing games, he would saunter up and snatch from us our balls, bats, spinning tops, and marbles. We would stand around pouting, sniffling, trying to keep back our tears, begging for our playthings. But Bigger would refuse. We never demanded that he give them back; we were afraid, and Bigger was bad. We had seen him clout boys when he was angry and we did not want to run that risk. We never recovered our toys unless we flattered him and made him feel that he was superior to us. Then, perhaps, if he felt like it, he condescended, threw them at us and then gave each of us a swift kick in the bargain, just to make us feel his utter contempt.

That was the way Bigger No. 1 lived. His life was a continuous challenge to others. At all times he *took* his way, right or wrong, and those who contradicted him had him to fight. And never was he happier than when he had someone cornered and at his mercy; it seemed that the deepest meaning of his squalid life was in him at such times.

I don't know what the fate of Bigger No. 1 was. His swaggering personality is swallowed up somewhere in the amnesia of my childhood. But I suspect that his end was violent. Anyway, he left a marked impression upon me; maybe it was because I longed secretly to be like him and was afraid. I don't know.

If I had known only one Bigger I would not have written *Native Son*. Let me call the next one Bigger No. 2; he was about seventeen and tougher than the first Bigger. Since I, too, had grown older, I was a little less afraid of him. And the hardness of this Bigger No. 2 was not directed toward me or the other Negroes, but toward the whites who ruled the South. He bought clothes and food on credit and would not pay for them. He lived in the dingy shacks of the white landlords and refused to pay rent. Of course, he had no money, but neither did we. We did without the necessities of life and starved ourselves, but he never would. When we asked him why he acted as he did, he would tell us (as though we were little children in a kindergarten) that the white folks had everything and he had nothing. Further, he would tell us that we were fools not to get what we wanted while we were alive in this world. We would listen and silently agree. We longed to believe and act as he did, but we were afraid. We were Southern Negroes and we were hungry and we wanted to live, but we were more willing to tighten our belts than risk conflict. Bigger No. 2 wanted to live and he did; he was in prison the last time I heard from him.

There was Bigger No. 3, whom the white folks called a 'bad nigger'. He carried his life in his hands in a literal fashion. I once worked as a ticket-taker in a Negro movie house (all movie houses in Dixie are Jim Crow; there are movies for whites and movies for blacks), and many times Bigger No. 3 came to the door and gave my arm a hard pinch and walked into the theater. Resentfully and silently, I'd nurse my bruised arm. Presently, the proprietor would come over and ask how things were going. I'd point into the darkened theater and say: 'Bigger's in there.' 'Did he pay?' the proprietor would ask. 'No, sir,' I'd answer. The proprietor would pull down the corners of his lips and speak through his teeth: 'We'll kill that goddamn nigger one of these days.' And the episode would end right there. But later on Bigger No. 3 was killed during the days of Prohibition: while delivering liquor to a customer he was shot through the back by a white cop.

And then there was Bigger No. 4, whose only law was death. The Jim Crow laws of the South were not for him. But as he laughed and cursed and broke them, he knew that some day he'd have to pay for his freedom. His rebellious spirit made him violate all the taboos and consequently he always oscillated between moods of intense elation and depression. He was never happier than when he had outwitted some foolish custom, and he was never more melancholy than when brooding over the impossibility of his ever being free. He had no job, for he regarded digging ditches for fifty cents a day as slavery. 'I can't live on that', he would say. Ofttimes I'd find him reading a book; he would stop and in a joking, wistful, and cynical manner ape the antics of the white folks. Generally, he'd end his mimicry in a depressed state and say: 'The white folks won't let us do nothing.' Bigger No. 4 was sent to the asylum for the insane.

Then there was Bigger No. 5, who always rode the Jim Crow streetcars without paying and sat wherever he pleased. I remember one morning his getting into a streetcar (all streetcars in Dixie are divided into two sections: one section is for whites and is labeled – FOR WHITES; the other section is for Negroes and is labeled – FOR COLORED) and sitting in the white section. The conductor went to him and said: 'Come on, nigger. Move over where you belong. Can't you read?' Bigger answered: 'Naw, I can't read.' The conductor flared up: 'Get out of that seat!' Bigger took out his knife, opened it, held it nonchalantly in his hand and replied: 'Make me.' The conductor turned red, blinked, clenched his fists, and walked away, stammering:

'The goddamn scum of the earth!' A small angry conference of white men took place in the front of the car and the Negroes sitting in the Jim Crow section overhead: 'That's that Bigger Thomas nigger and you'd better leave 'im alone.' The Negroes experienced an intense flash of pride and the streetcar moved on its journey without incident. I don't know what happened to Bigger No. 5. But I can guess.

The Bigger Thomases were the only Negroes I know of who consistently violated the Jim Crow laws of the South and got away with it, at least for a sweet brief spell. Eventually, the whites who restricted their lives made them pay a terrible price. They were shot, hanged, maimed, lynched, and generally hounded until they were either dead or their spirits broken.

There were many variations to this behavioristic pattern. Later on I encountered other Bigger Thomases who did not react to the locked-in Black Belts with the same extremity and violence. But before I use Bigger Thomas as a springboard for the examination of milder types, I'd better indicate more precisely the nature of the environment that produced these men, or the reader will be left with the impression that they were essentially and organically bad.

In Dixie there are two worlds, the white world and the black world, and they are physically separated. There are white schools and black schools, white churches and black churches, white businesses and black businesses, white graveyards and black graveyards, and, for all I know, a white God and a black God . . .

This separation was accomplished after the Civil War by the terror of the Ku Klux Klan, which swept the newly freed Negro through arson, pillage, and death out of the United States Senate, the House of Representatives, the many state legislatures, and out of the public, social, and economic life of the South. The motive for this assault was simple and urgent. The imperialistic tug of history had torn the Negro from his African home and had placed him ironically upon the most fertile plantation areas of the South; and, when the Negro was freed, he outnumbered the whites in many of these fertile areas.

Hence, a fierce and bitter struggle took place to keep the ballot from the Negro, for had he had a chance to vote, he would have automatically controlled the richest lands of the South and with them the social, political, and economic destiny of a third of the Republic. Though the South is politically a part of America, the problem that faced her was peculiar and the struggle between the whites and the blacks after the Civil War was in essence a struggle for power, ranging over thirteen states and involving the lives of tens of millions of people.

But keeping the ballot from the Negro was not enough to hold him in check; disfranchisement had to be supplemented by a whole panoply of rules, taboos, and penalties designed not only to insure peace (complete submission) but to guarantee that no real threat would ever arise. Had the Negro lived upon a common territory, separate from the bulk of the white population, this program of oppression might not have assumed such a brutal and violent form. But this war took place between people who were neighbors, whose homes adjoined, whose farms had common boundaries. Guns and disfranchisement, therefore, were not enough to make the black neighbor keep his distance. The white neighbor decided to limit the amount of education his black neighbor could receive; decided to keep him off the police force and out of the local national guards; to segregate him residentially; to Jim Crow him in public places; to restrict his participation in the professions and jobs; and to build up a vast, dense ideology of racial superiority that would justify any act of violence taken against him to defend white dominance; and further, to condition him to hope for little and to receive that little without rebelling.

But, because the blacks were so *close* to the very civilization which sought to keep them out, because they could not *help* but react in some way to its incentives and prizes, and because the very tissue of their consciousness received its tone and timbre from the strivings of that dominant civilization, oppression spawned among them a myriad variety of reactions, reaching from outright blind rebellion to a sweet, other-worldly submissiveness.

In the main, this delicately balanced state of affairs has not greatly altered since the Civil War, save in those parts of the South which have been industrialized or urbanized. So volatile and tense are these relations that if a Negro rebels against rule and taboo, he is lynched and the reason for the lynching is usually called 'rape', that catchword which has garnered such vile connotations that it can raise a mob anywhere in the South pretty quickly, even today.

Now for the variations in the Bigger Thomas pattern. Some of the Negroes living under these conditions got religion, felt that Jesus would redeem the void of living; felt that the more bitter life was in the present the happier it would be in the hereafter. Others, clinging still to that brief glimpse of post-Civil War freedom, employed a thousand ruses and stratagems of struggle to win their rights. Still others projected their hurts and longings into more naïve and mundane forms – blues, jazz, swing – and, without intellectual guidance, tried to build up a compensatory nourishment for themselves. Many labored under hot suns and then killed the restless ache with alcohol. Then there were those who strove for an education, and when they got it, enjoyed the financial fruits of it in the style of their bourgeois oppressors. Usually they went hand in hand with the powerful whites and helped to keep their groaning brothers in line, for that was the safest course of action. Those who did this called themselves 'leaders'. To give you an idea of how completely these 'leaders' worked with those who oppressed, I can tell you that I lived the first seventeen years of my life in the South without so much as hearing of or seeing one act of rebellion from *any* Negro, save the Bigger Thomases.

But why did Bigger revolt? No explanation based upon a hard and fast rule of conduct can be given. But there were always two factors psychologically dominant in his personality. First, through some quirk of circumstance, he had become estranged from the religion and the folk culture of his race. Second, he was trying to react to and answer the call of the dominant civilization whose glitter came to him through the newspapers, magazines, radios, movies, and the mere imposing sight and sound of daily American life. In many respects his emergence as a distinct type was inevitable.

As I grew older, I became familiar with the Bigger Thomas conditioning and its numerous shadings no matter where I saw it in Negro life. It was not, as I have already said, as blatant or extreme as in the originals; but it was there, nevertheless, like an underdeveloped negative.

Sometimes, in areas far removed from Mississippi, I'd hear a Negro say: 'I wish I didn't have to live this way. I feel like I want to burst.' Then the anger would pass; he would go back to his job and try to eke out a few pennies to support his wife and children.

Sometimes I'd hear a Negro say: 'God, I wish I had a flag and a country of my own.' But that mood would soon vanish and he would go his way placidly enough.

Sometimes I'd hear a Negro ex-soldier say: 'What in hell did I fight in the war for? They segregated me even when I was offering my life for my country.' But he, too, like the others, would soon forget, would become caught up in the tense grind of struggling for bread.

I've even heard Negroes, in moments of anger and bitterness, praise what Japan is doing in China, not because they believed in oppression (being objects of oppression themselves), but because they would suddenly sense how empty their lives were when looking at the dark faces of Japanese generals in the roto-gravure supplements of the Sunday newspapers. They would dream of what it would be like to live in a country where they could forget their color and play a responsible role in the vital processes of the nation's life.

I've even heard Negroes say that maybe Hitler and Mussolini are all right; that maybe Stalin is all right. They did not say this out of any intellectual comprehension of the forces at work in the world, but because they felt that these men 'did things', a phrase which is charged with more meaning than the mere words imply. There was in the back of their minds, when they said this, a wild and intense longing (wild and intense because it was suppressed!) to belong, to be identified, to feel that they

16

were alive as other people were, to be caught up forgetfully and exultingly in the swing of events, to feel the clean, deep, organic satisfaction of doing a job in common with others.

It was not until I went to live in Chicago that I first thought seriously of writing of Bigger Thomas. Two items of my experience combined to make me aware of Bigger as a meaningful and prophetic symbol. First, being free of the daily pressure of the Dixie environment, I was able to come into possession of my own feelings. Second, my contact with the labor movement and its ideology made me see Bigger clearly and feel what he meant.

I made the discovery that Bigger Thomas was not black all the time; he was white, too, and there were literally millions of him, everywhere. The extension of my sense of the personality of Bigger was the pivot of my life; it altered the complexion of my existence. I became conscious, at first dimly, and then later on with increasing clarity and conviction, of a vast, muddied pool of human life in America. It was as though I had put on a pair of spectacles whose power was that of an x-ray enabling me to see deeper into the lives of men. Wherever I picked up a newspaper, I'd no longer feel that I was reading the doings of whites alone (Negroes are rarely mentioned in the press unless they've committed some crime!), but of a complex struggle for life going on in my country, a struggle in which I was involved. I sensed, too, that the Southern scheme of oppression was but an appendage of a far vaster and in many respects more ruthless and impersonal commodity-profit machine.

Trade-union struggles and issues began to grow meaningful to me. The flow of goods across the seas, buoying and depressing the wages of men, held a fascination. The pronouncements of foreign governments, their policies, plans, and acts were calculated and weighted in relation to the lives of people about me. I was literally overwhelmed when, in reading the works of Russian revolutionists, I came across descriptions of the 'holiday energies of the masses', 'the locomotives of history', 'the conditions prerequisite for revolution', and so forth. I approached all of these new revelations in the light of Bigger Thomas, his hopes, fears, and despairs; and I began to feel far-flung kinships, and sense, with fright and abashment, the possibilities of *alliances* between the American Negro and other people possessing a kindred consciousness.

As my mind extended in this general and abstract manner, it was fed with even more vivid and concrete examples of the lives of Bigger Thomas. The urban environment of Chicago, affording a more stimulating life, made the Negro Bigger Thomases react more violently than even in the South. More than ever I began to see and understand the environmental factors which made for this extreme conduct. It was not that Chicago segregated Negroes more than the South, but that Chicago had more to offer, that Chicago's physical aspect – noisy, crowded, filled with the sense of power and fulfillment – did so much more to dazzle the mind with a taunting sense of possible achievement that the segregation it did impose brought forth from Bigger a reaction more obstreperous than in the South.

So the concrete picture and the abstract linkages of relationships fed each other, each making the other more meaningful and affording my emotions an opportunity to react to them with success and understanding. The process was like a swinging pendulum, each to and fro motion throwing up its tiny bit of meaning and significance, each stroke helping to develop the dim negative which had been implanted in my mind in the South.

During this period the shadings and nuances which were filling in Bigger's picture came, not so much from Negro life, as from the lives of whites I met and grew to know. I began to sense that they had their own kind of Bigger Thomas behavioristic pattern which grew out of a more subtle and broader frustration. The waves of recurring crime, the silly fads and crazes, the quicksilver changes in public taste, the hysteria and fears – all of these had long been mysteries to me. But now I looked back of them and felt the pinch and pressure of the environment that gave them their pitch and peculiar kind of being. I began to feel with my mind the inner tensions of the people I met. I don't mean to say that I think that environment *makes* consciousness (I suppose God makes that, if there is a God), but I do say that I felt and still feel that the environment supplies the instrumentalities through which the organism expresses itself, and if that environment is warped or tranquil, the mode and manner of behavior will be affected toward deadlocking tensions or orderly fulfilment and satisfaction.

Let me give examples of how I began to develop the dim negative of Bigger. I met white writers who talked of their responses, who told me how whites reacted to this lurid American scene. And, as they talked, I'd translate what they said in terms of Bigger's life. But what was more important still, I read their novels. Here, for the first time, I found ways and techniques of gauging meaningfully the effects of American civilization upon the personalities of people. I took these techniques, these ways of seeing and feeling, and twisted them, bent them, adapted them, until they became *my* ways of apprehending the locked-in life of the Black Belt areas. This association with white writers was the life preserver of my hope to depict Negro life in fiction, for my race possessed no fictional works dealing with such problems, had no background in such sharp and critical testing of experience, no novels that went with a deep and fearless will down to the dark roots of life.

Here are examples of how I culled the information relating to Bigger from my reading:

There is in me a memory of reading an interesting pamphlet telling of the friendship of Gorky and Lenin in exile. The booklet told of how Lenin and Gorky were walking down a London street. Lenin turned to Gorky and, pointing, said: 'Here is *their* Big Ben.' 'There is *their* Westminster Abbey.' 'There is *their* library.' And at once, while reading that passage, my mind stopped, teased, challenged with the effort to remember, to associate widely disparate but meaningful experiences in my life. For a moment nothing would come, but I remained convinced that I had heard the meaning of those words sometime, somewhere before. Then, with a sudden glow of satisfaction of having gained a little more knowledge about the world in which I lived, I'd end up by saying: 'That's Bigger. That's the Bigger Thomas reaction.'

In both instances the deep sense of exclusion was identical.

The feeling of looking at things with a painful and unwarrantable nakedness was an experience, I learned, that transcended national and racial boundaries. It was this intolerable sense of feeling and understanding so much, and yet living on a plane of social reality where the look of a world which one did not make or own struck one with a blinding objectivity and tangibility, that made me grasp the revolutionary impulse in my life and the lives of those about me and far away.

I remember reading a passage in a book dealing with old Russia which said: 'We must be ready to make endless sacrifices if we are to be able to overthrow the Czar.' And again I'd say to myself: 'I've heard that somewhere, sometime before.' And again I'd hear Bigger Thomas, far away and long ago, telling some white man who was trying to impose upon him: 'I'll kill you and go to hell and pay for it.' While living in America I heard from far away Russia the bitter accents of tragic calculation of how much human life and suffering it would cost a man to live as a man in a world that denied him the right to live with dignity. Actions and feelings of men ten thousand miles from home helped me to understand the moods and the impulses of those walking the streets of Chicago and Dixie.

I am not saying that I heard any talk of revolution in the South when I was a kid there. But I did hear the lispings, the whispers, the mutters which some day, under one stimulus or another, will surely grow into open revolt unless the conditions which produce Bigger Thomases are changed.

In 1932 another source of information was dramatically opened up to me and I saw data of a surprising nature that helped to clarify the personality of Bigger. From the moment that Hitler took power in Germany and began to oppress the Jews, I tried to keep track of what was happening. And on innumerable occasions I was startled to detect, either from the side of the Fascists or from the side of the oppressed, reactions, moods, phrases, attitudes that reminded me strongly of Bigger, that helped to bring out more clearly the shadowy outlines of the negative that lay in the back of my mind.

I read every account of the Fascist movement in Germany I could lay my hands on, and from page to page I encountered and recognized familiar emotional patterns. What struck me with particular force was the Nazi preoccupation with the construction of a society in which there would exist among all people (*German* people, of course!) *one* solidarity of ideals, *one* continuous circulation of fundamental beliefs, notions, and assumptions. I am not now speaking of the popular idea of regimenting people's thought; I'm speaking of the implicit, almost unconscious, or pre-conscious, assumptions and ideals upon which whole nations and races act and live. And while reading these Nazi pages I'd be reminded of the Negro preacher in the South telling of a life beyond this world, a life in which the color of men's skins would not matter, a life in which each man would know what was deep down in the hearts of his fellow man. And I could hear Bigger Thomas standing on a street corner in America expressing his agonizing doubts and chronic suspicions, thus: 'I ain't going to trust nobody. Everything is a racket and everybody is out to get what he can for himself. Maybe if we had a true leader, we could do something.' And I'd know that I was still on the track of learning about Bigger, still in the midst of the modern struggle for solidarity among men.

When the Nazis spoke of the necessity of a highly ritualized and symbolized life, I could hear Bigger Thomas on Chicago's South Side saying: 'Man, what we need is a leader like Marcus Garvey. We need a nation, a flag, an army of our own. We colored folks ought to organize into groups and have generals, captains, lieutenants, and so forth. We ought to take Africa and have a national home.' I'd know, while listening to these childish words, that a white man would smile derisively at them. But I could not smile, for I knew the truth of those simple words from the facts of my own life. The deeper hunger in those childish ideas was like a flash of lightning illuminating the whole dark inner landscape of Bigger's mind. Those words told me that the civilization which had given birth to Bigger contained no spiritual sustenance, had created no culture which could hold and claim his allegiance and faith, had sensitized him and had left him stranded, a free agent to roam the streets of our cities, a hot and whirling vortex of undisciplined and unchannelized impulses. The results of these observations made me feel more than ever estranged from the civilization in which I lived, and more than ever resolved toward the task of creating with words a scheme of images and symbols whose direction could enlist the sympathies, loyalties, and yearnings of the millions of Bigger Thomases in every land and race ...

But more than anything else, as a writer, I was fascinated by the similarity of the emotional tensions of Bigger in America and Bigger in Nazi Germany and Bigger in old Russia. All Bigger Thomases, white and black, felt tense, afraid, nervous, hysterical, and restless. From far away Nazi Germany and old Russia had come to me items of knowledge that told me that certain modern experiences were creating types of personalities whose existence ignored racial and national lines of demarcation, that these personalities carried with them a more universal drama-element than anything I'd ever encountered before; that these personalities were mainly imposed upon men and women living in a world whose fundamental assumptions could no longer be taken for granted: a world ridden with national and class strife; a world whose metaphysical meanings had vanished; a world in which God no longer existed as a daily focal point of men's lives; a world in which men could no longer retain their faith in an ultimate hereafter. It was a highly geared world whose nature was conflict and action, a world whose limited area and vision imperiously urged men to satisfy their organisms, a world that existed on a plane of animal sensation alone.

It was a world in which millions of men lived and behaved like drunkards, taking a stiff drink of hard life to lift them up for a thrilling moment, to give them a quivering sense of wild exultation and fulfillment that soon faded and let them down. Eagerly they took another drink, wanting to avoid the dull, flat look of things, then still another, this time stronger, and then they felt that their lives had meaning. Speaking figuratively, they were soon chronic alcoholics, men who lived by violence, through extreme action and sensation, through drowning daily in a perpetual nervous agitation.

From these items I drew my first political conclusions about Bigger: I felt that Bigger, an American product, a native son of this land, carried within him the potentialities of either Communism or Fascism. I don't mean to say that the Negro boy I depicted in *Native Son* is either a Communist or a Fascist. He is not either. But he is a product of a dislocated society; he is a dispossessed and disinherited man; he is all of this, and he lives amid the greatest possible plenty on earth and he is looking and feeling for a way out. Whether he'll follow some gaudy, hysterical leader who'll promise rashly to fill the void in him, or whether he'll come to an understanding with the millions of his kindred fellow workers under trade-union or revolutionary guidance depends upon the future drift of events in America. But, granting the emotional state, the tensity, the fear, the hate, the impatience, the sense of exclusion, the ache for violent action, the emotional and cultural hunger, Bigger Thomas, conditioned as his organism is, will not become an ardent, or even a lukewarm, supporter of the *status quo*.

The difference between Bigger's tensity and the German variety is that Bigger's, due to America's educational restrictions on the bulk of her Negro population, is in a nascent state, not yet articulate. And the difference between Bigger's longing for self-identification and the Russian principle of self-determination is that Bigger's, due to the effects of American oppression, which has not allowed for the forming of deep ideas of solidarity among Negroes, is still in a state of individual anger and hatred. Here, I felt, was *drama*! Who will be the first to touch off these Bigger Thomases in America, white and black?

For a long time I toyed with the idea of writing a novel in which a Negro Bigger Thomas would loom as a symbolic figure of American life, a figure who would hold within him the prophecy of our future. I felt strongly that he held within him, in a measure which perhaps no other contemporary type did, the outlines of action and feeling which we would encounter on a vast scale and in the days to come. Just as one sees when one walks into a medical research laboratory jars of alcohol containing abnormally large or distorted portions of the human body, just so did I see and feel that the conditions of life under which Negroes are forced to live in America contain the embryonic emotional prefigurations of how a large part of the body politic would react under stress.

So, with this much knowledge of myself and the world gained and known, why should I not try to work out on paper the problem of what will happen to Bigger? Why should I not, like a scientist in a laboratory, use my imagination and invent test-tube situations, place Bigger in them, and, following the guidance of my own hopes and fears, what I had learned and remembered, work out in fictional form an emotional statement and resolution of this problem?

But several things militated against my starting to work. Like Bigger himself, I felt a mental censor – product of the fears which a Negro feels from living in America – standing over me, draped in white, warning me not to write. This censor's warnings were translated into my own thought processes thus: 'What will white people think if I draw the picture of such a Negro boy? Will they not at once say: "See, didn't we tell you all along that niggers are like that? Now, look, one of their own kind has come along and drawn the picture for us!" ' I felt that if I drew the picture of Bigger truthfully, there would be many reactionary whites who would try to make of him something I did not intend. And yet, and this was what made it difficult, I knew that I could not write of Bigger convincingly if I did not depict him as he *was*: that is, resentful toward whites, sullen, angry, ignorant, emotionally unstable, depressed and unaccountably elated at times, and unstable even, because of his own lack of inner organization which American oppression has fostered in him, to unite with the members of his own race. And would not whites misread Bigger and, doubting his authenticity, say: 'This man is preaching hate against the whole white race'?

The more I thought of it the more I became convinced that if

I did not write of Bigger as I saw and felt him, if I did not try to make him a living personality and at the same time a symbol of all the larger things I felt and saw in him, I'd be reacting as Bigger himself reacted: that is, I'd be acting out of *fear* if I let what I thought whites would say constrict and paralyze me.

As I contemplated Bigger and what he meant, I said to myself: 'I must write this novel, not only for others to read, but to free *myself* of this sense of shame and fear.' In fact, the novel, as time passed, grew upon me to the extent that it became a necessity to write it; the writing of it turned into a way of living for me.

Another thought kept me from writing. What would my own white and black comrades in the Communist party say? This thought was the most bewildering of all. Politics is a hard and narrow game; its policies represent the aggregate desires and aspirations of millions of people. Its goals are rigid and simply drawn, and the minds of the majority of politicians are set, congealed in terms of daily tactical maneuvers. How could I create such complex and wide schemes of associational thought and feeling, such filigreed webs of dreams and politics, without being mistaken for a 'smuggler of reaction', 'an ideological confusionist', or 'an individualistic and dangerous element'? Though my heart is with the collectivist and proletarian ideal, I solved this problem by assuring myself that honest politics and honest feeling in imaginative repesentation ought to be able to meet on common healthy ground without fear, suspicion, and quarreling. Further, and more importantly, I steeled myself by coming to the conclusion that whether politicians accepted or rejected Bigger did not really matter; my task, as I felt it, was to free myself of this burden of impressions and feelings, recast them into the image of Bigger and make him *true*. Lastly, I felt that a right more immediately deeper than that of politics or race was at stake; that is, a *human* right, the right of a man to think and feel honestly. And especially did this personal and human right bear hard upon me, for temperamentally I am inclined to satisfy the claims of my own ideals rather than the expectations of others. It was this obscure need that had pulled me into the labor movement in the beginning and by exercising it I was but fulfilling what I felt to be the laws of my own growth.

There was another constricting thought that kept me from work. It deals with my own race. I asked myself: 'What will Negro doctors, lawyers, dentists, bankers, school teachers, social workers and business men, think of me if I draw such a picture of Bigger?' I knew from long and painful experience that the Negro middle and professional classes were the people of my own race who were more than others ashamed of Bigger and what he meant. Having narrowly escaped the Bigger Thomas reaction pattern themselves – indeed, still retaining traces of it within the confines of their own timid personalities – they would not relish being publicly reminded of the lowly, shameful depths of life above which they enjoyed their bourgeois lives. Never did they want people, especially *white* people, to think that their lives were so much touched by anything so dark and brutal as Bigger.

Their attitude toward life and art can be summed up in a single paragraph: 'But, Mr Wright, there are so many of us who are *not* like Bigger. Why don't you portray in your fiction the *best* traits of our race, something that will show the white people what we have done in *spite* of oppression? Don't represent anger and bitterness. Smile when a white person comes to you. Never let him feel that you are so small that what he had done to crush you has made you hate him! Oh, above all, save your *pride*!'

But Bigger won over all these claims; he won because I felt that I was hunting on the trail of more exciting and thrilling game. What Bigger meant had claimed me because I felt with all of my being that he was more important than what any person, white or black, would say or try to make of him, more important than any political analysis designed to explain or deny him, more important, even, than my own sense of fear, shame, and diffidence.

But Bigger was still not down upon paper. For a long time I had been writing of him in my mind, but I had yet to put him into an image, a breathing symbol draped out in the guise of the only form of life my native land had allowed me to know intimately, that is, the ghetto life of the American Negro. But the basic reason for my hesitancy was that another and far more complex problem had risen to plague me. Bigger, as I saw and felt him, was a snarl of many realities; he had in him many levels of life.

First, there was his personal and private life, that intimate existence that is so difficult to snare and nail down in fiction, that elusive core of being, that individual data of consciousness which in every man and woman is like that in no other. I had to deal with Bigger's dreams, his fleeting, momentary sensations, his yearning, visions, his deep emotional responses. Then I was confronted with that part of him that was dual in aspect, dim, wavering, that part of him which is so much a part of *all* Negroes and *all* whites that I realized that I could put it down upon paper only by feeling out its meaning first within the confines of my own life. Bigger was attracted and repelled by the American scene. He was an American, because he was a native son; but he was also a Negro nationalist in a vague sense because he was not allowed to live as an American. Such was his way of life and mine; neither Bigger nor I resided fully in either camp.

Of this dual aspect of Bigger's social consciousness, I placed the nationalistic side first, not because I agreed with Bigger's wild and intense hatred of white people, but because his hate had placed him, like a wild animal at bay, in a position where he was most symbolic and explainable. In other words, his nationalist complex was for me a concept through which I could grasp more of the total meaning of his life than I could in any other way. I tried to approach Bigger's *snarled* and *confused* nationalist feelings with *conscious* and *informed* ones of my own. Yet, Bigger was not nationalist enough to feel the need of religion or the folk culture of his own people. What made Bigger's social consciousness most complex was the fact that he was hovering unwanted between two worlds – between powerful America and his own stunted place in life – and I took upon myself the task of trying to make the reader feel this No Man's Land. The most that I could say of Bigger was that he felt the *need* for a whole life and *acted* out of that need; that was all.

Above and beyond all this, there was that American part of Bigger which is the heritage of us all, that part of him which we get from our seeing and hearing, from school, from the hopes and dreams of our friends; that part of him which the common people of America never talk of but take for granted. Among millions of people the deepest convictions of life are never discussed openly; they are felt, implied, hinted at tacitly and obliquely in their hopes and fears. We live by an idealism that makes us believe that the Constitution is a good document of government, that the Bill of Rights is a good legal and humane principle to safeguard our civil liberties, that every man and woman should have the opportunity to realize himself, to seek his own individual fate and goal, his own peculiar and untranslatable destiny. I don't say that Bigger knew this in the terms in which I'm speaking of it; I don't say that any such thought ever entered his head. His emotional and intellectual life was never that articulate. But he knew it emotionally, intuitively, for his emotions and his desires were developed, and he caught it, as most of us do, from the mental and emotional climate of our time. Bigger had all of this in him, dammed up, buried, implied, and I had to develop it in fictional form.

There was still another level of Bigger's life that I felt bound to account for and render, a level as elusive to discuss as it was to grasp in writing. Here again, I had to fall back upon my own feelings as a guide, for Bigger did not offer in his life any articulate verbal explanations. There seems to hover somewhere in that dark part of all our lives, in some more than in others, an objectless, timeless, spaceless element of primal fear and dread, stemming, perhaps, from our birth (depending upon whether one's outlook upon personality is Freudian or non-Freudian!), a fear and dread which exercises an impelling influence upon our lives all out of proportion to its obscurity. And, accompanying this *first fear*, is, for the want of a better name, a reflex urge toward ecstasy, complete submission, and trust. The springs of religion are here, and also the origins of rebellion. And in a boy like Bigger, young, unschooled, whose subjective life was clothed in the tattered rags of American 'culture', this primitive fear and ecstasy were naked, exposed, unprotected by religion or a framework of government or a scheme of society whose final faiths would gain his love and trust; unprotected by trade or profession, faith or belief; opened to every trivial blast of daily or hourly circumstance.

There was yet another level of reality in Bigger's life: the impliedly political. I've already mentioned that Bigger had in him impulses which I had felt were present in the vast upheavals of Russia and Germany. Well, somehow, I had to make these political impulses felt by the reader in terms of Bigger's daily actions, keeping in mind as I did so the probable danger of my being branded as a propagandist by those who would not like the subject matter.

Then there was Bigger's relationship with white America, both North and South, which I had to depict, which I had to make known once again, alas; a relationship whose effects are carried by every Negro, like scars, somewhere in his body and mind.

I had also to show what oppression had done to Bigger's relationships with his own people, how it had split him off from them, how it had baffled him; how oppression seems to hinder and stifle in the victim those very qualities of character which are so essential for an effective struggle against the oppressor.

Then there was the fabulous city in which Bigger lived, an indescribable city, huge, roaring, dirty, noisy, raw, stark, brutal; a city of extremes: torrid summers and sub-zero winters, white people and black people, the English language and strange tongues, foreign born and native born, scabby poverty and gaudy luxury, high idealism and hard cynicism! A city so young that, in thinking of its short history, one's mind, as it travels backward in time, is stopped abruptly by the barren stretches of wind-swept prairie! But a city old enough to have caught within the homes of its long, straight streets the symbols and images of man's age-old destiny, of truths as old as the mountains and seas, of dramas as abiding as the soul of man itself! A city which has become the pivot of the Eastern, Western, Northern, and Southern poles of the nation. But a city whose black smoke clouds shut out the sunshine for seven months of the year; a city in which, on a fine balmy May morning, one can sniff the stench of the stockyards; a city where people have grown so used to gangs and murders and graft that they have honestly forgotten that government can have a pretense of decency!

With all of this thought out, Bigger was still unwritten. Two events, however, came into my life and accelerated the process, made me sit down and actually start work on the typewriter, and just stop the writing of Bigger in my mind as I walked the streets.

The first event was my getting a job in the South Side Boy's Club, an institution which tried to reclaim the thousands of Negro Bigger Thomases from the dives and the alleys of the Black Belt. Here, on a vast scale, I had an opportunity to observe Bigger in all of his moods, actions, haunts. Here I felt for the first time that the rich folk who were paying my wages did not really give a good goddamn about Bigger, that their kindness was prompted at bottom by a selfish motive. They were paying me to distract Bigger with ping-pong, checkers, swimming, marbles, and baseball in order that he might not roam the streets and harm the valuable white property which adjoined the Black Belt. I am not condemning boys' clubs and ping-pong as such; but these little stopgaps were utterly inadequate to fill up the centuries-long chasm of emptiness which American civilization had created in these Biggers. I felt that I was doing a kind of dressed-up police work, and I hated it.

I would work hard with these Biggers, and when it would come time for me to go home I'd say to myself, under my breath so that no one could hear: 'Go to it, boys! Prove to the bastards that gave you these games that life is stronger than ping-pong ... Show them that full-blooded life is harder and hotter than they suspect, even though that life is draped in a black skin which at heart they despise ...'

They did. The police blotters of Chicago are testimony to how *much* they did. That was the only way I could contain myself for doing a job I hated; for a moment I'd allow myself, vicariously, to feel as Bigger felt – not much, just a little, just a *little* – but, still, there it was.

The second event that spurred me to write of Bigger was more personal and subtle. I had written a book of short stories which was published under the title of *Uncle Tom's Children*. When the reviews of that book began to appear, I realized that I had made an awfully naïve mistake. I found that I had written a book which even bankers' daughters could read and weep over and feel good about. I swore to myself that if I wrote another book, no one would weep over it; that it would be so hard and deep that they would have to face it without the consolation of tears. It was this that made me get to work in dead earnest.

Now, until this movement I did not stop to think very much about the plot of *Native Son*. The reason I did not is because I was not for one moment ever worried about it. I had spent years learning about Bigger, what had made him, what he meant; so, when the time came for writing, *what had made him and what he meant* constituted my plot. But the far-flung items of his life had to be couched in imaginative terms, terms known and acceptable to a common body of readers, terms which would, in the course of the story, manipulate the deepest held notions and convictions of their lives. That came easy. The moment I began to write, the plot fell out, so to speak. I'm not trying to oversimplify or make the process seem oversubtle. At bottom, what happened is very easy to explain.

Any Negro who has lived in the North or the South knows that times without number he has heard of some Negro boy being picked up on the streets and carted off to jail and charged with 'rape'. This thing happens so often that to my mind it had become a representative symbol of the Negro's uncertain position in America. Never for a second was I in doubt as to what kind of social reality or dramatic situation I'd put Bigger in, what kind of test-tube life I'd set up to evoke his deepest reactions. Life had made the plot over and over again, to the extent that I knew it by heart. So frequently do these acts recur that when I was halfway through the first draft of *Native Son* a case paralleling Bigger's flared forth in the newspapers of Chicago. (Many of the newspaper items and some of the incidents in *Native Son* are but fictionalized versions of the Robert Nixon case and rewrites of news stories from the *Chicago Tribune*.) Indeed, scarcely was *Native Son* off the press before Supreme Court Justice Hugo L. Black gave the nation a long and vivid account of the American police methods of handling Negro boys.

Let me describe this sterotyped situation: A crime wave is sweeping a city and citizens are clamoring for police action. Squad cars cruise the Black Belt and grab the first Negro boy who seems to be unattached and homeless. He is held for perhaps a week without charge or bail, without the privilege of communicating with anyone, including his own relatives. After a few days this boy 'confesses' anything that he is asked to confess, any crime that handily happens to be unsolved and on the calendar. Why does he confess? After the boy has been grilled night and day, hanged up by his thumbs, dangled by his feet out of twenty-story windows, and beaten (in places that leave no scars – cops have found a way to do that), he signs the papers before him, papers which are usually accompanied by a verbal promise to the boy that he will not go to the electric chair. Of course, he ends up by being executed or sentenced for life. If you think I'm telling tall tales, get chummy with some white cop who works in a Black Belt district and ask him for the lowdown.

When a black boy is carted off to jail in such a fashion, it is almost impossible to do anything for him. Even well-disposed Negro lawyers find it difficult to defend him, for the boy will plead guilty one day and then not guilty the next, according to the degree of pressure and persuasion that is brought to bear upon his frightened personality from one side or the other. Even the boy's own family is scared to death; sometimes fear of police intimidation makes them hesitate to acknowledge that the boy is a blood relation of theirs.

Such has been America's attitude toward these boys that if one is picked up and confronted in a police cell with ten white cops, he is intimidated almost to the point of confessing anything. So far removed are these practices from what the average American citizen encounters in his daily life that it takes a huge act of his imagination to believe that it is true; yet, this same average citizen, with his kindness, his American sportsmanship and good will, would probably act with the mob if a self-respecting Negro family moved into his apartment building to escape the Black Belt and its terrors and limitations . . .

Now, after all of this, when I sat down to the typewriter, I could not work; I could not think of a good opening scene for the book. I had definitely in mind the kind of emotion I wanted to evoke in the reader in that first scene, but I could not think of the type of concrete event that would convey the motif of the entire scheme of the book, that would sound, in varied form, the note that was to be resounded throughout its length, that would introduce to the reader just what kind of an organism Bigger's was and the environment that was bearing hourly upon it. Twenty or thirty times I tried and failed; then I argued that if I could not write the opening scene, I'd start with the scene that followed. I did. The actual writing of the book began with the scene in the pool room.

Now, for the writing. During the years in which I had met all of those Bigger Thomases, those varieties of Bigger Thomases, I had not consciously gathered material to write of them; I had not kept a notebook record of their sayings and doings. Their actions had simply made impressions upon my sensibilities as I lived from day to day, impressions which crystallized and coagulated into clusters and configurations of memory, attitudes, moods, ideas. And these subjective states, in turn, were automatically stored away somewhere in me. I was not even aware of the process. But, excited over the book which I had set myself to write, under the stress of emotion, these things came surging up, tangled, fused, knotted, entertaining me by the sheer variety and potency of their meaning and suggestiveness.

With the whole theme in mind, in an attitude almost akin to prayer, I gave myself up to the story. In an effort to capture some phase of Bigger's life that would not come to me readily, I'd jot down as much of it as I could. Then I'd read it over and over, adding each time a word, a phrase, a sentence until I felt that I had caught all the shadings of reality I felt dimly were there. With each of these rereadings and rewritings it seemed that I'd gather in facts and facets that tried to run away. It was an act of concentration, of trying to hold within one's center of attention all of that bewildering array of facts which science, politics, experience, memory, and imagination were urging upon me. And then, while writing, a new and thrilling relationship would spring up under the drive of emotion, coalescing and telescoping alien facts into a known and felt truth. That was the deep fun of the job: to feel within my body that I was pushing out to new areas of feeling, strange landmarks of emotion, tramping upon foreign soil, compounding new relationships of perceptions, making new and – until that very split second of time! – unheard-of and unfelt effects with words. It had a buoying and tonic impact upon me; my senses would strain and seek for more and more of such relationships; my temperature would rise as I worked. That is writing as I feel it, a kind of significant living.

The first draft of the novel was written in four months, straight through, and ran to some 576 pages. Just as a man rises in the mornings to dig ditches for his bread, so I'd work daily. I'd think of some abstract principle of Bigger's conduct and at once my mind would turn it into some act I'd seen Bigger perform, some act which I hoped would be familiar enough to the American reader to gain his credence. But in the writing of scene after scene I was guided by but one criterion: to tell the truth as I saw it and felt it. That is, to objectify in words some insight derived from my living in the form of action, scene, and dialogue. If a scene seemed improbable to me, I'd not tear it up, but ask myself: 'Does it reveal enough of what I feel to stand in spite of its unreality?' If I felt it did, it stood. If I felt that it did not, I ripped it out. The degree of morality in my writing depended upon the degree of felt life and truth I could put down upon the printed page. For example, there is a scene in *Native Son* where Bigger stands in a cell with a Negro preacher, Jan, Max, the State's Attorney, Mr Dalton, Mrs Dalton, Bigger's mother, his brother, his sister, Al, Gus, and Jack. While writing that scene, I knew that it was unlikely that so many people would ever be allowed to come into a murderer's cell. But I wanted those people in that cell to elicit a certain important emotional response from Bigger. And so the scene stood. I felt that what I wanted that scene to say to the reader was *more important than its surface reality or plausibility*.

Always, as I wrote, I was both reader and writer, both the conceiver of the action and the appreciator of it. I tried to write so that, in the same instant of time, the objective and subjective aspects of Bigger's life would be caught in a focus of prose. And always I tried to *render, depict*, not merely to tell the story. If a thing was cold, I tried to make the reader *feel* cold, and not just tell about it. In writing in this fashion, sometimes I'd find it necessary to use a stream of consciousness technique, then rise to an interior monologue, descend to a direct rendering of a dream state, then to a matter-of-fact depiction of what Bigger was saying, doing, and feeling. Then I'd find it impossible to say what I wanted to say without stepping in and speaking outright on my own; but when doing this I always made an effort to retain the mood of the story, explaining everything only in terms of Bigger's life and, if possible, in the rhythms of Bigger's thought (even though the words would be mine). Again, at other times, in the guise of the lawyer's speech and the newspaper items, or in terms of what Bigger would overhear or see from afar, I'd give what others were saying and thinking of him. But always, from the start to the finish, it was Bigger's story, Bigger's fear, Bigger's flight, and Bigger's fate that I tried to depict. I wrote with the conviction in mind (I don't know if this is right or wrong; I only know that I'm temperamentally inclined to feel this way) that the main burden of all serious fiction consists almost wholly of character-destiny and the items, social, political, and personal, of that character-destiny.

As I wrote I followed, almost unconsciously, many principles of the novel which my reading of the novels of other writers had made me feel were necessary for the building of a well-constructed book. For the most part the novel is rendered in the present; I wanted the reader to feel that Bigger's story was happening *now*, like a play upon the stage or a movie unfolding upon the screen. Action follows action, as in a prize fight. Wherever possible, I told of Bigger's life in close-up, slow-motion, giving the feel of the grain in the passing of time. I had long had the feeling that this was the best way to 'enclose' the reader's mind in a new world, to blot out all reality except that which I was giving him.

Then again, as much as I could, I restricted the novel to what Bigger saw and felt, to the limits of his feeling and thoughts, even when I was conveying *more* than that to the reader. I had the notion that such a manner of rendering made for a sharper effect, a more pointed sense of the character, his peculiar type of being and consciousness. Throughout there is but one point of view: Bigger's. This, too, I felt made for a richer illusion of reality.

I kept out of the story as much as possible, for I wanted the reader to feel that there was nothing between him and Bigger; that the story was a special *première* given in his own private theater.

I kept the scenes long, made as much happen within a short space of time as possible; all of which, I felt made for greater density and richness of effect.

In a like manner I tried to keep a unified sense of background throughout the story; the background would change, of course, but I tried to keep before the eyes of the reader at all times the forces and elements against which Bigger was striving.

And, because I had limited myself to rendering only what Bigger saw and felt, I gave no more reality to the other characters than that which Bigger himself saw.

This, honestly, is all I can account for in the book. If I

attempted to account for scenes and characters, to tell why certain scenes were written in certain ways, I'd be stretching facts in order to be pleasantly intelligible. All else in the book came from my feelings reacting upon the material, and any honest reader knows as much about the rest of what is in the book as I do; that is, if, as he reads, he is willing to let his emotions and imagination become as influenced by the materials as I did. As I wrote, for some reason or other, one image, symbol, character, scene, mood, feeling evoked its opposite, its parallel, its complementary, and its ironic counterpart. Why? I don't know. My emotions and imagination just like to work that way. One can account for just so much of life, and then no more. At least, not yet.

With the first draft down, I found that I could not end the book satisfactorily. In the first draft I had Bigger going smack to the electric chair; but I felt that two murders were enough for one novel. I cut the final scene and went back to worry about the beginning. I had no luck. The book was one-half finished, with the opening and closing scenes unwritten. Then, one night, in desperation – I hope that I'm not disclosing the hidden secrets of my craft! – I sneaked out and got a bottle. With the help of it, I began to remember many things which I could not remember before. One of them was that Chicago was overrun with rats. I recalled that I'd seen many rats on the streets, that I'd heard and read of Negro children being bitten by rats in their beds. At first I rejected the idea of Bigger battling a rat in his room; I was afraid that the rat would 'hog' the scene. But the rat would not leave me; he presented himself in many attractive guises. So, cautioning myself to allow the rat scene to disclose *only* Bigger, his family, their little room, and their relationships, I let the rat walk in, and he did his stuff.

Many of the scenes were torn out as I reworked the book. The mere rereading of what I'd written made me think of the possibility of developing themes which had been only hinted at in the first draft. For example, the entire guilt theme that runs through *Native Son* was woven in *after* the first draft was written.

At last I found out how to end the book; I ended it just as I had begun it, showing Bigger living dangerously, taking his life into his hands, accepting what life had made him. The lawyer, Max, was placed in Bigger's cell at the end of the novel to register the moral – or what *I* felt was the moral – horror of Negro life in the United States.

The writing of *Native Son* was to me an exciting, enthralling, and even a romantic experience. With what I've learned in the writing of this book, with all of its blemishes, imperfections, with all of its unrealized potentialities, I am launching out upon another novel, this time about the status of women in modern American society. This book, too, goes back to my childhood just as Bigger went, for, while I was storing away impressions of Bigger, I was storing away impressions of many other things that made me think and wonder. Some experience will ignite somewhere deep down in me the smoldering embers of new fires and I'll be off again to write yet another novel. It is good to live when one feels that such as that will happen to one. Life becomes sufficient unto life; the rewards of living are found in living.

I don't know if *Native Son* is a good book or a bad book. And I don't know if the book I'm working on now will be a good book or a bad book. And I really don't care. The mere writing of it will be more fun and a deeper satisfaction than any praise or blame from anybody.

I feel that I'm lucky to be alive to write novels today, when the whole world is caught in the pangs of war and change. Early American writers, Henry James and Nathaniel Hawthorne, complained bitterly about the bleakness and flatness of the American scene. But I think that if they were alive, they'd feel at home in modern America. True, we have no great church in America; our national traditions are still of such a sort that we are not wont to brag of them; and we have no army that's above the level of mercenary fighters; we have no group acceptable to the whole of our country upholding certain humane values; we have no rich symbols, no colorful rituals. We have only a money-grubbing, industrial civilization. But we do have in the Negro the embodiment of a past tragic enough to appease the spiritual hunger of even a James; and we have in the oppression of the Negro a shadow athwart our national life dense and heavy enough to satisfy even the gloomy broodings of a Hawthorne. And if Poe were alive, he would not have to invent horror; horror would invent him.

New York, 7 March 1940.

Even today is my complaint rebellious,
My stroke is heavier than my groaning.
                                    – Job

BOOK ONE

Fear

Brrrrrrriiiiiiiiiiiiiiiiiiiiiiinng!

An alarm clock clanged in the dark and silent room. A bed spring creaked. A woman's voice sang out impatiently:

'Bigger, shut that thing off!'

A surly grunt sounded above the tinny ring of metal. Naked feet swished dryly across the planks in the wooden floor and the clang ceased abruptly.

'Turn on the light, Bigger.'

'Awright,' came a sleepy mumble.

Light flooded the room and revealed a black boy standing in a narrow space between two iron beds, rubbing his eyes with the backs of his hands. From a bed to his right the woman spoke again:

'Buddy, get up from there! I got a big washing on my hands today and I want you-all out of here.'

Another black boy rolled from bed and stood up. The woman also rose and stood in her nightgown.

'Turn your heads so I can dress,' she said.

The two boys averted their eyes and gazed into a far corner of the room. The woman rushed out of her nightgown and put on a pair of step-ins. She turned to the bed from which she had risen and called:

'Vera! Get up from there!'

'What time is it, Ma?' asked a muffled, adolescent voice from beneath a quilt.

'Get up from there, I say!'

'O.K., Ma.'

A brown-skinned girl in a cotton gown got up and stretched her arms above her head and yawned. Sleepily, she sat on a chair and fumbled with her stockings. The two boys kept their faces averted while their mother and sister put on enough clothes to keep them from feeling ashamed; and the mother and sister did the same while the boys dressed. Abruptly, they all paused, holding their clothes in their hands, their attention caught by a light tapping in the thinly plastered walls of the room. They forgot their conspiracy against shame and their eyes strayed apprehensively over the floor.

'There he is again, Bigger!' the woman screamed, and the tiny one-room apartment galvanized into violent action. A chair toppled as the woman, half-dressed and in her stocking feet, scrambled breathlessly upon the bed. Her two sons, barefoot, stood tense and motionless, their eyes searching anxiously under the bed and chairs. The girl ran into a corner, half-stooped and gathered the hem of her slip into both of her hands and held it tightly over her knees.

'Oh! Oh!' she wailed.

'There he goes!'

The woman pointed a shaking finger. Her eyes were round with fascinated horror.

'Where?'

'I don't see 'im!'

'Bigger, he's behind the trunk!' the girl whimpered.

'Vera!' the woman screamed. 'Get up here on the bed! Don't let that thing *bite* you!'

Frantically, Vera climbed upon the bed and the woman caught hold of her. With their arms entwined about each other, the black mother and the brown daughter gazed open-mouthed at the trunk in the corner.

Bigger looked round the room wildly, then darted to a curtain and swept it aside and grabbed two heavy iron skillets from a wall above a gas stove. He whirled and called softly to his brother, his eyes glued to the trunk.

'Buddy!'

'Yeah?'

'Here; take this skillet.'

'O.K.'

'Now, get over by the door!'

'O.K.'

Buddy crouched by the door and held the iron skillet by its handle, his arm flexed and poised. Save for the quick, deep breathing of the four people, the room was quiet. Bigger crept on tiptoe toward the trunk with the skillet clutched stiffly in his hand, his eyes dancing and watching every inch of the wooden floor in front of him. He paused and, without moving an eye or muscle, called:

'Buddy!'

'Hunh?'

'Put that box in front of the hole so he can't get out!'

'O.K.'

Buddy ran to a wooden box and shoved it quickly in front of a gaping hole in the molding and then backed again to the door, holding the skillet ready. Bigger eased to the trunk and peered behind it cautiously. He saw nothing. Carefully, he stuck out his bare foot and pushed the trunk a few inches.

'There he is!' the mother screamed again.

A huge black rat squealed and leaped at Bigger's trouser-leg and snagged it in his teeth, hanging on.

'Goddamn!' Bigger whispered fiercely, whirling and kicking out his leg with all the strength of his body. The force of his movement shook the rat loose and it sailed through the air and struck a wall. Instantly, it rolled over and leaped again. Bigger dodged and the rat landed against a table leg. With clenched teeth, Bigger held the skillet; he was afraid to hurl it, fearing that he might miss. The rat squeaked and turned and ran in a narrow circle, looking for a place to hide; it leaped again past Bigger and scurried on dry rasping feet to one side of the box and then to the other, searching for the hole. Then it turned and reared upon its hind legs.

'Hit 'im, Bigger!' Buddy shouted.

'Kill 'im!' the woman screamed.

The rat's belly pulsed with fear. Bigger advanced a step and the rat emitted a long thin song of defiance, its black beady eyes glittering, its tiny forefeet pawing the air restlessly. Bigger swung the skillet; it skidded over the floor, missing the rat, and clattered to a stop against a wall.

'Goddamn!'

The rat leaped. Bigger sprang to one side. The rat stopped under a chair and let out a furious screak. Bigger moved slowly backward toward the door.

'Gimmie that skillet, Buddy,' he asked quietly, not taking his eyes from the rat.

Buddy extended his hand. Bigger caught the skillet and lifted it high in the air. The rat scuttled across the floor and stopped again at the box and searched quickly for the hole; then it reared once more and bared long yellow fangs, piping shrilly, belly quivering.

Bigger aimed and let the skillet fly with a heavy grunt. There was a shattering of wood as the box caved in. The woman screamed and hid her face in her hands. Bigger tiptoed forward and peered.

'I got 'im,' he muttered, his clenched teeth bared in a smile. 'By God, I got 'im.'

He kicked the splintered box out of the way and the flat black body of the rat lay exposed, its two long yellow tusks showing distinctly. Bigger took a shoe and pounded the rat's head, crushing it, cursing hysterically:

'You sonofa*bitch*!'

The woman on the bed sank to her knees and buried her face in the quilts and sobbed:

'Lord, Lord, have mercy . . .'

'Aw, Mama,' Vera whimpered, bending to her. 'Don't cry. It's dead now.'

The two brothers stood over the dead rat and spoke in tones of awed admiration.

'Gee, but he's a big bastard.'

'That sonofabitch could cut your throat.'

'He's over a foot long.'

'How in hell do they get so big?'

'Eating garbage and anything else they can get.'

'Look, Bigger, there's a three-inch rip in your pant-leg.'

'Yeah; he was after me, all right.'

'Please, Bigger, take 'im out,' Vera begged.

'Aw, don't be so scary,' Buddy said.

The woman on the bed continued to sob. Bigger took a piece of newspaper and gingerly lifted the rat by its tail and held it out at arm's length.

'Bigger, take 'im out,' Vera begged again.

Bigger laughed and approached the bed with the dangling rat, swinging it to and fro like a pendulum, enjoying his sister's fear.

'Bigger!' Vera gasped convulsively; she screamed and swayed and closed her eyes and fell headlong across her mother and rolled limply from the bed to the floor.

'Bigger, for God's sake!' the mother sobbed, rising and bending over Vera. 'Don't do that! Throw that rat out!'

He laid the rat down and started to dress.

'Bigger, help me lift Vera to the bed,' the mother said.

He paused and turned round.

'What's the matter?' he asked, feigning ignorance.

'Do what I asked you, will you, boy?'

He went to the bed and helped his mother lift Vera. Vera's eyes were closed. He turned away and finished dressing. He wrapped the rat in a newspaper and went out of the door and down the stairs and put it into a garbage can at the corner of an alley. When he returned to the room his mother was still bent over Vera, placing a wet towel upon her head. She straightened and faced him, her cheeks and eyes wet with tears and her lips tight with anger.

'Boy, sometimes I wonder what makes you act like you do.'

'What I do now?' he demanded belligerently.

'Sometimes you act the biggest fool I ever saw.'

'What you talking about?'

'You scared your sister with that rat and she *fainted*! Ain't you got no sense at *all*?'

'Aw, I didn't know she was that scary.'

'Buddy!' the mother called.

'Yessum.'

'Take a newspaper and spread it over that spot.'

'Yessum.'

Buddy opened out a newspaper and covered the smear of blood on the floor where the rat had been crushed. Bigger went to the window and stood looking out abstractedly into the street. His mother glared at his back.

'Bigger, sometimes I wonder why I birthed you,' she said bitterly.

Bigger looked at her and turned away.

'Maybe you oughtn't've. Maybe you ought to left me where I was.'

'You shut your sassy mouth!'

'Aw, for chrissakes!' Bigger said, lighting a cigarette.

'Buddy, pick up them skillets and put 'em in the sink,' the mother said.

'Yessum.'

Bigger walked across the floor and sat on the bed. His mother's eyes followed him.

'We wouldn't have to live in this garbage dump if you had any manhood in you,' she said.

'Aw, don't start that again.'

'How you feel, Vera?' the mother asked.

Vera raised her head and looked about the room as though expecting to see another rat.

'Oh, Mama!'

'You poor thing!'

'I couldn't help it. Bigger scared me.'

'Did you hurt yourself?'

'I bumped my head.'

'Here; take it easy. You'll be all right.'

'How come Bigger acts that way?' Vera asked, crying again.

'He's just crazy,' the mother said. 'Just plain dumb black crazy.'

'I'll be late for my sewing class at the Y.W.C.A.,' Vera said.

'Here; stretch out on the bed. You'll feel better in a little while,' the mother said.

She left Vera on the bed and turned a pair of cold eyes upon Bigger.

'Suppose you wake up some morning and find your sister dead? What would you think then?' she asked. 'Suppose those rats cut our veins at night when we sleep? Naw! Nothing like that ever bothers you! All you care about is your own pleasure! Even when the relief offers you a job you won't take it till they threaten to cut off your food and starve you! Bigger, honest, you the most no-countest man I ever seen in all my life!'

'You done told me that a thousand times,' he said, not looking round.

'Well, I'm telling you agin! And mark my word, some of these days you going to set down and *cry*. Some of these days you going to wish you had made something out of yourself, instead of just a tramp. But it'll be too late then.'

'Stop prophesying about me,' he said.

'I prophesy much as I please! And if you don't like it, you can get out. We can get along without you. We can live in one room just like we living now, even with you gone,' she said.

'Aw, for chrissakes!' he said, his voice filled with nervous irritation.

'You'll regret how you living some day,' she went on. 'If you don't stop running with that gang of yours and do right you'll end up where you never thought you would. You think I don't know what you boys is doing, but I do. And the gallows is at the end of the road you traveling, boy. Just remember that.' She turned and looked at Buddy. 'Throw that box outside, Buddy.'

'Yessum.'

There was silence. Buddy took the box out. The mother went behind the curtain to the gas stove. Vera sat up in bed and swung her feet to the floor.

'Lay back down, Vera,' the mother said.

'I feel all right now, Ma. I got to go to my sewing class.'

'Well, if you feel like it, set the table,' the mother said, going behind the curtain again. 'Lord, I get so tired of this I don't know what to do,' her voice floated plaintively from behind the

47

curtain. 'All I ever do is try to make a home for you children and you don't care.'

'Aw, Ma,' Vera protested. 'Don't say that.'

'Vera sometimes I just want to lay down and quit.'

'Ma, please don't say that.'

'I can't last many more years, living like this.'

'I'll be old enough to work soon, Ma.'

'I reckon I'll be dead then. I reckon God'll call me home.'

Vera went behind the curtain and Bigger heard her trying to comfort his mother. He shut their voices out of his mind. He hated his family because he knew that they were suffering and that he was powerless to help them. He knew that the moment he allowed himself to feel to its fullness how they lived, the shame and misery of their lives, he would be swept out of himself with fear and despair. So he held toward them an attitude of iron reserve; he lived with them, but behind a wall, a curtain. And toward himself he was even more exacting. He knew that the moment he allowed what his life meant to enter fully into his consciousness, he would either kill himself or someone else. So he denied himself and acted tough.

He got up and crushed his cigarette upon the window sill. Vera came into the room and placed knives and forks upon the table.

'Get ready to eat, you-all,' the mother called.

He sat at the table. The odor of frying bacon and boiling coffee drifted to him from behind the curtain. His mother's voice floated to him in song.

> 'Life is like a mountain railroad
>   With an engineer that's brave
> We must make the run successful
>   From the cradle to the grave...'

The song irked him and he was glad when she stopped and came into the room with a pot of coffee and a plate of crinkled bacon. Vera brought the bread in and they sat down. His mother closed her eyes and lowered her head and mumbled,

'Lord, we thank Thee for the food You done placed before us

for the nourishment of our bodies. Amen.' She lifted her eyes
and without changing her tone of voice, said, 'You going to
have to learn to get up earlier than this, Bigger, to hold a
job.'

He did not answer or look up.

'You want me to pour you some coffee?' Vera asked.

'Yeah.'

'You going to take the job, ain't you, Bigger?' his mother
asked.

He laid down his fork and stared at her.

'I told you last night I was going to take it. How many times
you want to ask me?'

'Well, don't bite her head off,' Vera said. 'She only asked you
a question.'

'Pass the bread and stop being smart.'

'You know you have to see Mr Dalton at five-thirty,' his
mother said.

'You done said that ten times.'

'I don't want you to forget, son.'

'And you know how you can forget,' Vera said.

'Aw, lay off Bigger,' Buddy said. 'He told you he was going
to take the job.'

'Don't tell 'em nothing,' Bigger said.

'You shut your mouth, Buddy, or get up from this table,' the
mother said. 'I'm not going to take any stinking sass from you.
One fool in the family's enough.'

'Lay off, Ma,' Buddy said.

'Bigger's setting here like he ain't glad to get a job,' she
said.

'What you want me to do? Shout?' Bigger asked.

'Oh, Bigger !' his sister said.

'I wish you'd keep your big mouth out of this !' he told his
sister.

'If you get that job,' his mother said in a low, kind tone of
voice, busy slicing a loaf of bread, 'I can fix up a nice place for
you children. You could be comfortable and not have to live like
pigs.'

'Bigger ain't decent enough to think of nothing like that,' Vera said.

'God, I wish you-all would let me eat,' Bigger said.

His mother talked on as though she had not heard him and he stopped listening.

'Ma's talking to you, Bigger,' Vera said.

'So *what*?'

'Don't be that way, Bigger!'

He laid down his fork and his strong black fingers gripped the edge of the table; there was silence save for the tinkling of his brother's fork against a plate. He kept staring at his sister till her eyes fell.

'I wish you'd let me eat,' he said again.

As he ate he felt that they were thinking of the job he was to get that evening and it made him angry; he felt that they had tricked him into a cheap surrender.

'I need some carfare,' he said.

'Here's all I got,' his mother said, pushing a quarter to the side of his plate.

He put the quarter in his pocket and drained his cup of coffee in one long swallow. He got his coat and cap and went to the door.

'You know, Bigger,' his mother said, 'if you don't take that job the relief'll cut us off. We won't have any food.'

'I told you I'd take it!' he shouted and slammed the door.

He went down the steps into the vestibule and stood looking out into the street through the plate glass of the front door. Now and then a street car rattled past over steel tracks. He was sick of his life at home. Day in and day out there was nothing but shouts and bickering. But what could he do? Each time he asked himself that question his mind hit a blank wall and he stopped thinking. Across the street directly in front of him, he saw a truck pull to a stop at the curb and two white men in overalls got out with pails and brushes. Yes, he could take the job at Dalton's and be miserable, or he could refuse it and starve. It maddened him to think that he did not have a wider choice of action. Well, he could not stand here all day like this.

What was he to do with himself? He tried to decide if he wanted to buy a ten-cent magazine, or go to a movie, or go to the poolroom and talk with the gang, or just loaf around. With his hands deep in his pockets, another cigarette slanting across his chin, he brooded and watched the men at work across the street. They were pasting a huge colored poster to a signboard. The poster showed a white face.

'That's Buckley!' He spoke softly to himself. 'He's running for State's Attorney again.' The men were slapping the poster with wet brushes. He looked at the round florid face and wagged his head. 'I bet that sonofabitch rakes off a million bucks in graft a year. Boy, if I was in his shoes for just one day I'd *never* have to worry again.'

When the men were through they gathered up their pails and brushes and got into the truck and drove off. He looked at the poster: the white face was fleshy but stern; one hand was uplifted and its index finger pointed straight out into the street at each passer-by. The poster showed one of those faces that looked straight at you when you looked at it and all the while you were walking and turning your head to look at it it kept looking unblinkingly back at you until you got so far from it you had to take your eyes away, and then it stopped, like a movie blackout. Above the top of the poster were tall red letters: IF YOU BREAK THE LAW, YOU CAN'T WIN!

He snuffed his cigarette and laughed silently. 'You crook,' he mumbled, shaking his head. 'You let whoever pays *you* off win!' He opened the door and met the morning air. He went along the sidewalk with his head down, fingering the quarter in his pocket. He stopped and searched all of his pockets; in his vest pocket he found a lone copper cent. That made a total of twenty-six cents, fourteen cents of which would have to be saved for carfare to Mr Dalton's; that is, if he decided to take the job. In order to buy a magazine and go to the movies he would have to have at least twenty cents more. 'Goddammit, I'm always broke!' he mumbled.

He stood on the corner in the sunshine, watching cars and people pass. He needed more money; if he did not get more than he had now he would not know what to do with himself for the rest of the day. He wanted to see a movie; his senses hungered for it. In a movie he could dream without effort; all he had to do was lean back in a seat and keep his eyes open.

He thought of Gus and G.H. and Jack. Should he go to the poolroom and talk with them? But there was no use in his going unless they were ready to do what they had been long planning to do. If they could, it would mean some sure and quick money. From three o'clock to four o'clock in the after-noon there was no policeman on duty in the block where Blum's Delicatessen was and it would be safe. One of them could hold a gun on Blum and keep him from yelling; one could watch the front door; one could watch the back; one could get the money from the box under the counter. Then all four of them could lock Blum in the store and run out through the back and duck down the alley and meet an hour later, either at Doc's poolroom or at the South Side Boy's Club, and split the money.

Holding up Blum ought not take more than two minutes, at the most. And it would be their last job. But it would be the toughest one that they had ever pulled. All the other times they had raided newsstands, fruit stands, and apartments. And, too, they had never held up a white man before. They had always robbed Negroes. They felt that it was much easier and safer to rob their own people, for they knew that white policemen never really searched diligently for Negroes who committed crimes against other Negroes. For months they had talked of robbing Blum's, but had not been able to bring themselves to do it. They had the feeling that the robbing of Blum's would be a violation of ultimate taboo; it would be a trespassing into territory where the full wrath of an alien white world would be turned loose upon them; in short, it would be a symbolic chal-lenge of the white world's rule over them; a challenge which they yearned to make, but were afraid to. Yes; if they could rob Blum's, it would be a real hold-up, in more senses than one. In comparison, all of their other jobs had been play.

'Good-bye, Bigger.'

He looked up and saw Vera passing with a sewing kit dangling from her arm. She paused at the corner and came back to him.

'Now, what you want?'

'Bigger, please ... You're getting a good job now. Why don't you stay away from Jack and Gus and G.H. and keep out of trouble?'

'You keep your big mouth out of my business!'

'But, Bigger!'

'Go on to school, will you!'

She turned abruptly and walked on. He knew that his mother had been talking to Vera and Buddy about him, telling them that if he got into any more trouble he would be sent to prison and not just to the reform school, where they had sent him last time. He did not mind what his mother said to Buddy about him. Buddy was all right. Tough, plenty. But Vera was a sappy girl; she did not have any more sense than to believe everything she was told.

He walked toward the poolroom. When he got to the door he saw Gus half a block away, coming toward him. He stopped and waited. It was Gus who had first thought of robbing Blum's.

'Hi, Bigger!'

'What you saying, Gus?'

'Nothing. Seen G.H. or Jack yet?'

'Naw. You?'

'Naw. Say, got a cigarette?'

'Yeah.'

Bigger took out his pack and gave Gus a cigarette; he lit his and held the match for Gus. They leaned their backs against the red-brick wall of a building, smoking, their cigarettes slanting white across their black chins. To the east Bigger saw the sun burning a dazzling yellow. In the sky above him a few big white clouds drifted. He puffed silently, relaxed, his mind pleasantly vacant of purpose. Every slight movement in the street evoked a casual curiosity in him. Automatically, his eyes followed each car as it whirred over the smooth black asphalt. A

53

woman came by and he watched the gentle sway of her body until she disappeared into a doorway. He sighed, scratched his chin and mumbled.

'Kinda warm today.'

'Yeah,' Gus said.

'You get more heat from this sun than from them old radiators at home.'

'Yeah; them old white landlords sure don't give much heat.'

'And they always knocking at your door for money.'

'I'll be glad when summer comes.'

'Me too,' Bigger said.

He stretched his arms above his head and yawned; his eyes moistened. The sharp precision of the world of steel and stone dissolved into blurred waves. He blinked and the world grew hard again, mechanical, distinct. A weaving motion in the sky made him turn his eyes upward; he saw a slender streak of billowing white blooming against the deep blue. A plane was writing high up in the air.

'Look !' Bigger said.

'What?'

'That plane writing up there,' Bigger said, pointing.

'Oh !'

They squinted at a tiny ribbon of unfolding vapor that spelled out the word: USE ... The plane was so far away that at times the strong glare of the sun blanked it from sight.

'You can hardly see it,' Gus said.

'Looks like a little bird,' Bigger breathed with childlike wonder.

'Them white boys sure can fly,' Gus said.

'Yeah,' Bigger said, wistfully. 'They get a chance to do everything.'

Noiselessly, the tiny plane looped and veered, vanishing and appearing, leaving behind it a long trail of white plumage, like coils of fluffy paste being squeezed from a tube; a plume-coil that grew and swelled and slowly began to fade into the air at the edges. The plane wrote another word: SPEED ...

'How high you reckon he is?' Bigger asked.

'I don't know. Maybe a hundred miles; maybe a thousand.'

'I could fly one of them things if I had a chance,' Bigger mumbled reflectively, as though talking to himself.

Gus pulled down the corners of his lips, stepped out from the wall, squared his shoulders, doffed his cap, bowed low, and spoke with mock deference:

'Yessuh.'

'You go to hell,' Bigger said, smiling.

'Yessuh,' Gus said again.

'I *could* fly a plane if I had a chance,' Bigger said.

'If you wasn't black and if you had some money and if they'd let you go to that aviation school, you *could* fly a plane,' Gus said.

For a moment Bigger contemplated all the 'ifs' that Gus had mentioned. Then both boys broke into hard laughter, looking at each other, through squinted eyes. When their laughter subsided, Bigger said in a voice that was half-question and half-statement:

'It's funny how the white folks treat us, ain't it?'

'It better be funny,' Gus said.

'Maybe they right in not wanting us to fly,' Bigger said. ' 'Cause if I took a plane up I'd take a couple of bombs along and drop 'em as sure as hell . . .'

They laughed again, still looking upward. The plane sailed and dipped and spread another word against the sky: GAS-OLINE . . .

'Use Speed Gasoline,' Bigger mused, rolling the words slowly from his lips. 'God, I'd like to fly up there in that sky.'

'God'll let you fly when He gives you your wings up in heaven,' Gus said.

They laughed again, reclining against the wall, smoking, the lids of their eyes drooped softly against the sun. Cars whizzed past on rubber tires. Bigger's face was metallically black in the strong sunlight. There was in his eyes a pensive, brooding amusement, as of a man who had been long confronted and tantalized by a riddle whose answer seemed always just on the verge of escaping him, but prodding him irresistibly on to seek its solution. The silence irked Bigger; he was anxious to do something to evade looking so squarely at this problem.

'Let's play "white",' Bigger said, referring to a game of play-acting in which he and his friends imitated the ways and manners of white folks.

'I don't feel like it,' Gus said.

'General!' Bigger pronounced in a sonorous tone, looking at Gus expectantly.

'Aw, hell! I don't want to play,' Gus whined.

'You'll be court-martialed,' Bigger said, snapping out his words with military precision.

'Nigger, you nuts!' Gus laughed.

'General!' Bigger tried again, determinedly.

Gus looked wearily at Bigger, then straightened, saluted, and answered:

'Yessuh.'

'Send your men over the river at dawn and attack the enemy's left flank,' Bigger ordered.

'Yessuh.'

'Send the Fifth, Sixth, and Seventh Regiments,' Bigger said, frowning. 'And attack with tanks, gas, planes, and infantry.'

'Yessuh!' Gus said again, saluting and clicking his heels.

For a moment they were silent, facing each other, their shoulders thrown back, their lips compressed to hold down the mounting impulse to laugh. Then they guffawed, partly at themselves and partly at the vast white world that sprawled and towered in the sun before them.

'Say, what's a "left flank"?' Gus asked.

'I don't know,' Bigger said. 'I heard it in the movies.'

They laughed again. After a bit they relaxed and leaned against the wall, smoking. Bigger saw Gus cup his left hand to his ear, as though holding a telephone receiver; and cup his right hand to his mouth, as though talking into a transmitter.

'Hello,' Gus said.

'Hello,' Bigger said. 'Who's this?'

'This is Mr J. P. Morgan speaking,' Gus said.

'Yessuh, Mr Morgan,' Bigger said; his eyes filled with mock adulation and respect.

'I want you to sell twenty thousand shares of U.S. Steel in the market this morning,' Gus said.

'At what price, suh?' Bigger asked.

'Aw, just dump 'em at any price,' Gus said with casual irritation. 'We're holding too much.'

'Yessuh,' Bigger said.

'And call me at my club at two this afternoon and tell me if the President telephoned,' Gus said.

'Yessuh, Mr Morgan,' Bigger said.

Both of them made gestures signifying that they were hanging up telephone receivers; then they bent double, laughing.

'I bet that's *just* the way they talk,' Gus said.

'I wouldn't be surprised,' Bigger said.

They were silent again. Presently, Bigger cupped his hand to his mouth and spoke through an imaginary telephone transmitter.

'Hello.'

'Hello,' Gus answered. 'Who's this?'

'This is the President of the United States speaking,' Bigger said.

'Oh, yessuh, Mr President,' Gus said.

'I'm calling a cabinet meeting this afternoon at four o'clock and you, as Secretary of State, *must* be there.'

'Well, now, Mr President,' Gus said, 'I'm pretty busy. They raising sand over there in Germany and I got to send 'em a note . . .'

'But this is important,' Bigger said.

'What you going to take up at this cabinet meeting?' Gus asked.

'Well, you see, the niggers is raising sand all over the country,' Bigger said, struggling to keep back his laughter. 'We've got to do something with these black folks . . .'

'Oh, if it's about the niggers, I'll be right there, Mr President,' Gus said.

They hung up imaginary receivers and leaned against the

wall and laughed. A streetcar rattled by, Bigger sighed and swore.

'Goddammit!'

'What's the matter?'

'They don't let us do *nothing*.'

'Who?'

'The *white* folks.'

'You talk like you just now finding that out,' Gus said.

'Naw. But I just can't get used to it,' Bigger said. 'I swear to God I can't. I know I oughtn't think about it, but I can't help it. Every time I think about it I feel like somebody's poking a red-hot iron down my throat. Goddammit, look! We live here and they live there. We black and they white. They got things and we ain't. They do things and we can't. It's just like living in jail. Half the time I feel like I'm on the outside of the world peeping in through a knot-hole in the fence . . .'

'Aw, ain't no use feeling that way about it. It don't help none,' Gus said.

'You know one thing?' Bigger said.

'What?'

'Sometimes I feel like something awful's going to happen to me,' Bigger spoke with a tinge of bitter pride in his voice.

'What you mean?' Gus asked, looking at him quickly. There was fear in Gus's eyes.

'I don't know. I just feel that way. Every time I get to thinking about me being black and they being white, me being here and they being there, I feel like something awful's going to happen to me . . .'

'Aw, for chrissakes! There ain't nothing you can do about it. How come you want to worry yourself? You black and they make the laws . . .'

'Why they make us live in one corner of the city? Why don't they let us fly planes and run ships . . .'

Gus hunched Bigger with his elbow and mumbled good-naturedly, 'Aw, nigger, quit thinking about it. You'll go nuts.'

The plane was gone from the sky and the white plumes of floating smoke were thinly spread, vanishing. Because he was

restless and had time on his hands, Bigger yawned again and
hoisted his arms high above his head.

'Nothing ever happens,' he complained.

'What you want to happen?'

'Anything,' Bigger said with a wide sweep of his dingy
palm, a sweep that included all the possible activities of the
world.

Then their eyes were riveted; a slate-colored pigeon swooped
down to the middle of the steel car tracks and began strutting to
and fro with ruffled feathers, its fat neck bobbing with regal
pride. A streetcar rumbled forward and the pigeon rose swiftly
through the air on wings stretched so taut and sheer that Bigger
could see the gold of the sun through their translucent tips. He
tilted his head and watched the slate-colored bird flap and
wheel out of sight over the edge of a high roof.

'Now, if I could only do that,' Bigger said.

Gus laughed.

'Nigger, you nuts.'

'I reckon we the only things in this city that can't go where
we want to go and do what we want to do.'

'Don't think about it,' Gus said.

'I can't help it.'

'That's why you feeling like something awful's going to
happen to you,' Gus said. 'You think too much.'

'What in hell can a man do?' Bigger asked, turning to Gus.

'Get drunk and sleep it off.'

'I can't. I'm broke.'

Bigger crushed his cigarette and took out another one and
offered the package to Gus. They continued smoking. A huge
truck swept past, lifting scraps of white paper into the sunshine;
the bits settled down slowly.

'Gus?'

'Hunh?'

'You know where the white folks live?'

'Yeah,' Gus said, pointing eastward. 'Over across the "line";
over there on Cottage Grove Avenue.'

'Naw; they don't,' Bigger said.

'What you mean?' Gus asked, puzzled. 'Then, where do they live?'

Bigger doubled his fist and struck his solar plexus.

'Right down here in my stomach,' he said.

Gus looked at Bigger searchingly, then away, as though ashamed.

'Yeah; I know what you mean,' he whispered.

'Every time I think of 'em, I *feel* 'em,' Bigger said.

'Yeah; and in your chest and throat, too,' Gus said.

'It's like fire.'

'And sometimes you can't hardly breathe . . .'

Bigger's eyes were wide and placid, gazing into space.

'That's when I feel like something awful's going to happen to me . . .' Bigger paused, narrowed his eyes. 'Naw; it ain't like something going to happen to me. It's . . . It's like I was going to do something I can't help . . .'

'Yeah!' Gus said with uneasy eagerness. His eyes were full of a look compounded of fear and admiration for Bigger. 'Yeah; I know what you mean. It's like you going to fall and don't know where you going to land . . .'

Gus's voice trailed off. The sun slid behind a big white cloud and the street was plunged in cool shadow; quickly the sun edged forth again and it was bright and warm once more. A long sleek black car, its fenders glinting like glass in the sun, shot past them at high speed and turned a corner a few blocks away. Bigger pursed his lips and sang:

'Zoooooooooom!'

'They got everything,' Gus said.

'They own the world,' Bigger said.

'Aw, what the hell,' Gus said. 'Let's go in the poolroom.'

'O.K.'

They walked toward the door of the poolroom.

'Say, you taking that job you told us about?' Gus asked.

'I don't know.'

'You talk like you don't want it.'

'Oh, hell, yes! I want the job,' Bigger said.

They looked at each other and laughed. They went inside.

The poolroom was empty, save for a fat, black man who held a half-smoked, unlit cigar in his mouth and leaned on the front counter. To the rear burned a single green-shaded bulb.

'Hi, Doc,' Bigger said.

'You boys kinda early this morning,' Doc said.

'Jack or G.H. around yet?' Bigger asked.

'Naw,' Doc said.

'Let's shoot a game,' Gus said.

'I'm broke,' Bigger said.

'I got some money.'

'Switch on the light. The balls are racked,' Doc said.

Bigger turned on the light. They lagged for first shot. Bigger won. They started playing. Bigger's shots were poor; he was thinking of Blum's, fascinated with the idea of the robbery, and a little afraid of it.

'Remember what we talked about so much?' Bigger asked in a flat, neutral tone.

'Naw.'

'Old Blum.'

'Oh,' Gus said. 'We ain't talked about that for a month. How come you think of it all of a sudden?'

'Let's clean the place out.'

'I don't know.'

'It was your plan from the start,' Bigger said.

Gus straightened and stared at Bigger, then at Doc who was looking out of the front window.

'You going to tell Doc? Can't you never learn to talk low?'

'Aw, I was just asking you, do you want to try it?'

'Naw.'

'How come? You scared 'cause he's a white man?'

'Naw. But Blum keeps a gun. Suppose he beats us to it?'

'Aw, you scared; that's all. He's a white man and you scared.'

'The hell I'm scared,' Gus, hurt and stung, defended himself.

Bigger went to Gus and placed an arm about his shoulders.

'Listen, you won't have to go in. You just stand at the door and keep watch, see? Me and Jack and G. H.'ll go in. If anybody comes along, you whistle and we'll go out the back way. That's all.'

The front door opened; they stopped talking and turned their heads.

'Here comes Jack and G.H. now,' Bigger said.

Jack and G.H. walked to the rear of the poolroom.

'What you guys doing?' Jack asked.

'Shooting a game. Wanna play?' Bigger asked.

'You asking 'em to play and I'm paying for the game,' Gus said.

They all laughed and Bigger laughed with them but he stopped quickly. He felt that the joke was on him and he took a seat alongside the wall and propped his feet upon the rungs of a chair, as though he had not heard. Gus and G.H. kept on laughing.

'You niggers is crazy,' Bigger said. 'You laugh like monkeys and you ain't got nerve enough to do nothing but talk.'

'What you mean?' G.H. asked.

'I got a haul all figured out,' Bigger said.

'What haul?'

'Old Blum's.'

There was silence. Jack lit a cigarette. Gus looked away, avoiding the conversation.

'If old Blum was a black man, you-all would be itching to go. 'Cause he's white, everybody's scared.'

'I ain't scared,' Jack said. 'I'm with you.'

'You say you got it all figured out?' G.H. asked.

Bigger took a deep breath and looked from face to face. It seemed to him that he should not have to explain.

'Look, it'll be easy. There ain't nothing to be scared of. Between three and four ain't nobody in the store but the old man. The cop is way down at the other end of the block. One of us'll stay outside and watch. Three of us'll go in, see? One of us'll throw a gun on old Blum; one of us'll make for the cash box under the counter; one of us'll make for the back door and have it open so we can make a quick get-away down the back alley ... That's all. It won't take three minutes.'

'I thought we said we wasn't never going to use a gun,' G.H. said. 'And we ain't bothered no white folks before.'

'Can't you see? This is something *big*,' Bigger said.

He waited for more objections. When none were forthcoming, he talked again.

'We can do it, if you niggers ain't scared.'

Save for the sound of Doc's whistling up front, there was silence. Bigger watched Jack closely; he knew that the situation was one in which Jack's word would be decisive. Bigger was afraid of Gus, because he knew that Gus would not hold out if Jack said yes. Gus stood at the table, toying with a cue stick, his eyes straying lazily over the billiard balls scattered about the table in the array of an unfinished game. Bigger rose and sent the balls whirling with a sweep of his hand, then looked straight at Gus as the gleaming balls kissed and rebounded from the rubber cushions, zig-zagging across the table's green cloth. Even though Bigger had asked Gus to be with him in the robbery, the fear that Gus would really go made the muscles of Bigger's stomach tighten; he was hot all over. He felt as if he wanted to sneeze and could not; only it was more nervous than wanting to sneeze. He grew hotter, tighter; his nerves were taut and his teeth were on edge. He felt that something would soon snap within him.

'Goddammit! Say something, somebody!'

'I'm in,' Jack said again.

'I'll go if the rest goes,' G.H. said.

Gus stood without speaking and Bigger felt a curious sensation—half-sensual, half-thoughtful. He was divided and pulled against himself. He had handled things just right so far; all but Gus had consented. The way things stood now there were three against Gus, and that was just as he had wanted it to be. Bigger was afraid of robbing a white man and he knew that Gus was afraid, too. Blum's store was small and Blum was alone, but Bigger could not think of robbing him without being flanked by his three pals. But even with his pals he was afraid. He had argued all of his pals but one into consenting to the robbery, and toward the lone man who held out he felt a hot

63

hate and fear; he had transferred his fear of the whites to Gus. He hated Gus because he knew that Gus was afraid, as even he was; and he feared Gus because he felt that Gus would consent and then he would be compelled to go through with the robbery. Like a man about to shoot himself and dreading to shoot and yet knowing that he has to shoot and feeling it all at once and powerfully, he watched Gus and waited for him to say yes. But Gus did not speak. Bigger's teeth clamped so tight that his jaws ached. He edged toward Gus, not looking at Gus, but feeling the presence of Gus over all his body, through him, in and out of him, and hating himself and Gus because he felt it. Then he could not stand it any longer. The hysterical tensity of his nerves urged him to speak, to free himself. He faced Gus, his eyes red with anger and fear, his fists clenched and held stiffly to his sides.

'You black sonofabitch,' he said in a voice that did not vary in tone. 'You scared 'cause he's a white man.'

'Don't cuss me, Bigger,' Gus said quietly.

'I *am* cussing you!'

'You don't have to cuss me,' Gus said.

'Then why don't you use that black tongue of yours?' Bigger asked. 'Why don't you say what you going to do?'

'I don't have to use my tongue unless I *want* to!'

'You bastard! You scared bastard!'

'You ain't my boss,' Gus said.

'You yellow!' Bigger said. 'You scared to rob a white man.'

'Aw, Bigger. Don't say that,' G.H. said. 'Leave 'im alone.'

'He's yellow,' Bigger said. 'He won't go with us.'

'I didn't say I wouldn't go,' Gus said.

'Then, for chrissakes, say what you going to do,' Bigger said.

Gus leaned on his cue stick and gazed at Bigger and Bigger's stomach tightened as though he were expecting a blow and were getting ready for it. His fists clenched harder. In a split second he felt how his fist and arm and body would feel if he hit Gus squarely in the mouth, drawing blood; Gus would fall and he would walk out and the whole thing would be over and the robbery would not take place. And his thinking and feeling in this way made the choking tightness rising from the pit of his stomach to his throat slacken a little.

'You see, Bigger,' began Gus in a tone that was a compromise between kindness and pride. 'You see, bigger, you the cause of all the trouble we ever have. It's your hot temper. Now, how come you want to cuss me? Ain't I got a right to make up my mind? Naw; that ain't your way. You start cussing. You say I'm scared. It's *you* who's scared. You scared I'm going to say yes and you'll have to go through with the job . . .'

'Say that again! Say that again and I'll take one of these balls and sink it in your goddamn mouth,' Bigger said, his pride wounded to the quick.

'Aw, for chrissakes,' Jack said.

'You *see* how he is,' Gus said.

'Why don't you say what you going to do?' Bigger demanded.

'Aw, I'm going with you-all,' Gus said in a nervous tone that sought to hide itself; a tone that hurried on to other things. 'I'm going, but Bigger don't have to act like that. He don't have to cuss me.'

'Why didn't you say that at first?' Bigger asked; his anger amounted almost to frenzy. 'You make a man want to sock you!'

'. . . I'll help on the haul,' Gus continued, as though Bigger had not spoken. 'I'll help just like I always help. But I'll be goddamn if I'm taking orders from *you*, Bigger! You just a scared coward! You calling me scared so nobody'll see how scared *you* is!'

Bigger leaped at him, but Jack ran between them. G.H. caught Gus's arm and led him aside.

'Who's asking you to take orders?' Bigger said. 'I never want to give orders to a piss-sop like you!'

'You boys cut out that racket back there!' Doc called.

They stood silently about the pool table. Bigger's eyes followed Gus as Gus put his cue stick in the rack and brushed chalk dust from his trousers and walked a little distance away. Bigger's stomach burned and a hazy black cloud hovered a moment before his eyes, and left. Mixed images of violence ran like sand through his mind, dry and fast, vanishing. He could stab Gus with his knife; he could slap him; he could kick him; he could trip him up and send him sprawling on his face. He could do a lot of things to Gus for making him feel this way.

'Come on, G.H.' Gus said.

'Where we going?'

'Let's walk.'

'O.K.'

'What we gonna do?' Jack asked. 'Meet here at three?'

'Sure,' Bigger said. 'Didn't we just decide?'

'I'll be here,' Gus said, with his back turned.

When Gus and G.H. had gone Bigger sat down and felt cold sweat on his skin. It was planned now and he would have to go through with it. His teeth gritted and the last image he had seen of Guss going through the door lingered in his mind. He could have taken one of the cue sticks and gripped it hard and swung it at the back of Gus's head, feeling the impact of the hard wood cracking against the bottom of the skull. The tight feeling was still in him and he knew that it would remain until they were actually doing the job, until they were in the store taking the money.

'You and Gus sure don't get along none,' Jack said, shaking his head.

Bigger turned and looked at Jack; he had forgotten that Jack was still there.

'Aw, that yellow black bastard,' Bigger said.

'He's all right,' Jack said.

'He's scared,' Bigger said. 'To make him ready for a job, you have to make him scared two ways. You have to make him more scared of what'll happen to him if he don't do the job than of what'll happen to him if he pulls the job.'

'If we going to Blum's today, we oughtn't fuss like this,' Jack said. 'We got a job on our hands, a real job.'

'Sure. Sure, I know,' Bigger said.

Bigger felt an urgent need to hide his growing and deepening feeling of hysteria; he had to get rid of it or else he would succumb to it. He longed for a stimulus powerful enough to focus his attention and drain off his energies. He wanted to run. Or listen to some swing music. Or laugh or joke. Or read a *Real Detective Story Magazine*. Or go to a movie. Or visit Bessie. All that morning he had lurked behind his curtain of indifference and looked at things, snapping and glaring at whatever had tried to make him come out into the open. But now he was out; the thought of the job at Blum's and the tilt he had had with Gus had snared him into things and his self-trust was gone. Confidence could only come again now through action so violent that it would make him forget. These were the rhythms of his life: indifference and violence; periods of abstract brooding and periods of intense desire; moments of silence and moments of anger – like water ebbing and flowing from the tug of a faraway, invisible force. Being this way was a need of his as deep as eating. He was like a strange plant blooming in the day and wilting at night; but the sun that made it bloom and the cold darkness that made it wilt were never seen. It was his own sun and darkness, a private and personal sun and darkness. He was bitterly proud of his swiftly changing moods and boasted when he had to suffer the results of them. It was the way he was, he would say; he could not help it, he would say, and his head would wag. And it was his sullen stare and the violent action that followed that made Gus and Jack and G.H. hate and fear him as much as he hated and feared himself.

'Where you want to go?' Jack asked. 'I'm tired of setting.'

'Let's walk,' Bigger said.

They went to the front door. Bigger paused and looked round the poolroom with a wild and exasperated expression, his lips tightening with resolution.

'Goin'?' Doc asked, not moving his head.

'Yeah,' Bigger said.

'See you later,' Jack said.

They walked along the street in the morning sunshine. They waited leisurely at corners for cars to pass; it was not that they feared cars, but they had plenty of time. They reached South Parkway smoking freshly lit cigarettes.

'I'd like to see a movie,' Bigger said.

'*Trader Horn*'s running again at the Regal. They're bringing a lot of old pictures back.'

'How much is it?'

'Twenty cents.'

'O.K. Let's see it.'

Bigger strode silently beside Jack for six blocks. It was noon when they reached Forty-seventh Street and South Parkway. The Regal was just opening. Bigger lingered in the lobby and looked at the colored posters while Jack bought the tickets. Two features were advertised: one, *The Gay Woman*, was pictured on the posters in images of white men and white women lolling on beaches, swimming, and dancing in night clubs; the other, *Trader Horn*, was shown on the posters in terms of black men and black women dancing against a wild background of barbaric jungle. Bigger looked up and saw Jack standing at his side.

'Come on. Let's go in,' Jack said.

'O.K.'

He followed Jack into the darkened movie. The shadows were soothing to his eyes after the glare of the sun. The picture had not started and he slouched far down in a seat and listened to a pipe organ shudder in waves of nostalgic tone, like a voice humming hauntingly within him. He moved restlessly, looking round as though expecting to see someone sneaking up on him. The organ sang forth full, then dropped almost to silence.

'You reckon we'll do all right at Blum's?' he asked in a drawling voice tinged with uneasiness.

'Aw, sure,' Jack said; but his voice, too, was uneasy.

'You know, I'd just as soon go to jail as take that damn relief job,' Bigger said.

'Don't say that. Everything'll be all right.'

'You reckon it will?'

'Sure.'

'I don't give a damn.'

'Let's think about how we'll do it, not about how we'll get caught.'

'Scared?'

'Naw. You?'

'Hell, naw !'

They were silent, listening to the organ. It sounded for a long moment on a trembling note, then died away. Then it stole forth again in whispering tones that could scarcely be heard.

'We better take our guns along this time,' Bigger said.

'O.K. But we gotta be careful. We don't wanna kill nobody.'

'Yeah. But I'll feel safer with a gun this time.'

'Gee, I wished it was three o'clock now. I wished it was over.'

'Me too.'

The organ sighed into silence and the screen flashed with the rhythm of moving shadows. There was a short newsreel which Bigger watched without much interest. Then came *The Gay Woman* in which, amid scenes of cocktail drinking, dancing, golfing, swimming, and spinning roulette wheels, a rich young white woman kept clandestine appointments with her lover while her millionaire husband was busy in the offices of a vast paper mill. Several times Bigger nudged Jack in the ribs with his elbow as the giddy young woman duped her husband and kept from him the knowledge of what she was doing.

'She sure got her old man fooled,' Bigger said.

'Looks like it. He's so busy making money he don't know what's going on,' Jack said. 'Them rich chicks'll do anything.'

'Yeah. And she's a hot looking number, all right,' Bigger said. 'Say, maybe I'll be working for folks like that if I take that relief job. Maybe I'll be driving 'em around . . .'

'Sure,' Jack said. 'Man you ought to take that job. You don't know what you might run into. My ma used to work for rich white folks and you ought to hear the tales she used to tell . . .'

'What she say?' Bigger asked eagerly.

'Ah, man, them rich white women'll go to bed with anybody, from a poodle on up. Shucks, they even have their chauffeurs. Say, if you run into anything on that new job that's too much for you to handle, let me know . . .'

They laughed. The play ran on and Bigger saw a night club

floor thronged with whirling couples and heard a swing band playing music. The rich young woman was dancing and laughing with her lover.

'I'd like to be invited to a place like that just to find out what it feels like,' Bigger mused.

'Man, if them folks saw you they'd run,' Jack said. 'They'd think a gorilla broke loose from the zoo and put on a tuxedo.'

They bent over low in their seats and giggled without restraint. When Bigger sat up again he saw the picture flashing on. A tall waiter was serving two slender glasses of drinks to the rich young woman and her lover.

'I bet their mattresses is stuffed with paper dollars,' Bigger said.

'Man, them folks don't even have to turn over in their sleep,' Jack said. 'A butler stands by their beds at night, and when he hears 'em sigh, he gently rolls 'em over . . .'

They laughed again, then fell silent abruptly. The music accompanying the picture dropped to a low, rumbling note and the rich young woman turned and looked toward the front door of the night club from which a chorus of shouts and screams was heard.

'I bet it's her husband,' Jack said.

'Yeah,' Bigger said.

Bigger saw a sweating, wild-eyed young man fight his way past a group of waiters and whirling dancers.

'He looks like a crazy man,' Jack said.

'What you reckon he wants?' Bigger asked, as though he himself was outraged at the sight of the frenzied intruder.

'Damn if I know,' Jack muttered preoccupiedly.

Bigger watched the wild young man elude the waiters and run in the direction of the rich woman's table. The music of the swing band stopped and men and women scurried frantically into corners and doorways. There were shouts: *Stop 'im! Grab 'im!* The wild man halted a few feet from the rich woman and reached inside of his coat and drew forth a black object. There were more screams: *He's got a bomb! Stop 'im!* Bigger saw the woman's lover leap to the center of the floor, fling his hands high into the air and catch the bomb just as the man threw it. As the rich woman fainted, her lover hurled the bomb out of a window, shattering a pane. Bigger saw a white flash light up the night outside as the bomb exploded deafeningly. Then he was looking at the wild man who was now pinned to the floor by a dozen hands. He heard a woman scream: *He's a Communist!*

'Say, Jack?'

'Hunh?'

'What's a Communist?'

'A Communist is a red, ain't he?'

'Yeah; but what's a red?'

'Damn if I know. It's a race of folks who live in Russia, ain't it?'

'They must be wild.'

'Looks like it. That guy was trying to kill somebody.'

The scenes showed the wild man weeping on his knees and cursing through his tears. *I wanted to kill 'im*, he sobbed. Bigger now understood that the wild bomb-thrower was a Communist who had mistaken the rich woman's lover for her husband and had tried to kill him.

'Reds must don't like rich folks,' Jack said.

'They sure must don't,' Bigger said. 'Every time you hear about one, he's trying to kill somebody or tear things up.'

The picture continued and showed the rich young woman in a fit of remorse, telling her lover that she thanked him for saving her life, but that what had happened had taught her that her husband needed her. *Suppose it had been he?* she whimpered.

'She's going back to her old man,' Bigger said.

'Oh, yeah,' Jack said. 'They got to kiss in the end.'

Bigger saw the rich young woman rush home to her millionaire husband. There were long embraces and kisses as the rich woman and the rich man vowed never to leave each other and to forgive each other.

'You reckon folks really act like that?' Bigger asked, full of the sense of a life he had never seen.

'Sure, man. They rich,' Jack said.

'I wonder if this guy I'm going to work for is a rich man like that?' Bigger asked.

'Maybe so,' Jack said.

'Shucks. I got a great mind to take that job,' Bigger said.

'Sure. You don't know what you might see.'

They laughed. Bigger turned his eyes to the screen, but he did not look. He was filled with a sense of excitement about his new job. Was what he had heard about rich white people really true? Was he going to work for people like you saw in the movies? If he were, then he'd see a lot of things from the inside; he'd get the dope, the low-down. He looked at *Trader Horn* unfold and saw pictures of naked black men and women whirling in wild dances and heard drums beating and then gradually the African scene changed and was replaced by images in his own mind of white men and women dressed in black and white clothes, laughing, talking, drinking, and dancing. Those were smart people: they knew how to get hold of money, millions of it. Maybe if he were working for them something would happen and he would get some of it. He would see just how they did it. Sure, it was all a game and white people knew how to play it. And rich white people were not so hard on Negroes: it was the poor whites who hated Negroes. They hated Negroes because they didn't have their share of the money. His mother had always told him that rich white people liked Negroes better than they did poor whites. He felt that if he were a poor white and did not get his share of the money, then he would deserve to be kicked. Poor white people were stupid. It was the right white people who were smart and knew how to treat people. He remembered hearing somebody tell a story of a Negro chauffeur who had married a rich white girl and the girl's family had shipped the couple out of the country and had supplied them with money.

Yes, his going to work for the Daltons was something big. Maybe Mr Dalton was a millionaire. Maybe he had a daughter who was a hot kind of girl; maybe she spent lots of money; maybe she'd like to come to the South Side and see the sights sometimes. Or maybe she had a secret sweetheart and only he would know about it because he would have to drive her around; maybe she would give him money not to tell.

He was a fool for wanting to rob Blum's just when he was about to get a good job. Why hadn't he thought of that before? Why take a fool's chance when other things, big things, could happen? If something slipped up this afternoon he would be out of a job and in jail, maybe. And he wasn't so hot about robbing Blum's, anyway. He frowned in the darkened movie, hearing the roll of tom-toms and the screams of black men and women dancing free and wild, men and women who were adjusted to their soil and at home in their world, secure from fear and hysteria.

'Come on, Bigger,' Jack said. 'We gotta go.'

'Hunh?'

'It's twenty to three.'

He rose and walked down the dark aisle over the soft, invisible carpet. He had seen practically nothing of the picture, but he did not care. As he walked into the lobby his insides tightened again with the thought of Gus and Blum's.

'Swell, wasn't it?'

'Yeah; it was a killer,' Bigger said.

He walked alongside Jack briskly until they came to Thirty-ninth Street.

'We better get our guns,' Bigger said.

'Yeah.'

'We got about fifteen minutes.'

'O.K.'

'So long.'

He walked home with a mounting feeling of fear. When he reached his doorway, he hesitated about going up. He didn't want to rob Blum's; he was scared. But he had to go through with it now. Noiselessly, he went up the steps and inserted his key in the lock; the door swung in silently and he heard his mother singing behind the curtain.

> 'Lord, I want to be a Christian,
> In my heart, in my heart,
> Lord, I want to be a Christian,
> In my heart, in my heart...'

He tiptoed into the room and lifted the top mattress of his bed and pulled forth the gun and slipped it inside of his shirt. Just as he was about to open the door his mother paused in her singing.

'That you, Bigger?'

He stepped quickly into the outer hallway and slammed the door and bounded headlong down the stairs. He went to the vestibule and swung through the door into the street, feeling that ball of hot tightness growing larger and heavier in his stomach and chest. He opened his mouth to breathe. He headed for Doc's and came to the door and looked inside. Jack and G.H. were shooting pool at a rear table. Gus was not there. He felt a slight lessening of nervous tension and swallowed. He looked up and down the street; very few people were out and the cop was not in sight. A clock in a window across the street told him that it was twelve minutes to three. Well, this was it; he had to go in. He lifted his left hand and wiped sweat from his forehead in a long slow gesture. He hesitated a moment longer at the door, then went in, walking with firm steps to the rear table. He did not speak to Jack or G.H., nor they to him. He lit a cigarette with shaking fingers and watched the spinning billiard balls roll and gleam and clack over the green stretch of cloth, dropping into holes after bounding to and fro from the rubber cushions. He felt impelled to say something to ease the swelling in his chest. Hurriedly, he flicked his cigarette into a spittoon and, with twin eddies of blue smoke jutting from his black nostrils, shouted hoarsely,

'Jack, I betcha two bits you can't make it!'

Jack did not answer; the ball shot straight across the table and vanished into a side pocket.

'You would've lost,' Jack said.

'Too late now,' Bigger said. 'You wouldn't bet, so *you* lost.'

He spoke without looking. His entire body hungered for keen sensation, something exciting and violent to relieve the tautness. It was now ten minutes to three and Gus had not come. If Gus stayed away much longer, it would be too late. And Gus knew that. If they were going to do anything, it certainly ought to be done before folks started coming into the streets to buy their food for supper, and while the cop was down at the other end of the block.

'That bastard!' Bigger said. 'I knew it!'

'Oh, he'll be along,' Jack said.

'Sometimes I'd like to cut his yellow heart out,' Bigger said, fingering the knife in his pocket.

'Maybe he's hanging around some meat,' G.H. said.

'He's just scared,' Bigger said. 'Scared to rob a white man.'

The billiard balls clacked. Jack chalked his cue stick and the metallic noise made Bigger grit his teeth until they ached. He didn't like that noise; it made him feel like cutting something with his knife.

'If he makes us miss this job, I'll fix 'im, so help me,' Bigger said. 'He oughtn't to be late. Every time somebody's late, things go wrong. Look at the big guys. You don't ever hear of them being late, do you? Naw! They work like clocks!'

'Ain't none of us got more guts'n Gus,' G.H. said. 'He's been with us every time.'

'Aw, shut your trap,' Bigger said.

'There you go again, Bigger,' G.H. said. 'Gus was just talking about how you act this morning. You get too nervous when something's coming off . . .'

'Don't tell me I'm nervous,' Bigger said.

'If we don't do it today, we can do it tomorrow,' Jack said.

'Tomorrow's Sunday, fool!'

'Bigger, for chrissakes! Don't holler!' Jack said tensely.

Bigger looked at Jack hard and long, then turned away with a grimace.

'Don't tell the world what we're trying to do,' Jack whispered in a mollifying tone.

Bigger walked to the front of the store and stood looking out of the plate glass window. Then, suddenly, he felt sick. He saw Gus coming along the street. And his muscles stiffened. He was going to do something to Gus; just what, he did not know. As Gus neared he heard him whistling: 'The Merry-Go-Round Broke Down . . .' The door swung in.

'Hi, Bigger,' Gus said.

Bigger did not answer. Gus passed him and started toward the rear tables. Bigger whirled and kicked him hard. Gus flopped on his face with a single movement of his body. With a look that showed that he was looking at Gus on the floor and at Jack and G.H. at the rear table and at Doc – looking at them all at once in a kind of smiling, roving, turning-slowly glance – Bigger laughed, softly at first, then harder, louder, hysterically; feeling something like hot water bubbling inside of him and trying to come out. Gus got up and stood quiet, his mouth open and his eyes dead-black with hate.

'Take it easy, boys,' Doc said, looking up from behind his counter, and then bending over again.

'What you kick me for?' Gus asked.

' 'Cause I wanted to,' Bigger said.

Gus looked at Bigger with lowered eyes. G.H. and Jack leaned on their cue sticks and watched silently.

'I'm going to fix you one of these days,' Gus threatened.

'Say that again,' Bigger said.

Doc laughed, straightening and looking at Bigger.

"Lay off the boy, Bigger.'

Gus turned and walked toward the rear tables. Bigger, with an amazing bound, grabbed him in the back of his collar.

'I asked you to say that again!'

'Quit, Bigger!' Gus spluttered, choking, sinking to his knees.

'Don't tell me to quit!'

The muscles of his body gave a tightening lunge and he saw his fist come down on the side of Gus's head; he had struck him really before he was conscious of doing so.

'Don't hurt 'im,' Jack said.

'I'll kill 'im,' Bigger said through shut teeth, tightening his hold on Gus's collar, choking him harder.

'T-turn m-m-m-me l-loose.' Gus gurgled, struggling.

'Make me!' Bigger said, drawing his fingers tighter.

Gus was very still, resting on his knees. Then, like a taut bow finding release, he sprang to his feet, shaking loose from Bigger and turning to get away. Bigger staggered back against the wall breathless for a moment. Bigger's hand moved so swiftly that nobody saw it; a gleaming blade flashed. He made a long step, as graceful as an animal leaping, threw out his left foot and tripped Gus to the floor. Gus turned over to rise, but Bigger was on top of him, with his knife open and ready.

'Get up! Get up and I'll slice your tonsils!'

Gus lay still.

'That's all right, Bigger,' Gus said in surrender. 'Lemme up.'

'You trying to make a fool out of me, ain't you?'

'Naw,' Gus said, his lips scarcely moving.

'You goddamn right you ain't,' Bigger said.

His face softened a bit and the hard glint in his bloodshot eyes died. But he still knelt with the open knife. Then he stood.

'Get up!' he said.

'Please, Bigger!'

'You want me to slice you?'

He stooped again and placed the knife at Gus's throat. Gus did not move and his large black eyes looked pleadingly. Bigger was not satisfied: he felt his muscles tightening again.

'Get up! I ain't going to ask you no more!'

Slowly, Gus stood. Bigger held the open blade an inch from Gus's lips.

'Lick it,' Bigger said, his body tingling with elation.

Gus's eyes filled with tears.

'Lick it, I said! You think I'm playing?'

Gus looked round the room without moving his head, just rolling his eyes in a mute appeal for help. But no one moved. Bigger's left fist was slowly lifting to strike. Gus's lips moved toward the knife; he stuck out his tongue and touched the blade. Gus's lips quivered and the tears streamed down his cheeks.

'Hahahaha!' Doc laughed.

'Aw, leave 'im alone,' Jack called.

Bigger watched Gus with lips twisted in a crooked smile.

'Say, Bigger, ain't you scared 'im enough?' Doc asked.

Bigger did not answer. His eyes gleamed hard again, pregnant with another idea.

'Put your hands up, way up!' he said.

Gus swallowed and stretched his hands high along the wall.

'Leave 'im alone, Bigger,' G.H. called weakly.

'I'm doing this,' Bigger said.

He put the tip of the blade into Gus's shirt and then made an arc with his arm, as though cutting a circle.

'How would you like me to cut your belly button out?'

Gus did not answer. Sweat trickled down his temples. His lips hung wide, loose.

'Shut them liver lips of yours!'

Gus did not move a muscle. Bigger pushed the knife harder into Gus's stomach.

'Bigger!' Gus said in a tense whisper.

'Shut your mouth!'

Gus shut his mouth. Doc laughed, Jack and G.H. laughed. Then Bigger stepped back and looked at Gus with a smile.

'You clown,' he said. 'Put your hands down and set on that chair.' He watched Gus sit. 'That ought to teach you not to be late next time, see?'

'We ain't late, Bigger. We still got time . . .'

'Shut up! It *is* late!' Bigger insisted commandingly.

Bigger turned aside; then, hearing a sharp scrape on the floor, stiffened. Gus sprang from the chair and grabbed a billiard ball from the table and threw it with a half-sob and half-curse. Bigger flung his hands upward to shield his face and the impact of the ball struck his wrist. He had shut his eyes when he had glimpsed the ball sailing through the air toward him and when he opened his eyes Gus was flying through the rear door and at the same time he heard the ball hit the floor and roll away. A hard pain throbbed in his hand. He sprang forward, cursing.

'You sonofabitch!'

He slipped on a cue stick lying in the middle of the floor and tumbled forward.

'That's enough now, Bigger,' Doc said, laughing.

Jack and G.H. also laughed. Bigger rose and faced them, holding his hurt hand. His eyes were red and he stared with speechless hate.

'Just keep laughing,' he said.

'Behave yourself, boy,' Doc said.

'Just keep laughing,' Bigger said again, taking out his knife.

'Watch what you're doing now,' Doc cautioned.

'Aw, Bigger,' Jack said, backing away toward the rear door.

'You done spoiled things now,' G.H. said. 'I reckon that was what you wanted . . .'

'You go to hell!' Bigger shouted, drowning out G.H.'s voice.

Doc bent down behind the counter and when he stood up he had something in his hand which he did not show. He stood there laughing. White spittle showed at the corners of Bigger's lips. He walked to the billiard table, his eyes on Doc. Then he began to cut the green cloth on the table with long sweeping strokes of his arm. He never took his eyes from Doc's face.

'Why, you sonofabitch!' Doc said. 'I ought to shoot you, so help me God! Get out, before I call a cop!'

Bigger walked slowly past Doc, looking at him, not hurrying, and holding the open knife in his hand. He paused in the doorway and looked back. Jack and G.H. were gone.

'Get out of here!' Doc said, showing a gun.

'Don't you like it?' Bigger asked.

'Get out before I shoot you!' Doc said. 'And don't you ever set your black feet inside here again!'

Doc was angry and Bigger was afraid. He shut the knife and slipped it in his pocket and swung through the door to the street. He blinked his eyes from the bright sunshine; his nerves were so taut that he had difficulty in breathing. Halfway down the block he passed Blum's store; he looked out of the corners of his eyes through the plate glass window and saw that Blum was alone and the store was empty of customers. Yes; they would have had time to rob the store; in fact, they still had time. He had lied to Gus and G.H. and Jack. He walked on; there was not a policeman in sight. Yes; they could have robbed the store and could have gotten away. He hoped the fight he had had with Gus covered up what he was trying to hide. At least the fight made him feel the equal of them. And he felt the equal of Doc, too; had he not slashed his table and dared him to use his gun?

He had an overwhelming desire to be alone; he walked to the middle of the next block and turned into an alley. He began to laugh, softly, tensely; he stopped still in his tracks and felt something warm roll down his cheek and he brushed it away. 'Jesus,' he breathed. 'I laughed so hard I cried.' Carefully, he dried his face on his coat sleeve, then stood for two whole minutes staring at the shadow of a telephone pole on the alley pavement. Suddenly he straightened and walked on with a single expulsion of breath. 'What the hell!' He stumbled violently over a tiny crack in the pavement. 'Goddamn!' he said. When he reached the end of the alley, he turned into a street, walking slowly in the sunshine, his hands jammed deep into his pockets, his head down, depressed.

He went home and sat in a chair by the window, looking out dreamily.

'That you, Bigger?' his mother called from behind the curtain.

'Yeah,' he said.

'What you run in here and run out for, a little while ago?'

'Nothing.'

'Don't you go and get into no trouble, now, boy.'

'Aw, Ma! Leave me alone.'

He listened awhile to her rubbing clothes on the metal washboard, then he gazed abstractedly into the street, thinking of how he had felt when he fought Gus in Doc's poolroom. He was relieved and glad that in an hour he was going to see about that job at the Dalton place. He was disgusted with the gang; he knew that what had happened today put an end to his being with them in any more jobs. Like a man staring regretfully but hopelessly at the stump of a cut-off arm or leg, he knew that the fear of robbing a white man had had hold of him when he started that fight with Gus; but he knew it in a way that kept it from coming to his mind in the form of a hard and sharp idea. His confused emotions had made him feel instinctively that it would be better to fight Gus and spoil the plan of the robbery than to confront a white man with a gun. But he kept this knowledge of his fear thrust firmly down in him; his courage to live depended upon how successfully his fear was hidden from his consciousness. He had fought Gus because Gus was late; that was the reason his emotions accepted and he did not try to justify himself in his own eyes, or in the eyes of the gang. He did not think enough of them to feel that he had to; he did not consider himself as being responsible to them for what he did, even though they had been involved as deeply as he in the planned robbery. He felt that same way toward everyone. As long as he could remember, he had never been responsible to anyone. The moment a situation became so that it exacted something of him, he rebelled. That was the way he lived; he passed his days trying to defeat or gratify powerful impulses in a world he feared.

*

Outside his window he saw the sun dying over the rooftops in the western sky and watched the first shade of dusk fall. Now and then a streetcar ran past. The rusty radiator hissed at the far end of the room. All day long it had been springlike; but now dark clouds were slowly swallowing the sun. All at once the street lamps came on and the sky was black and close to the house-tops.

Inside his shirt he felt the cold metal of the gun resting against his naked skin; he ought to put it back between the mattresses. No! He would keep it. He would take it with him to the Dalton place. He felt that he would be safer if he took it. He was not planning to use it and there was nothing in particular that he was afraid of, but there was in him an uneasiness and distrust that made him feel that he ought to have it along. He was going among white people, so he would take his knife and his gun; it would make him feel that he was the equal of them, give him a sense of completeness. Then he thought of a good reason why he should take it; in order to get to the Dalton place, he had to go through a white neighborhood. He had not heard of any Negroes being molested recently, but he felt that it was always possible.

Far away a clock boomed five times. He sighed and got up

and yawned and stretched his arms high above his head to loosen the muscles of his body. He got his overcoat, for it was growing cold outdoors; then got his cap. He tiptoed to the door, wanting to slip out without his mother hearing him. Just as he was about to open it, she called,

'Bigger!'

He stopped and frowned.

'Yeah, Ma.'

'You going to see about that job?'

'Yeah.'

'Ain't you going to eat?'

'I ain't got time now.'

She came to the door, wiping her soapy hands upon an apron.

'Here; take this quarter and buy you something.'

'O.K.'

'And be careful, son.'

He went out and walked south to Forty-sixth Street, then eastward. Well, he would see in a few moments if the Daltons for whom he was to work were like the people he had seen and heard in the movie. But while walking through this quiet and spacious white neighborhood, he did not feel the pull and mystery of the thing as strongly as he had in the movie. The houses he passed were huge: lights glowed softly in windows. The streets were empty, save for an occasional car that zoomed past on swift rubber tires. This was a cold and distant world; a world of white secrets carefully guarded. He could feel a pride, a certainty, and a confidence in these streets and houses. He came to Drexel Boulevard and began to look for 4605. When he came to it, he stopped and stood before a high, black, iron picket fence, feeling constricted inside. All he had felt in the movie was gone; only fear and emptiness filled him now.

Would they expect him to come in the front way or back? It was queer that he had not thought of that. Goddamn! He walked the length of the picket fence in front of the house, seeking for a walk leading to the rear. But there was none. Other than the front gate, there was only a driveway, the entrance to which was securely locked. Suppose a policeman saw him wandering in a white neighborhood like this? It would be thought that he was trying to rob or rape somebody. He grew angry. Why had he come to take this goddamn job? He could have stayed among his own people and escaped feeling this fear and hate. This was not his world; he had been foolish in thinking that he would have liked it. He stood in the middle of the sidewalk with his jaws clamped tight; he wanted to strike something with his fist. Well ... Goddamn! There was nothing to do but go in the front way. If he were doing wrong, they could not kill him, at least; all they could do was to tell him that he could not get the job.

Timidly, he lifted the latch on the gate and walked to the steps. He paused, waiting for someone to challenge him. Nothing happened. Maybe nobody was home? He went to the door and saw a dim light burning in a shaded niche above a doorbell. He pushed it and was startled to hear a soft gong sound within. Maybe he had pushed it too hard? Aw, what the hell! He had to do better than this; he relaxed his taut muscles and stood at ease, waiting. The doorknob turned. The door opened. He saw a white face. It was a woman.

'Hello!'

'Yessum,' he said.

'You want to see somebody?'

'Er ... Er ... I want to see Mr Dalton.'

'Are you the Thomas boy?'

'Yessum.'

'Come in.'

He edged through the door slowly, then stopped halfway. The woman was so close to him that he could see a tiny mole at the corner of her mouth. He held his breath. It seemed that there was not room enough for him to pass without actually touching her.

'Come on in,' the woman said.

'Yessum,' he whispered.

He squeezed through and stood uncertainly in a softly lighted hallway.

'Follow me,' she said.

With cap in hand and shoulders sloped, he followed, walking over a rug so soft and deep that it seemed he was going to fall at each step he took. He went into a dimly lit room.

'Take a seat,' she said. 'I'll tell Mr Dalton that you're here and he'll be out in a moment.'

'Yessum.'

He sat and looked up at the woman; she was staring at him and he looked away in confusion. He was glad when she left. That old bastard! What's so damn funny about me? I'm just like she is . . . He felt that the position in which he was sitting was too awkward and found that he was on the very edge of the chair. He rose slightly to sit farther back; but when he sat he sank down so suddenly and deeply that he thought the chair had collapsed under him. He bounded halfway up, in fear; then, realizing what had happened, he sank distrustfully down again. He looked round the room; it was lit by dim lights glowing from a hidden source. He tried to find them by roving his eyes, but could not. He had not expected anything like this; he had not thought that this world would be so utterly different from his own that it would intimidate him. On the smooth walls were several paintings whose nature he tried to make out, but failed. He would have liked to examine them, but dared not. Then he listened; a faint sound of piano music floated to him from somewhere. He was sitting in a white home; dim lights burned round him; strange objects challenged him; and he was feeling angry and uncomfortable.

'All right. Come this way.'

He started at the sound of a man's voice.

'Suh?'

'Come this way.'

Misjudging how far back he was sitting in the chair, his first attempt to rise failed and he slipped back, resting on his side. Grabbing the arms of the chair, he pulled himself upright and found a tall, lean, white-haired man holding a piece of paper in his hand. The man was gazing at him with an amused smile that made him conscious of every square inch of skin on his black body.

'Thomas?' the man asked. 'Bigger Thomas?'

'Yessuh,' he whispered; not speaking, really; but hearing his words issue involuntarily from his lips, as of a force of their own.

'Come this way.'

'Yessuh.'

He followed the man out of the room and down a hall. The man stopped abruptly. Bigger paused, bewildered; then he saw coming slowly towards him a tall, thin, white woman, walking silently, her hands lifted delicately in the air and touching the walls to either side of her. Bigger stepped back to let her pass. Her face and hair were completely white; she seemed to him like a ghost. The man took her arm gently and held her for a moment. Bigger saw that she was old and her gray eyes looked stony.

'Are you all right?' the man asked.

'Yes,' she answered.

'Where's Peggy?'

'She's preparing dinner. I'm quite all right, Henry.'

'You shouldn't be alone this way. When is Mrs Patterson coming back?' the man asked.

'She'll be back Monday. But Mary's here. I'm all right; don't worry about me. Is someone with you?'

'Oh, yes. This is the boy the relief sent.'

'The relief people were very anxious for you to work for us,' the woman said; she did not move her body or face as she talked, but she spoke in a tone of voice that indicated that she was speaking to Bigger. 'I hope you'll like it here.'

'Yessum,' Bigger whispered faintly, wondering as he did so if he ought to say anything at all.

'How far did you go in school?'

'To the eighth grade, mam.'

'Don't you think it would be a wise procedure to inject him into his new environment at once, so he could get the feel of things?' the woman asked, addressing herself by the tone of her voice to the man now.

'Well, tomorrow'll be time enough,' the man said hesitantly.

'I think it's important emotionally that he feels free to trust his environment,' the woman said. 'Using the analysis contained in the case record the relief sent us, I think we should evoke an immediate feeling of confidence ...'

'But that's too abrupt,' the man said.

Bigger listened, blinking and bewildered. The long strange words they used made no sense to him; it was another language. He felt from the tone of their voices that they were having a difference of opinion about him, but he could not determine what it was about. It made him uneasy, tense, as though there were influences and presences about him which he could feel but not see. He felt strangely blind.

'Well, let's try it,' the woman said.

'Oh, all right. We'll see. We'll see,' the man said.

The man let go of the woman and she walked on slowly, the long white fingers of her hands just barely touching the walls. Behind the woman, following at the hem of her dress, was a big white cat, pacing without sound. She's blind! Bigger thought in amazement.

'Come on; this way,' the man said.

'Yessuh.'

He wondered if the man had seen him staring at the woman. He would have to be careful here. There were so many strange things. He followed the man into a room.

'Sit down.'

'Yessuh,' he said, sitting.

'That was Mrs Dalton,' the man said. 'She's blind.'

'Yessuh.'

'She has a very deep interest in colored people.'

'Yessuh,' Bigger whispered. He was conscious of the effort to breathe; he licked his lips and fumbled nervously with his cap.

'Well, I'm Mr Dalton.'

'Yessuh.'

'Do you think you'd like driving a car?'

'Oh, yessuh.'

'Did you bring the paper?'

'Suh?'

'Didn't the relief give you a note to me?'

'Oh, yessuh!'

He had completely forgotten about the paper. He stood to reach into his vest pocket and, in doing so, dropped his cap. For a moment his impulses were deadlocked; he did not know if he should pick up his cap and then find the paper, or find the paper and then pick up his cap. He decided to pick up his cap.

'Put your cap here,' said Mr Dalton, indicating a place on his desk.

'Yessuh.'

Then he was stone-still; the white cat bounded past him and leaped upon the desk; it sat looking at him with large placid eyes and mewed plaintively.

'What's the matter, Kate?' Mr Dalton asked, stroking the cat's fur and smiling. Mr Dalton turned back to Bigger. 'Did you find it?'

'Nawsuh. But I got it here, somewhere.'

He hated himself at that moment. Why was he acting and feeling this way? He wanted to wave his hand and blot out the white man who was making him feel like this. If not that, he wanted to blot himself out. He had not raised his eyes to the level of Mr Dalton's face once since he had been in the house. He stood with his knees slightly bent, his lips partly open, his shoulders stooped; and his eyes held a look that went only to the surface of things. There was an organic conviction in him that this was the way white folks wanted him to be when in their presence; none had ever told him that in so many words, but their manner had made him feel that they did. He laid the cap down, noticing that Mr Dalton was watching him closely. Maybe he was not acting right? Goddamn! Clumsily, he searched for the paper. He could not find it at first and he felt called upon to say something for taking so long.

'I had it right here in my vest pocket,' he mumbled.

'Take your time.'

'Oh, here it is.'

He drew the paper forth. It was crumpled and soiled. Nervously, he straightened it out and handed it to Mr Dalton, holding it by its very tip end.

'All right, now,' said Mr Dalton. 'Let's see what you've got here. You live at 3721 Indiana Avenue?'

'Yessuh.'

Mr Dalton paused, frowned, and looked up at the ceiling.

'What kind of building is that over there?'

'You mean where I live, suh?'

'Yes.'

'Oh, it's just an old building.'

'Where do you pay rent?'

'Down on Thirty-first Street.'

'To the South Side Real Estate Company?'

'Yessuh.'

Bigger wondered what all these questions could mean; he had heard that Mr Dalton owned the South Side Real Estate Company, but he was not sure.

'How much rent do you pay?'

'Eight dollars a week.'

'For how many rooms?'

'We just got one, suh.'

'I see . . . Now, Bigger, tell me, how old are you?'

'I'm twenty, suh.'

'Married?'

'Nawsuh.'

'Sit down. You needn't stand. And I won't be long.'

'Yessuh.'

He sat. The white cat still contemplated him with large, moist eyes.

'Now, you have a mother, a brother, and a sister?'

'Yessuh.'

'There are four of you?'

'Yessuh, there's four of us,' he stammered, trying to show that he was not as stupid as he might appear. He felt a need to speak more, for he felt that maybe Mr Dalton expected it. And he suddenly remembered the many times his mother had told him not to look at the floor when talking with white folks or asking for a job. He lifted his eyes and saw Mr Dalton watching him closely. He dropped his eyes again.

'They call you Bigger?'

'Yessuh.'

'Now, Bigger, I'd like to talk with you a little . . .'

Yes, goddammit! He knew what was coming. He would be asked about that time he had been accused of stealing auto tires and had been sent to the reform school. He felt guilty, condemned. He should not have come here.

'The relief people said some funny things about you. I'd like to talk to you about them. Now, you needn't feel ashamed with me,' said Mr Dalton, smiling. 'I was a boy myself once and I think I know how things are. So just be yourself . . .' Mr Dalton pulled out a package of cigarettes. 'Here; have one.'

'Nawsuh; thank you, suh.'

'You don't smoke?'

'Yessuh. But I just don't want one now.'

'Now, Bigger, the relief people said you were a very good worker when you were interested in what you were doing. Is that true?'

'Well, I do my work, suh.'

'But they said you were always in trouble. How do you explain that?'

'I don't know, suh.'

'Why did they send you to the reform school?'

His eyes glared at the floor.

'They said I was stealing!' he blurted defensively. 'But I wasn't.'

'Are you sure?'

'Yessuh.'

'Well, how did you get mixed up in it?'

'I was with some boys and the police picked us up.'

Mr Dalton said nothing. Bigger heard a clock ticking somewhere behind him and he had a foolish impulse to look at it. But he restrained himself.

'Well, Bigger, how do you feel about it now?'

'Suh? 'Bout what?'

'If you had a job, would you steal now?'

'Oh, nawsuh. I don't steal.'

'Well,' said Mr Dalton, 'they say you can drive a car and I'm going to give you a job.'

He said nothing.

'You think you can handle it?'

'Oh, yessuh.'

'The pay calls for $20 a week, but I'm going to give you $25. The extra $5 is for yourself, for you to spend as you like. You will get the clothes you need and your meals. You're to sleep in the back room, above the kitchen. You can give the $20 to your mother to keep your brother and sister in school. How does that sound?'

'It sounds all right. Yessuh.'

'I think we'll get along.'

'Yessuh.'

'I don't think we'll have any trouble.'

'Nawsuh.'

'Now, Bigger,' said Mr Dalton, 'since that's settled, let's see what you'll have to do every day. I leave every morning for my office at nine. It's a twenty-minute drive. You are to be back at ten and take Miss Dalton to school. At twelve, you call for Miss Dalton at the University. From then until night you are more or less free. If either Miss Dalton or I go out at night, of course, you do the driving. You work every day, but we don't get up till noon on Sundays. So you will have Sunday mornings to yourself, unless something unexpected happens. You get one full day off every two weeks.'

'Yessuh.'

'You think you can handle that?'

'Oh, yessuh.'

'And any time you're bothered about anything, come and see me. Let's talk it over.'

'Yessuh.'

'Oh, Father!' a girl's voice sang out.

'Yes, Mary,' said Mr Dalton.

Bigger turned and saw a white girl walk into the room. She was very slender.

'Oh, I didn't know you were busy.'

'That's all right, Mary. What is it?'

Bigger saw that the girl was looking at him.

'Is this the new chauffeur, Father?'

'What do you want, Mary?'

'Will you get the tickets for the Thursday concert?'

'At Orchestra Hall?'

'Yes.'

'Yes. I'll get them.'

'Is this the new chauffeur?'

'Yes,' said Mr Dalton. 'This is Bigger Thomas.'

'Hello, Bigger,' the girl said.

Bigger swallowed. He looked at Mr Dalton, then felt that he should not have looked.

'Good evening, mam.'

The girl came close to him and stopped just opposite his chair.

'Bigger, do you belong to a union?' she asked.

'Now, Mary!' said Mr Dalton, frowning.

'Well, Father, he should,' the girl said, turning to him, then back to Bigger. 'Do you?'

'Mary . . .' said Mr Dalton.

'I'm just asking him a question, Father!'

Bigger hesitated. He hated the girl then. Why did she have to do this when he was trying to get a job?

'No'm,' he mumbled, his head down and his eyes glowering.

'And why not?' the girl asked.

Bigger heard Mr Dalton mumble something. He wished Mr Dalton would speak and end this thing. He looked up and saw Mr Dalton staring at the girl. She's making me lose my job! he thought. Goddamn! He knew nothing about unions, except that they were considered bad. And what did she mean by talking to him this way in front of Mr Dalton, who, surely, didn't like unions?

'We can settle about the union later, Mary,' said Mr Dalton.

'But you wouldn't mind belonging to a union, would you?' the girl asked.

'I don't know, mam,' Bigger said.

'Now, Mary, you can see that the boy is new,' said Mr. Dalton. 'Leave him alone.'

The girl turned and poked out a red tongue at him.

'All right, Mr Capitalist!' She turned again to Bigger. 'Isn't he a capitalist, Bigger?'

Bigger looked at the floor and did not answer. He did not know what a capitalist was.

The girl started to leave, but stopped.

'Oh, Father, if he hasn't anything else to do, let him drive me to my lecture at the University tonight.'

'I'm talking to him now, Mary. He'll be through in a moment.'

The girl picked up the cat and walked from the room. There was a short interval of silence. Bigger wished the girl had not said anything about unions. Maybe he would not be hired now. Or, if hired, maybe he would be fired soon if she kept acting like that. He had never seen anyone like her before. She was not a bit the way he had imagined she would be.

'Oh, Mary!' Mr Dalton called.

'Yes, Father,' Bigger heard her answer from the hallway.

Mr Dalton rose and left the room. He sat still, listening. Once or twice he thought he heard the girl laugh, but he was not sure. The best thing he could do was to leave that crazy girl alone. He had heard about unions; in his mind unions and Communists were linked. He relaxed a little, then stiffened when he heard Mr Dalton walk back into the room. Wordlessly, the white man sat behind the desk and picked up the paper and looked at it in a long silence. Bigger watched him with lowered eyes; he knew that Mr Dalton was thinking of something other than that paper. In his heart he cursed the crazy girl. Maybe Mr Dalton was deciding not to hire him. Goddamn! Maybe he would not get the extra five dollars a week now. *Goddamn that woman!* She spoiled everything! Maybe Mr Dalton would feel that he could not trust him.

'Oh, Bigger,' said Mr Dalton.

'Yessuh.'

'I want you to know why I'm hiring you.'

'Yessuh.'

'You see, Bigger, I'm a supporter of the National Association for the Advancement of Colored People. Did you ever hear of that organization?'

'Nawsuh.'

'Well, it doesn't matter,' said Mr Dalton. 'Have you had your dinner?'

'Nawsuh.'

'Well, I think you'll do.'

Mr Dalton pushed a button. There was silence. The woman who had answered the front door came in.

'Yes, Mr Dalton.'

'Peggy, this is Bigger. He's going to drive for us. Give him something to eat, and show him where he's to sleep and where the car is.'

'Yes, Mr Dalton.'

'And, Bigger, at eight-thirty, drive Miss Dalton out to the University and wait for her,' said Mr Dalton.

'Yessuh.'

'That's all now.'

'Yessuh.'

'Come with me,' Peggy said.

Bigger rose and got his cap and followed the woman through the house to the kitchen. The air was full of the scent of food cooking and pots bubbled on the stove.

'Sit here,' Peggy said, clearing a place for him at a white-topped table. He sat and rested his cap on his knees. He felt a little better now that he was out of the front part of the house, but still not quite comfortable.

'Dinner isn't quite ready yet,' Peggy said. 'You like bacon and eggs?'

'Yessum.'

'Coffee?'

'Yessum.'

He sat looking at the white walls of the kitchen and heard the woman stir about behind him.

'Did Mr Dalton tell you about the furnace?'

'No'm.'

'Well, he must have forgotten it. You're supposed to attend to that, too. I'll show you where it is before you go.'

'You mean I got to keep the fire going, mam?'

'Yes. But it's easy. Did you ever fire before?'

'No'm.'

'You can learn. There's nothing to it.'

'Yessum.'

Peggy seemed kind enough, but maybe she was being kind in order to shove her part of the work on him. Well, he would wait and see. If she got nasty, he would talk to Mr Dalton about her. He smelt the odor of frying bacon and realized that he was very hungry. He had forgotten to buy a sandwich with the quarter his mother had given him, and he had not eaten since morning. Peggy placed a plate, knife, fork, spoon, sugar, cream, and bread before him; then she dished up the bacon and eggs.

'You can get more if you want it.'

The food was good. This was not going to be a bad job. The only thing bad so far was that crazy girl. He chewed his bacon and eggs while some remote part of his mind considered in amazement how different this rich girl was from the one he had seen in the movies. This woman he had watched on the screen had not seemed dangerous and his mind had been able to do with her as it liked, but this rich girl walked over everything, put herself in the way and, what was strange beyond understanding, talked and acted so simply and directly that she confounded him. He had quite forgotten that Peggy was in the kitchen and when his plate was empty he took a soft piece of bread and began to sop it clean, carrying the bread to his mouth in huge chunks.

'You want some more?'

He stopped chewing and laid the bread aside. He had not wanted to let her see him do that; he did that only at home.

'No'm,' he said. 'I got a plenty.'

'You reckon you'll like it here?' Peggy asked.

'Yessum. I hope so.'

'This is a swell place,' Peggy said. 'About as good as you'll find anywhere. The last colored man who worked for us stayed ten years.'

Bigger wondered why she said 'us'. She must stand in with the old man and old woman pretty good, he thought.

'Ten years?' he said.

'Yes; ten years. His name was Green. He was a good man, too.'

'How came he to leave?'

'Oh, he was smart, that Green was. He took a job with the government. Mrs Dalton made him go to night school. Mrs Dalton's always trying to help somebody.'

Yes; Bigger knew that. But he was not going to any night school. He looked at Peggy; she was bent over the sink, washing dishes. Her words had challenged him and he felt he had to say something.

'Yessum, he was smart,' he said. 'And ten years is a long time.'

'Oh, it wasn't so long,' Peggy said. 'I've been here twenty years myself. I always was one for sticking to a job. I always say when you get a good place, then stick there. A rolling stone gathers no moss, and it's true.'

Bigger said nothing.

'Everything's simple and nice around here,' Peggy said. 'They've got millions, but they live like human beings. They don't put on airs and strut. Mrs Dalton believes that people should be that way.'

'Yessum.'

'They're Christian people and believe in everybody working hard, and living a clean life. Some people think we ought to have more servants than we do, but we get along. It's just like one big family.'

'Yessum.'

'Mr Dalton's a fine man,' Peggy said.

'Oh, yessum. He is.'

95

'You know, he does a lot for your people.'

'My people?' asked Bigger, puzzled.

'Yes, the colored people. He gave over five million dollars to colored schools.'

'Oh!'

'But Mrs Dalton's the one who's really nice. If it wasn't for her, he would not be doing what he does. She made him rich. She had millions when he married her. Of course, he made a lot of money himself afterwards out of real estate. But most of the money's hers. She's blind, poor thing. She lost her sight ten years ago. Did you see her yet?'

'Yessum.'

'Was she alone?'

'Yessum.'

'Poor thing! Mrs Patterson, who takes care of her, is away for the week-end and she's all alone. Isn't it too bad, about her?'

'Oh, yessum,' he said, trying to get into his voice some of the pity for Mrs Dalton that he thought Peggy expected him to feel.

'It's really more than a job you've got here,' Peggy went on. 'It's just like home. I'm always telling Mrs Dalton that this is the only home I'll ever know. I wasn't in this country but two years before I started working here . . .'

'Oh,' said Bigger, looking at her.

'I'm Irish, you know,' she said. 'My folks in the old country feel about England like the colored folks feel about this country. So I know something about colored people. Oh, these are fine people, fine as silk. Even the girl. Did you meet her yet?'

'Yessum.'

'Tonight?'

'Yessum.'

Peggy turned and looked at him sharply.

'She's a sweet thing, she is,' she said. 'I've known her since she was two years old. To me she's still a baby and will always be one. But she's kind of wild, she is. Always in hot water. Keeps her folks worried to death, she does. She runs around with a wild and crazy bunch of reds . . .'

'*Reds!*' Bigger exclaimed.

'Yes. But she don't mean nothing by it,' Peggy said. 'Like her mother and father, she feels sorry for people and she thinks the reds'll do something for 'em. The Lord only knows where she got her wild ways, but she's got 'em. If you stay around here, you'll get to know her. But don't you pay no attention to her red friends. They just keep up a lot of fuss.'

Bigger wanted to ask her to tell him more about the girl, but thought that he had better not do that now.

'If you're through, I'll show you the furnace and the car, and where your room is,' she said and turned the fire low under the pots on the stove.

'Yessum.'

He rose and followed her out of the kitchen, down a narrow stairway at the end of which was the basement. It was dark: Bigger heard a sharp click and the light came on.

'This way . . . What did you say your name was?'

'Bigger, mam.'

'What?'

'Bigger.'

He smelt the scent of coal and ashes and heard fire roaring. He saw a red bed of embers glowing in the furnace.

'This is the furnace,' she said.

'Yessum.'

'Every morning you'll find the garbage here; you burn it and put the bucket on the dumb-waiter.'

'Yessum.'

'You never have to use a shovel for coal. It's a self-feeder. Look, see?'

Peggy pulled a lever and there came a loud rattle of fine lumps of coal sliding down a metal chute. Bigger stooped and saw, through the cracks of the furnace, the coal spreading out fanwise over the red bed of fire.

'That's fine,' he mumbled in admiration.

'And you don't have to worry about water, either. It fills itself.'

Bigger liked that; it was easy; it would be fun, almost.

'Your biggest trouble will be taking out the ashes and sweeping. And keep track of how the coal runs; when it's low, tell me or Mr Dalton and we'll order some more.'

'Yessum. I can handle it.'

'Now, to get to your room all you have to do is go up these back stairs. Come on.'

He followed up a stretch of stairs. She opened a door and switched on a light and Bigger saw a large room whose walls were covered with pictures of girls' faces and prize fighters.

'This was Green's room. He was always one for pictures. But he kept things neat and nice. It's plenty warm here. Oh, yes; before I forget. Here are the keys to the room and the garage and the car. Now, I'll show you the garage. You have to get to it from the outside.'

He followed her down the steps and outside into the driveway. It was much warmer.

'Looks like snow,' Peggy said.

'Yessum.'

'This is the garage,' she said, unlocking and pushing open a door which, as it swung in, made lights come on automatically. 'You always bring the car out and wait at the side door for the folks. Let's see. You say you're driving Miss Dalton tonight?'

'Yessum.'

'Well, she leaves at eight-thirty. So you're free until then. You can look over your room if you want to.'

'Yessum. I reckon I will.'

Bigger went behind Peggy down the stairs and back into the basement. She went to the kitchen and he went to his room. He stood in the middle of the floor, looking at the walls. There were pictures of Jack Johnson, Joe Louis, Jack Dempsey, and Henry Armstrong; there were others of Ginger Rogers, Jean Harlow, and Janet Gaynor. The room was large and had two radiators. He felt the bed; it was soft. Gee! He would bring Bessie here some night. Not right at once; he would wait until he had learned the ropes of the place. A room all to himself! He could bring a pint of liquor up here and drink it in peace. He would not have to slip around any more. He would not have to sleep with Buddy and stand Buddy's kicking all night long. He lit a cigarette and stretched himself full length upon the bed. Ohhhh . . . This was not going to be bad at all. He looked at his dollar watch; it was seven. In a little while he would go down and examine the car. And he would buy himself another watch, too. A dollar watch was not good enough for a job like this; he would buy a gold one. There were a lot of new things he could get. Oh, boy! This would be an easy life. Everything was all right, except that girl. She worried him. She might cause him to lose his job if she kept talking about unions. She was a funny girl, all right. Never in his life had he met anyone like her. She puzzled him. She was rich, but she didn't act like she was rich. She acted like . . . Well, he didn't know exactly what she did act like. In all of the white women he had met, mostly on jobs and at relief stations, there was always a certain coldness and reserve; they stood their distance and spoke to him from afar. But this girl waded right in and hit him between the eyes with her words and ways. Aw, hell! What good was there in thinking about her like this? Maybe she was all right. Maybe he would just have to get used to her; that was all. I bet she spends a plenty of dough, he thought. And the old man had given five million dollars to colored people. If a man could give five million dollars away, the millions must be as common to him as nickels. He rose up and sat on the edge of the bed.

What make of car was he to drive? He had not thought to look when Peggy had opened the garage door. He hoped it would be a Packard, or a Lincoln, or a Rolls Royce. Boy! Would he drive! Just wait! Of course, he would be careful when he was driving Miss or Mr Dalton. But when he was alone he would burn up the pavement; he would make those tires smoke!

He licked his lips; he was thirsty. He looked at his watch; it was ten past eight. He would go to the kitchen and get a drink of water and then drive the car out of the garage. He went down the steps, through the basement to the stairs leading to the kitchen door. Though he did not know it, he walked on tiptoe. He eased the door open and peeped in. What he saw

99

made him suck his breath in; Mrs Dalton in flowing white clothes was standing stonestill in the middle of the kitchen floor. There was silence, save for the slow ticking of a large clock on a white wall. For a moment he did not know if he should go in or go back down the steps; his thirst was gone. Mrs Dalton's face was held in an attitude of intense listening and her hands were hanging loosely at her sides. To Bigger her face seemed to be capable of hearing in every pore of the skin and listening always to some low voice speaking. Sitting quietly on the floor beside her was the white cat, its large black eyes fastened upon him. It made him uneasy just to look at her and that white cat; he was about to close the door and tiptoe softly back down the stairs when she spoke.

'Are you the new boy?'

'Yessum.'

'Did you want something?'

'I didn't mean to disturb you, mam. I – I . . . I just wanted a drink of water.'

'Well, come on in. I think you'll find a glass somewhere.'

He went to the sink, watching her as he walked, feeling that she could see him even though he knew that she was blind. His skin tingled. He took a glass from a narrow shelf and filled it from a faucet. As he drank he stole a glance at her over the rim of the glass. Her face was still, tilted, waiting. It reminded him of a dead man's face he had once seen. Then he realized that Mrs Dalton had turned and listened to the sound of his feet as he had walked. She knows exactly where I'm standing, he thought.

'You like your room?' she asked; and as she spoke he realized that she had been standing there waiting to hear the sound of his glass as it had clinked on the sink.

'Oh, yessum.'

'I hope you're a careful driver.'

'Oh, yessum. I'll be careful.'

'Did you ever drive before?'

'Yessum. But it was a grocery truck.'

He had the feeling that talking to a blind person was like talking to someone whom he himself could scarcely see.

'How far did you say you went in school, Bigger?'

'To the eighth grade, mam.'

'Did you ever think of going back?'

'Well, I gotta work now, mam.'

'Suppose you had the chance to go back?'

'Well, I don't know, mam.'

'The last man who worked here went to night school and got an education.'

'Yessum.'

'What would you want to be if you had an education?'

'I don't know, mam.'

'Did you ever think about it?'

'No'm.'

'You would rather work?'

'I reckon I would, mam.'

'Well, we'll talk about that some other time. I think you'd better get the car for Miss Dalton now.'

'Yessum.'

He left her standing in the middle of the kitchen floor, exactly as he had found her. He did not know just how to take her; she made him feel that she would judge all he did harshly but kindly. He had a feeling toward her that was akin to that which he held toward his mother. The difference in his feelings toward Mrs Dalton and his mother was that he felt that his mother wanted him to do the things *she* wanted him to do, and he felt that Mrs Dalton wanted him to do the things she felt that *he* should have wanted to do. But he did not want to go to night school. Night school was all right; but he had other plans. Well, he didn't know just what they were right now, but he was working them out.

The night air had grown warmer. A wind had risen. He lit a cigarette and unlocked the garage; the door swung in and again he was surprised and pleased to see the lights spring on automatically. These people's got everything, he mused. He examined the car; it was a dark blue Buick, with steel spoke wheels and of a new make. He stepped back from it and looked it over; then he opened the door and looked at the dashboard.

He was a little disappointed that the car was not so expensive as he had hoped, but what it lacked in price was more than made up for in color and style. 'It's all right,' he said half-aloud. He got in and backed it into the driveway and turned it round and pulled it up to the side door.

'Is that you, Bigger?'

The girl stood on the steps.

'Yessum.'

He got out and held the rear door open for her.

'Thank you.'

He touched his cap and wondered if it were the right thing to do.

'Is it that university-school out there on the Midway, mam?'

Through the rear mirror above him he saw her hesitate before answering.

'Yes; that's the one.'

He pulled the car into the street and headed south, driving about thirty-five miles an hour. He handled the car expertly, picking up speed at the beginning of each block and slowing slightly as he approached each street intersection.

'You drive well,' she said.

'Yessum,' he said proudly.

He watched her through the rear mirror as he drove; she was kind of pretty, but very little. She looked like a doll in a show window: black eyes, white face, red lips. And she was not acting at all now as she had acted when he first saw her. In fact, she had a remote look in her eyes. He stopped the car at Forty-seventh Street for a red light; he did not have to stop again until he reached Fifty-first Street where a long line of cars formed in front of him and a long line in back. He held the steering wheel lightly, waiting for the line to move forward. He had a keen sense of power when driving; the feel of a car added something to him. He loved to press his foot against a pedal and sail along, watching others stand still, seeing the asphalt road unwind under him. The lights flashed from red to green and he nosed the car forward.

'Bigger!'

'Yessum.'

'Turn at this corner and pull up on a side street.'

'Here, mam?'

'Yes; here.'

Now what on earth did this mean? He pulled the car off Cottage Grove Avenue and drew to a curb. He turned to look at her and was startled to see that she was sitting on the sheer edge of the back seat, her face some six inches from his.

'I scare you?' she asked softly, smiling.

'Oh, no'm,' he mumbled, bewildered.

He watched her through the mirror. Her tiny white hands dangled over the back of the front seat and her eyes looked out vacantly.

'I don't know how to say what I'm going to say,' she said.

He said nothing. There was a long silence. What in all hell did this girl want? A street car rumbled by. Behind him, reflected in the rear mirror, he saw the traffic lights flash from green to red, and back again. Well, whatever she was going to say, he wished she would say it and get it over. This girl was strange. She did the unexpected every minute. He waited for her to speak. She took her hands from the back of the front seat and fumbled in her purse.

'Gotta match?'

'Yessum.'

He dug a match from his vest pocket.

'Strike it,' she said.

He blinked. He struck the match and held the flame for her. She smoked awhile in silence.

'You're not a tattletale, are you?' she asked with a smile.

He opened his mouth to reply, but no words came. What she had asked and the tone of voice in which she had asked it made him feel that he ought to have answered in some way; but what?

'I'm not going to the University,' she said at last. 'But you can forget that. I want you to drive me to the Loop. But if anyone should ask you, then I went to the University, see, Bigger?'

'Yessum, it's all right 'with me,' he mumbled.

'I think I can trust you.'

'Yessum.'

'After all, I'm on your side.'

Now, what did *that* mean? She was on *his* side. What side was he on? Did she mean that she liked people? Well, he had heard that about her whole family. Was she really crazy? How much did her folks know of how she acted? But if she were really crazy, why did Mr Dalton let him drive her out?

'I'm going to meet a friend of mine who's also a friend of yours,' she said.

'Friend of mine!' he could not help exclaiming.

'Oh, you don't know him yet,' she said, laughing.

'Oh.'

'Go to the Outer Drive and then to 16 Lake Street.'

'Yessum.'

Maybe she was talking about the reds? *That* was it! But none of his friends were reds. What was all this? If Mr Dalton should ask him if he had taken her to the University, he would have to say yes and depend upon her to back him up. But suppose Mr Dalton had someone watching, someone who would tell where he had really taken her? He had heard that many rich people had detectives working for them. If only he knew what this was all about he would feel much better. And she had said that she was going to meet someone who was a friend of his. He didn't want to meet any Communists. They didn't have any money. He felt that it was all right for a man to go to jail for robbery, but to go to jail for fooling around with reds was bunk. Well, he would drive her; that was what he had been hired for. But he was going to watch his step in this business. The only thing he hoped was that she would not make him lose his job. He pulled the car off the Outer Drive at Seventh Street, drove north on Michigan Boulevard to Lake Street, then headed west for two blocks, looking for number 16.

'It's right here, Bigger.'

'Yessum.'

He pulled to a stop in front of a dark building.

'Wait,' she said, getting out of the car.

He saw her smiling broadly at him, almost laughing. He felt that she knew every feeling and thought he had at that moment and he turned his head away in confusion. Goddamn that woman!

'I won't be long,' she said.

She started off, then turned back.

'Take it easy, Bigger. You'll understand it better bye and bye.'

'Yessum,' he said, trying to smile; but couldn't.

'Isn't there a song like that, a song your people sing?'

'Like what, mam?'

'We'll understand it better bye and bye?'

'Oh, yessum.'

She was an odd girl, all right. He felt something in her over and above the fear she inspired in him. She responded to him as if he were human, as if he lived in the same world as she. And he had never felt that before in a white person. But why? Was this some kind of game? The guarded feeling of freedom he had while listening to her was tangled with the hard fact that she was white and rich, a part of the world of people who told him what he could and could not do.

He looked at the building into which she had gone; it was old and unpainted; there were no lights in the windows or doorway. Maybe she was meeting her sweetheart? If that was all, then things would straighten out. But if she had gone to meet those Communists? And what were Communists like, anyway? Was *she* one? What made people Communists? He remembered seeing many cartoons of Communists in newspapers and always they had flaming torches in their hands and wore beards and were trying to commit murder or set things on fire. People who acted that way were crazy. All he could recall having heard about Communists was associated in his mind with darkness, old houses, people speaking in whispers, and trade unions on strike. And this was something like it.

He stiffened; the door into which she had gone opened. She

came out, followed by a young white man. They walked to the car; but, instead of getting into the back seat, they came to the side of the car and stood, facing him.

'Oh, Bigger, this is Jan. And Jan, this is Bigger Thomas.'

Jan smiled broadly, then extended an open palm toward him. Bigger's entire body tightened with suspense and dread.

'How are you, Bigger?'

Bigger's right hand gripped the steering wheel and he wondered if he ought to shake hands with this white man.

'I'm fine,' he mumbled.

Jan's hand was still extended. Bigger's right hand raised itself about three inches, then stopped in mid-air.

'Come on and shake,' Jan said.

Bigger extended a limp palm, his mouth open in astonishment. He felt Jan's fingers tighten about his own. He tried to pull his hand away, ever so gently, but Jan held on, firmly, smiling.

'We may as well get to know each other,' Jan said. 'I'm a friend of Mary's.'

'Yessuh,' he mumbled.

'First of all,' Jan continued, putting his foot upon the running-board, 'don't say *sir* to me. I'll call you Bigger and you'll call me Jan. That's the way it'll be between us. How's that?'

Bigger did not answer. Mary was smiling. Jan still gripped his hand and Bigger held his head at an oblique angle, so that he could, by merely shifting his eyes, look at Jan and then out into the street whenever he did not wish to meet Jan's gaze. He heard Mary laughing softly.

'It's all right, Bigger,' she said. 'Jan *means* it.'

He flushed warm with anger. Goddam her soul to hell! Was she laughing at him? Were they making fun of him? What was it that they wanted? Why didn't they leave him alone? He was not bothering them. Yes, anything could happen with people like these. His entire mind and body were painfully concentrated into a single sharp point of attention. He was trying desperately to understand. He felt foolish sitting behind the steering wheel like this and letting a white man hold his hand.

What would people passing along the street think? He was very conscious of his black skin and there was in him a prodding conviction that Jan and men like him had made it so that he would be conscious of that black skin? Did not white people despise a black skin? Then why was Jan doing this? Why was Mary standing there so eagerly, with shining eyes? What could they get out of this? Maybe they did not depise him? But they made him feel his black skin by just standing there looking at him, one holding his hand and the other smiling. He felt he had no physical existence at all right then; he was something he hated, the badge of shame which he knew was attached to a black skin. It was a shadowy region, a No Man's Land, the ground that separated the white world from the black that he stood upon. He felt naked, transparent; he felt that this white man, having helped to put him down, having helped to deform him, held him up now to look at him and be amused. At that moment he felt toward Mary and Jan a dumb, cold, and inarticulate hate.

'Let me drive awhile,' Jan said, letting go of his hand and opening the door.

Bigger looked at Mary. She came forward and touched his arm.

'It's all right, Bigger,' she said.

He turned in the seat to get out, but Jan stopped him.

'No; stay in and move over.'

He slid over and Jan took his place at the wheel. He was still feeling his hand strangely; it seemed that the pressure of Jan's fingers had left an indelible imprint. Mary was getting into the front seat, too.

'Move over, Bigger,' she said.

He moved closed to Jan. Mary pushed herself in, wedging tightly between him and the outer door of the car. There were white people to either side of him; he was sitting between two vast white looming walls. Never in his life had he been so close to a white woman. He smelt the odor of her hair and felt the soft pressure of her thigh against his own. Jan headed the car back to the Outer Drive, weaving in and out of the line of traffic. Soon they were speeding along the lake front, past a huge flat sheet of dully gleaming water. The sky was heavy with snow clouds and the wind was blowing strong.

'Isn't it glorious tonight?' she asked.

'God, yes!' Jan said.

Bigger listened to the tone of their voices, to their strange accents, to the exuberant phrases that flowed so freely from their lips.

'That sky!'

'And that water!'

'It's so beautiful it makes you ache just to look at it,' said Mary.

'This is a beautiful world, Bigger,' Jan said, turning to him. 'Look at that skyline!'

Bigger looked without turning his head; he just rolled his eyes. Stretching to one side of him was a vast sweep of tall buildings flecked with tiny squares of yellow light.

'We'll own all that some day, Bigger,' Jan said with a wave of his hand. 'After the revolution it'll be ours. But we'll have to fight for it. What a world to win, Bigger! And when that day comes, things'll be different. There'll be no white and no black; there'll be no rich and no poor.'

Bigger said nothing. The car whirred along.

'We seem strange to you, don't we, Bigger?' Mary asked.

'Oh, no'm,' he breathed softly, knowing that she did not believe him, but finding it impossible to answer her in any other way.

His arms and legs were aching from being cramped into so small a space, but he dared not move. He knew that they would not have cared if he had made himself more comfortable, but his moving would have called attention to himself and his black body. And he did not want that. These people made him feel things he did not want to feel. If he were white, if he were like them, it would have been different. But he was black. So he sat still, his arms and legs aching.

'Say, Bigger,' asked Jan, 'where can we get a good meal on the South Side?'

'Well,' Bigger said, reflectively.

'We want to go a *real* nice place,' Mary said, turning to him gayly.

'You want to go a night club?' Bigger asked in a tone that indicated that he was simply mentioning names and not recommending places to go.

'No; we want to eat.'

'Look, Bigger. We want one of those places where colored people eat, not one of those show places.'

What *did* these people want? When he answered his voice was neutral and toneless.

'Well, there's Ernie's Kitchen Shack . . .'

'That sounds good!'

'Let's go there, Jan,' Mary said.

'O.K.,' Jan said. 'Where is it?'

'It's at Forty-seventh Street and Indiana,' Bigger told them.

Jan swung the car off the Outer Drive at Thirty-first Street and drove westward to Indiana Avenue. Bigger wanted Jan to drive faster, so that they could reach Ernie's Kitchen Shack in the shortest possible time. That would allow him a chance to sit in the car and stretch out his cramped and aching legs while they ate. Jan turned onto Indiana Avenue and headed south. Bigger wondered what Jack and Gus and G.H. would say if they saw him sitting between two white people in a car like this. They would tease him about such a thing as long as they could remember it. He felt Mary turn in her seat. She placed her hand on his arm.

'You know, Bigger, I've long wanted to go into those houses,' she said, pointing to the tall, dark apartment buildings looming to either side of them, 'and just *see* how your people live. You know what I mean? I've been to England, France, and Mexico, but I don't know how people live ten blocks from me. We know so *little* about each other. I just want to *see*. I want to *know* these people. Never in my life have I been inside a Negro home. Yet they *must* live like we live. They're *human* . . . There are twelve million of them . . . They live in our country . . . In the same city with us . . .' her voice trailed off wistfully.

There was silence. The car sped through the Black Belt, past tall buildings holding black life. Bigger knew that they were thinking of his life and the life of his people. Suddenly he wanted to seize some heavy object in his hand and grip it with all the strength of his body and in some strange way rise up and stand in naked space above the speeding car and with one final blow blot it out – with himself and them in it. His heart was beating fast and he struggled to control his breath. This thing was getting the better of him; he felt that he should not give way to his feelings like this. But he could not help it. Why didn't they leave him alone? What had he done to them? What good could they get out of sitting here making him feel so miserable?

'Tell me where it is, Bigger,' Jan said.

'Yessuh.'

Bigger looked out and saw that they were at Forty-sixth Street.

'It's at the end of the next block, suh.'

'Can I park along here somewhere?'

'Oh; yessuh.'

'Bigger, *please*! Don't say *sir* to me . . . I don't *like* it. You're a man just like I am; I'm no better than you. Maybe other white men like it. But I don't. Look, Bigger . . .'

'Yes . . .' Bigger paused, swallowed, and looked down at his black hands. 'O.K.,' he mumbled, hoping that they did not hear the choke in his voice.

'You see, Bigger . . .' Jan began.

Mary reached her hand round the back of Bigger and touched Jan's shoulder.

'Let's get out,' she said hurriedly.

Jan pulled the car to the curb and opened the door and stepped out. Bigger slipped behind the steering wheel again, glad to have room at last for his arms and legs. Mary got out of the other door. Now, he could get some rest. So intensely taken up was he with his own immediate sensations, that he did not look up until he felt something strange in the long silence. When he did look he saw, in a split second of time, Mary turn her eyes away from his face. She was looking at Jan and Jan was looking at her. There was no mistaking the meaning of the look in their eyes. To Bigger it was plainly a bewildered and questioning look, a look that asked: What on earth is wrong with him? Bigger's teeth clamped tight and he stared straight before him.

'Aren't you coming with us, Bigger?' Mary asked in a sweet tone that made him want to leap at her.

The people in Ernie's Kitchen Shack knew him and he did not want them to see him with these white people. He knew that if he went in they would ask one another: *Who're them white folks Bigger's hanging around with?*

'I – I . . . I don't want to go in . . .' he whispered breathlessly.

'Aren't you hungry?' Jan asked.

'Naw; I ain't hungry.'

Jan and Mary came close to the car.

'Come and sit with us anyhow,' Jan said.

'I . . . I . . .' Bigger stammered.

'It'll be all right,' Mary said.

'I can stay here. Somebody has to watch the car,' he said.

'Oh, to hell with the car!' Mary said. 'Come on in.'

'I don't want to eat,' Bigger said stubbornly.

'Well,' Jan sighed. 'If that's the way you feel about it, we won't go in.'

Bigger felt trapped. Oh, goddamn! He saw in a flash that he could have made all of this very easy if he had simply acted from the beginning as if they were doing nothing unusual. But he did not understand them; he distrusted them, really hated them. He was puzzled as to why they were treating him this way. But, after all, this was his job and it was just as painful to sit here and let them stare at him as it was to go in.

'O.K.,' he mumbled angrily.

He got out and slammed the door. Mary came close to him and caught his arm. He stared at her in a long silence; it was the first time he had ever looked directly at her, and he was able to do so only because he was angry.

'Bigger,' she said, 'you don't have to come in unless you

really want to. Please, don't think .... Oh, Bigger ... We're not trying to make you feel badly ...'

Her voice stopped. In the dim light of the street lamp Bigger saw her eyes cloud and her lips tremble. She swayed against the car. He stepped backward, as though she were contaminated with an invisible contagion. Jan slipped his arm about her waist, supporting her. Bigger heard her sob softly. Good God! He had a wild impulse to turn around and walk away. He felt ensnared in a tangle of deep shadows, shadows as black as the night that stretched above his head. The way he had acted had made her cry, and yet the way she had acted had made him feel that he had to act as he had toward her. In his relations with her he felt that he was riding a seesaw; never were they on a common level; either he or she was up in the air. Mary dried her eyes and Jan whispered something to her. Bigger wondered what he could say to his mother, or to the relief, or Mr Dalton, if he left them. They would be sure to ask why he had walked off his job, and he would not be able to tell.

'I'm all right, now, Jan,' he heard Mary say. 'I'm sorry. I'm just a fool, I suppose ... I acted a ninny.' She lifted her eyes to Bigger. 'Don't mind me, Bigger. I'm just silly, I guess ...'

He said nothing.

'Come on, Bigger,' Jan said in a voice that sought to cover up everything. 'Let's eat.'

Jan caught his arm and tried to pull him forward, but Bigger hung back. Jan and Mary walked toward the entrance of the café and Bigger followed, confused and resentful. Jan went to a small table near a wall.

'Sit down, Bigger.'

Bigger sat. Jan and Mary sat in front of him.

'You like fried chicken?' Jan asked.

'Yessuh,' he whispered.

He scratched his head. How on earth could he learn not to say *yessuh* and *yessum* to white people in one night when he had been saying it all his life long? He looked before him in such a way that his eyes would not meet theirs. The waitress came and Jan ordered three beers and three portions of fried chicken.

'Hi, Bigger!'

He turned and saw Jack waving at him, but staring at Jan and Mary. He waved a stiff palm in return. Goddamn! Jack walked away hurriedly. Cautiously, Bigger looked round; the waitresses and several people at other tables were staring at him. They all knew him and he knew what they were wondering as he would have wondered if he had been in their places. Mary touched his arm.

'Have you ever been here before, Bigger?'

He groped for neutral words, words that would convey information but not indicate any shade of his own feelings.

'A few times.'

'It's very nice,' Mary said.

Somebody put a nickel in an automatic phonograph and they listened to the music. Then Bigger felt a hand grab his shoulder.

'Hi, Bigger! Where you been?'

He looked up and saw Bessie laughing in his face.

'Hi,' he said gruffly.

'Oh, 'scuse me. I didn't know you had company,' she said, walking away with her eyes upon Jan and Mary.

'Tell her to come over, Bigger,' Mary said.

Bessie had gone to a far table and was sitting with another girl.

'She's over there now,' Bigger said.

The waitress brought the beer and chicken.

'This is simply grand!' Mary exclaimed.

'You got something there,' Jan said, looking at Bigger. 'Did I say that right, Bigger!'

Bigger hesitated.

'That's the way they say it,' he spoke flatly.

Jan and Mary were eating. Bigger picked up a piece of chicken and bit it. When he tried to chew he found his mouth dry. It seemed that the very organic functions of his body had altered; and when he realized why, when he understood the cause, he could not chew the food. After two or three bites, he stopped and sipped his beer.

'Eat your chicken,' Mary said. 'It's good!'

'I ain't hungry,' he mumbled.

'Want some more beer?' Jan asked after a long silence.

Maybe if he got a little drunk it would help him.

'I don't mind,' he said.

Jan ordered another round.

'Do they keep anything stronger than beer here?' Jan asked.

'They got anything you want,' Bigger said.

Jan ordered a fifth of rum and poured a round. Bigger felt the liquor warming him. After a second drink Jan began to talk.

'Where were you born, Bigger?'

'In the South.'

'Whereabouts?'

'Mississippi.'

'How far did you go in school?'

'To the eighth grade.'

'Why did you stop?'

'No money.'

'Did you go to school in the North or South?'

'Mostly in the South. I went two years up here.'

'How long have you been in Chicago?'

'Oh, about five years.'

'You like it here?'

'It'll do.'

'You live with your people?'

'My mother, brother, and sister.'

'Where's your father?'

'Dead.'

'How long ago was that?'

'He got killed in a riot when I was a kid – in the South.'

There was silence. The rum was helping Bigger.

'And what was done about it?' Jan asked.

'Nothing, as far as I know.'

'How do you feel about it?'

'I don't know.'

'Listen, Bigger, that's what we want to *stop*. That's what we Communists are fighting. We want to stop people from treating others that way. I'm a member of the Party. Mary sympathizes. Don't you think if we got together we could stop things like that?'

'I don't know,' Bigger said; he was feeling the rum rising to his head. 'There's a lot of white people in the world.'

'You've read about the Scottsboro boys?'

'I heard about 'em.'

'Don't you think we did a good job in helping to keep 'em from killing those boys?'

'It was all right.'

'You know, Bigger,' said Mary, 'we'd like to be friends of yours.'

He said nothing. He drained his glass and Jan poured another round. He was getting drunk enough to look straight at them now. Mary was smiling at him.

'You'll get used to us,' she said.

Jan stoppered the bottle of rum.

'We'd better go,' he said.

'Yes,' Mary said. 'Oh, Bigger, I'm going to Detroit at nine in the morning and I want you to take my small trunk down to the station. Tell Father and he'll let you make up your time. You better come for the trunk at eight-thirty.'

'I'll take it down.'

Jan paid the bill and they went back to the car. Bigger got behind the steering wheel. He was feeling good. Jan and Mary got into the back seat. As Bigger drove he saw her resting in Jan's arms.

'Drive around in the park awhile, will you, Bigger?'

'O.K.'

He turned into the Washington Park and pulled the car slowly round and round the long gradual curves. Now and then he watched Jan kiss Mary in the reflection of the rear mirror above his head.

'You got a girl, Bigger?' Mary asked.

'I got a girl,' he said.

'I'd like to meet her some time.'

He did not answer. Mary's eyes stared dreamily before her, as

if she were planning future things to do. Then she turned to Jan
and laid her hand tenderly upon his arm.

'How was the demonstration?'

'Pretty good. But the cops arrested three comrades.'

'Who were they?'

'A Y. C. L.-er and two Negro women. Oh, by the way, Mary.
We need money for bail badly.'

'How much?'

'Three thousand.'

'I'll mail you a check.'

'Swell.'

'Did you work hard today?'

'Yeah. I was at a meeting until three this morning. Ma and
I've been trying to raise bail money all day today.'

'Max is a darling, isn't he?'

'He's one of the best lawyers we've got.'

Bigger listened; he knew that they were talking communism
and he tried to understand. But he couldn't.

'Jan.'

'Yes, honey.'

'I'm coming out of school this spring and I'm going to join
the Party.'

'*Gee*, you're a brick !'

'But I'll have to be careful.'

'Say, how's about your working with me, in the office?'

'No, I want to work among Negroes. That's where people are
needed. It seems as though they've been pushed out of everything.'

'That's true.'

'When I see what they've done to those people, it makes me
so mad . . .'

'Yes; it's awful.'

'And I feel so helpless and useless. I want to *do* something.'

'I knew all along you'd come through.'

'Say, Jan, do you know many Negroes? I want to meet some.'

'I don't know any very well. But you'll meet them when
you're in the Party.'

'They have so much *emotion*! What a people! If we could ever get them going . . .'

'We can't have a revolution without 'em,' Jan said. 'They've got to be organized. They've got spirit. They'll give the Party something it needs.'

'And their songs – the spirituals! Aren't they marvelous?' Bigger saw her turn to him. 'Say, Bigger, can you sing?'

'I can't sing,' he said.

'Aw, Bigger,' she said, pouting. She tilted her head, closed her eyes and opened her mouth.

> 'Swing low, sweet chariot,
> Coming fer to carry me home . . .'

Jan joined in and Bigger smiled derisively. Hell, that ain't the tune, he thought.

'Come on, Bigger, and help us sing it,' Jan said.

'I can't sing,' he said again.

They were silent. The car purred along. Then he heard Jan speaking in low tones.

'Where's the bottle?'

'Right here.

'I want a sip.'

'I'll take one, too, honey.'

'Going heavy tonight, ain't you?'

'About as heavy as you.'

They laughed. Bigger drove in silence. He heard the faint, musical gurgle of liquor.

'Jan!'

'What?'

'That was a *big* sip!'

'Here; you get even.'

Through the rear mirror he saw her tilt the bottle and drink.

'Maybe Bigger wants another one, Jan. Ask him.'

'Oh, say, Bigger! Here; take a swig!'

He slowed the car and reached back for the bottle; he tilted it twice, taking two huge swallows.

'Woooow!' Mary laughed.

'You took a *swig*, all right,' Jan said.

Bigger wiped his mouth with the back of his hand and continued driving slowly through the dark park. Now and then he heard the half-empty bottle of rum gurgling. They getting plastered, he thought, feeling the effect of the rum creeping outward to his fingers and upward to his lips. Presently, he heard Mary giggle. Hell, she's plastered already! The car rolled slowly round and round the sloping curves. The rum's soft heat was spreading fanwise out from his stomach, engulfing his whole body. He was not driving: he was simply sitting and floating along smoothly through darkness. His hands rested lightly on the steering wheel and his body slouched lazily down in the seat. He looked at the mirror; they were drinking again. They plastered, all right, he thought. He pulled the car softly round the curves, looking at the road before him one second and up at the mirror the next. He heard Jan whispering; then he heard them both sigh. His lips were numb. I'm almost drunk, he thought. His sense of the city and park fell away; he was floating in the car and Jan and Mary were in back, kissing. A long time passed.

'It's one o'clock, honey,' Mary said. 'I better go in.'

'O.K. But let's drive a little more. It's great here.'

'Father says I'm a bad girl.'

'I'm sorry, darling.'

'I'll call you in the morning before I go.'

'Sure. What time?'

'About eighty-thirty.'

'Gee, but I hate to see you go to Detroit.'

'I hate to go too. But I got to. You see, honey, I got to make up for being bad with you down in Florida. I got to do what Mother and Father say for awhile.'

'I hate to see you go just the same.'

'I'll be back in a couple of days.'

'A couple of days is a long time.'

'You're silly, but you're sweet,' she said, laughing and kissing him.

'You better drive on, Bigger,' Jan called.

Bigger drove out of the park onto Cottage Grove Avenue and headed north. The city streets were empty and quiet and dark and the tires of the car hummed over the asphalt. When he reached Forty-sixth Street, a block from the Dalton home, he heard a streetcar rumbling faintly behind him, far down the avenue.

'Here comes my car,' Jan said, turning to peer through the rear window.

'Oh, gee, honey!' Mary said. 'You've got such a long way to go. If I had time, I'd ride you home. But I've been out so late as it is that Mama's going to be suspicious.'

'Don't worry. I'll be all right.'

'Oh, say! Let Bigger drive you home.'

'Nonsense! Why should he drive me all that distance this time of morning?'

'Then you'd better take this car, honey.'

'No. I'll see you home first.'

'But, honey, the cars run only every half hour when it's late like this,' Mary said. 'You'll get ill, waiting out here in the cold. Look, you take this car. I'll get home all right. It's only a block . . .'

'Are you sure you'll be all right?'

'Of course. I'm in sight of home now. There; see . . .'

Through the rear mirror Bigger saw her pointing to the Dalton home.

'O.K.,' Jan said. 'You'd better stop here and let me off, Bigger.'

He stopped the car. Bigger heard them speak in whispers.

'Good-bye, Jan.'

'Good-bye, honey.'

'I'll call you tomorrow?'

'Sure.'

Jan stood at the front door of the car and held out his palm. Bigger shook timidly.

'It's been great meeting you, Bigger,' Jan said.

'O.K.,' Bigger mumbled.

'I'm damn glad I know you. Look. Have another drink.'

Bigger took a big swallow.

'You better give me one, too, Jan. It'll make me sleep,' Mary said.

'You're sure you haven't had enough?'

'Aw, come on, honey.'

She got out of the car and stood on the curb. Jan gave her the bottle and she tilted it.

'Whoa!' Jan said.

'What's the matter?'

'I don't want you to pass out.'

'I can hold it.'

Jan tilted the bottle and emptied it, then laid it in the gutter. He fumbled clumsily in his pockets for something. He swayed; he was drunk.

'You lose something, honey?' Mary lisped; she, too, was drunk.

'Naw; I got some stuff here I want Bigger to read. Listen, Bigger, I got some pamphlets here. I want you to read 'em, see?'

Bigger held out his hand and received a small batch of booklets.

'O.K.'

'I really want you to read 'em, now. We'll have a talk 'bout 'em in a coupla days . . .' His speech was thick.

'I'll read 'em,' Bigger said, stifling a yawn and stuffing the booklets into his pocket.

'I'll see that he reads 'em,' Mary said.

Jan kissed her again. Bigger heard the Loop-bound car rumbling forward.

'Well, good-bye,' he said.

'Goo'-bye, honey,' Mary said. 'I'm gonna ride up front with Bigger.'

She got into the front seat. The streetcar clanged to a stop. Jan swung onto it and it started north. Bigger drove toward Drexel Boulevard. Mary slumped down in the seat and sighed. Her legs sprawled wide apart. The car rolled along. Bigger's head was spinning.

'You're very nice, Bigger,' she said.

He looked at her. Her face was pasty white. Her eyes were glassy. She was very drunk.

'I don't know,' he said.

'My! But you say the *fun*niest things,' she giggled.

'Maybe,' he said.

She leaned her head on his shoulder.

'You don't mind, do you?'

'I don't mind.'

'You know, for *three* hours you haven't said *yes* or *no*.'

She doubled up with laughter. He tightened with hate. Again she was looking inside of him and he did not like it. She sat up and dabbed at her eyes with a handkerchief. He kept his eyes straight in front of him and swung the car into the driveway and brought it to a stop. He got out and opened the door. She did not move. Her eyes were closed.

'We're here,' he said.

She tried to get up and slipped back into the seat.

'Aw, shucks!'

She's drunk, *really* drunk, Bigger thought. She stretched out her hand.

'Here; gimme a lift. I'm wobbly . . .'

She was resting on the small of her back and her dress was pulled up so far that he could see where her stockings ended on her thighs. He stood looking at her for a moment; she raised her eyes and looked at him. She laughed.

'Help me, Bigger. I'm stuck.'

He helped her and his hands felt the softness of her body as she stepped to the ground. Her dark eyes looked at him feverishly from deep sockets. Her hair was in his face, filling him with its scent. He gritted his teeth, feeling a little dizzy.

'Where's my hat? I dropped it shomewhere . . .'

She swayed as she spoke and he tightened his arms about her, holding her up. He looked around; her hat was lying on the running board.

'Here it is,' he said.

As he picked it up he wondered what a white man would

think seeing him here with her like this. Suppose old man Dalton saw him now? Apprehensively, he looked up at the big house. It was dark and silent.

'Well,' Mary sighed. 'I suppose I better go to bed . . .'

He turned her loose, but had to catch her again to keep her off the pavement. He led her to the steps.

'Can you make it?'

She looked at him as though she had been challenged.

'Sure. Turn me loose . . .'

He took his arm from her and she mounted the steps firmly and then stumbled loudly on the wooden porch. Bigger made a move toward her, but stopped, his hands outstretched, frozen with fear. Good God, she'll wake up everybody! She was half-bent over, resting on one knee and one hand, looking back at him in amused astonishment. That girl's crazy! She pulled up and walked slowly back down the steps, holding onto the railing. She swayed before him, smiling.

'I sure am drunk . . .'

He watched her with a mingled feeling of helplessness, admiration, and hate. If her father saw him here with her now, his job would be over. But she was beautiful, slender, with an air that made him feel that she did not hate him with the hate of other white people. But, for all of that, she was white and he hated her. She closed her eyes slowly, then opened them; she was trying desperately to take hold of herself. Since she was not able to get to her room alone, ought he to call Mr Dalton or Peggy? Naw . . . That would betray her. And, too, in spite of his hate for her, he was excited standing here watching her like this. Her eyes closed again and she swayed toward him. He caught her.

'I'd better help you,' he said.

'Let's go the back way, Bigger. I'll stumble sure as hell . . . and wake up everybody . . . if we go up the front . . .'

Her feet dragged on the concrete as he led her to the basement. He switched on the light, supporting her with his free hand.

'I didn't know I was sho drunk,' she mumbled.

He led her slowly up the narrow stairs to the kitchen door, his hand circling her waist and the tips of his fingers feeling the soft swelling of her breasts. Each second she was leaning more heavily against him.

'Try to stand up,' he whispered fiercely as they reached the kitchen door.

He was thinking that perhaps Mrs Dalton was standing in flowing white and staring with stony blind eyes in the middle of the floor, as she had been when he had come for the glass of water. He eased the door back and looked. The kitchen was empty and dark, save for a faint blue hazy light that seeped through a window from the winter sky.

'Come on.'

She pulled heavily on him, her arm about his neck. He pushed the door in and took a step inside and stopped, waiting, listening. He felt her hair brush his lips. His skin glowed warm and his muscles flexed; he looked at her face in the dim light, his senses drunk with the odor of her hair and skin. He stood for a moment, then whispered in excitement and fear:

'Come on; you got to get to your room.'

He led her out of the kitchen into the hallway; he had to walk her a step at a time. The hall was empty and dark; slowly he half-walked and half-dragged her to the back stairs. Again he hated her; he shook her.

'Come on; wake up!'

She did not move or open her eyes; finally she mumbled something and swayed limply. His fingers felt the soft curves of her body and he was still, looking at her, enveloped in a sense of physical elation. This little bitch! he thought. Her face was touching his. He turned her round and began to mount the steps, one by one. He heard a slight creaking and stopped. He looked, straining his eyes in the gloom. But there was no one. When he got to the top of the steps she was completely limp and was still trying to mumble something. Goddamn! He could move her only by lifting her bodily. He caught her in his arms and carried her down the hall, then paused. Which was her door? Goddamn!

'Where's your room?' he whispered.

She did not answer. Was she completely out? He could not leave her here; if he took his hands from her she would sink to the floor and lie there all night. He shook her hard, speaking as loudly as he dared.

'Where's your room?'

Momentarily, she roused herself and looked at him with blank eyes.

'Where's your room?' he asked again.

She rolled her eyes toward a door. He got her as far as the door and stopped. Was this really her room? Was she too drunk to know? Suppose he opened the door to Mr and Mrs Dalton's room? Well, all they could do was fire him. It wasn't his fault that she was drunk. He felt strange, possessed, or as if he were acting upon a stage in front of a crowd of people. Carefully, he freed one hand and turned the knob of the door. He waited; nothing happened. He pushed the door in quietly; the room was dark and silent. He felt along the wall with his fingers for the electric switch and could not find it. He stood, holding her in his arms, fearful, in doubt. His eyes were growing used to the darkness and a little light seeped into the room from the winter sky through a window. At the far end of the room he made out the shadowy form of a white bed. He lifted her and brought her into the room and closed the door softly.

'Here; wake up, now.'

He tried to stand her on her feet and found her weak as jelly. He held her in his arms again, listening in the darkness. His senses reeled from the scent of her hair and skin. She was much smaller than Bessie, his girl, but much softer. Her face was buried in his shoulder; his arms tightened about her. Her face turned slowly and he held his face still, waiting for her face to come round, in front of his. Then her head leaned backward, slowly, gently; it was as though she had given up. Her lips, faintly moist in the hazy blue light, were parted and he saw the furtive glints of her white teeth. Her eyes were closed. He stared at her dim face, the forehead capped with curly black hair. He eased his hand, the fingers spread wide, up the center of her back and her face came toward him and her lips touched his, like something he had imagined. He stood her on her feet and she swayed against him.

He lifted her and laid her on the bed. Something urged him to leave at once, but he leaned over her, excited, looking at her face in the dim light, not wanting to take his hands from her breasts. She tossed and mumbled sleepily. He tightened his fingers on her breasts, kissing her again, feeling her move toward him. He was aware only of her body now; his lips trembled. Then he stiffened. The door behind him had creaked.

He turned and a hysterical terror seized him, as though he were falling from a great height in a dream. A white blur was standing by the door, silent, ghostlike. It filled his eyes and gripped his body. It was Mrs Dalton. He wanted to knock her out of his way and bolt from the room.

'Mary!' she spoke softly, questioningly.

Bigger held his breath. Mary mumbled again; he bent over her, his fists clenched in fear. He knew that Mrs Dalton could not see him; but he knew that if Mary spoke she would come to the side of the bed and discover him, touch him. He waited tensely, afraid to move for fear of bumping into something in the dark and betraying his presence.

'Mary!'

He felt Mary trying to rise and quickly he pushed her head back to the pillow.

'She must be asleep,' Mrs Dalton mumbled.

He wanted to move from the bed, but was afraid he would stumble over something and Mrs Dalton would hear him, would know that someone besides Mary was in the room. Frenzy dominated him. He held his hand over her mouth and his head was cocked at an angle that enabled him to see Mary and Mrs Dalton by merely shifting his eyes. Mary mumbled and tried to rise again. Frantically, he caught a corner of the pillow and brought it to her lips. He had to stop her from mumbling, or he would be caught. Mrs Dalton was moving slowly toward him and he grew tight and full, as though about to explode. Mary's fingernails tore at his hands and he caught the pillow and covered her entire face with it, firmly. Mary's body surged upward and he pushed downward upon the pillow with all of his weight, determined that she must not move or make any sound that would betray him. His eyes were filled with the white blur moving toward him in the shadows of the room. Again Mary's body heaved and he held the pillow in a grip that took all of his strength. For a long time he felt the sharp pain of her fingernails biting into his wrists. The white blur was still.

'Mary? Is that you?'

He clenched his teeth and held his breath, intimidated to the core by the awesome white blur floating toward him. His muscles flexed taut as steel and he pressed the pillow, feeling the bed give slowly, evenly, but silently. Then suddenly her fingernails did not bite into his wrists. Mary's fingers loosened. He did not feel her surging and heaving against him. Her body was still.

'Mary! is that *you*?'

He could see Mrs Dalton plainly now. As he took his hands from the pillow he heard a long slow sigh go up from the bed into the air of the darkened room, a sigh which afterwards, when he remembered it, seemed final, irrevocable.

'Mary! Are you ill?'

He stood up. With each of her movements toward the bed his body made a movement to match hers, away from her, his feet not lifting themselves from the floor, but sliding softly and silently over the smooth deep rug, his muscles flexed so taut they ached. Mrs Dalton now stood over the bed. Her hands reached out and touched Mary.

'Mary! Are you asleep? I heard you moving about ...'

Mrs Dalton straightened suddenly and took a quick step back.

'You're dead drunk! You *stink* with whiskey!'

She stood silently in the hazy blue light, then she knelt at the side of the bed. Bigger heard her whispering. She's praying, he thought in amazement and the words echoed in his mind as though someone had spoken them aloud. Finally, Mrs Dalton stood up and her face tilted to that upward angle at which she always held it. He waited, his teeth clamped, his fists clenched. She moved slowly toward the door; he could scarcely see her now. The door creaked; then silence.

He relaxed and sank to the floor, his breath going in a long gasp. He was weak and wet with sweat. He stayed crouched and bent, hearing the sound of his breathing filling the darkness. Gradually, the intensity of his sensations subsided and he was aware of the room. He felt that he had been in the grip of a weird spell and was now free. The fingertips of his right hand were pressed deeply into the soft fibers of the rug and his whole body vibrated from the wild pounding of his heart. He had to get out of the room, and quickly. Suppose that had been *Mr* Dalton? His escape had been narrow enough, as it was.

He stood and listened. Mrs Dalton might be out there in the hallway. How could he get out of the room? He all but shuddered with intensity of his loathing for this house and all it had made him feel since he had first come into it. He reached his hand behind him and touched the wall; he was glad to have something solid at his back. He looked at the shadowy bed and remembered Mary as some person he had not seen in a long time. She was still there. Had he hurt her? He went to the bed and stood over her; her face lay sideways on the pillow. His hand moved toward her, but stopped in mid-air. He blinked his eyes and stared at Mary's face; it was darker than when he had first bent over her. Her mouth was open and her eyes bulged glassily. Her bosom, her bosom, her – her bosom was not moving! He could not hear her breath coming and going now as he had when he had first brought her into the room! He bent and moved her head with his hand and found that she was relaxed and limp. He snatched his hand away. Thought and feeling were balked in him; there was something he was trying to tell himself desperately, but could not. Then, convulsively, he sucked his breath in and huge words formed slowly, ringing in his ears: *She's dead* . . .

The reality of the room fell from him; the vast city of white people that sprawled outside took its place. She was dead and he had killed her. He was a murderer, a Negro murderer, a black murderer. He had killed a white woman. He had to get away from here. Mrs Dalton had been in the room while he was there, but she had not known it. But, *had* she? No! Yes! Maybe she had gone for help? No. If she had known she would have screamed. She didn't know. He had to slip out of the house. Yes. He could go home to bed and tomorrow he could tell them that he had driven Mary home and had left her at the side door.

In the darkness his fear made live in him an element which he reckoned with as 'them'. He had to construct a case for 'them'. But, *Jan*! Oh ... Jan would give him away. When it was found that she was dead Jan would say that he had left them together in the car at Forty-sixth Street and Cottage Grove Avenue. But he would tell them that that was not true. And, after all, was not Jan a *red*? Was not his word as good as Jan's? He would say that Jan had come home with them. No one must know that he was the last person who had been with her.

Fingerprints! He had read about them in magazines. His fingerprints would give him away, surely! They could prove that he had been inside of her' room! But suppose he told them that he had come to get the trunk? That was it! The *trunk*! His fingerprints had a right to be there. He looked round and saw her trunk on the other side of the bed, open, the top standing up. He could take the trunk to the basement and put the car into the garage and then go home. *No!* There was a better way. He would not put the car into the garage! He would say that Jan had come to the house and he had left Jan outside in the car. But there was still a *better way*! Make them think that Jan did it. Reds'd do anything. Didn't the papers say so? He would tell them that he had brought Jan and Mary home in the car and Mary had asked him to go with her to her room to get the trunk – and Jan was *with* them! – and he had got the trunk and taken it to the basement and when he had gone he had left Mary and Jan – who had come back down – sitting in the car, kissing ... *That's it!*

He heard a clock ticking and searched for it with his eyes; it was at the head of Mary's bed, its white dial glowing in the blue darkness. It was five minutes past three. Jan had left them at Forty-sixth Street and Cottage Grove. *Jan didn't leave at Forty-sixth Street; he rode with us . . .*

He went to the trunk and eased the top down and dragged it over the rug to the middle of the floor. He lifted the top and felt inside; it was half-empty.

Then he was still, barely breathing, filled with another idea. Hadn't Mr Dalton said that they did not get up early on Sunday mornings? Hadn't Mary said that she was going to Detroit? If Mary were missing when they got up, would they not think that she had already gone to Detroit? He . . . *Yes!* He could, he could put her *in* the trunk! She was small. Yes; put her in the trunk. She had said that she would be gone for three days. For three days, then, maybe no one would know. He would have three days of time. She was a crazy girl anyhow. She was always running around with reds, wasn't she? Anything could happen to her. People would think that she was up to some of her crazy ways when they missed her. Yes, reds'd do anything. Didn't the papers say so?

He went to the bed; he would have to lift her into the trunk. He did not want to touch her, but he knew he had to. He bent over her. His hands were outstretched, trembling in mid-air. He had to touch her and lift her and put her in the trunk. He tried to move his hands and could not. It was as though he expected her to scream when he touched her. Goddamn! It all seemed foolish! He wanted to laugh. It was unreal. Like a nightmare. He had to lift a dead woman and was afraid. He felt that he had been dreaming of something like this for a long time, and then, suddenly, it was true. He heard the clock ticking. Time was passing. It would soon be morning. He had to act. He could not stand here all night like this; he might go to the electric chair. He shuddered and something cold crawled over his skin. Goddamn!

He pushed his hand gently under her body and lifted it. He stood with her in his arms; she was limp. He took her to the trunk and involuntarily jerked his head round and saw a white blur standing at the door and his body was instantly wrapped in a sheet of blazing terror and a hard ache seized his head and then the white blur went away. *I thought that was her* ... His heart pounded.

He stood with her body in his arms in the silent room and cold facts battered him like waves sweeping in from the sea: she was dead; she was white; she was a woman; he had killed her; he was black; he might be caught; he did not want to be caught; if he were they would kill him.

He stooped to put her in the trunk. Could he get her in? He looked again toward the door, expecting to see the white blur; but nothing was there. He turned her on her side in his arms; He was breathing hard and his body trembled. He eased her down, listening to the soft rustle of her clothes. He pushed her head into a corner, but her legs were too long and would not go in.

He thought he heard a noise and straightened; it seemed to him that his breathing was as loud as wind in a storm. He listened and heard nothing. He had to get her legs in! Bend her legs at the knees, he thought. Yes, almost. A little more ... He bent them some more. Sweat dripped from his chin onto his hands. He doubled her knees and pushed her completely into the trunk. That much was done. He eased the top down and fumbled into the darkness for the latch and heard it click loudly.

He stood up and caught hold of one of the handles of the trunk and pulled. The trunk would not move. He was weak and his hands were slippery with sweat. He gritted his teeth and caught the trunk with both hands and pulled it to the door. He opened the door and looked into the hall: it was empty and silent. He stood the trunk on end and carried his right hand over his left shoulder and stooped and caught the strap and lifted the trunk to his back. Now, he would have to stand up. He strained; the muscles of his shoulders and legs quivered with effort. He rose, swaying, biting his lips.

Putting one foot carefully before the other, he went down the hall, down the stairs, then through another hall to the kitchen and paused. His back ached and the strap cut into his palm like fire. The trunk seemed to weigh a ton. He expected the white blur to step before him at any moment and hold out its hand and touch the trunk and demand to know what was in it. He wanted to put the trunk down and rest; but he was afraid that he would not be able to lift it again. He walked across the kitchen floor, down the steps, leaving the kitchen door open behind him. He stood in the darkened basement with the trunk upon his back and listened to the roaring draft of the furnace and saw the coals burning red through the cracks. He stooped, waiting to hear the bottom of the trunk touch the concrete floor. He bent more and rested on one knee. Goddamn! His hand, seared with fire, slipped from the strap and the trunk hit the floor with a loud clatter. He went forward and squeezed his right hand in his left to still the fiery pain.

He stared at the furnace. He trembled with another idea. He – he could, he – he could put her, he could put her *in* the furnace. He would *burn* her! That was the safest thing of all to do. He went to the furnace and opened the door. A huge red bed of coals blazed and quivered with molten fury.

He opened the trunk. She was as he had put her; her head buried in one corner and her knees bent and doubled toward her stomach. He would have to lift her again. He stooped and caught her shoulders and lifted her in his arms. He went to the door of the furnace and paused. The fire seethed. Ought he to put her in head or feet first? Because he was tired and scared, and because her feet were nearer, he pushed her in, feet first. The heat blasted his hands.

He had all but her shoulders in. He looked into the furnace; her clothes were ablaze and smoke was filling the interior so that he could scarcely see. The draft roared upward, droning in his ears. He gripped her shoulders and pushed hard, but the body would not go any farther. He tried again, but her head still remained out. Now ... Goddamn! He wanted to strike something with his fist. What could he do? He stepped back and looked.

A noise made him whirl; two green burning pools – pools of accusation and guilt – stared at him from a white blur that sat perched upon the edge of the trunk. His mouth opened in a silent scream and his body became hotly paralyzed. It was the white cat and its round green eyes gazed past him at the white face hanging limply from the fiery furnace door. *God!* He closed his mouth and swallowed. Should he catch the cat and kill it and put it in the furnace, too? He made a move. The cat stood up; its white fur bristled; its back arched. He tried to grab it and it bounded past him with a long wail of fear and scampered up the steps and through the door and out of sight. Oh! He had left the kitchen door open. *That* was it. He closed the door and stood again before the furnace, thinking, Cats can't talk . . .

He got his knife from his pocket and opened it and stood by the furnace, looking at Mary's white throat. Could he do it? He had to. Would there be blood? Oh, Lord! He looked round with a haunted and pleading look in his eyes. He saw a pile of old newspapers stacked carefully in a corner. He got a thick wad of them and held them under the head. He touched the sharp blade to the throat, just touched it, as if expecting the knife to cut the white flesh of itself, as if he did not have to put pressure behind it. Wistfully, he gazed at the edge of the blade resting on the white skin; the gleaming metal reflected the tremulous fury of the coals. Yes; he *had* to. Gently, he sawed the blade into the flesh and struck a bone. He gritted his teeth and cut harder. As yet there was no blood anywhere but on the knife. But the bone made it difficult. Sweat crawled down his back. Then blood crept outward in widening circles of pink on the newspapers, spreading quickly now. He whacked at the bone with the knife. The head hung limply on the newspapers, the curly black hair dragging about in blood. He whacked harder, but the head would not come off.

He paused, hysterical. He wanted to run from the basement and go as far as possible from the sight of this bloody throat. But he could not. He must not. He *had* to burn this girl. With eyes glazed, with nerves tingling with excitement, he looked about the basement. He saw a hatchet. *Yes!* That would do it. He spread a neat layer of newspapers beneath the head, so that the blood would not drip on the floor. He got the hatchet, held the head at a slanting angle with his left hand and, after pausing in an attitude of prayer, sent the blade of the hatchet into the bone of the throat with all the strength of his body. The head rolled off.

He was not crying, but his lips were trembling and his chest was heaving. He wanted to lie down upon the floor and sleep off the horror of this thing. But he had to get out of here. Quickly, he wrapped the head in the newspapers and used the wad to push the bloody trunk of the body deeper into the furnace. Then he shoved the head in. The hatchet went next.

Would there be coal enough to burn the body? No one would come down here before ten o'clock in the morning, maybe. He looked at his watch. It was four o'clock. He got another piece of paper and wiped his knife with it. He put the paper into the furnace and the knife into his pocket. He pulled the lever and coal rattled against the sides of the tin chute and he saw the whole furnace blaze and the draft roared still louder. When the body was covered with coal, he pushed the lever back. Now!

Then, abruptly, he stepped back from the furnace and looked at it, his mouth open. Hell! Folks'd *smell* it! There would be an odor and someone would look in the furnace. Aimlessly, his eyes searched the basement. There! That ought to do it! He saw the smutty blades of an electric exhaust fan high up in the wall of the basement, back of the furnace. He found the switch and threw it. There was a quick whir, then a hum. Things would be all right now; the exhaust fan would suck the air out of the basement and there would be no scent.

He shut the trunk and pushed it into a corner. In the morning he would take it to the station. He looked around to see if he had left anything that would betray him; he saw nothing.

He went out of the back door; a few fine flakes of snow were floating down. It had grown colder. The car was still in the driveway. Yes; he would leave it there.

Jan and Mary were sitting in the car, kissing. They said, Good night, Bigger ... And he said, Good night ... And he touched his hand to his cap ...

As he passed the car he saw the door was still open. Mary's purse was on the floor. He took it and closed the door. Naw! Leave it open; he opened it and went on down the driveway.

The streets were empty and silent. The wind chilled his wet body. He tucked the purse under his arm and walked. What would happen now? Ought he to run away? He stopped at a street corner and looked into the purse. There was a thick roll of bills; tens and twenties . . . Good! He would wait until morning to decide what to do. He was tired and sleepy.

He hurried home and ran up the steps and went on tiptoe into the room. His mother and brother and sister breathed regularly in sleep. He began to undress, thinking, *I'll tell 'em I left her with Jan in the car after I took the trunk down in the basement. In the morning I'll take the trunk to the station, like she told me . . .*

He felt something heavy sagging in his shirt; it was the gun. He took it out; it was warm and wet. He shoved it under the pillow. *They can't say I did it. If they do, they can't prove it.*

He eased the covers of the bed back and slipped beneath them and stretched out beside Buddy; in five minutes he was sound asleep.

BOOK TWO

Flight

It seemed to Bigger that no sooner had he closed his eyes than he was wide awake again, suddenly and violently, as though someone had grabbed his shoulders and had shaken him. He lay on his back in bed, hearing and seeing nothing. Then, like an electric switch being clicked on, he was aware that the room was filled with pale daylight. Somewhere deep in him a thought formed: It's morning. Sunday morning. He lifted himself on his elbows and cocked his head in an attitude of listening. He heard his mother and brother and sister breathing softly, in deep sleep. He saw the room and saw snow falling past the windows; but his mind formed no image of any of these. They simply existed, unrelated to each other; the snow and the daylight and the soft sound of breathing cast a strange spell upon him, a spell that waited for the wand of fear to touch it and endow it with reality and meaning. He lay in bed, only a few seconds from deep sleep, caught in a deadlock of impulses, unable to rise to the land of the living.

Then, in answer to a foreboding call from a dark part of his mind, he leaped from bed and landed on his bare feet in the middle of the room. His heart raced; his lips parted; his legs trembled. He struggled to come fully awake. He relaxed his taut muscles, feeling fear, remembering that he had killed Mary, had smothered her, had cut her head off and put her body in the fiery furnace.

This was Sunday morning and he had to take the trunk to the station. He glanced about and saw Mary's shiny black purse lying atop his trousers on a chair. Good God! Though the air of the room was cold, beads of sweat broke onto his forehead and his breath stopped. Quickly, he looked round; his mother and sister were still sleeping. Buddy slept in the bed from which he

135

had just arisen. Throw that purse away! Maybe he had forgotten other things? He searched the pockets of his trousers with nervous fingers and found the knife. He snapped it open and tiptoed to the window. Dried ridges of black blood were on the blade! He had to get rid of these at once. He put the knife into the purse and dressed hurriedly and silently. Throw the knife and purse into a garbage can. That's it! He put on his coat and found stuffed in a pocket the pamphlets Jan had given him. Throw these away, too! Oh, but ... Naw! He paused and gripped the pamphlets in his black fingers as his mind filled with a cunning idea. Jan had given him these pamphlets and he would keep them and show them to the police if he were ever questioned. That's it! He would take them to his room at Dalton's and put them in a dresser drawer. He would say that he had not even opened them and had not wanted to. He would say that he had taken them only because Jan had insisted. He shuffled the pamphlets softly, so that the paper would not rustle, and read the titles: *Race Prejudice on Trial. The Negro Question in the United States. Black and White Unite and Fight.* But that did not seem so dangerous. He looked at the bottom of the pamphlet and saw a black and white picture of a hammer and a curving knife. Below it he read a line that said: *Issued by the Communist Party of the United States.* Now, *that* did seem dangerous. He looked further and saw a pen-and-ink drawing of a white hand clasping a black hand in solidarity and remembered the moment when Jan had stood on the running board of the car and had shaken hands with him. That had been an awful moment of hate and shame. Yes, he would tell them that he was afraid of reds, that he had not wanted to sit in the car with Jan and Mary, that he had not wanted to eat with them. He would say that he had done so only because it had been his job. He would tell them that it was the first time he had ever sat at a table with white people.

He stuffed the pamphlets into his coat pocket and looked at his watch. It was ten minutes until seven. He had to hurry and pack his clothes. He had to take that trunk to the station at eight-thirty.

Then fear rendered his legs like water. Suppose Mary had not burned? Suppose she was still there, exposed to view? He wanted to drop everything and rush back and see. But maybe even something worse had happened; maybe they had discovered that she was dead and maybe the police were looking for him? Should he not leave town right now? Gripped by the same impelling excitement that had had hold of him when he was carrying Mary up the stairs he stood in the middle of the room. *No*; he would stay. Things were with him; no one suspected that she was dead. He would carry through and blame the thing upon Jan. He got his gun from beneath the pillow and put it in his shirt.

He tiptoed from the room, looking over his shoulder at his mother and sister and brother sleeping. He went down the steps to the vestibule and into the street. It was white and cold. Snow was falling and an icy wind blew. The streets were empty. Tucking the purse under his arm, he walked to an alley where a garbage can stood covered with snow. Was it safe to leave it here? The men on the garbage trucks would empty the can early in the morning and no one would be prying round on a day like this, with all the snow and its being Sunday. He lifted the top of the can and pushed the purse deep into a frozen pile of orange peels and mildewed bread. He replaced the top and looked around; no one was in sight.

He went back to the room and got his suitcase from under the side of the bed. His folks were still sleeping. In order to pack his clothes, he had to get to the dresser on the other side of the room. But how could he get there, with the bed on which his mother and sister slept standing squarely in the way? Goddamn! He wanted to wave his hand and blot them out? They were always too close to him, so close that he could never have any way of his own. He eased to the bed and stepped over it. His mother stirred slightly, then was still. He pulled open a dresser drawer and took out his clothes and piled them in the suitcase. While he worked there hovered before his eyes an image of Mary's head lying on the wet newspapers, the curly black ringlets soaked with blood.

'Bigger!'

He sucked his breath in and whirled about, his eyes glaring. His mother was leaning on her elbow in bed. He knew at once that he should not have acted frightened.

'What's the matter, boy?' she asked in a whisper.

'Nothing,' he answered, whispering too.

'You jumped like something bit you.'

'Aw, leave me alone. I got to pack.'

He knew that his mother was waiting for him to give an account of himself, and he hated her for that. Why couldn't she wait until he told her of his own accord? And yet he knew that if she waited, he would never tell her.

'You get the job?'

'Yeah.'

'What they paying you?'

'Twenty.'

'You started already?'

'Yeah.'

'When?'

'Last night.'

'I wondered what made you so late.'

'I had to work,' he drawled with impatience.

'You didn't get in until after four.'

He turned and looked at her.

'I got in at *two*.'

'It was after *four*, Bigger,' she said, turning and straining her eyes to look at an alarm clock above her head. 'I tried to wait up for you, but I couldn't. When I heard you come in, I looked up at the clock and it was after four.'

'*I* know when I got in, Ma.'

'But, Bigger, it was after *four*.'

'It was just a little after *two*.'

'Oh, Lord! If you *want* it two, then let it be two, for all I care. You act like you scared of something.

'Now, what you want to start a fuss for?'

'A fuss? *Boy!*'

'Before I get out of bed, you pick on me.'

'Bigger, I'm not picking on you honey. I'm glad you got the job.'

'You don't talk like it.'

He felt that his acting in this manner was a mistake. If he kept on talking about the time he had gotten in last night, he would so impress it upon her that she would remember it and perhaps say something later on that would hurt him. He turned away and continued packing. He had to do better than this; he had to control himself.

'You want to eat?'

'Yeah.'

'I'll fix you something.'

'O.K.'

'You going to stay on the place?'

'Yeah.'

He heard her getting out of bed; he did not dare look round now. He had to keep his head turned while she dressed.

'How you like the people, Bigger?'

'They all right.'

'You don't act like you glad.'

'Oh, Ma! For chrissakes! You want me to *cry*!'

'Bigger, sometimes I wonder what makes you act like you do.'

He had spoken in the wrong tone of voice; he had to be careful. He fought down the anger rising in him. He was in trouble enough without getting into a fuss with his mother.

'You got a good job, now,' his mother said. 'You ought to work hard and keep it and try to make a man out of yourself. Some day you'll want to get married and have a home of your own. You got your chance now. You always said you never had a chance. Now, you got one.'

He heard her move about and he knew that she was dressed enough for him to turn round. He strapped the suitcase and set it by the door; then he stood at the window, looking wistfully out at the feathery flakes of falling snow.

'Bigger, what's wrong with you?'

He whirled.

'Nothing,' he said, wondering what change she saw in him.

'Nothing. You just worry me, that's all,' he concluded, feeling that even if he did say something wrong he had to fight her off him now. He wondered just how his words *really* did sound. Was the tone of his voice this morning different from other mornings? Was there something unusual in his voice since he had killed Mary? Could people tell he had done something wrong by the way he acted? He saw his mother shake her head and go behind the curtain to prepare breakfast. He heard a yawn; he looked and saw that Vera was leaning on her elbow, smiling at him.

'You get the job?'

'Yeah.'

'How much you making?'

'Aw, Vera. Ask Ma. I done told her everything.'

'Goody! Bigger got a job!' sang Vera.

'Aw, shut up,' he said.

'Leave him alone, Vera,' the mother said.

'What's the matter?'

'What's the matter with 'im *all* the time?' asked the mother.

'Oh, Bigger,' said Vera, tenderly and plaintively.

'That boy just ain't got no sense, that's all,' the mother said. 'He won't even speak a decent word to you.'

'Turn your head so I can dress,' Vera said.

Bigger looked out of the window. He heard someone say, 'Aw!' and he knew that Buddy was awake.

'Turn your head, Buddy,' Vera said.

'O.K.'

Bigger heard his sister rushing into her clothes.

'You can look now,' Vera said.

He saw Buddy sitting up in bed, rubbing his eyes. Vera was sitting on the edge of a chair, with her right foot hoisted upon another chair, buckling her shoes. Bigger stared vacantly in her direction. He wished that he could rise up through the ceiling and float away from this room, forever.

'I wish you wouldn't look at me,' Vera said.

'Hunh?' said Bigger, looking in surprise at her pouting lips. Then he noticed what she meant and poked out his lips at her.

Quickly, she jumped up and threw one of her shoes at him. It sailed past his head and landed against the window, rattling the panes.

'I told you not to look at me!' Vera screamed.

Bigger stood up, his eyes red with anger.

'I just wish you had hit me,' he said.

'You, Vera!' the mother called.

'Ma, make 'im stop looking at me,' Vera wailed.

'Wasn't nobody looking at her,' Bigger said.

'You looked under my dress when I was buttoning my shoes!'

'I just *wish* you had hit me,' Bigger said again.

'I ain't no dog!' Vera said.

'Come on in the kitchen and dress, Vera,' the mother said.

'He makes me feel like a dog,' Vera sobbed with her face buried in her hands, going behind the curtain.

'Boy,' said Buddy, 'I tried to keep awake till you got in last night, but I couldn't. I had to go to bed at three. I was so sleepy I could hardly keep my eyes open.'

'I was here before then,' Bigger said.

'Aw, naw! I was up . . .'

'*I* know when I got in!'

They looked at each other in silence.

'O.K.,' Buddy said.

Bigger was uneasy. He felt that he was not handling himself right.

'You get the job?' Buddy asked.

'Yeah.'

'Driving?'

'Yeah.'

'What kind of a car is it?'

'A Buick.'

'Can I ride with you some time?'

'Sure; as soon as I get settled.'

Buddy's questions made him feel a little more at ease; he always liked the adoration Buddy showed him.

'Gee! That's the kind of job I want,' Buddy said.

'It's easy.'

'Will you see if you can find me one?'

'Sure. Give me time.'

'Got a cigarette?'

'Yeah.'

They were silent, smoking. Bigger was thinking of the furnace. Had Mary burned? He looked at his watch; it was seven o'clock. Ought he go over right now, without waiting for breakfast? Maybe he had left something lying round that would let them know Mary was dead. But if they slept late on Sunday mornings, as Mr Dalton had said, they would have no reason to be looking round down there.

'Bessie was by last night,' Buddy said.

'Yeah?'

'She said she saw you in Ernie's Kitchen Shack with some white folks.'

'Yeah. I was driving 'em last night.'

'She was talking about you and her getting married.'

'Humph!'

'How come gals that way, Bigger? Soon's a guy get a good job, they want to marry?'

'Damn if I know.'

'You got a good job now. You can get a better gal than Bessie,' Buddy said.

Although he agreed with Buddy, he said nothing.

'I'm going to tell Bessie!' Vera called.

'If you do, I'll break your neck,' Bigger said.

'Hush that kind of talk in here,' the mother said.

'Oh, yeah,' Buddy said. 'I met Jack last night. He said you almost murdered old Gus.'

'I ain't having nothing to do with that gang no more,' Bigger said emphatically.

'But Jack's all right,' Buddy said.

'Well, Jack, but none of the rest.'

Gus and G.H. and Jack seemed far away to Bigger now, in another life, and all because he had been in Dalton's home for a few hours and had killed a white girl. He looked round the

room, seeing it for the first time. There was no rug on the floor
and the plastering on the walls and ceiling hung loose in many
places. There were two worn iron beds, four chairs, an old
dresser, and a drop-leaf table on which they ate. This was much
different from Dalton's home. Here all slept in one room; there
he would have a room for himself alone. He smelt food cooking
and remembered that one could not smell food cooking in
Dalton's home; pots could not be heard rattling all over the
house. Each person lived in one room and had a little world of
his own. He hated this room and all the people in it, including
himself. Why did he and his folks have to live like this? What
had they ever done? Perhaps they had not done anything.
Maybe they had to live this way precisely because none of them
in all their lives had ever done anything, right or wrong, that
mattered much.

    'Fix the table, Vera. Breakfast's ready,' the mother called.

    'Yessum.'

Bigger sat at the table and waited for food. Maybe this would
be the last time he would eat here. He felt it keenly and it
helped him to have patience. Maybe some day he would be
eating in jail. Here he was sitting with them and they did not
know that he had murdered a white girl and cut her head off
and burnt her body. The thought of what he had done, the
awful horror of it, the daring associated with such actions,
formed for him for the first time in his fear-ridden life a barrier
of protection between him and a world he feared. He had
murdered and had created a new life for himself. It was something that was all his own, and it was the first time in his life he
had had anything that others could not take from him. Yes; he
could sit here calmly and eat and not be concerned about what
his family thought or did. He had a natural wall from behind
which he could look at them. His crime was an anchor weigh-
ing him safely in time; it added to him a certain confidence
which his gun and knife did not. He was outside of his family
now, over and beyond them; they were incapable of even thinking that he had done such a deed. And he had done something
which even he had not thought possible.

Though he had killed by accident, not once did he feel the need to tell himself that it had been an accident. He was black and he had been alone in a room where a white girl had been killed; therefore he had killed her. That was what everybody would say anyhow, no matter what he said. And in a certain sense he knew that the girl's death had not been accidental. He had killed many times before, only on those other times there had been no handy victim of circumstance to make visible or dramatic his will to kill. His crime seemed natural; he felt that all of his life had been leading to something like this. It was no longer a matter of dumb wonder as to what would happen to him and his black skin; he knew now. The hidden meaning of his life – a meaning which others did not see and which he had always tried to hide – had spilled out. No; it was no accident, and he would never say that it was. There was in him a kind of terrified pride in feeling and thinking that some day he would be able to say publicly that he had done it. It was as though he had an obscure but deep debt to fulfill to himself in accepting the deed.

Now that the ice was broken, could he not do other things? What was there to stop him? While sitting there at the table waiting for his breakfast, he felt that he was arriving at something which had long eluded him. Things were becoming clear; he would know how to act from now on. The thing to do was to act just like others acted, live like they lived, and while they were not looking, do what you wanted. They would never know. He felt in the quiet presence of his mother, brother, and sister a force, inarticulate and unconscious, making for living without thinking, making for peace and habit, making for a hope that blinded. He felt that they wanted and yearned to see life in a certain way; they needed a certain picture of the world; there was one way of living they preferred above all others; and they were blind to what did not fit. They did not want to see what others were doing if that doing did not feed their own desires. All one had to do was to be bold, do something nobody thought of. The whole thing came to him in the form of a powerful and simple feeling; there was in everyone a greater hunger to believe that made him blind, and if he could see while others were blind, then he could get what he wanted and never be caught at it. Now, who on earth would think that he, a black timid Negro boy, would murder and burn a rich white girl and would sit and wait for his breakfast like this! Elation filled him.

He sat at the table watching the snow fall past the window and many things became plain. No, he did not have to hide behind a wall or a curtain now; he had a safer way of being safe, an easier way. What he had done last night had proved that. Jan was blind. Mary had been blind. Mr Dalton was blind. And Mrs Dalton was blind; yes, blind in more ways than one. Bigger smiled slightly. Mrs Dalton had not known that Mary was dead while she had stood over the bed in that room last night. She had thought that Mary was drunk, because she was used to Mary's coming home drunk. And Mrs Dalton had not known that he was in the room with her; it would have been the last thing she would have thought of. He was black and would not have figured in her thoughts on such an occasion. Bigger felt that a lot of people were like Mrs Dalton, blind . . .

'Here you are, Bigger,' his mother said, setting a plate of grits on the table.

He began to eat, feeling much better after thinking out what had happened to him last night. He felt he could control himself now.

'Ain't you-all eating?' he asked, looking around.

'You go on and eat. You got to go. We'll eat later,' his mother said.

He did not need any money, for he had the money he had gotten from Mary's purse; but he wanted to cover his tracks carefully.

'You got any money, Ma?'

'Just a little, Bigger.'

'I need some.'

'Here's a half. That leaves me exactly one dollar to last till Wednesday.'

He put the half-dollar in his pocket. Buddy had finished dressing and was sitting on the edge of the bed. Suddenly, he saw Buddy, saw him in the light of Jan. Buddy was soft and vague; his eyes were defenseless and their glance went only to the surface of things. It was strange that he had not noticed that before. Buddy, too, was blind. Buddy was sitting there longing for a job like his. Buddy, too, went round and round in a groove and did not see things. Buddy's clothes hung loosely compared with the way Jan's hung. Buddy seemed aimless, lost, with no sharp or hard edges, like a chubby puppy. Looking at Buddy and thinking of Jan and Mr Dalton, he saw in Buddy a certain stillness, an isolation, meaninglessness.

'How come you looking at me that way, Bigger?'

'Hunh?'

'You looking at me so funny.'

'I didn't know it. I was thinking.'

'What?'

'Nothing.'

His mother came into the room with more plates of food and he saw how soft and shapeless she was. Her eyes were tired and sunken and darkly ringed from a long lack of rest. She moved about slowly, touching objects with her fingers as she passed them, using them for support. Her feet dragged over the wooden floor and her face held an expression of tense effort. Whenever she wanted to look at anything, even though it was near her, she turned her entire head and body to see it and did not shift her eyes. There was in her heart, it seemed, a heavy and delicately balanced burden whose weight she did not want to assume by disturbing it one whit. She saw him looking at her.

'Eat your breakfast, Bigger.'

'I'm eating.'

Vera brought her plate and sat opposite him. Bigger felt that even though her face was smaller and smoother than his mother's, the beginning of the same tiredness was already there. How different Vera was from Mary! He could see it in the very way Vera moved her hand when she carried the fork to her mouth; she seemed to be shrinking from life in every gesture she made. The very manner in which she sat showed a fear so deep as to be an organic part of her: she carried the food to her mouth in tiny bits, as if dreading its choking her, or fearing that it would give out too quickly.

'Bigger!' Vera wailed.

'Hunh?'

'You stop now,' Vera said, laying aside her fork and slapping her hand through the air at him.

'What?'

'Stop looking at me, Bigger!'

'Aw, shut up and eat your breakfast!'

'Ma, make 'im stop looking at me!'

'I ain't looking at her, Ma!'

'You *is*!' Vera said.

'Eat your breakfast, Vera, and hush,' said the mother.

'He just keeps watching me, Ma!'

'Gal, you crazy!' said Bigger.

'I ain't no crazy'n you!'

'Now, *both* of you hush,' said the mother.

'I ain't going to eat with him watching me,' Vera said, getting up and sitting on the edge of the bed.

'Go on and eat your grub!' Bigger said, leaping to his feet and grabbing his cap. 'I'm getting out of here.'

'What's wrong with you, Vera?' Buddy asked.

'Tend to your business!' Vera said, tears welling to her eyes.

'Will you children *please* hush,' the mother wailed.

'Ma, you oughtn't let 'im treat me that way,' Vera said.

Bigger picked up his suitcase. Vera came back to the table, drying her eyes.

'When will I see you again, Bigger?' the mother asked.

'I don't know,' he said, slamming the door.

He was halfway down the steps when he heard his name called.

'Say, Bigger!'

He stopped and looked back. Buddy was running down the steps. He waited, wondering what was wrong.

'What you want?'

Buddy stood before him, diffident, smiling.

'I – I . . .'

'What's the matter?'

'Shucks, I just thought . . .'

Bigger stiffened with fright.

'Say, what you so excited about?'

'Aw, I reckon it ain't nothing. I just thought maybe you was in trouble . . .'

Bigger mounted the steps and stood close to Buddy.

'Trouble? What you mean?' he asked in a frightened whisper.

'I – I just thought you was kind of nervous. I wanted to help you, that's all. I – I just thought . . .'

'How come you think that?'

Buddy held out a roll of bills in his hand.

'You dropped it on the floor,' he said.

Bigger stepped back, thunder-struck. He felt in his pocket for the money; it was not there. He took the money from Buddy and stuffed it hurriedly in his pocket.

'Did Ma see it?'

'Naw.'

He gazed at Buddy in a long silence. He knew that Buddy was yearning to be with him, aching to share his confidence; but that could not happen now. He caught Buddy's arm in a tight grip.

'Listen, don't tell nobody, see? Here,' he said, taking out the roll and peeling off a bill. 'Here; take this and buy something. But don't tell *no*body.'

'Gee! Thanks. I – I won't tell. But can I help you?'

'Naw; naw . . .'

Buddy started back up the steps.

'Wait,' Bigger said.

Buddy came back and stood facing him, his eyes eager, shining. Bigger looked at him, his body as taught as that of an animal about to leap. But his brother would not betray him. He could trust Buddy. He caught Buddy's arm again and squeezed it until Buddy flinched with pain.

'Don't you tell *no*body, hear?'

'Naw; naw ... I *won't* ...'

'Go on back, now.'

Buddy ran up the steps, out of sight. Bigger stood brooding in the shadows of the stairway. He thrust the feeling from him, not with shame, but with impatience. He had felt toward Buddy for an instant as he had felt toward Mary when she lay upon the bed with the white blur moving toward him in the hazy blue light of the room. But he won't tell, he thought.

He went down the steps and into the street. The air was cold and the snow had stopped. Overhead the sky was clearing a little. As he neared the corner drug store, which stayed open all night, he wondered if any of the gang was around. Maybe Jack or G.H. was hanging out and had not gone home, as they sometimes did. Though he felt he was cut off from them forever, he had a strange hankering for their presence. He wanted to know how he would feel if he saw them again. Like a man reborn, he wanted to test and taste each thing now to see how it went; like a man risen up well from a long illness, he felt deep and wayward whims.

He peered through the frosted glass; yes, G.H. was there. He opened the door and went in. G.H. sat at the fountain, talking to the soda-jerker. Bigger sat next to him. They did not speak. Bigger bought two packages of cigarettes and shoved one of them to G.H., who looked at him in surprise.

'This for *me*?' G.H. asked.

Bigger waved his palm and pulled down the corners of his lips.

'Sure.'

G.H. opened the pack.

'Jesus, I sure needed one. Say, you working now?'

'Yeah.'

'How you like it?'

'Aw, swell,' Bigger said, crossing his fingers. He was trembling with excitement; sweat was on his forehead. He was excited and something was impelling him to become more excited. It was like a thirst springing from his blood. The door opened and Jack came in.

'Say, how is it, Bigger?'

Bigger wagged his head.

'Honky dory,' he said. 'Here; gimme another pack of cigarettes,' he told the clerk. 'This is for you, Jack.'

'Jesus, you in clover, sure 'nough,' Jack said, glimpsing the thick roll of bills.

'Where's Gus?' Bigger asked.

'He'll be along in a minute. We been hanging out at Clara's all night.'

The door opened again; Bigger turned and saw Gus step inside. Gus paused.

'Now, you-all don't fight,' Jack said.

Bigger bought another package of cigarettes and tossed it toward Gus. Gus caught it and stood, bewildered.

'Aw, come on, Gus. Forget it,' Bigger said.

Gus came forward slowly; he opened the package and lit one.

'Bigger, you sure is crazy,' Gus said with a shy smile.

Bigger knew that Gus was glad that the fight was over. Bigger was not afraid of them now; he sat with his feet propped upon his suitcase, looking from one to the other with a quiet smile.

'Lemme have a dollar,' Jack said.

Bigger peeled off a dollar bill for each of them.

'Don't say I never give you nothing,' he said, laughing.

'Bigger, you sure is one more crazy nigger,' Gus said again, laughing with joy.

But he had to go; he could not stay here talking with them. He ordered three bottles of beer and picked up his suitcase.

'Ain't you going to drink one, too?' G.H. asked.

'Naw! I got to go.'

'We'll be seeing you!'

'So long!'

He waved at them and swung through the door. He walked over the snow, feeling giddy and elated. His mouth was open and his eyes shone. It was the first time he had ever been in their presence without feeling fearful. He was following a strange path into a strange land and his nerves were hungry to see where it led. He lugged his suitcase to the end of the block, and stood waiting for a streetcar. He slipped his fingers into his vest pocket and felt the crisp roll of bills. Instead of going to Daltons', he could take a streetcar to a railway station and leave town. But what would happen if he left? If he ran away now it would be thought at once that he knew something about Mary, as soon as she was missed. No; it would be far better to stick it out and see what happened. It might be a long time before anyone would think that Mary was killed and a still longer time before anyone would think that he had done it. And when Mary was missed, would they not think of the reds first?

The streetcar rumbled up and he got on and rode to Forty-seventh street, where he transferred to an eastbound car. He looked anxiously at the dim reflection of his black face in the sweaty windowpane. Would any of the white faces all about him think that he had killed a rich white girl? No! They might think he would steal a dime, rape a woman, get drunk, or cut somebody; but to kill a millionaire's daughter and burn her body? He smiled a little, feeling a tingling sensation enveloping all his body. He saw it all very sharply and simply: act like other people thought you ought to act, yet do what you wanted. In a certain sense he had been doing just that in a loud and rough manner all his life, but it was only last night when he had smothered Mary in her room while her blind mother had stood with outstretched arms that he had seen how clearly it could be done. Although he was trembling a little, he was not really afraid. He was eager, tremendously excited. I can take care of them, he thought, thinking of Mr and Mrs Dalton.

There was only one thing that worried him; he had to get that lingering image of Mary's bloody head lying on those news-papers from before his eyes. If that were done, then he would be all right. Gee, what a fool she was, he thought, remembering how Mary had acted. Carrying on that way! Hell, she *made* me do it! I couldn't help it! She should've known better! She should've left me alone, goddammit! He did not feel sorry for Mary; she was not real to him, not a human being; he had not known her long or well enough for that. He felt that his murder of her was more than amply justified by the fear and shame she had made him feel. It seemed that her actions had evoked fear and shame in him. But when he thought hard about it it seemed impossible that they could have. He really did not know just where that fear and shame had come from; it had just been there, that was all. Each time he had come in contact with her it had risen hot and hard.

It was not Mary he was reacting to when he felt that fear and shame. Mary had served to set off his emotions, emotions conditioned by many Marys. And now that he had killed Mary he felt a lessening of tension in his muscles; he had shed an invisible burden he had long carried.

As the car lurched over the snow he lifted his eyes and saw black people upon the snow-covered sidewalks. Those people had feelings of fear and shame like his. Many a time he had stood on street corners with them and talked of white people as long sleek cars zoomed past. To Bigger and his kind white people were not really people; they were a sort of great natural force, like a stormy sky looming overhead, or like a deep whirling river stretching suddenly at one's feet in the dark. As long as he and his black folks did not go beyond certain limits, there was no need to fear that white force. But whether they feared it or not, each and every day of their lives they lived with it; even when words did not sound its name, they acknowledged its reality. As long as they lived here in this prescribed corner of the city, they paid mute tribute to it.

There were rare moments when a feeling and longing for solidarity with other black people would take hold of him. He would dream of making a stand against that white force, but that dream would fade when he looked at the other black people near him. Even though black like them, he felt there was too much difference between him and them to allow for a common binding and a common life. Only when threatened with death could that happen; only in fear and shame, with their backs against a wall, could that happen. But never could they sink their differences in hope.

As he rode, looking at the black people on the sidewalks, he felt that one way to end fear and shame was to make all those black people act together, rule them, tell them what to do, and make them do it. Dimly, he felt that there should be one direction in which he and all other black people could go whole-heartedly; that there should be a way in which gnawing hunger and restless aspiration could be fused; that there should be a manner of acting that caught the mind and body in certainty and faith. But he felt that such would never happen to him and his black people, and he hated them and wanted to wave his hand and blot them out. Yet, he still hoped, vaguely. Of late he had liked to hear tell of men who could rule others, for in actions such as these he felt that there was a way to escape from this tight morass of fear and shame that sapped at the base of his life. He liked to hear of how Japan was conquering China; of how Hitler was running the Jews to the ground; of how Mussolini was invading Spain. He was not concerned with whether these acts were right or wrong; they simply appealed to him as possible avenues of escape. He felt that some day there would be a black man who would whip the black people into a tight band and together they would act and end fear and shame. He never thought of this in precise mental images; he felt it; he would feel it for a while and then forget. But hope was always waiting somewhere deep down in him.

It was fear that had made him fight Gus in the poolroom. If he had felt certain of himself and of Gus, he would not have fought. But he knew Gus, as he knew himself, and he knew that one of them might fail through fear at the decisive moment. How could he think of going to rob Blum's that way? He distrusted and feared Gus and knew that Gus distrusted and feared him; and the moment he tried to band himself and Gus together to do something, he would hate Gus and himself. Ultimately, though, his hate and hope turned outward from himself and Gus: his hope toward a vague benevolent something that would help and lead him, and his hate toward the whites; for he felt that they ruled him, even when they were far away and not thinking of him, ruled him by conditioning him in his relations to his own people.

The streetcar crawled through the snow; Drexel Boulevard was the next stop. He lifted the suitcase and stood at the door. In a few minutes he would know if Mary had burned. The car stopped; he swung off and walked through snow as deep as his ankles, heading for Daltons'.

When he got to the driveway he saw that the car was standing just as he had left it, but all covered with a soft crust of snow. The house loomed white and silent. He unlatched the gate and went past the car, seeing before his eyes an image of Mary, her bloody neck just inside the furnace and her head with its curly black hair lying upon the soggy newspapers. He paused. He could turn round now and go back. He could get into the car and be miles from here before anybody knew it. But why run away unless there was a good reason? He had some money to make a run for it when the time came. And he had his gun. His fingers trembled so that he had difficulty in unlocking the door; but they were not trembling from fear. It was a kind of eagerness he felt, a confidence, a fulness, a freedom; his whole life was caught up in a supreme and meaningful act. He pushed the door in, then was stone-still, sucking his breath in softly. In the red glare of the furnace stood a shadowy figure, Is that Mrs Dalton? But it was taller and stouter than Mrs Dalton. Oh, it was Peggy! She stood with her back to him, a little bent. She seemed to be peering hard into the furnace. She didn't hear me come in, he thought. *Maybe I ought to go!* But before he could move Peggy turned around.

'Oh, good morning, Bigger.'

He did not answer.

'I'm glad you came. I was just about to put more coal into the fire.'

'I'll fix it, mam.'

He came forward, straining his eyes to see if any traces of Mary were in the furnace. When he reached Peggy's side he saw that she was staring through the cracks of the door at the red bed of livid coals.

'The fire was very hot last night,' Peggy said. 'But this morning it got low.'

'I'll fix it,' Bigger said, standing and not daring to open the door of the furnace while she stood there beside him in the red darkness.

He heard the dull roar of the draft going upwards and wondered if she suspected anything. He knew that he should have turned on the light; but what if he did and the light revealed part of Mary in the furnace?

'I'll fix it, mam,' he said again.

Quickly, he wondered if he would have to kill her to keep her from telling if she turned on the light and saw something that made her think that Mary was dead? Without turning his head he saw an iron shovel resting in a near-by corner. His hands clenched. Peggy moved from his side toward a light that swung from the ceiling at the far end of the room near the stairs.

'I'll give you some light,' she said.

He moved silently and quickly toward the shovel and waited to see what would happen. The light came on, blindingly bright; he blinked. Peggy stood near the steps holding her right hand tightly over her breast. She had on a kimono and was trying to hold it closely about her. Bigger understood at once. She was not even thinking of the furnace; she was just a little ashamed of having been seen in the basement in her kimono.

'Has Miss Dalton come down yet?' she asked over her shoulder as she went up the steps.

'No'm. I haven't seen her.'

'You just come?'

'Yessum.'

She stopped and looked back at him.

'But the car, it's in the driveway.'

'Yessum,' he said simply, not volunteering any information.

'Then it stayed out all night?'

'I don't know, mam.'

'Didn't you put it in the garage?'

'No'm. Miss Dalton told me to leave it out.'

'Oh! Then it *did* stay out all night. That's why it's covered with snow.'

'I reckon so, mam.'

Peggy shook her head and sighed.

'Well, I suppose she'll be ready for you to take her to the station in a few minutes.'

'Yessum.'

'I see you brought the trunk down.'

'Yessum. She told me to bring it down last night.'

'Don't forget it,' she said, going through the kitchen door.

For a long time after she had gone he did not move from his tracks. Then, slowly, he looked round the basement, turning his head like an animal with eyes and ears alert, searching to see if anything was amiss. The room was exactly as he had left it last night. He walked about, looking closer. All at once he stopped, his eyes widening. Directly in front of him he saw a small piece of blood-stained newspaper lying in the livid reflection cast by the cracks in the door of the furnace. Had Peggy seen that? He ran to the light and turned it out and ran back and looked at the piece of paper. He could barely see it. That meant that Peggy had not seen it. How about Mary? Had she burned? He turned the light back on and picked up the piece of paper. He glanced to the left and right to see if anyone was watching, then opened the furnace door and peered in, his eyes filled with the vision of Mary and her bloody throat. The inside of the furnace breathed and quivered in the grip of fiery coals. But there was no sign of the body, even though the body's image hovered before his eyes, between his eyes and the bed of coals burning hotly. Like the oblong mound of fresh clay of a newly made grave, the red coals revealed the bent outlines of Mary's body. He had the feeling that if he simply touched that red oblong mound with his finger it would cave in and Mary's body would come into full view, unburnt. The coals had the appearance of having burnt the body beneath, leaving the glowing embers formed into a shell of red hotness with a hollowed space in the center, keeping still in the embrace of the quivering coals the huddled shape of Mary's body. He blinked his eyes and became aware that he still held the piece of paper in his hand. He lifted it to the level of the door and the draft sucked it from his fingers; he watched it fly into the red trembling heat, smoke, turn black, blaze, then vanish. He shut off the fan; there was no danger of scent now.

He shut the door and pulled the lever for more coal. The rattling of the tiny lumps against the tin sides of the chute came loudly to his ears as the oblong mound of red fire turned gradually black and blazed from the fanwise spreading of coal whirling into the furnace. He shut off the lever and stood up; things were all right so far. As long as no one poked round in that fire, things would be all right. He himself did not want to poke in it, for fear that some part of Mary was still there. If things could go on like this until afternoon, Mary would be burned enough to make him safe. He turned and looked at the trunk again. Oh! He must not forget! He had to put those Communist pamphlets in his room right away. He ran back of the furnace, up the steps to his room and placed the pamphlets smoothly and neatly in a corner of his dresser drawer. Yes, they would have to be stacked neatly. No one must think that he had read them.

He went back to the basement and stood uncertainly in front of the furnace. He felt that he had left something undone, something that would betray him. Maybe he ought to shake the ashes down? Yes. The fire must not become so clogged with cinders that it would not burn. At the moment he stooped to grasp the protruding handle of the lower bin to shake it to and fro, a vivid image of Mary's face as he had seen it upon the bed in the blue light of the room gleamed at him from the smoldering embers and he rose abruptly, giddy and hysterical with guilt and fear. His hands twitched; he could not shake the ashes now. He had to get out into the air, away from this basement whose very walls seemed to loom closer about him each second, making it difficult for him to breathe.

He went to the trunk, grasped its handle and dragged it to the door, lifted it to his back, carried it to the car and fastened it to the running board. He looked at his watch; it was eight-twenty. Now, he would have to wait for Mary to come out. He took his seat at the steering wheel and waited for five minutes. He would ring the bell for her. He looked at the steps leading up to the side door of the house, remembered how Mary had stumbled last night and how he had held her up. Then, involuntarily, he started in fright as a full blast of intense sunshine fell from the sky, making the snow leap and glitter and sparkle about him in a world of magic whiteness without sound. It's getting late! He would have to go in and ask for Miss Dalton. If he stayed here too long it would seem that he was not expecting her to come down. He got out of the car and walked up the steps to the side door. He looked through the glass; no one was in sight. He tried to open the door and found it locked. He pushed the bell, hearing the gong sound softly within. He waited a moment, then saw Peggy hurrying down the hall. She opened the door.

'Hasn't she come out yet?'

'No'm. And it's getting late.'

'Wait. I'll call her.'

Peggy, still dressed in the kimono, ran up the stairs, the same stairs up which he had half-dragged Mary and the same stairs down which he had stumbled with the trunk last night. Then he saw Peggy coming back down the stairs, much slower than she had gone up. She came to the door.

'She ain't here. Maybe she's gone. What did she tell you?'

'She said to drive her to the station and to take her trunk, mam.'

'Well, she ain't in her room and she ain't in Mrs Dalton's room. And Mr Dalton's asleep. Did she tell you she was going this morning?'

'That's what she told me last night, mam.'

'She told you to bring the trunk down last night?'

'Yessum.'

Peggy thought a moment, looking past him at the snow-covered car.

'Well, you better take the trunk on. Maybe she didn't stay here last night.'

'Yessum.'

He turned and started down the steps.

'Bigger!'

'Yessum.'

'You say she told you to leave the car out, all *night*?'

'Yessum.'

'Did she say she was going to use it again?'

'No'm. You see,' Bigger said, feeling his way, 'he was in it . . .'

'*Who?*'

'The gentleman.'

'Oh; yes. Take the trunk on. I suppose Mary was up to some of her pranks.'

He got into the car and pulled it down the driveway to the street, then headed northward over the snow. He wanted to look back and see if Peggy was watching him, but dared not. That would make her think that he thought that something was wrong, and he did not want to give that impression now. Well, at least he had one person thinking it as he wanted it thought.

He reached the La Salle Street Station, pulled the car to a platform, backed into a narrow space between other cars, hoisted the trunk up, and waited for a man to give him a ticket for the trunk. He wondered what would happen if no one called for it. Maybe they would notify Mr Dalton. Well, he would wait and see. He had done his part. Miss Dalton had asked him to take the trunk to the station and he had done it.

He drove as hurriedly back to the Daltons' as the snow-covered streets would allow. He wanted to be back on the spot and see what would happen, to be there with his fingers on the pulse of time. He reached the driveway and nosed the car into the garage, locked it, and then stood wondering if he ought to go to his room or to the kitchen. It would be better to go straight to the kitchen as though nothing had happened. He had not as yet eaten his breakfast as far as Peggy was concerned, and his coming into the kitchen would be thought natural. He went through the basement, pausing to look at the roaring furnace, and then went to the kitchen door and stepped in softly. Peggy stood at the gas stove with her back to him. She turned and gave him a brief glance.

'You make it all right?'

'Yessum.'

'You see her down there?'

'No'm.'

'Hungry?'

'A little, mam.'

'A little?' Peggy laughed. 'You'll get used to how this house is run on Sundays. Nobody gets up early and when they do they're almost famished.'

'I'm all right, mam.'

'That was the only kick Green had while he was working here,' Peggy said. 'He swore we starved him on Sundays.'

Bigger forced a smile and looked down at the black and white linoleum on the floor. What would she think if she knew? He felt very kindly toward Peggy just then; he felt he had something of value which she could never take from him even if she despised him. He heard the phone ring in the hall-way. Peggy straightened and looked at him as she wiped her hands on her apron.

'Who on earth's calling here this early on a Sunday morning?' she mumbled.

She went out and he sat, waiting. Maybe that was Jan asking about Mary. He remembered that Mary had promised to call him. He wondered how long it took to go to Detroit. Five or six hours? It was not far. Mary's train had already gone. About four o'clock she would be due in Detroit. Maybe someone had planned to meet her? If she was not on the train, would they call or wire about it? Peggy came back, went to the stove and continued cooking.

'Things'll be ready in a minute,' she said.

'Yessum.'

Then she turned to him.

'Who was the gentleman with Miss Dalton last night?'

'I don't know, mam. I think she called him Jan, or something like that.'

'Jan? He just called,' Peggy said. She tossed her head and her lips tightened. 'He's a no-good one, if there ever was one. One of them anarchists who's agin the government.'

Bigger listened and said nothing.

'What on earth a good girl like Mary wants to hang around with that crazy bunch for, God only knows. Nothing good'll come of it, just you mark my word. If it wasn't for that Mary and her wild ways, this household would run like a clock. It's such a pity, too. Her mother's the very soul of goodness. And there never was a finer man than Mr Dalton ... But later on Mary'll settle down. They all do. They think they're missing something unless they kick up their heels when they're young and foolish ...'

She brought a bowl of hot oatmeal and milk to him and he began to eat. He had difficulty in swallowing, for he had no appetite. But he forced the food down. Peggy talked on and he wondered what he should say to her; he found that he could say nothing. Maybe she was not expecting him to say anything. Maybe she was talking to him because she had no one else to talk to, like his mother did sometimes. Yes; he would see about that fire again when he got to the basement. He would fill that furnace as full of coal as it would get and make sure that Mary burned in a hurry. The hot cereal was making him sleepy and he suppressed a yawn.

'What all I got to do today, mam?'

'Just wait on call. Sunday's a dull day. Maybe Mr or Mrs Dalton'll go out.'

'Yessum.'

He finished the oatmeal.

'You want me to do anything now?'

'No. But you're not through eating. You want some ham and eggs?'

'No'm. I got a plenty.'

'Well, it's right here for you. Don't be afraid to ask for it.'

'I reckon I'll see about the fire now.'

'All right, Bigger. Just you listen for the bell about two o'clock. Till then I don't think there'll be anything.'

He went to the basement. The fire was blazing. The embers glowed red and the draft droned upward. It did not need any coal. Again he looked round the basement, into every nook and corner, to see if he had left any trace of what had happened last night. There was none.

He went to his room and lay on the bed. Well; here he was now. What would happen? The room was quiet. No! He heard something! He cocked his head, listening. He caught faint sounds of pots and pans rattling in the kitchen below. He got up and walked to the far end of the room; the sounds came louder. He heard the soft but firm tread of Peggy as she walked across the kitchen floor. She's right under me, he thought. He stood still, listening. He heard Mrs Dalton's voice, then Peggy's. He stooped and put his ear to the floor. Were they talking about Mary? He could not make out what they were saying. He stood up and looked round. A foot from him was the door of the clothes closet. He opened it; the voices came clearly. He went into the closet and the planks squeaked; he stopped. Had they heard him? Would they think he was snooping? Oh! He had an idea! He got his suitcase and opened it and took out an armful of clothes. If anyone came into the room it would seem that he was putting his clothes away. He went into the closet and listened.

'. . . you mean the car stayed out all *night* in the drive-way?'

'Yes; he said she told him to leave it there.'

'What time was that?'

'I don't know, Mrs Dalton. I didn't ask him.'

'I don't understand this at all.'

'Oh, she's all right. I don't think you need worry.'

'But she didn't even leave a note, Peggy. That's not like Mary. Even when she ran away to New York that time she at least left a note.'

'Maybe she hasn't gone. Maybe something came up and she stayed out all night, Mrs Dalton.'

'But why would she leave the car out?'

'I don't know.'

'And he said a man was with her?'

'It was that Jan, I think, Mrs Dalton.'

'Jan?'

162

'Yes; the one who was with her in Florida.'

'She just *won't* leave those awful people alone.'

'He called here this morning, asking for her.'

'Called *here*?'

'Yes.'

'And what did he say?'

'He seemed sort of peeved when I told him she was gone.'

'What can that poor child be up to? She told me she was not seeing him any more.'

'Maybe *she* had him to call, Mrs Dalton . . .'

'What do you mean?'

'Well, mam, I was kind of thinking that maybe she's with him again, like that time she was in Florida. And maybe she had him to call to see if we knew she was gone . . .'

'Oh, Peggy!'

'Oh, I'm sorry, mam . . . Maybe she stayed with some friends of hers?'

'But she was in her *room* at two o'clock this morning, Peggy. Whose house would she go to at that hour?'

'Mrs Dalton, I noticed something when I went to her room this morning.'

'What?'

'Well, mam, it looked like her bed wasn't slept in at all. The cover wasn't even pulled back. Looks like somebody had just stretched out awhile and then got up . . .'

'Oh!'

Bigger listened intently, but there was silence. They knew that something was wrong now. He heard Mrs Dalton's voice again, quavering with doubt and fear.

'Then she *didn't* sleep here last night?'

'Looks like she didn't.'

'Did that boy say Jan was in the car?'

'Yes. I thought something was strange about the car being left out in the snow all night, and so I asked him. He said she told him to leave the car there and he said Jan was in it.'

'Listen, Peggy . . .'

'Yes, Mrs Dalton.'

'Mary was drunk last night. I hope nothing's happened to her.'

'Oh, what a pity!'

'I went to her room just after she came in . . . She was too drunk to talk. She was *drunk*, I tell you. I never thought she'd come home in that condition.'

'She'll be all right, Mrs Dalton I *know* she will.'

There was another long silence. Bigger wondered if Mrs Dalton was on her way to his room. He went back to the bed and lay down, listening. There were no sounds. He lay a long time, hearing nothing; then he heard footsteps in the kitchen again. He hurried into the closet.

'Peggy!'

'Yes, Mrs Dalton.'

'Listen, I just felt around in Mary's room. Something's wrong. She didn't finish packing her trunk. At least half of her things are still there. She said she was planning to go to some dances in Detroit and she didn't take the new things she bought.'

'Maybe she didn't go to Detroit.'

'But where *is* she?'

Bigger stopped listening, feeling fear for the first time. He had not thought that the trunk was not fully packed. How could he explain that she had told him to take a half-packed trunk to the station? Oh, shucks! The girl was drunk. That was it. Mary was so drunk that she didn't know what she was doing. He would say that she had told him to take it and he had just taken it; that's all. If someone asked him why he had taken a half-packed trunk to the station, he would tell them that that was no different from all the other foolish things that Mary had told him to do that night. Had not people seen him eating with her and Jan in Ernie's Kitchen Shack? He would say that both of them were drunk and that he had done what they told him because it was his job. He listened again to the voices.

'. . . and after a while send that boy to me. I want to talk to him.'

'Yes, Mrs Dalton.'

Again he lay on the bed. He would have to go over his story and make it foolproof. Maybe he had done wrong in taking that trunk? Maybe it would have been better to have carried Mary down in his arms and burnt her? But he had put her in the trunk because of the fear of someone's seeing her in his arms. That was the only way he could have gotten her down out of the room. Oh, hell, what had happened had happened and he would stick to his story. He went over the story again, fastening every detail firmly in his mind. He would say that she had been drunk, sloppy drunk. He lay on the soft bed in the warm room listening to the steam hiss in the radiator and thinking drowsily and lazily of how drunk she had been and of how he had lugged her up the steps and of how he had pushed the pillow over her face and of how he had put her in the trunk and of how he had struggled with the trunk on the dark stairs and of how his fingers had burned while he stumbled down the stairs with the heavy trunk going *bump-bump-bump* so loud that surely all the world must have heard it . . .

He jumped awake, hearing a knock at the door. His heart raced. He sat up and stared sleepily around the room. Had someone knocked? He looked at his watch; it was three o'clock. Gee! He must have slept through the bell that was to ring at two. The knock came again.

'O.K.!' he mumbled.

'This is Mrs Dalton!'

'Yessum. Just a minute.'

He reached the door in two long steps, then stood a moment trying to collect himself. He blinked his eyes and wet his lips. He opened the door and saw Mrs Dalton smiling before him, dressed in white, her pale face held as it had been when she was standing in the darkness while he had smothered Mary on the bed.

'Y-y-yes, mam,' he stammered. 'I – I was asleep . . .'

'You didn't get much sleep last night, did you?'

'No'm,' he drawled, afraid of what she might mean.

'Peggy rang for you three times, and you didn't answer.'

'I'm sorry, mam . . .'

'That's all right. I wanted to ask you about last night ... Oh, you took the trunk to the station, didn't you?' she asked.

'Yessum. This morning,' he said, detecting hesitancy and confusion in her voice.

'I see,' said Mrs Dalton. She stood with her face tilted upward in the semi-darkness of the hallway. He had his hand on the doorknob, waiting, his muscles taut. He had to be careful with his answers now. And yet he knew he had a certain protection; he knew that a certain element of shame would keep Mrs Dalton from asking him too much and letting him know that she was worried. He was a boy and she was an old woman. He was the hired and she was the hirer. And there was a certain distance to be kept between them.

'You left the car in the driveway last night, didn't you?'

'Yessum. I was about to put it up,' he said, indicating that his only concern was with keeping his job and doing his duties. 'But she told me to leave it.'

'And was someone with her?'

'Yessum. A gentleman.'

'That must have been pretty late, wasn't it?'

'Yessum. A little before two, mam.'

'And you took the trunk down a little before two?'

'Yessum. She told me to.'

'She took you to her room?'

He did not want her to think that he had been alone in the room with Mary. Quickly, he recast the story in his mind.

'Yessum. They went up ...'

'Oh, *he* was with her?'

'Yessum.'

'I see ...'

'Anything wrong, mam?'

'Oh, no! I – I – I ... No; there's nothing wrong.'

She stood in the doorway and he looked at her light-gray blind eyes, eyes almost as white as her face and hair and dress. He knew that she was really worried and wanted to ask him more questions. But he knew that she would not want to hear him tell of how drunk her daughter had been. After all, he was black and she was white. He was poor and she was rich. She would be ashamed to let him think that something was so wrong in her family that she had to ask him, a black servant, about it. He felt confident.

'Will there be anything right now, mam?'

'No. In fact, you may take the rest of the day off, if you like. Mr Dalton is not feeling well and we're not going out.'

'Thank you, mam.'

She turned away and he shut the door; he stood listening to the soft whisper of her shoes die away down the hall, then on the stairs. He pictured her groping her way, her hands touching the walls. She must know this house like a book, he thought. He trembled with excitement. She was white and he was black; she was rich and he was poor; she was old and he was young; she was the boss and he was the worker. He was safe; yes. When he heard the kitchen door open and shut he went to the closet and listened again. But there were no sounds.

Well, he would go out. To go out now would be the answer to the feeling of strain that had come over him while talking to Mrs Dalton. He would go and see Bessie. That was it! He got his cap and coat and went to the basement. The suction of air through the furnace moaned and the fire was white-hot; there was enough coal to last until he came back.

He went to Forty-seventh Street and stood on the corner to wait for a car. Yes, Bessie was the one he wanted to see now. Funny, he had not thought of her much during the last day and night. Too many exciting things had been happening. He had had no need to think of her. But now he had to forget and relax and he wanted to see her. She was always home on Sunday afternoons. He wanted to see her very badly; he felt that he would be stronger to go through tomorrow if he saw her.

The streetcar came and he got on, thinking of how things had gone that day. No; he did not think they would suspect him of anything. He was black. Again he felt the roll of crisp bills in his pocket; if things went wrong he could always run away. He wondered how much money was in the roll; he had not even counted it. He would see when he got to Bessie's. No;

he need not be afraid. He felt the gun nestling close to his skin. That gun could always make folks stand away and think twice before bothering him.

But of the whole business there was one angle that bothered him; he should have gotten more money out of it; he should have *planned* it. He had acted too hastily and accidentally. Next time things would be much different; he would plan and arrange so that he would have money enough to keep him a long time. He looked out of the car window and then round at the white faces near him. He wanted suddenly to stand up and shout, telling them that he had killed a rich white girl, a girl whose family was known to all of them. Yes; if he did that a look of startled horror would come over their faces. But, no. He would not do that, even though the satisfaction would be keen. He was so greatly outnumbered that he would be arrested, tried, and executed. He wanted the keen thrill of startling them, but felt that the cost was too great. He wished that he had the power to say what he had done without fear of being arrested; he wished that he could be an idea in their minds; that his black face and the image of his smothering Mary and cutting off her head and burning her could hover before their eyes as a terrible picture of reality which they could see and feel and yet not destroy. He was not satisfied with the way things stood now; he was a man who had come in sight of a goal, then had won it, and in winning it had seen just within his grasp another goal, higher, greater. He had learned to shout and had shouted and no ear had heard him; he had just learned to walk and was walking but could not see the ground beneath his feet; he had long been yearning for weapons to hold in his hands and suddenly found that his hands held weapons that were invisible.

The car stopped a block from Bessie's home and he got off. When he reached the building in which she lived, he looked up to the second floor and saw a light burning in her window. The street lamps came on suddenly, lighting up the snow-covered sidewalks with a yellow sheen. It had gotten dark early. The lamps were round hazy balls of light frozen into motionlessness, anchored in space and kept from blowing away in the icy wind by black steel posts. He went in and rang the bell and, in answer to a buzzer, mounted the stairs and found Bessie smiling at him in her door.

'Hello, stranger!'

'Hi, Bessie.'

He stood face to face with her, then reached for her hands. She shied away.

'What's the matter?'

'You know what's the matter.'

'Naw, I don't.'

'What you reaching for me for?'

'I want to kiss you, honey.'

'You don't want to kiss me.'

'Why?'

'I ought to be asking *you* that.'

'What's the matter?'

'I saw you with your white friends last night.'

'Aw; they wasn't my friends.'

'Who was they?'

'I work for 'em.'

'And you eat with 'em.'

'Aw, Bessie . . .'

'You didn't even *speak* to me.'

'I *did*!'

'You just growled and waved your hand.'

'Aw, baby. I was working then. You understand.'

'I thought maybe you was 'shamed of me, sitting there with that white gal all dressed in silk and satin.'

'Aw, hell, Bessie. Come on. Don't act that way.'

'You really want to kiss me?'

'Sure. What you think I came here for?'

'How come you so long seeing me, then?'

'I told you I been working, honey. You saw me last night. Come on. Don't act this way.'

'I don't know,' she said, shaking her head.

He knew that she was trying to see how badly he missed her,

trying to see how much power she still had over him. He grabbed her arm and pulled her to him, kissing her long and hard, feeling as he did so that she was not responding. When he took his lips away he looked at her with eyes full of reproach and at the same time he felt his teeth clamping and his lips tingling slightly with rising passion.

'Let's go in,' he said.

'If you want to.'

'Sure I want to.'

'You stayed away so long.'

'Aw, don't be that way.'

They went in.

'How come you acting so cold tonight?' he asked.

'You could have dropped me a postcard,' she said.

'Aw, I just forgot it.'

'Or you could've phoned.'

'Honey, I was busy.'

'Looking at that old white gal, I reckon.'

'Aw, hell!'

'You don't move me no more.'

'The hell I don't.'

'You could've come by just for five minutes.'

'Baby, I was busy.'

When he kissed her this time she responded a little. To let her know that he loved her he circled her waist with his arm and squeezed her tightly.

'I'm tired tonight,' she sighed.

'Who *you* been seeing?'

'*Nobody*.'

'What you doing tired?'

'If you want to talk that way you can leave right now. I didn't ask you who you been seeing to make you stay away this long, did I?'

'You all on edge tonight.'

'You could have just said, "Hello, dog!"'

'Really, honey. I was busy.'

'You was setting there at that table with them white folks like you was a lawyer or something. You wouldn't even look at me when I spoke to you.'

'Aw, forget it. Let's talk about something else.'

He attempted to kiss her again and she shied away.

'Come on, honey.'

'Who *you* been with?'

'Nobody. I swear. I been working. And I been thinking hard about you. I been missing you. Listen, I got a room all my own where I'm working. Some nights you can stay there with me, see? Gee, I been missing you awful, honey. Soon's I got time I came right over.'

He stood looking at her in the dim light of the room. She was teasing him and he liked it. At least it took him away from that terrible image of Mary's head lying on the bloody newspaper. He wanted to kiss her again, but deep down he did not really mind her standing off from him; it made him hunger more keenly for her. She was looking at him wistfully, half-leaning against a wall, her hands on her hips. Then suddenly he knew how to draw her out, to drive from her mind all thought of her teasing him. He reached into his pocket and drew forth the roll of bills. Smiling, he held it in his palm and spoke as though to himself:

'Well, I reckon somebody else might like this if you don't.'

She came a step forward.

'Bigger! Gee! Where you get all that money from?'

'Wouldn't you like to know?'

'How much is it?'

'What you care?'

She came to his side.

'How much is it, really?'

'What you want to know for?'

'Let me see it. I'll give it back to you.'

'I'll let you see it, but it'll have to stay in *my* hand, see?'

He watched the expression of coyness on her face change to one of amazement as she counted the bills.

'Lord, Bigger! Where you get this money from?'

'Wouldn't you like to know?' he said, slipping his arm about her waist.

'Is it yours?'

'What in hell you reckon I'm doing with it?'

'Tell me where you get it from, honey.'

'You going to be sweet to me?'

He felt her body growing gradually less stiff; but her eyes were searching his face.

'You ain't got into nothing, is you?'

'You going to be sweet to me?'

'Oh, Bigger!'

'Kiss me, honey.'

He felt her relax completely; he kissed her and she drew him to the bed. They sat down. Gently, she took the money from his hand.

'How much is it?' he asked.

'Don't you know?'

'Naw.'

'Didn't you *count* it?'

'Naw.'

'Bigger, where you get this money from?'

'Maybe I'll tell you some day,' he said, leaning back and resting his head on the pillow.

'You into something.'

'How much is there?'

'A hundred and twenty-five dollars.'

'You going to be sweet to me?'

'But, Bigger, *where* you get this money from?'

'What do that matter?'

'You going to buy me something?'

'Sure.'

'What?'

'Anything you want.'

They were silent for a moment. Finally, his arm about her waist felt her body relax into a softness he knew and wanted. She rested her head on the pillow; he put the money in his pocket and leaned over her.

'Gee, honey. I been wanting you bad.'

'For real?'

'Honest to God.'

He leaned over her, full of desire, and lowered his head to hers and kissed her. When he took his lips away for breath he heard her say:

'Don't stay away so long from me, hear, honey?'

'I won't.'

'You love me?'

'Sure.'

He kissed her again and he felt her arm lifting above his head and he heard the click as the light went out. He kissed her again, hard.

'Bessie?'

'Hunh?'

'Come on, honey.'

They were still a moment longer; then she rose. He waited. He heard her clothes rustling in the darkness; she was undressing. He got up and began to undress. Gradually, he began to see in the darkness; she was on the other side of the bed, her presence like a shadow in the denser darkness surrounding her. He heard the bed creak as she lay down. He went to her, folding her in his arms, mumbling.

'Gee, kid.'

He felt two soft palms holding his face tenderly and the thought and image of the whole blind world which had made him ashamed and afraid fell away as he felt her as a fallow field beneath him stretching out under a cloudy sky waiting for rain, and he floated on a wild tide, rising and sinking with the ebb and flow of her blood, being willingly dragged into a warm night sea to rise renewed to the surface to face a world he hated and wanted to blot out of existence, clinging close to a fountain whose warm waters washed and cleaned his senses, cooled them, made them strong and keen again to see and smell and touch and taste and hear, cleared them to end the tiredness and to reforge in him a new sense of time and space; – after he had been tossed to dry upon a warm sunlit rock under a white sky he lifted his hand slowly and heavily and touched Bessie's lips with his fingers and mumbled.

'Gee, kid.'

'Bigger.'

He took his hand away and relaxed. He did not feel that he wanted to step forth and resume where he had left off living; not just yet. He was lying at the bottom of a deep dark pit upon a pallet of warm wet straw and at the top of the pit he could see the cold blue of the distant sky. Some hand had reached inside of him and had laid a quiet finger of peace upon the restless tossing of his spirit and had made him feel that he did not need to long for a home now. Then, like the long withdrawing sound of a receding wave, the sense of night and sea and warmth went from him and he lay in the darkness, gazing with vacant eyes at the shadowy ceiling, hearing his and her breathing.

'Bigger?'

'Hunh?'

'You like your job?'

'Yeah. Why?'

'I just asked.'

'You swell.'

'You mean that?'

'Sure.'

'Where you working?'

'Over on Drexel.'

'Where?'

'In the 4600 block.'

'Oh !'

'What?'

'Nothing.'

'But, what?'

'Oh, I just happen to think of something.'

'Tell me. What is it?'

'It ain't nothing, Bigger, honey.'

What did she mean by asking all these questions? He wondered if she had detected anything in him. Then he wondered if he were not letting fear get the better of him by thinking always in terms of Mary and of her having been smothered and burnt.

But he wanted to know why she had asked where he worked.

'Come on, honey. Tell me what you thinking.'

'It ain't nothing much, Bigger. I used to work over in that section, not far from where the Loeb folks lived.'

'Loeb?'

'Yeah. One of the families of one of the boys that killed that Franks boy. Remember?'

'Naw; what you mean?'

'You remember hearing people talk about Loeb and Leopold.'

'Oh!'

'The ones who killed the boy and tried to get money from the boy's family . . .'

. . . by sending notes to them Bigger was not listening. The world of sound fell abruptly away from him and a vast picture appeared before his eyes, a picture teeming with so much meaning that he could not react to it all at once. He lay, his eyes unblinking, his heart pounding, his lips slightly open, his breath coming and going so softly that it seemed he was not breathing at all. *you remember them aw you ain't even listening* He said nothing. *how come you won't listen when I talk to you* Why could he, why could he not, not send a letter to the Daltons, asking for money? *Bigger* He sat up in bed, staring into the darkness. *what's the matter honey* He could ask for ten thousand, or maybe twenty. *Bigger what's the matter I'm talking to you* He did not answer; his nerves were taut with the hard effort to remember something. Now! Yes, Loeb and Leopold had planned to have the father of the murdered boy get on a train and throw the money out of the window while passing some spot. He leaped from bed and stood in the middle of the floor *Bigger* He could, yes, he could have them pack the money in a shoe box and have them throw it out of a car somewhere on the South Side. He looked round in the darkness, feeling Bessie's fingers on his arm. He came to himself and sighed.

'What's the matter, honey?' she asked.

'Hunh?'

'What's on your mind?'

'Nothing.'

'Come on and tell me. You worried?'

'Naw; naw . . .'

'Now, I told *you* what was on my mind, but you won't tell me what's on *yours*. That ain't fair.'

'I just forgot something. That's all.'

'That ain't what you was thinking about,' she said.

He sat back on the bed, feeling his scalp tingle with excitement. Could he do it? This was what had been missing and this was what would make the thing complete. But this thing was so big he would have to take time and think it over carefully.

'Honey, tell me where you get that money?'

'What money?' he asked in a tone of feigned surprise.

'Aw, Bigger. I know something's wrong. You worried. You got something on your mind. I can tell it.'

'You want me to make up something to tell you?'

'All right; if that's the way you feel about it.'

'Aw, Bessie . . .'

'You didn't have to come here tonight.'

'Maybe I shouldn't've come.'

'You don't have to come no more.'

'Don't you love me?'

'About as much as you love me.'

'How much is that?'

'You ought to know.'

'Aw, let's stop fussing,' he said.

He felt the bed sag gently and heard the bed-covers rustling as she pulled them over her. He turned his head and stared at the dim whites of her eyes in the darkness. Maybe, yes, maybe he could, maybe he could use her. He leaned and stretched himself on the bed beside her; she did not move. He put his hand upon her shoulder, pressing it just softly enough to let her know that he was thinking about her. His mind tried to grasp and encompass as much of her life as it could, tried to understand and weigh it in relation to his own, as his hand rested on her shoulder. Could he trust her? How much could he tell her? Would she act with him, blindly, believing his word?

'Come on. Let's get dressed and go out and get something to drink,' she said.

'O.K.'

'You ain't acting like you always act tonight.'

'I got something on my mind.'

'Can't you tell me?'

'I don't know.'

'Don't you trust me?'

'Sure.'

'Then why don't you tell me?'

He did not answer. Her voice had come in a whisper, a whisper he had heard many times when she wanted something badly. It brought to him a full sense of her life, what he had been thinking and feeling when he had placed his hand upon her shoulder. The same deep realization he had had that morning at home at the breakfast table, while watching Vera and Buddy and his mother came back to him; only it was Bessie he was looking at now and seeing how blind she was. He felt the narrow orbit of her life: from her room to the kitchen of the white folks was the farthest she ever moved. She worked long hours, hard and hot hours seven days a week, with only Sunday afternoons off; and when she did get off she wanted fun, hard and fast fun, something to make her feel that she was making up for the starved life she led. It was her hankering for sensation that he liked about her. Most nights she was too tired to go out; she only wanted to get drunk. She wanted liquor and he wanted her. So he would give her the liquor and she would give him herself. He had heard her complain about how hard the white folks worked her; she had told him over and over again that she lived their lives when she was working in their homes, not her own. That was why, she told him, she drank. He knew why she liked him; he gave her money for drinks. He knew that if he did not give it to her someone else would; she would see to that. Bessie, too, was very blind. What ought he tell her? She might come in just handy. Then he realized that whatever he chose to tell her ought not to be anything that would make her feel in any way out of it; she ought to be made to feel that she knew it all. Goddamn! He just simply could not get used to acting like he ought. He should not have made her think that something was happening that he did not want her to know.

'Give me time, honey, and I'll tell you,' he said, trying to straighten things out.

'You don't have to unless you want to.'

'Don't be that way.'

'You just can't treat me any old way, Bigger.'

'I ain't trying to, honey.'

'You can't play me cheap.'

'Take it easy. I know what I'm doing.'

'I hope you do.'

'For chrissakes!'

'Aw, come on. I want a drink.'

'Naw; listen . . .'

'Keep your business. You don't have to tell me. But don't you come running to me when you need a friend, see?'

'When we get a couple of drinks, I'll tell you all about it.'

'Suit yourself.'

He saw her waiting at the door for him; he put on his coat and cap and they walked slowly down the stairs, saying nothing. It seemed warmer outside, as though it were going to snow again. The sky was low and dark. The wind blew. As he walked beside Bessie his feet sank into the soft snow. The streets were empty and silent, stretching before him white and clean under the vanishing glow of a long string of street lamps. As he walked he saw out of the corners of his eyes Bessie striding beside him, and it seemed that his mind could feel the soft swing of her body as it went forward. He yearned suddenly to be back in bed with her, feeling her body warm and pliant to his. But the look on her face was a hard and distant one; it separated him from her body by a great suggestion of space. He had not really wanted to go out with her tonight; but her questions and suspicions had made him say yes when she had wanted to go for a drink. As he walked beside her he felt that there were two Bessies: one a body that he had just had and wanted badly again; the other was in Bessie's face; it asked questions; it bargained and sold the other Bessie to advantage. He wished he could clench his fist and swing his arm and blot out, kill, sweep away the Bessie on Bessie's face and leave the other helpless and yielding before him. He would then gather her up and put her in his chest, his stomach, some place deep inside him, always keeping her there even when he slept, ate, talked; keeping her there to feel and know that she was his to have and hold whenever he wanted to.

'Where we going?'

'Wherever you want to.'

'Let's go to the Paris Grill.'

'O.K.'

They turned a corner and walked to the middle of the block to the grill, and went in. An automatic phonograph was playing. They went to a rear table. Bigger ordered two sloe gin fizzes. They sat silent, looking at each other, waiting. He saw Bessie's shoulders jerking in rhythm to the music. Would she help him? Well, he would ask her; he would frame the story so that she would not have to know everything. He knew that he should have asked her to dance, but the excitement that had hold of him would not let him. He was feeling different tonight from every other night; he did not need to dance and sing and clown over the floor in order to blot out a day and night of doing nothing. He was full of excitement. The waitress brought the drinks and Bessie lifted hers.

'Here's to you, even if you don't want to talk and even if you is acting queer.'

'Bessie, I'm worried.'

'Aw, come on and drink,' she said.

'O.K.'

They sipped.

'Bigger?'

'Hunh?'

'Can't I help you in what you doing?'

'Maybe.'

'I want to.'

'You trust me?'

'I have so far.'

'I mean now?'

'Yes; if you tell me what to trust you for?'

'Maybe I can't do that.'

'Then you don't trust me.'

'It's got to be that way, Bessie.'

'If I trusted you, would you tell me?'

'Maybe.'

'Don't say "maybe", Bigger.'

'Listen, honey,' he said, not liking the way he was talking to her, but afraid of telling her outright. 'The reason I'm acting this way is I got something big on.'

'What?'

'It'll mean a lot of money.'

'I wish you'd either tell me or quit talking about it.'

They were silent; he saw Bessie drain her glass.

'I'm ready to go,' she said.

'Aw . . .'

'I want to get some sleep.'

'You mad?'

'Maybe.'

He did not want her to be that way. How could he make her stay? How much could he tell her? Could he make her trust him without telling everything? He suddenly felt she would come closer to him if he made her feel that he was in danger. That's it! Make her feel concerned about him.

'Maybe I'll have to get out of town soon,' he said.

'The police?'

'Maybe.'

'What you do?'

'I'm planning to do it now.'

'But where you get that money?'

'Look, Bessie, if I have to leave town and wanted dough, would you help me if I split with you?'

'If you took me with you, you wouldn't have to split.'

He was silent; he had not thought of Bessie's being with him. A woman was a dangerous burden when a man was running away. He had read of how men had been caught because of women, and he did not want that to happen to him. But, if, yes, but if he told her, yes, just enough to get her to work with him?

'O.K.,' he said. 'I'll say this much : I'll take you if you help me.'

'You really mean that?'

'Sure.'

'Then you going to tell me?'

Yes, he could dress the story up. Why even mention Jan? Why not tell it so that if she were ever questioned she would say the things that he wanted her to say, things that would help him? He lifted the glass and drained the liquor and set it down and leaned forward and toyed with the cigarette in his fingers. He spoke with bated breath.

'Listen, here's the dope, see? The gal where I'm working, the daughter of the old man who's rich, a millionaire, has done run off with a red, see?'

'Eloped?'

'Hunh? Er . . . Yeah; eloped.'

'With a *red*?'

'Yeah; one of them Communists.'

'Oh ! What's wrong with her?'

'Aw; she's crazy. Nobody don't know she's gone, so last night I took the money from her room, see?'

'Oh !'

'They don't know where she is.'

'But what you going to do?'

'They don't know where she is,' he said again.

'What you mean?'

He sucked his cigarette; he saw her looking at him, her black eyes wide with eager interest. He liked that look. In one way, he hated to tell her, because he wanted to keep her guessing. He wanted to take as long as possible in order to see that look of complete absorption upon her face. It made him feel alive and gave him a heightened sense of the value of himself.

'I got an idea,' he said.

'Oh, Bigger, *tell* me!'

'Don't talk so loud!'

'Well, *tell* me!'

'They don't know where the girl is. They might think she's kidnaped, see?' His whole body was tense and as he spoke his lips trembled.

'Oh, that was what you was so excited about when I told you about Loeb and Leopold . . .'

'Well, what you think?'

'Would they *really* think she's kidnaped?'

'We can *make* 'em think it.'

She looked into her empty glass. Bigger beckoned the waitress and ordered two more drinks. He took a deep swallow and said,

'The gal's gone, see? They don't know where she is? Don't nobody know. But they might think somebody did if they was told, see?'

'You mean . . . You mean we could say *we* did it? You mean write to 'em . . .'

'. . . and ask for money, sure,' he said. 'And get it, too. You see, we cash in, 'cause nobody else is trying to.'

'But suppose she shows up?'

'She won't.'

'How you know?'

'I just know she won't.'

'Bigger, you *know* something about that girl. You know where she is?'

'That's all right about where she is. I know we won't have to worry about her showing up, see?'

'Oh, Bigger, this is *crazy*!'

'Then, hell, we won't talk about it no more!'

'Oh, I don't mean that.'

'Then what *do* you mean?'

'I mean we got to be careful.'

'We can get ten thousand dollars.'

'How?'

'We can have 'em leave the money somewhere. They'll think they can get the girl back . . .'

'Bigger, you know where that girl is?' she said, giving her voice a tone of half-question and half-statement.

'Naw.'

'Then it'll be in the papers. She'll show up.'

'She won't.'

'How you know?'

'She just won't.'

He saw her lips moving, then heard her speak softly, leaning toward him.

'Bigger, you ain't done nothing to that girl, is you?'

He stiffened with fear. He felt suddenly that he wanted something in his hand, something solid and heavy: his gun, a knife, a brick.

'If you say that again, I'll slap you back from this table!'

'Oh!'

'Come on, now. Don't be a fool.'

'Bigger, you oughtn't've done it . . .'

'You going to help me? Say yes or no.'

'Gee, Bigger . . .'

'You scared? You scared after letting me take that silver from Mrs Heard's home? After letting me get Mrs Macy's radio? You scared now?'

'I don't know.'

'You wanted me to tell you; well I told you. That's a woman, always. You want to know something then you run like a rabbit.'

'But we'll get *caught*.'

'Not if we do right.'

'But how could we do it, Bigger?'

'I'll figure it out.'

'But I want to know.'

'It'll be easy.'

'But how?'

'I can fix it so you can pick up the money and nobody'll bother you.'

'They catch people who do things like that.'

'If you scared they *will* catch you.'

'How could I pick up the money?'

'We'll tell 'em where to leave it.'

'But they'll have police watching.'

'Not if they want the gal back. We got a club over 'em, see? And I'll be watching, too. I work in the house where they live. If they try to doublecross us, I'll let you know.'

'You reckon we could do it?'

'We could have 'em throw the money out of a car. You could be in some spot to see if they send anybody to watch. If you see anybody around, then you don't touch the money, see? But they want the gal; they won't watch.'

There was a long silence.

'Bigger, I don't know,' she said.

'We could go to New York, to Harlem, if we had money. New York's a real town. We could lay low for awhile.'

'But suppose they mark the money?'

'They won't. And if they do, I'll tell you. You see, I'm right there in the house.'

'But if we run off, they'll think we did it. They'll be looking for us for years, Bigger . . .'

'We won't run right away. We'll lay low for awhile.'

'I don't know, Bigger.'

He felt satisfied; he could tell by the way she looked that if he pushed her hard enough she would come in with him. She was afraid and he could handle her through her fear. He looked at his watch; it was getting late. He ought to go back and have a look at that furnace.

'Listen, I got to go.'

He paid the waitress and they went out. There was another way to bind her to him. He drew forth the roll of bills, peeled off one for himself, and held out the rest of the money toward her.

'Here,' he said. 'Get something and save the rest for me.'

'Oh!'

She looked at the money and hesitated.

'Don't you want it?'

'Yeah,' she said, taking the roll.

'If you string along with me, you'll get plenty more.'

They stopped in front of her door; he stood looking at her.

'Well,' he said. 'What you think?'

'Bigger, honey. I – I don't know,' she said plaintively.

'You wanted me to tell you.'

'I'm scared.'

'Don't you trust me?'

'But we ain't never done nothing like this before. They'll look everywhere for us for something like this. It ain't like coming to where I work at night when the white folks is gone out of town and stealing something. It ain't . . .'

'It's up to you.'

'I'm scared, Bigger.'

'Who on earth'll think *we* did it?'

'I don't know. You really think they don't know where the girl is?'

'I know they don't.'

'*You* know?'

'Naw.'

'She'll turn up.'

'She won't. And, anyhow, she's a crazy girl. They might even think she's in it herself, just to get money from her family. They might think the reds is doing it. They won't think *we* did. They don't think we got enough guts to do it. They think niggers is too scared . . .'

'I don't know.'

'Did I ever tell you wrong?'

'Naw; but we ain't never done nothing like this before.'

'Well, I ain't wrong now.'

'When do you want to do it?'

'Soon as they begin to worry about the gal.'

'You really reckon we could?'

'I told you what I think.'

'Naw; Bigger! I ain't going to do it. I think you . . .'

He turned abruptly and walked away from her.

'Bigger!'

She ran over the snow and tugged at his sleeve. He stopped, but did not turn round. She caught his coat and pulled him about. Under the yellow sheen of a street lamp they confronted each other, silently. All about them was the white snow and the night; they were cut off from the world and were conscious only of each other. He looked at her without expression, waiting. Her eyes were fastened fearfully and distrustfully upon his face. He held his body in an attitude that suggested that he was delicately balanced upon a hairline, waiting to see if she would push him forward or draw him back. Her lips smiled faintly and she lifted her hand and touched his face with her fingers. He knew that she was fighting out in her feelings the question of just how much he meant to her. She grabbed his hand and squeezed it, telling him in the pressure of her fingers that she wanted him.

'But, Bigger, honey . . . Let's don't do that. We getting along all right like we is now . . .'

He drew his hand away.

'I'm going,' he said.

'When I'll see you, honey?'

'I don't know.'

He started off again and she overtook him and encircled him with her arms.

'Bigger, honey . . .'

'Come on, Bessie. What you going to do?'

She looked at him with round, helpless black eyes. He was still poised, wondering if she would pull him toward her, or let him fall alone. He was enjoying her agony, seeing and feeling the worth of himself in her bewildered desperation. Her lips trembled and she began to cry.

'What you going to do?' he asked again.

'If I do it, it's 'cause you want me to,' she sobbed.

He put his arm about her shoulders.

'Come on, Bessie,' he said. 'Don't cry.'

She stopped and dried her eyes; he looked at her closely. She'll do it, he thought.

'I got to go,' he said.

'I ain't going in right now.'

'Where you going?'

He found that he was afraid of what she did, now that she was working with him. His peace of mind depended upon knowing what she did and why.

'I'm going to get a pint.'

That was all right; she was feeling as he knew she always felt.

'Well, I'll see you tomorrow night, hunh?'

'O.K., honey. But be careful.'

'Look, Bessie, don't you worry none. Just trust me. No matter what happens, they won't catch us. And they won't even know you had anything to do with it.'

'If they start after us, where could we hide, Bigger? You know we's black. We can't go just *any*where.'

He looked round the lamp-lit, snow-covered street.

'There's plenty of places,' he said. 'I know the South Side from A to Z. We could even hide out in one of those old buildings, see? Like I did last time. Nobody ever looks into 'em.'

He pointed across the street to a black, looming, empty apartment building.

'Well,' she sighed.

'I'm going,' he said.

'So long, honey.'

He walked toward the car line; when he looked back he saw her still standing in the snow; she had not moved. She'll be all right, he thought. She'll go along.

Snow was falling again; the streets were long paths leading through a dense jungle, lit here and there with torches held high in invisible hands. He waited ten minutes for a car and none came. He turned the corner and walked, his head down, his hands dug into his pockets, going to Dalton's.

He was confident. During the last day and night new fears

had come, but new feelings had helped to allay those fears. The moment when he had stood above Mary's bed and found that she was dead the fear of electrocution had entered his flesh and blood. But at home at the breakfast table with his mother and sister and brother, seeing how blind they were; and overhearing Peggy and Mrs Dalton talking in the kitchen, a new feeling had been born in him, a feeling that all but blotted out the fear of death. As long as he moved carefully and knew what he was about, he could handle things, he thought. As long as he could take his life into his own hands and dispose of it as he pleased, as long as he could decide just when and where he would run to, he need not be afraid.

He felt that he had his destiny in his grasp. He was more alive than he could ever remember having been; his mind and attention were pointed, focused toward a goal. For the first time in his life he moved consciously between two sharply defined poles: he was moving away from the threatening penalty of death, from the death-like times that brought him that tightness and hotness in his chest; and he was moving toward that sense of fulness he had so often but inadequately felt in magazines and movies.

The shame and fear and hate which Mary and Jan and Mr Dalton and that huge rich house had made rise so hard and hot in him had now cooled and softened. Had he not done what they thought he never could? His being black and at the bottom of the world was something which he could take with a new-born strength. What his knife and gun had once meant to him, his knowledge of having secretly murdered Mary now meant. No matter how they laughed at him for his being black and clown-like, he could look them in the eyes and not feel angry. The feeling of being always enclosed in the stifling embrace of an invisible force had gone from him.

As he turned into Drexel Boulevard and headed toward Daltons', he thought of how restless he had been, how he was consumed always with a body hunger. Well, in a way he had settled that tonight; as time passed he would make it more definite. His body felt free and easy now that he had lain with

Bessie. That she would do what he wanted was what he had sealed in asking her to work with him in this thing. She would be bound to him by ties deeper than marriage. She would be his; her fear of capture and death would bind her to him with all the strength of her life; even as what he had done last night had bound him to this new path with all the strength of his own life.

He turned off the sidewalk and walked up the Dalton driveway, went into the basement and looked through the bright cracks of the furnace door. He saw a red heap of seething coals and heard the upward hum of the draft. He pulled the lever, hearing the rattle of coal against tin and seeing the quivering embers grow black. He shut off the coal and stooped and opened the bottom door of the furnace. Ashes were piling up. He would have to take the shovel and clean them out in the morning and make sure that no unburnt bones were left. He had closed the door and started to the rear of the furnace, going to his room, when he heard Peggy's voice.

'Bigger!'

He stopped and before answering he felt a keen sensation of excitement flush over all his skin. She was standing at the head of the stairs, in the door leading to the kitchen.

'Yessum.'

He went to the bottom of the steps and looked upward.

'Mrs Dalton wants you to pick up the trunk at the station . . .'

'The *trunk*?'

He waited for Peggy to answer his surprised question. Perhaps he should not have asked it in that way?

'They called up and said that no one had claimed it. And Mr Dalton got a wire from Detroit. Mary never got there.'

'Yessum.'

She came all the way down the stairs and looked round the basement, as though seeking some missing detail. He stiffened; if she saw something that would make her ask him about Mary he would take the iron shovel and let her have it straight across her head and then take the car and make a quick getaway.

'Mr Dalton's worried,' Peggy said. 'You know, Mary didn't

pack the new clothes she bought to take with her on the trip. And poor Mrs Dalton's been pacing the floor and phoning Mary's friends all day.'

'Don't nobody know where she is?' Bigger asked.

'Nobody. Did Mary tell you to take the trunk like it *was*?'

'Yessum,' he said, knowing that this was the first hard hurdle. 'It was locked and standing in a corner. I took it down and put it right where you saw it this morning.'

'Oh, Peggy!' Mrs Dalton's voice called.

'Yes!' Peggy answered.

Bigger looked up and saw Mrs Dalton at the head of the stairs, standing in white as usual and with her face tilted trustingly upward.

'Is the boy back yet?'

'He's down here now, Mrs Dalton.'

'Come to the kitchen a moment, will you, Bigger?' she asked.

'Yessum.'

He followed Peggy into the kitchen. Mrs Dalton had her hands clasped tightly in front of her and her face was still tilted, higher now, and her white lips were parted.

'Peggy told you about picking up the trunk?'

'Yessum. I'm on my way now.'

'What time did you leave here last night?'

'A little before two, mam.'

'And she told you to take the trunk down?'

'Yessum.'

'And she told you not to put the car up?'

'Yessum.'

'And it was just where you left it last night when you came this morning?'

'Yessum.'

Mrs Dalton turned her head as she heard the inner kitchen door open; Mr Dalton stood in the doorway.

'Hello, Bigger.'

'Good day, suh.'

'How are things?'

'Fine, suh.'

'The station called about the trunk a little while ago. You'll have to pick it up.'

'Yessuh. I'm on my way now, suh.'

'Listen, Bigger. What happened last night?'

'Well, nothing, suh. Miss Dalton told me to take the trunk down so I could take it to the station this morning; and I did.'

'Was Jan *with* you?'

'Yessuh. All three of us went upstairs when I brought 'em in in the car. We went to the room to get the trunk. Then I took it down and put it in the basement.'

'Was Jan drunk?'

'Well, I don't know, suh. They was drinking . . .'

'And what happened?'

'Nothing, suh. I just took the trunk to the basement and left. Miss Dalton told me to leave the car out. She said Mr Jan would take care of it.'

'What were they talking about?'

Bigger hung his head.

'I don't know, suh.'

He saw Mrs Dalton lift her right hand and he knew that she meant for Mr Dalton to stop questioning him so closely. He felt her shame.

'That's all right, Bigger,' Mrs Dalton said. She turned to Mr Dalton. 'Where do you suppose this Jan would be now?'

'Maybe he's at the Labor Defender office.'

'Can you get in touch with him?'

'Well,' said Mr Dalton, standing near Bigger and looking hard at the floor. 'I could. But I'd rather wait. I still think Mary's up to some of her foolish pranks. Bigger, you'd better get that trunk.'

'Yessuh.'

He got the car and drove through the falling snow toward the Loop. In answering their questions he felt that he had succeeded in turning their minds definitely in the direction of Jan. If things went at this pace he would have to send the ransom note right away. He would see Bessie tomorrow and get things settled. Yes; he would ask for ten thousand dollars. He would have Bessie stand in the window of an old building at some well-lighted street corner with a flashlight. In the note he would tell Mr Dalton to put the money in a shoe box and drop it in the snow at the curb; he would tell him to keep his car moving and his lights blinking and not to drop the money until he saw the flashlight blink three times in the window... Yes; that's how it would be. Bessie would see the lights of Mr Dalton's car blinking and after the car was gone she would pick up the box of money. It would be easy.

He pulled the car into the station, presented the ticket, got the trunk, hoisted it to the running board, and headed again for the Dalton home. When he reached the driveway the snow was falling so thickly that he could not see ten feet in front of him. He put the car into the garage, set the trunk in the snow, locked the garage door, lifted the trunk to his back and carried it to the entrance of the basement. Yes; the trunk was light; it was half-empty. No doubt they would question him again about that. Next time he would have to go into details and he would try to fasten hard in his mind the words he spoke so that he could repeat them a thousand times, if necessary. He could, of course, set the trunk in the snow right now and take a streetcar and get the money from Bessie and leave town. But why do that? He could handle this thing. It was going his way. They were not suspecting him and he would be able to tell the moment their minds turned in his direction. And, too, he was glad he had let Bessie keep that money. Suppose he were searched here on the job? For them to find money on him was alone enough to fasten suspicion upon him definitely. He unlocked the door and took the trunk inside; his back was bent beneath its weight and he walked slowly with his eyes on the wavering red shadows on the floor. He heard the fire singing in the furnace. He took the trunk to the corner in which he had placed it the night before. He put it down and stood looking at it. He had an impulse to open it and look inside. He stooped to fumble with the metal clasp, then started violently, jerking upright.

'Bigger !'

Without answering and before he realized what he was doing, he whirled, his eyes wide with fear and his hand half-raised, as though to ward off a blow. The moment of whirling brought him face to face with what seemed to his excited senses an army of white men. His breath stopped and he blinked his eyes in the red darkness, thinking that he should be acting more calmly. Then he saw Mr Dalton and another white man standing at the far end of the basement; in the red shadows their faces were white discs of danger floating still in the air.

'Oh!' he said softly.

The white man at Mr Dalton's side was squinting at him; he felt that tight, hot, choking fear returning. The white man clicked on the light. He had a cold, impersonal manner that told Bigger to be on his guard. In the very look of the man's eyes Bigger saw his own personality reflected in narrow, restricted terms.

'What's the matter, boy?' the man asked.

Bigger said nothing; he swallowed, caught hold of himself and came forward slowly. The white man's eyes were steadily upon him. Panic seized Bigger as he saw the white man lower his head, narrow his eyes still more, sweep back his coat and ram his hands into his pants' pockets, revealing as he did so a shining badge on his chest. Words rang in Bigger's mind: This is a cop! He could not take his eyes off the shining bit of metal. Abruptly, the man changed his attitude and expression, took his hands from his pocket and smiled a smile that Bigger did not believe.

'I'm not the law, boy. So don't be scared.'

Bigger clamped his teeth; he had to control himself. He should not have let that man see him staring at his badge.

'Yessuh,' he said.

'Bigger, this is Mr Britten,' Mr Dalton said. 'He's a private investigator attached to the staff of my office . . .'

'Yessuh,' Bigger said again, his tension slackening.

'He wants to ask you some questions. So just be calm and try to tell him whatever he wants to know.'

'Yessuh.'

'First of all, I want to have a look at that trunk,' Britten said.

Bigger stood aside as they passed him. He glanced quickly at the furnace. It was still very hot, droning. Then he, too, went to the trunk, standing discreetly to one side, away from the two white men, looking with surface eyes at what they were doing. He shoved his hands deep into his pockets; he stood in a peculiar attitude that allowed him to respond at once to whatever they said or did and at the same time to be outside and away from them. He watched Britten turn the trunk over and bend to it and try to work the lock. I got to be careful, Bigger thought. One little slip now and I'll spoil the whole thing. Sweat came onto his neck and face. Britten could not unlock the trunk and he looked upward, at Bigger.

'It's locked. You got a key, boy?'

'Nawsuh.'

Bigger wondered if this were a trap; he decided to play safe and speak only when he was spoken to.

'You mind if I break it?'

'Go right ahead,' Mr Dalton said. 'Say, Bigger, get Mr Britten the hatchet.'

'Yessuh,' he answered mechanically.

He thought rapidly, his entire body stiff. Should he tell them that the hatchet was somewhere in the house and offer to go after it and take the opportunity and run away? How much did they really suspect him? Was this whole thing a ruse to confuse and trap him? He glanced sharply and intently at their faces; they seemed to be waiting only for the hatchet. Yes; he would take a chance and stay; he would lie his way out of this. He turned and went to the spot where the hatchet had been last night, the spot from which he had taken it to cut off Mary's head. He stooped and pretended to search. Then he straightened.

'It ain't here now ... I – I saw it about here yesterday,' he mumbled.

'Well, never mind,' Britten said. 'I think I can manage.'

Bigger eased back toward them, waiting, watching. Britten lifted his foot and gave the lock a short, stout kick with the heel of his shoe and it sprang open. He lifted out the tray and looked inside. It was half-empty and the clothes were disarrayed and tumbled.

'You see?' Mr Dalton said. 'She didn't take all of her things.'

'Yes. In fact, she didn't need a trunk at all from the looks of this,' Britten said.

'Bigger, was the trunk locked when she told you to take it down?' Mr Dalton asked.

'Yessuh,' Bigger said, wondering if that answer was the safest.

'Was she too drunk to know what she was doing, Bigger?'

'Well, they went into the room,' he said. 'I went in after them. Then she told me to take the trunk down. That's all happened.'

'She could have put these things into a small suitcase,' Britten said.

The fire sang in Bigger's ears and he saw the red shadows dance on the walls. Let them try to find out who did it! His teeth were clamped hard, until they ached.

'Sit down, Bigger,' Britten said.

Bigger looked at Britten, feigning surprise.

'Sit on the trunk,' Britten said.

'Me?'

'Yeah. Sit down.'

He sat.

'Now, take your time and think hard. I want to ask you some questions.'

'Yessuh.'

'What time did you take Miss Dalton from here last night?'

'About eighty-thirty, suh.'

Bigger knew that this was it. This man was here to find out everything. This was an examination. He would have to point his answers away from himself quite definitely. He would have to tell his story. He would let each of the facts of his story fall slowly, as thought he did not realize the significance of them. He would answer only what was asked.

'You drove her to school?'

He hung his head and did not answer.

'Come on, boy!'

'Well, mister, you see, I'm just working here . . .'

'What do you mean?'

Mr Dalton come close and looked hard into his face.

'Answer his questions, Bigger.'

'Yessuh.'

'You drove her to school?' Britten asked again.

Still, he did not answer.

'I asked you a question, boy!'

'Nawsuh. I didn't drive her to school.'

'Where did you take her?'

'Well, suh. She told me, after I got as far as the park, to turn round and take her to the Loop.'

'She didn't go to *school*?' Mr Dalton asked, his lips hanging open in surprise.

'Nawsuh.'

'Why didn't you tell me this before, Bigger?'

'She told me not to.'

There was silence. The furnace droned. Huge red shadows swam across the walls.

'Where did you take her, then?' Britten asked.

'To the Loop, suh.'

'Whereabouts in the Loop?'

'To Lake Street, suh.'

'Do you remember the number?'

'Sixteen, I think, suh.'

'Sixteen Lake Street?'

'Yessuh.'

'That's the Labor Defender office,' Mr Dalton said, turning to Britten. 'This Jan's a Red.'

'How long was she in there?' Britten asked.

'About half-hour, I reckon, suh.'

'Then what happened?'

'Well, I waited in the car . . .'

'She stayed there till *you* brought her home?'

'Nawsuh.'

'She came out . . .'

'*They* came out . . .'

'This man Jan was with her, then?'

'Yessuh. He was with her. Seems to me she went in there to get him. She didn't say anything; she just went in and stayed awhile and then came out with him.'

'Then you drove 'em . . .'

'*He* drove,' Bigger said.

'Weren't *you* driving?'

'Yessuh. But he wanted to drive and she told me to let him.'

There was another silence. They wanted him to draw the picture and he would draw it like he wanted it. He was trembling with excitement. In the past had they not always drawn the picture for him? He could tell them anything he wanted and what could they do about it? It was his word against Jan's, and Jan was a red.

'You waited somewhere for 'em?' Britten asked; the tone of curt hostility had suddenly left his voice.

'Nawsuh. I was in the car . . .'

'And where did they go?'

He wanted to tell of how they had made him sit between them; but he thought that he would tell that later on, when he was telling how Jan and Mary had made him feel.

'Well, Mr Jan asked me where was a good place to eat. The only one I knew about where white folks,' he said 'white folks' very slowly, so that they would know that he was conscious of what was meant, 'ate on the South Side was Ernie's Kitchen Shack.'

'You took them there?'

'Mr Jan drove the car, suh.'

'How long did they stay there?'

'Well, we must've stayed . . .'

'Weren't you waiting in the car?'

'Nawsuh. You see, mister, I did what they told me. I was only working for 'em . . .'

'Oh!' Britten said. 'I suppose he made you *eat* with 'im?'

'I didn't want to, mister. I swear I didn't. He kept worrying me till I went in.'

Britten walked away from the trunk, running the fingers of his left hand nervously through his hair. Again he turned to Bigger.

'They got drunk, hunh?'

'Yessuh. They was drinking.'

'What did this Jan say to you?'

'He talked about the Communists . . .'

'How much did they drink?'

'It seemed like a lot to me, suh.'

'Then you brought 'em home?'

'I drove 'em through the park, suh.'

'*Then* you brought 'em home?'

'Yessuh. That was nearly two.'

'How drunk was Miss Dalton?'

'Well, she couldn't hardly stand up, suh. When we got home, he had to lift her up the steps,' Bigger said with lowered eyes.

'That's all right boy. You can talk to us about it,' Britten said. 'Just how drunk was she?'

'She passed out,' Bigger said.

Britten looked at Dalton.

'She could not have left this house by herself,' Britten said. 'If Mrs Dalton's right, then she could *not* have left.' Britten stared at Bigger and Bigger felt that some deep question was on Britten's mind.

'What else happened?'

He would shoot now; he would let them have some of it.

'Well, I told you Miss Dalton told me to take the trunk. I said that 'cause she told me not to tell about me taking her to the Loop. It was Mr Jan who told me to take the trunk down and not put the car away.'

'*He* told you not to put the car away and to take the trunk?'

'Yessuh. That's right.'

'Why didn't you tell us this before, Bigger?' asked Mr Dalton.

'She told me not to, suh.'

198

'How was this Jan acting?' Britten asked.

'He was drunk,' said Bigger, feeling that now was the time to drag Jan in definitely. 'Mr Jan was the one who told me to take the trunk down and leave the car in the snow. I told you Miss Dalton told me that, but he told me. I would've been giving the whole thing away if I had told about Mr Jan.'

Britten walked toward the furnace and back again; the furnace droned as before. Bigger hoped that no one would try to look into it now; his throat grew dry. Then he started nervously as Britten whirled and pointed his finger into his face.

'What did he say about the Party?'

'Suh?'

'Aw, come on, boy! Don't stall! Tell me what he said about the Party!'

'The party? He asked me to sit at his table . . .'

'I mean the *Party*!'

'It wasn't a party, mister. He made me sit at his table and he bought chicken and told me to eat. I didn't want to, but he made me and it was my job.'

Britten came close to Bigger and narrowed his gray eyes.

'What unit are you in?'

'Suh?'

'Come on, *Comrade*, tell me what unit you are in?'

Bigger gazed at him, speechless, alarmed.

'Who's your organizer?'

'I don't know what you mean,' Bigger said, his voice quavering.

'Don't you read the *Daily*?'

'Daily what?'

'Didn't you know Jan before you came to work here?'

'Nawsuh. *Naw*suh!'

'Didn't they send you to Russia?'

Bigger stared and did not answer. He knew now that Britten was trying to find out if he were a Communist. It was something he had not counted on, ever. He stood up, trembling. He had not thought that this thing could cut two ways. Slowly, he shook his head and backed away.

'Nawsuh. You got me wrong. I ain't never fooled around with them folks. Miss Dalton and Mr Jan was the first ones I ever met, so help me God!'

Britten followed Bigger till Bigger's head struck the wall. Bigger looked squarely into his eyes. Britten, with a movement so fast that Bigger did not see it, grabbed him in the collar and rammed his head hard against the wall. He saw a flash of red.

'You *are* a Communist, *you goddamn* black sonofabitch! And you're going to tell me about Miss Dalton and that Jan bastard!'

'*Naw*suh! I ain't no Communist! *Naw*suh!'

'Well, what's *this*?' Britten jerked from his pocket the small packet of pamphlets that Bigger had put in his dresser drawer, and held them under his eyes. 'You know you're lying! Come on, talk!'

'Nawsuh! You got me wrong! Mr Jan gave me them things! He and Miss Dalton told me to read 'em . . .'

'Didn't you know Miss Dalton before?'

'Nawsuh!'

'Wait, Britten!' Mr Dalton laid his hand on Britten's arm. 'Wait. There's something to what he says. She tried to talk to him about unions when she first saw him yesterday. If that Jan gave him those pamphlets, then he knows nothing about it.'

'You're sure?'

'I'm positive. I thought at first, when you brought me those pamphlets, that he must have known something. But I don't think he does. And there's no use blaming him for something he didn't do.'

Britten loosened his fingers from Bigger's collar and shrugged his shoulders. Bigger relaxed, still standing, his head resting against the wall, aching. He had not thought that anyone would dare think that he, a black Negro, would be Jan's partner. Britten was his enemy. He knew that the hard light in Britten's eyes held him guilty because he was black. He hated Britten so hard and hot, while standing there with sleepy eyes and parted lips, that he would gladly have grabbed the iron shovel from the corner and split his skull in two. For a split second a roaring noise in his ears blotted out sound. He struggled to control himself; then he heard Britten talking.

'. . . got to get hold of that Jan.'

'That seems to be the next thing,' said Mr Dalton, sighing.

Bigger felt that if he said something directly to Mr Dalton, he could swing things round again in his favor; but he did not know just how to put it.

'You suppose she ran off?' he heard Britten ask.

'I don't know,' Mr Dalton said.

Britten turned to Bigger and looked at him; Bigger kept his eyes down.

'Boy, I just want to know, are you telling the truth?'

'Yessuh. I'm telling the truth. I just started to work here last night. I ain't done nothing. I did just what they told me to do.'

'You sure he's all right?' Britten asked Dalton.

'He's all right.'

'If you don't want me to work for you, Mr Dalton,' Bigger said, 'I'll go home. I didn't want to come here,' he continued, feeling that his words would awaken in Mr Dalton a sense of why he was here, 'but they sent me anyhow.'

'That's true,' Mr Dalton told Britten. 'He's referred to me from the relief. He's been in a reform school and I'm giving him a chance . . .' Mr Dalton turned to Bigger. 'Just forget it, Bigger. We had to make sure. Stay on and do your work. I'm sorry this had to happen. Don't let it break you down.'

'Yessuh.'

'O.K.,' said Britten. 'If you say he's O.K., then it's O.K. with me.'

'Go to your room, Bigger,' said Mr Dalton.

'Yessuh.'

Head down, he walked to the rear of the furnace and upstairs into his room. He turned the latch on the door and hurried to the closet to listen. The voices came clearly. Britten and Mr Dalton had come into the kitchen.

'My, but it was hot down there,' said Mr Dalton.

'Yes.'

'. . . I'm a little sorry you bothered him. He's here to try to get a new slant on things.'

'Well, you see 'em one way and I see 'em another. To me, a nigger's a nigger.'

'But he's a sort of problem boy. He's not really bad.'

'You got to be rough with 'em, Dalton. See how I got that dope out of 'im? He wouldn't've told you that.'

'But I don't want to make a mistake here. It wasn't his fault. He was doing what that crazy daughter of mine told him. I don't want to do anything I'll regret. After all, these black boys never get a chance . . .'

'They don't need a chance, if you ask me. They get in enough trouble without it.'

'Well, as long as they do their work, let's let 'em be.'

'Just as you say. You want me to stay on the job?'

'Sure. We must see this Jan. I can't understand Mary's going away and not saying anything.'

'I can have 'im picked up.'

'No, no! Not that way. Those reds'll get hold of it and they'll raise a stink in the papers.'

'Well, what do you want me to do?'

'I'll try to get 'im to come here. I'll phone his office, and if he's not there I'll phone his home.'

Bigger heard their footsteps dying away. A door slammed and then all was quiet. He came out of the closet and looked in the dresser drawer where he had put the pamphlets. Yes, Britten had searched his room; his clothes were mussed and tumbled. He would know how to handle Britten next time. Britten was familiar to him; he had met a thousand Brittens in his life. He stood in the center of the room, thinking. When Britten questioned Jan, would Jan deny having been with Mary at all, in order to protect her? If he did, that would be in his favor. If Britten wanted to check on his story about Mary's not going to school last night, he could. If Jan said that they had not been drinking it could be proved that they had been drinking by folks in the café. If Jan lied about one thing, it would be readily believed that he would lie about others. If Jan said that he had not come to the house, who would believe him after it was seen that he had lied about his not drinking and about Mary's going to school? If Jan tried to protect Mary, as he thought he would, he would only succeed in making a case against himself.

Bigger went to the window and looked out at the white curtain of falling snow. He thought of the kidnap note. Should he try to get money from them now? Hell, yes! He would show that Britten bastard! He would work fast. But he would wait until after Jan had told his story. He should see Bessie tonight. And he ought to pick out the pencil and paper he would use. And he must not forget to use gloves when he wrote the note so that no fingerprints would be on the paper. He'd give that Britten something to worry about, all right. Just wait.

Because he could go now, run off if he wanted to and leave it all behind, he felt a certain sense of power, a power born of a latent capacity to live. He was conscious of this quiet, warm, clean, rich house, this room with this bed so soft, the wealthy white people moving in luxury to all sides of him, whites living in a smugness, a security, a certainty that he had never known. The knowledge that he had killed a white girl they loved and regarded as their symbol of beauty made him feel the equal of them, like a man who had been somehow cheated, but had now evened the score.

The more the sense of Britten seeped into him the more did he feel the need to face him once again and let him try to get something from him. Next time he would do better; he had let Britten trap him on that Communist business. He should have been on the lookout for that; but the lucky thing was that he knew that Britten had done all his tricks at once, had shot his bolt, had played all his cards. Now that the thing was out in the open, he would know how to act. And furthermore, Britten might want him as a witness against Jan. He smiled while he lay in the darkness. If that happened, he would be safe in sending the ransom note. He could send it just when they thought they had pinned the disappearance of Mary upon Jan. That would throw everything into confusion and would make them want to reply and give the money at once and save the girl.

The warm room lulled his blood and a deepening sense of fatigue drugged him with sleep. He stretched out more fully on the bed, sighed, turned on his back, swallowed, and closed his eyes. Out of the surrounding silence and darkness came the quiet ringing of a distant church bell, thin, faint, but clear. It tolled, soft, then loud, then still louder, so loud that he wondered where it was. It sounded suddenly directly above his head and when he looked it was not there but went on tolling and with each passing moment he felt an urgent need to run and hide as though the bell were sounding a warning and he stood on a street corner in a red glare of light like that which came from the furnace and he had a big package in his arms so wet and slippery and heavy that he could scarcely hold onto it and he wanted to know what was in the package and he stopped near an alley corner and unwrapped it and the paper fell away and he saw – it was his *own* head – his own head lying with black face and half-closed eyes and lips parted with white teeth showing and hair wet with blood and the red glare grew brighter like light shining down from a red moon and red stars on a hot summer night and he was sweating and breathless from running and the bell clanged so loud that he could hear the iron tongue clapping against the metal sides each time it swung to and fro and he was running over a street paved with black coal and his shoes kicked tiny lumps rattling against tin cans and he knew that very soon he had to find some place to hide but there was no place and in front of him white people were coming to ask about the head from which the newspapers had fallen and which was now slippery with blood in his naked hands and he gave up and stood in the middle of the street in the red darkness and cursed the booming bell and the white people and felt that he did not give a damn what happened to him and when the people closed in he hurled the bloody head squarely into their faces *dongdongdong* ...

He opened his eyes and looked about him in the darkened room, hearing a bell ring. He sat up. The bell sounded again. How long had it been ringing? He got to his feet, swaying from stiffness, trying to shake off sleep and that awful dream.

'Yessum,' he mumbled.

The bell rang again, insistently. He fumbled in the dark for the light chain and pulled it. Excitement quickened within him. Had something happened? Was this the police?

'Bigger!' a mufflled voice called.

'Yessuh.'

He braced himself for whatever was coming and stepped to the door. As he opened it he felt it being pushed in by someone who seemed determined to get in in a hurry. Bigger backed away, blinking his eyes.

'We want to talk to you,' said Britten.

'Yessuh.'

He did not hear what Britten said after that, for he saw directly behind Britten a face that made him hold his breath. It was not fear he felt, but a tension, a supreme gathering of all the forces of his body for a showdown.

'Go on in, Mr Erlone,' Mr Dalton said.

Bigger saw Jan's eyes looking at him steadily. Jan stepped into the room and Mr Dalton followed. Bigger stood with his lips slightly parted, his hands hanging loosely by his sides, his eyes watchful, but veiled.

'Sit down, Erlone,' Britten said.

'This is all right,' Jan said. 'I'll stand.'

Bigger saw Britten pull from his coat pocket the packet of pamphlets and hold them under Jan's eyes. Jan's lips twisted into a faint smile.

'Well,' Jan said.

'You're one of those tough reds, hunh?' Britten asked.

'Come on. Let's get this over with,' Jan said. 'What do you want?'

'Take it easy,' Britten said. 'You got plenty of time. I know your kind. You like to rush and have things your way.'

Bigger saw Mr Dalton standing to one side, looking anxiously from one to the other. Several times Mr Dalton made as if to say something, then checked himself, as though uncertain.

'Bigger,' Britten asked, 'is this the man Miss Dalton brought here last night?'

Jan's lips parted. He stared at Britten, then at Bigger.

'Yessuh,' Bigger whispered, struggling to control his feelings, hating Jan violently because he knew he was hurting him; wanting to strike Jan with something because Jan's wide, incredulous stare made him feel hot guilty to the very core of him.

'You didn't bring me here, Bigger!' Jan said. 'Why do you tell them that?'

Bigger did not answer; he decided to talk only to Britten and Mr Dalton. There was silence. Jan was staring at Bigger; Britten and Mr Dalton were watching Jan. Jan made a move toward Bigger, but Britten's arm checked him.

'Say, what *is* this!' Jan demanded. 'What're you making this boy lie for?'

'I suppose you're going to tell us you weren't drunk last night, hunh?' asked Britten.

'What business is that of yours?' Jan shot at him.

'Where's Miss Dalton?' Britten asked.

Jan looked round the room, puzzled.

'She's in Detroit,' he said.

'You know your story by heart, don't you?' Britten said.

'Say, Bigger, what're they doing to you? Don't be afraid. Speak *up*!' said Jan.

Bigger did not answer; he looked stonily at the floor.

'Where did Miss Dalton tell you she was going?' Britten asked.

'She told me she was going to Detroit.'

'Did you see her last night?'

Jan hesitated.

'No.'

'You didn't give these pamphlets to the boy last night?'

Jan shrugged his shoulders, smiled and said:

'All right. I saw her. So what? You know why I didn't say so in the first place . . .'

'No. We *don't* know,' Britten said.

'Well, Mr Dalton here doesn't like reds, as you call 'em, and I didn't want to get Miss Dalton into trouble.'

'Then, you *did* meet her last night?'

'Yes.'

'Where is she?'

'If she's not in Detroit, then I don't know where she is.'

'You gave these pamphlets to this boy?'

'Yes; I did.'

'You and Miss Dalton were drunk last night . . .'

'Aw, come on! We weren't drunk. We had a little to drink . . .'

'You brought her home about two?'

Bigger stiffened and waited.

'Yeah.'

'You told the boy to take her trunk down to the basement?'

Jan opened his mouth, but no words came. He looked at Bigger, then back to Britten.

'Say, what is this?'

'Where's my daughter, Mr Erlone?' Mr Dalton asked.

'I tell you I don't know.'

'Listen, let's be frank, Mr Erlone,' said Mr Dalton. 'We know my daughter was drunk last night when you brought her here. She was too drunk to leave here by herself. Do you know where she is?'

'I – I didn't come here last night,' Jan stammered.

Bigger sensed that Jan had said that he had come home with Mary last night in order to make Mr Dalton believe that he would not have left his daughter alone in a car with a strange chauffeur. And Bigger felt that after Jan admitted that they had been drinking, he was bound to say that he had brought the girl home. Unwittingly, Jan's desire to protect Mary had helped him. Jan's denial of having come to the home would not be believed now; it would make Mr Dalton and Britten feel that he was trying to cover up something of even much greater seriousness.

'You didn't come *home* with her?' Mr Dalton asked.

'No!'

'You didn't tell the boy to take the trunk down?'

'Hell, no! Who says I did? I left the car and took a trolley home.' Jan turned and faced Bigger. 'Bigger, what're you telling these people?'

Bigger did not answer.

'He's just told us what you did last night,' Britten said.

'Where's Mary . . . Where's Miss Dalton?' Jan asked.

'We're waiting for you to tell us,' said Britten.

'D-d-didn't she go to Detroit?' Jan stammered.

'No,' said Mr Dalton.

'I called here this morning and Peggy told me she had.'

'You called here just to see if the family had missed her, didn't you?' asked Britten.

Jan walked over to Bigger.

'Leave 'im alone!' Britten said.

'Bigger,' Jan said, 'why did you tell these men I came here?'

'You say you didn't come here at *all* last night?' Mr Dalton asked again.

'Absolutely not. Bigger, *tell* 'em when I left the car.'

Bigger said nothing.

'Come on, Erlone. I don't know what you're up to, but you've been lying ever since you've been in this room. You said you didn't come here last night, and then you say you did. You said you weren't drunk last night, then you say you were. You said you didn't see Miss Dalton last night, then you say you did. Come on, now. Tell us where Miss Dalton is. Her father and mother want to know.'

Bigger saw Jan's bewildered eyes.

'Listen, I've told you all I know,' said Jan, putting his hat back on. 'Unless you tell me what this joke's all about, I'm getting on back home . . .'

'Wait a minute,' said Mr Dalton.

Mr Dalton came forward a step, and fronted Jan.

'You and I don't agree. Let's forget that. I want to know where my daughter is . . .'

'Is this a game?' asked Jan.

'No; no . . .' said Mr Dalton. 'I want to know. I'm worried . . .'

'I tell you, I don't know!'

'Listen, Mr Erlone. Mary's the only girl we've got. I don't want her to do anything rash. Tell her to come back. Or you bring her back.'

'Mr Dalton, I'm telling you the truth . . .'

'Listen,' Mr Dalton said. 'I'll make it all right with you . . .'

Jan's face reddened.

'What do you mean?' he asked.

'I'll make it worth your while . . .'

'You son . . .' Jan stopped. He walked to the door.

'Let 'im go,' said Britten. 'He can't get away. I'll phone and have 'im picked up. He knows more than he's telling . . .'

Jan paused in the doorway, looking at all three of them. Then he went out. Bigger sat on the edge of the bed and heard Jan's feet run down the stairs. A door slammed; then silence. Bigger saw Mr Dalton gazing at him queerly. He did not like that look. But Britten was jotting something on a pad, his face pale and hard in the yellow glare of the suspended electric bulb.

'You're telling us the truth about all this, aren't you, Bigger?' Mr Dalton asked.

'Yessuh.'

'He's all right,' Britten said. 'Come on; let's get to a phone. I'm having that guy picked up for questioning. It's the only thing to do. And I'll have some men go over Miss Dalton's room. We'll find out what happened. I'll bet my right arm that goddamn red's up to something!'

Britten went out and Mr Dalton followed, leaving Bigger still on the edge of the bed. When he heard the door slam, he got up and grabbed his cap and went softly down the stairs into the basement. He stood a moment looking through the cracks into the humming fire, blindingly red now. But how long would it keep that way, if he did not shake the ashes down? He remembered the last time he had tried and how hysterical he had felt. He must do better than this. He stooped and touched the handle of the ash bin with the fingers of his right hand, keeping his eyes averted as he did so. He imagined that if he shook it he would see pieces of bone falling into the bin and he knew that he would not be able to endure it. He jerked upright and, lashed by fiery whips of fear and guilt, backed hurriedly to the door. For the life of him, he could not bring himself to shake those ashes. But did it really matter? No. He tried to console himself with the thought that he was safe. No one would look into the bin. Why should they? No one suspected him; things were going along smoothly; he would be able to send the kidnap note and get the money without bothering about the ashes before anyone discovered that Mary was dead and in the fire. Then he went into the driveway, through the falling snow to the street. He had to see Bessie at once; the kidnap note had to be sent right away; there was no time to lose. If Mr Dalton, Britten, or Peggy missed him and asked him where he had been, he would say that he had gone out to get a package of cigarettes. But with all the excitement, no one would probably think of him. And they were after Jan now; he was safe.

'Bigger!'

He stopped, whirled, his hand reaching inside of his shirt for his gun. He saw Jan standing in the doorway of a store. As Jan came forward Bigger backed away. Jan stopped.

'For chrissakes! Don't be afraid of me. I'm not going to hurt you.'

In the pale yellow sheen of the street lamp they faced each other; huge wet flakes of snow floated down slowly, forming a delicate screen between them. Bigger had his hand inside of his shirt, on his gun. Jan stood staring, his mouth open.

'What's all this about, Bigger? I haven't done anything to you, have I? Where's Mary?'

Bigger felt guilty; Jan's presence condemned him. Yet he knew of no way to atone for his guilt; he felt he had to act as he was acting.

'I don't want to talk to you,' he mumbled.

'But what have I done to you?' Jan asked desperately.

Jan had done nothing to him, and it was Jan's innocence that made anger rise in him. His fingers tightened about the gun.

'I don't want to talk to you,' he said again.

He felt that if Jan continued to stand there and make him feel this awful sense of guilt, he would have to shoot him in spite of himself. He began to tremble, all over; his lips parted and his eyes widened.

'Go 'way,' Bigger said.

'Listen, Bigger, if these people are bothering you, just tell me. Don't be scared. I'm used to this sort of thing. Listen now. Let's go somewhere and get a cup of coffee and talk this thing over.'

Jane came forward again and Bigger drew his gun. Jan stopped; his face whitened.

'For God's sake, man! What're you doing? Don't shoot ... I haven't bothered you ... Don't ...'

'Leave me alone,' Bigger said, his voice tense and hysterical. 'Leave me alone! Leave me alone!'

Jan backed away from him.

'Leave me alone!' Bigger's voice rose to a scream.

Jan backed farther away, then turned and walked rapidly off, looking back over his shoulder. When he reached the corner he ran through the snow, out of sight. Bigger stood still, the gun in his hand. He had utterly forgotten where he was; his eyes were still riveted on that point in space where he had last seen Jan's retreating form. The tension in him slackened and he lowered the gun until it hung at his side, loosely in his fingers. He was coming back into possession of himself; for the past three minutes it seemed he had been under a strange spell, possessed by a force which he hated, but which he had to obey. He was startled when he heard soft footsteps coming toward him in the snow. He looked and saw a white woman. The woman saw him and paused; she turned abruptly and ran across the street. Bigger shoved the gun in his pocket and ran to the corner. He looked back; the woman was vanishing through the snow, in the opposite direction.

In him as he walked was a cold, driving will. He would go through with this; he would work fast. He had encountered in Jan a much stronger determination than he had thought would be there. If he sent the kidnap note, it would have to be done before Jan could prove that he was completely innocent. At that moment he did not care if he was caught. If only he could cower Jan and Britten into awe, into fear of him and his black skin and his humble manners!

He reached a corner and went into a drug store. A white clerk came to him.

'Give me a envelope, some paper, and a pencil,' he said.

He paid the money, put the package into his pocket and went out to the corner to wait for a car. One came; he got on and rode eastward, wondering what kind of note he would write. He rang the bell for the car to stop, got off and walked through the quiet Negro streets. Now and then he passed an empty building, white and silent in the night. He would make Bessie hide in one of these buildings and watch for Mr Dalton's car. But the ones he passed were too old; if one went into them they might collapse. He walked on. He had to find a building where Bessie could stand in a window and see the package of money when it was thrown from the car. He reached Langley Avenue and walked westward to Wabash Avenue. There were many empty buildings with black windows, like blind eyes, buildings like skeletons standing with snow on their bones in the winter winds. But none of them were on corners. Finally, at Michigan Avenue and East Thirty-sixth Place, he saw the one he wanted. It was tall, white, silent, standing on a well-lighted corner. By looking from any of the front windows Bessie would be able to see in all four directions. Oh! He had to have a flashlight! He went to a drug store and bought one for a dollar. He felt in the inner pocket of his coat for his gloves. Now, he was ready. He crossed the street and stood waiting for a car. His feet were cold and he stamped them in the snow, surrounded by people waiting, too, for a car. He did not look at them; they were simply blind people, blind like his mother, his brother, his sister, Peggy, Britten, Jan, Mr Dalton, and the sightless Mrs Dalton and the quiet empty houses with their black gaping windows.

He looked around the street and saw a sign on a building: THIS PROPERTY IS MANAGED BY THE SOUTH SIDE REAL ESTATE COMPANY. He had heard that Mr Dalton owed the South Side Real Estate Company, and the South Side Real Estate Company owned the house in which he lived. He paid eight dollars a week for one rat-infested room. He had never seen Mr Dalton until he had come to work for him; his mother always took the rent to the real estate office. Mr Dalton was somewhere far away, high up, distant, like a god. He owned property all over the Black Belt, and he owned property where white folks lived, too. But Bigger could not live in a building across the 'line'. Even though Mr Dalton gave millions of dollars for Negro education, he would rent houses to Negroes only in this prescribed area, this corner of the city tumbling down from rot. In a sullen way Bigger was conscious of this. Yes; he would send the kidnap note. He would jar them out of their senses.

When the car came he rode south and got off at Fifty-first Street and walked to Bessie's. He had to ring five times before the buzzer answered. Goddammit, I bet she's drunk! he thought. He mounted the steps and saw her peering at him through the door with eyes red from sleep and alcohol. His doubt of her made him fearful and angry.

'Bigger?' she asked.

'Get on back in the room,' he said.

'What's the matter?' she asked, backing away, her mouth open.

'Let me in! Open the door!'

She threw the door wide, almost stumbling as she did so.

'Turn on the light.'

'What's the matter, Bigger?'

'How many times do you want me to ask you to turn on the light?'

She turned it on.

'Pull them shades.'

She lowered the shades. He stood watching her. Now, I don't want any trouble out of her. He went to the dresser and pushed the jars and combs and brushes aside and took the package from his pocket and laid it in the cleared space.

'Bigger?'

He turned and looked at her.

'What?'

'You ain't planning to do that, sure 'nough?'

'What the hell you think?'

'Bigger, naw!'

He caught her arm and squeezed it in a grip of fear and hate.

'You ain't going to turn away from me now! Not now, goddamn you!'

She said nothing. He took off his cap and coat and threw them on the bed.

'They're wet, Bigger!'

'So what?'

'I ain't doing this,' she said.

'Like hell you ain't!'

'You can't make me!'

'You done helped me to steal enough from the folks you worked for to put you in jail already.'

She did not answer; he turned from her and got a chair and pulled it up to the dresser. He unwrapped the package and balled the paper into a knot and threw it into a corner of the room. Instinctively, Bessie stooped to pick it up. Bigger laughed and she straightened suddenly. Yes; Bessie was blind. He was about to write a kidnap note and she was worried about the cleanliness of her room.

'What's the matter?' she asked.

'Nothing.'

He was smiling grimly. He took out the pencil; it was not sharpened.

'Gimme a knife.'

'Ain't you got one?'

'Hell, naw! Get me a knife!'

'What you do with your knife?'

He stared at her, remembering that she knew that he had had a knife. An image of blood gleaming on the metal blade in the glare of the furnace came before his eyes and fear rose in him hotly.

'You want me to slap you?'

She went behind a curtain. He sat looking at the paper and pencil. She came back with a butcher knife.

'Bigger, please . . . I don't want to do it.'

'Got any liquor?'

'Yeah . . .'

'Get you a shot and set on that bed and keep quiet.'

She stood undecided, then got the bottle from under a pillow and drank. She lay on the bed, on her stomach, her face turned so that she could see him. He watched her through the looking-glass of the dresser. He sharpened the pencil and spread out the piece of paper. He was about to write when he remembered that he did not have his gloves on. Goddamn!

'Gimme my gloves.'

'Hunh?'

'Get my gloves out of the inside of my coat pocket.'

She swayed to her feet and got the gloves and stood back of his chair, holding them limply in her hands.

'Give 'em here.'

'Bigger ...'

'Give me the gloves and get back on that bed, will you?'

He snatched them from her and gave her a shove and turned back to the dresser.

'Bigger ...'

'I ain't asking you but once more to shut up!' he said, pushing the knife out of the way so he could write.

He put on the gloves and took up the pencil in a trembling hand and held it poised over the paper. He should disguise his handwriting. He changed the pencil from his right to his left hand. He would not write it; he would print it. He swallowed with dry throat. Now, what would be the best kind of note? He thought, I want you to put ten thousand ... Naw; that would not do. Not 'I'. It would be better to say 'we'. *We got your daughter*, he printed slowly in big round letters. That was better. He ought to say something to let Mr Dalton think that Mary was still alive. He wrote: *She is safe*. Now, tell him not to go to the police. No! Say something about Mary first! He bent and wrote: *She wants to come home* ... Now tell, him not to go to the police. *Don't go to the police if you want your daughter back safe*. Naw; that ain't good. His scalp tingled with excitement; it seemed that he could feel each strand of hair upon his head. He read the line over and crossed out 'safe' and wrote 'alive'. For a moment he was frozen, still. There was in his stomach a slow, cold, vast rising movement, as though he held within the embrace of his bowels the swing of planets through space. He was giddy. He caught hold of himself, focused his attention to write again. Now, about the money. How much? Yes; make it ten thousand. *Get ten thousand in 5 and 10 bills and put it in a shoe box* ... That's good. He had read that somewhere ... *and tomorrow night ride your car up and down Michigan Avenue from 35th Street to 40th Street*: That would make it hard for anybody to tell just where Bessie would be hiding. He wrote: *Blink your headlights some. When you see a light in a window blink three times throw the box in the snow and drive off. Do what this letter say*. Now, he would sign it. But how? It should be signed in some way that would throw them off the trail. Oh, yes! Sign it 'Red'. He printed, *Red*. Then, for some reason, he thought that that was not enough. Oh, yes. He would make one of those signs, like the ones he had seen on the Communist pamphlets. He wondered how they were made. There was a hammer and a round kind of knife. He drew a hammer, with a curving knife. But it did not look right. He examined it and discovered that he had left the handle off the knife. He sketched it in. Now, it was complete. He read it over. Oh! He had left out something. He had to put in the time when he wanted them to bring the money. He bent and printed again: *p.s. Bring the money at midnight*. He sighed, lifted his eyes and saw Bessie standing behind him. He turned and looked at her.

'Bigger, you ain't really going to do that?' she whispered in horror.

'Sure.'

'*Where*'s that girl?'

'I don't know.'

'You *do* know. You wouldn't be doing this if you didn't know.'

'Aw, what difference do it make?'

She looked straight into his eyes and whispered,

'Bigger, did you kill that girl?'

His jaw clamped tight and he stood up. She turned from him and flung herself upon the bed, sobbing. He began to feel cold;

he discovered that his body was covered with sweat. He heard a
soft rustle and looked down at his hand; the kidnap note was
shaking in his trembling fingers. But I ain't scared, he told
himself. He folded the note, put it into an envelope, sealed it by
licking the flap, and shoved it in his pocket. He lay down on
the bed beside Bessie and took her in his arms. He tried to
speak to her and found his throat so husky that no words
came.

'Come on, kid,' he whispered finally.

'Bigger, what's happened to you?'

'It ain't nothing. You ain't got much to do.'

'I don't *want* to.'

'Don't be scared.'

'You told me you was never going to kill nobody.'

'I ain't killed nobody.'

'You *did*! I see it in your eyes. I see it all over you.'

'Don't you trust me, baby?'

'Where's that girl, Bigger?'

'I don't know.'

'How you know she won't turn up?'

'She just won't.'

'You *did* kill her.'

'Aw, forget the girl.'

She stood up.

'If you killed *her* you'll kill *me*,' she said. 'I ain't in this.'

'Don't be a fool. I love you.'

'You told me you *never* was going to kill.'

'All right. They white folks. They done killed plenty of
us.'

'That don't make it right.'

He began to doubt her; he had never heard this tone in her
voice before. He saw her tear-wet eyes looking at him in stark
fear and he remembered that no one had seen him leave his
room. To stop Bessie who now knew too much would be easy.
He could take the butcher knife and cut her throat. He had to
make certain of her, one way or the other, before he went back
to Dalton's. Quickly, he stooped over her, his fists clenched. He

was feeling as he had felt when he stood over Mary's bed with the white blur drawing near; an iota more of fear would have sent him plunging again into murder.

'I don't want no playing from you now.'

'I'm scared, Bigger,' she whimpered.

She tried to get up; he knew she had seen the mad light in his eyes. Fear sheathed him in fire. His words came in a thick whisper.

'Keep still, now. I ain't playing. Pretty soon they'll be after me, maybe. And I ain't going to let 'em catch me, see? I ain't going to let 'em! The first thing they'll do in looking for me is to come to you. They'll grill you about me and you, you drunk fool, you'll tell! You'll tell if you ain't in it, too. If you ain't in it for your life, you'll tell.'

'Naw; Bigger!' she whimpered tensely. At that moment she was too scared even to cry.

'You going to do what *I* say?'

She wrenched herself free and rolled across the bed and stood up on the other side. He ran round the bed and followed her as she backed into a corner. His voice hissed from his throat:

'I ain't going to leave you behind to snitch!'

'I ain't going to snitch! I *swear* I ain't.'

He held his face a few inches from hers. He had to bind her to him.

'Yeah; I killed the girl,' he said. 'Now you know. You got to help me. You in it as deep as me! You done spent some of the money . . .'

She sank to the bed again, sobbing, her breath catching in her throat. He stood looking down at her, waiting for her to quiet. When she had control of herself, he lifted her and stood her upon her feet. He reached under the pillow and brought out the bottle and took out the stopper and put his hand round her and tilted her head.

'Here; take a shot.'

'Naw.'

'*Drink* . . .'

He carried the bottle to her lips; she drank a small swallow.

When he attempted to put the bottle away, she took it from him.

'That's enough, now. You don't want to get sloppy drunk.'

He turned her loose and she lay back on the bed, limp, whimpering. He bent to her.

'Listen, Bessie.'

'Bigger, please! Don't do this to me! *Please!* All I do is work, work like a dog! From morning till night. I ain't got no happiness. I ain't never had none. I ain't got nothing and you do this to me. After how good I been to you. Now you just spoil my whole life. I've done everything for you I know how and you do this to me. *Please*, Bigger . . .' She turned her head away and stared at the floor. 'Lord, don't let this happen to me! I ain't done nothing for this to come to me! I just work! I ain't had no happiness, no nothing. I just work. I'm black and I work and don't bother nobody . . .'

'Go on,' Bigger said, nodding his head affirmatively; he knew the truth of all she spoke without her telling it. 'Go on and see what that gets you.'

'But I don't want to do it, Bigger. They'll catch us. God *knows* they will.'

'I ain't going to leave you here to snitch on me.'

'I won't tell. Honest, I won't. I cross my heart and swear by God, I won't. You can run away . . .'

'I ain't got no money.'

'You *have* got money. I paid rent out of what you gave me and I bought some liquor. But the rest is there.'

'That ain't enough. I got to have some real dough.'

She cried again. He got the knife and stood over her.

'I can stop it all right now,' he said.

She started up, her mouth opening to scream.

'If you scream, I'll *have* to kill you. So help me God!'

'Naw; naw! Bigger, don't! *Don't!*'

Slowly, his arm relaxed and hung at his side; she fell to sobbing again. He was afraid that he would have to kill her before it was all over. She would not do to take along, and he could not leave her behind.

'All right,' he said. 'But you better do the right thing.'

He put the knife on the dresser and got the flashlight from his overcoat pocket and then stood over her with the letter and flashlight in his hand.

'Come on,' he said. 'Get your coat on.'

'Not tonight, Bigger! Not tonight . . .'

'It won't be tonight. But I got to show you what to do.'

'But it's cold. It's snowing . . .'

'Sure. And nobody'll see us. Come *on* !'

She pulled up; he watched her struggle into her coat. Now and then she paused and looked at him, blinking back her tears. When she was dressed, he put on his coat and cap and led her to the street. The air was thick with snow. The wind blew hard. It was a blizzard. The street lamps were faint smudges of yellow. They walked to the corner and waited for a car.

'I'd rather do anything but this,' she said.

'Stop now. We're in it.'

'Bigger, honey, I'd run off with you. I'd work for you, baby. We don't have to do this. Don't you believe I love you?'

'Don't try that on me now.'

The car came; he helped her on and sat down beside her and looked past her face at the silent snow flying white and wild outside the window. He brought his eyes farther round and looked at her; she was staring with blank eyes, like a blind woman waiting for some word to tell her where she was going. Once she cried and he gripped her shoulder so tightly that she stopped, more absorbed in the painful pressure of steel-like fingers than in her fate. They got off at Thirty-sixth Place and walked over to Michigan Avenue. When they reached the corner, Bigger stopped and made her stop by gripping her arm again. They were in front of the high, white, empty building with black windows.

'Where we going?'

'Right here.'

'Bigger,' she whimpered.

'Come on, now. Don't start that !'

'But I don't *want* to.'

'You *got* to.'

He looked up and down the street, past ghostly lamps that shed a long series of faintly shimmering cones of yellow against the snowy night. He took her to the front entrance which gave into a vast pool of inky silence. He brought out the flashlight and focused the round spot on a rickety stairway leading upward into a still blacker darkness. The planks creaked as he led her up. Now and then he felt his shoes sink into a soft, cushy substance. Cobwebs brushed his face. All around him was the dank smell of rotting timber. He stopped abruptly as something with dry whispering feet flitted across his path, emitting as the rush of its flight died a thin, piping wail of lonely fear.

'Ooow !'

Bigger whirled and centered the spot of light on Bessie's face. Her lips were drawn back, her mouth was open, and her hands were lifted midway to white-rimmed eyes.

'What you trying to do?' he asked. 'Tell the whole world we in here?'

'Oh, Bigger !'

'Come on !'

After a few feet he stopped and swung the light. He saw dusty walls, walls almost like those of the Dalton home. The doorways were wider than those of any house in which he had ever lived. Some rich folks lived here once, he thoughf. Rich white folks. That was the way most houses on the South Side were, ornate, old, stinking; homes once of rich white people, now inhabited by Negroes or standing dark and empty with yawning black windows. He remembered that bombs had been thrown by whites into houses like these when the Negroes had first moved into the South Side. He swept the disc of yellow and walked gingerly down a hall and into a room at the front of the house. It was feebly lit from the street lamps outside; he switched off the flashlight and looked round. The room had six large windows. By standing close to any of them, the streets in all four directions were visible.

'See, Bessie . . .'

He turned to look at her and found that she was not there. He called tensely:

'Bessie!'

There was no answer; he bounded to the doorway and switched on the flashlight. She was leaning against a wall, sobbing. He went to her, caught her arm and yanked her back into the room.

'Come on! You got to do better than this.'

'I'd rather have you kill me right now,' she sobbed.

'Don't you say that again!'

She was silent. His black open palm swept upward in a swift narrow arc and smacked solidly against her face.

'You want me to wake you up?'

She bent her head to her knees; he caught hold of her arm again and dragged her to the window. He spoke like a man who had been running and was out of breath:

'Now, look. All you got to do is come here tomorrow night, see? Ain't nothing going to bother you. I'm seeing to everything. Don't you worry none. You just do what I say. You come here and just watch. About twelve o'clock a car'll come along. It'll be blinking its headlights, see? When it comes, you just raise this flashlight and blink it three times, see? Like this. Remember that. Then watch that car. It'll throw out a package. Watch that package, 'cause the money'll be in it. It'll go into the snow. Look and see if anybody's about. If you see nobody, then go and get the package and go home. But don't go straight home. Make sure nobody's watching you, nobody's following you, see? Ride three or four street cars and transfer fast. Get off about five blocks from home and look behind you as you walk, see? Now, look. You can see up and down Michigan and Thirty-sixth. You can see if anybody's watching. I'll be in the white folks' house all day tomorrow. If they put anybody out to watch, I'll let you know not to come.'

'Bigger . . .'

'Come on, now.'

'Take me home.'

'You going to do it?'

She did not answer.

'You already in it,' he said. 'You got part of the money.'

'I reckon it don't make no difference,' she sighed.

'It'll be easy.'

'It won't. I'll get caught. But it don't make no difference. I'm lost anyhow. I was lost when I took up with you. I'm lost and it don't matter . . .'

'Come on.'

He led her back to the car stop. He said nothing as they waited in the whirling snow. When he heard the car coming, he took her purse from her, opened it and put the flashlight inside. The car stopped; he helped her on, put seven cents in her trembling hand and stood in the snow watching her black face through the window white with ice as the car moved off slowly through the night.

He walked to Daltons' through the snow. His right hand was in his coat pocket, his fingers about the kidnap note. When he reached the driveway, he looked about the street carefully. There was no one. He looked at the house; it was white, huge, silent. He walked up the steps and stood in front of the door. He waited a moment to see what would happen. So deeply conscious was he of violating dangerous taboo, that he felt that the very air or sky would suddenly speak, commanding him to stop. He was sailing fast into the face of a cold wind that all but sucked his breath from him; but he liked it. Around him were silence and night and snow falling, falling as though it had fallen from the beginning of time and would always fall till the end of the world. He took the letter out of his pocket and slipped it under the door. Turning, he ran down the steps and round the house. *I done it! I done it now! They'll see it tonight or in the morning . . .* He went to the basement door, opened it and looked inside; no one was there. Like an enraged beast, the furnace throbbed with heat, suffusing a red glare over everything. He stood in front of the cracks and watched the restless embers. *Had Mary burned completely?* He wanted to poke around in the coals to see, but dared not; he flinched from it even in thought. He pulled the lever for more coal, then went to his room.

When he stretched out on his bed in the dark he found that

his whole body was trembling. He was cold and hungry. While lying there shaking, a hot bath of fear, hotter than his blood, engulfed him, bringing him to his feet. He stood in the middle of the floor, seeing vivid images of his gloves, his pencil, and paper. How on earth had he forgotten them? He had to burn them. He would do it right now. He pulled on the light and went to his overcoat and got the gloves and pencil and paper and stuffed them into his shirt. He went to the door, listened a moment, then went into the hall and down the stairs to the furnace. He stood a moment before the gleaming cracks. Hurriedly, he opened the door and dumped the gloves and pencil and paper in; he watched them smoke, blaze; he closed the door and heard them burn in a furious whirlwind of draft.

A strange sensation enveloped him. Something tingled in his stomach and on his scalp. His knees wobbled, giving way. He stumbled to the wall and leaned against it weakly. A wave of numbness spread fanwise from his stomach over his entire body, including his head and eyes, making his mouth gape. Strength ebbed from him. He sank to his knees and pressed his fingers to the floor to keep from tumbling over. An organic sense of dread seized him. His teeth chattered and he felt sweat sliding down his armpits and back. He groaned, holding as still as possible. His vision was blurred; but gradually it cleared. Again he saw the furnace. Then he realized that he had been on the verge of collapse. Soon the glare and drone of the fire came to his eyes and ears. He closed his mouth and gritted his teeth; the peculiar paralyzing numbness was leaving.

When he was strong enough to stand without support, he rose to his feet and wiped his forehead on his sleeve. He had strained himself from a too long lack of sleep and food; and the excitement was sapping his energy. He should go to the kitchen and ask for his dinner. Surely, he should not starve like this. He mounted the steps to the door and knocked timidly; there was no answer. He turned the knob and pushed the door in and saw the kitchen flooded with light. On a table were spread several white napkins under which was something that looked like plates of food. He stood gazing at it, then went to the table and lifted the corners of the napkins. There were sliced bread and steak and fried potatoes and gravy and string beans and spinach and a huge piece of chocolate cake. His mouth watered. Was this for him? He wondered if Peggy was around. Ought he try to find her? But he disliked the thought of looking for her; that would bring attention to himself, something which he hated. He stood in the kitchen, wondering if he ought to eat, but afraid to do so. He rested his black fingers on the edge of the white table and a silent laugh burst from his parted lips as he saw himself for a split second in a lurid objective light: he had killed a rich white girl and had burned her body after cutting her head off and had lied to throw the blame on someone else and had written a kidnap note demanding ten thousand dollars and yet he stood here afraid to touch food on the table, food which undoubtedly was his own.

'Bigger?'

'Hunh?' he answered before he knew who had called.

'Where've you been? Your dinner's been waiting for you since five o'clock. There's a chair. Eat . . .'

as much as you want . . . He stopped listening. In Peggy's hand was the kidnap note. *I'll heat your coffee go ahead and eat* Had she opened it? Did she know what was in it? No; the envelope was still sealed. She came to the table and removed the napkins. His knees were shaking with excitement and sweat broke out on his forehead. His skin felt as though it were puckering up from a blast of heat. *don't you want the steak warmed* The question reached him from far away and he shook his head without really knowing what she meant. *don't you feel well*.

'This is all right,' he murmured.

'You oughtn't starve yourself that way.'

'I wasn't hungry.'

'You're hungrier than you think,' she said.

She set a cup and saucer at his plate, then laid the letter on the edge of the table. It held his attention as though it were a steel magnet and his eyes were iron. She got the coffee pot and poured his cup full. No doubt she had just gotten the letter from under the door and had not yet had time to give it to Mr Dalton. She placed a small jar of cream at his plate and took up the letter again.

'I've got to give this to Mr Dalton,' she said. 'I'll be back in a moment.'

'Yessum,' he whispered.

She left. He stopped chewing and stared before him, his mouth dry. But he *had* to eat. Not to eat now would create suspicion. He shoved the food in and chewed each mouthful awhile, then washed it down with swallows of hot coffee. When the coffee gave out, he used cold water. He strained his ears to catch sounds. But none came. Then the door swung in silently and Peggy came back. He could see nothing in her round red face. Out of the corners of his eyes he watched her go to the stove and putter with pots and pans.

'Want more coffee?'

'No'm.'

'You ain't scared of all this trouble we're having round here, are you, Bigger?'

'Oh, no'm,' he said, wondering if something in his manner had made her ask that.

'That poor Mary!' Peggy sighed. 'She acts like such a ninny. Imagine a girl keeping her parents worried sick all the time. But there are children for you these days.'

He hurried with his eating, saying nothing; he wanted to get out of the kitchen. The thing was in the open now; not all of it, but some of it. Nobody knew about Mary yet. He saw in his mind a picture of the Dalton family distraught and horrified when they found that Mary was kidnaped. That would put them a certain distance from him. They would think that white men did it; they would never think that a black, timid Negro did that. They would go after Jan. The 'Red' he had signed the letter and the hammer and curving knife would make them look for Communists.

'You got enough?'

'Yessum.'

'You better clean the ashes out of the furnace in the morning, Bigger.'

'Yessum.'

'And be ready for Mr Dalton at eight.'

'Yessum.'

'Your room all right?'

'Yessum.'

The door swung in violently. Bigger started in fright. Mr Dalton came into the kitchen, his face ashy. He stared at Peggy and Peggy, holding a dish towel in her hand, stared at him. In Mr Dalton's hand was the letter, opened.

'What's the matter, Mr Dalton?'

'Who . . . Where did . . . Who gave you this?'

'What?'

'This *letter*.'

'Why, nobody. I got it from the door.'

'When?'

'A few minutes ago. Anything wrong?'

Mr Dalton looked round the entire kitchen, not at anything in particular, but just round the entire stretch of four walls, his eyes wide and unseeing. He looked back at Peggy; it was as if he had thrown himself upon her mercy; was waiting for her to say some word that would take the horror away.

'W-what's the matter, Mr Dalton?' Peggy asked again.

Before Mr Dalton could answer Mrs Dalton groped her way into the kitchen, her white hands held high. Bigger watched her fingers tremble through the air till they touched Mr Dalton's shoulder. They gripped his coat hard enough to tear it from his body. Bigger, without moving an eyelid, felt his skin grow hot and his muscles stiffen.

'Henry! Henry!' Mrs Dalton called. 'What's the matter?'

Mr Dalton did not hear her; he still stared at Peggy.

'Did you see who left this letter?'

'No, Mr Dalton.'

'You, Bigger?'

'Nawsuh,' he whispered, his mouth full of dry food.

'Henry, tell me! *Please!* For Heaven's sake!'

Mr Dalton put his arm about Mrs Dalton's waist and held her close to him.

'It's . . . It's about Mary . . . It's . . . She . . .'

'What? Where is she?'

'They . . . They got her! They kidnaped her!'

'Henry! No!' Mrs Dalton screamed.

'Oh, no!' Peggy whimpered, running to Mr Dalton.

'My baby,' Mrs Dalton sobbed.

'She's been kidnaped,' Mr Dalton said, as though he had to say the words over again to convince himself.

Bigger's eyes were wide, taking in all three of them in one constantly roving glance. Mrs Dalton continued to sob and Peggy sank into a chair, her face in her hands. Then she sprang up and ran out of the room, crying:

'Lord, don't let them kill her!'

Mrs Dalton swayed. Mr Dalton lifted her and staggered, trying to get her through the door. As he watched Mr Dalton there flashed through Bigger's mind a quick image of how he had lifted Mary's body in his arms the night before. He rose and held the door open for Mr Dalton and watched him walk unsteadily down the dim hallway with Mrs Dalton in his arms.

He was alone in the kitchen now. Again the thought that he had the chance to walk out of here and be clear of it all came to him, and again he brushed it aside. He was tensely eager to stay and see how it would all end, even if that end swallowed him in blackness. He felt that he was living upon a high pinnacle where bracing winds whipped about him. There came to his ears a muffled sound of sobs. Then suddenly there was silence. What's happening? Would Mr Dalton phone the police now? He strained to listen, but no sounds came. He went to the door and took a few steps into the hallway. There were still no sounds. He looked about to make sure that no one was watching him, then crept on tiptoe down the hall. He heard voices. Mr Dalton was talking to someone. He crept farther; yes, he would hear . . . *I want to talk to Britten please.* Mr Dalton was phoning, *come right over please yes at once something awful has happened I don't want to talk about it over the phone.* That meant that when Britten came back he would be questioned again, *yes right away I'll be waiting.*

He had to get back to his room. He tiptoed along the hall, through the kitchen, down the steps, and into the basement. The torrid cracks of the furnace gleamed in the crimson darkness and he heard the throaty undertone of the draft devouring the air. Was she burnt? But even if she were not, who would think of looking in the furnace for her? He went to his room, into the closet, closed the door and listened. Silence. He came out, left the door open and, in order to get to the closet quickly and without sound, pulled off his shoes. He lay again on the bed, his mind whirling with images born of a multitude of impulses. He could run away; he could remain; he could even go down and confess what he had done. The mere thought that these avenues of action were open to him made him feel free, that his life was his, that he held his future in his hands. But they would never think that he had done it; not a meek black boy like him.

He bounded off the bed, listening, thinking that he had heard voices. He had been so deeply taken up with his own thoughts that he did not know if he had actually heard anything or had imagined it. Yes; he heard faint footsteps below. He hurried to the closet. The footsteps ceased. There came to him the soft sound of sobbing. It was Peggy. Her sobbing quieted, then rose to a high pitch. He stood for a long time, listening to Peggy's sobs and the long moan of the wind sweeping through the night outside. Peggy's sobs ceased and her footsteps sounded once more. Was she going to answer the doorbell? Footsteps came gain; Peggy had gone to the front of the house for something and had come back. He heard a heavy voice, a man's. At first he could not identify it; then he realized that it was Britten's.

'. . . and you found the note?'

'Yes.'

'How long ago?'

'About an hour.'

'You're sure you didn't see anyone leave it?'

'It was sticking under the door.'

'Think, now. Did you see anybody about the house or drive-way?'

'No. The boy and me, that's all that's been around here.'

'And where's the boy now?'

'Upstairs in his room, I think.'

'Did you ever see this handwriting before?'

'No, Mr Britten.'

'Can you guess, can you think, imagine who would send such a note?'

'No. Not a soul in this whole wide world, Mr Britten,' Peggy wailed.

Britten's voice ceased. There was the sound of other heavy feet. Chairs scraped over the floor. More people were in the kitchen. Who were they? Their movements sounded like those of men. Then Bigger heard Britten speaking again.

'Listen, Peggy. Tell me, how *does* this boy act?'

'What do you mean, Mr Britten?'

'Does he seem intelligent? Does he seem to be *acting*?'

'I don't know, Mr Britten. He's just like all the other colored boys.'

'Does he say "yes mam" and "no mam"?'

'Yes, Mr Britten. He's polite.'

'But does he seem to be trying to appear like he's more ignorant than he *really* is?'

'I don't know, Mr Britten.'

'Have you missed anything around the house since he's been here?'

'No; nothing.'

'Has he ever insulted you, or anything?'

'Oh, no! No!'

'What kind of a boy is he?'

'He's just a quiet colored boy. That's all I can say . . .'

'Did you ever see him reading anything?'

'No, Mr Britten.'

'Does he speak more intelligently at some times than at others?'

'No, Mr Britten. He talked always the same, to me.'

'Has he ever done anything that would make you think he knows something about this note?'

'No, Mr Britten.'

'When you speak to him, does he hesitate before he answers, as though he's thinking up what to say?'

'No, Mr Britten. He talks and acts natural-like.'

'When he talks, does he wave his hands around a lot, like he's been around a lot of Jews?'

'I never noticed, Mr Britten.'

'Did you ever hear 'im call anybody *comrade*?'

'No, Mr Britten.'

'Does he pull off his cap when he comes in the house?'

'I never noticed. I think so, Mr Britten.'

'Has he ever sat down in your presence without being asked, like he was used to being around white people?'

'No, Mr Britten. Only when I told him to.'

'Does he speak first, or does he wait until he's spoken to?'

'Well, Mr Britten. He seemed always to wait until we spoke to him before he said anything.'

'Now, listen, Peggy. Think and try to remember if his voice goes *up* when he talks, like Jews when they talk. Know what I mean? You see, Peggy, I'm trying to find out if he's been around Communists . . .'

'No, Mr Britten. He talks just like all other colored folks to me.'

'Where did you say he is now?'

'Upstairs in his room.'

When Britten's voice ceased Bigger was smiling. Yes; Britten was trying to trap him, trying to make out a case against him; but he could not find anything to go upon. Was Britten coming to talk to him now? There came the sound of other voices.

'It's a ten-to-one chance that she's dead.'

'Yeah. They usually bump 'em off. They're scared of 'em after they get 'em. They think they might identify them afterwards.'

'Did the old man say he was going to pay?'

'Sure. He wants his daughter back.'

'That's just ten thousand dollars shot to hell, if you ask me.'

'But he wants the girl.'

'Say, I bet it's those reds trying to raise money.'

'Yeah!'

'Maybe that's how they get their dough. They say that guy, Bruno Hauptmann, the one who snatched the Lindy baby, did it for the Nazis. They needed the money.'

'I'd like to shoot every one of them goddamn bastards, red or no red.'

There was the sound of a door opening and more footsteps.

'You have any luck with the old man?'

'Not yet.' It was Britten's voice.

'He's pretty washed up, eh?'

'Yeah; and who wouldn't be?'

'He won't call the cops?'

'Naw; he's scared stiff.'

'It might seem hard on the family, but if you let them snatchers know they can't scare money out of you, they'll stop.'

'Say, Brit, try 'im again.'

'Yeah; tell 'im there ain't nothing to do now but to call the cops.'

'Aw, I don't know. I hate to worry 'im.'

'Well, after all, it's *his* daughter. Let him handle it.'

'But listen, Brit. When they pick up this Erlone fellow, he's going to tell the cops and the papers'll have the story anyway. So call 'em now. The sooner they get started the better.'

'Naw; I'll wait for the old man to give the signal.'

Bigger knew that Mr Dalton had not wanted to notify the police; that much was certain. But how long would he hold out? The police would know everything as soon as Jan was picked up, for Jan would tell enough to make the police and the newspapers investigate. But if Jan were confronted with the fact of the kidnaping of Mary, what would happen? Could Jan prove an alibi? If he did, then the police would start looking for someone else. They would start questioning him again; they would want to know why he had lied about Jan's being in the house. But would not the word 'Red' which he had signed to the ransom note throw them off the track and make them still think that Jan or his comrades did it? Why would anybody want to think that Bigger had kidnaped Mary? Bigger came out of the closet and wiped sweat from his forehead with his sleeve. He had knelt so long that his blood had almost stopped and needlelike pains shot from the bottom of his feet to the calves of his legs. He went to the window and looked out at the swirling snow. He could hear wind rising; it was a blizzard all right. The snow moved in no given direction, but filled the world with a vast white storm of flying powder. The sharp currents of wind could be seen in whorls of snow twisting like miniature tornadoes.

The window overlooked an alley, to the right of which was Forty-fifth Street. He tried the window to see if it would open; he lifted it a few inches, then all the way with a loud and screechy sound. Had anyone heard him? He waited; nothing happened. Good! If the worst came to the worst, he could jump out of this window, right here, and run away. It was two stories to the ground and there was a deep drift of snow just below him. He lowered the window and lay again on the bed, waiting. The sound of firm feet came on the stairs. Yes; someone was coming up! His body grew rigid. A knock came at the door.

'Yessuh!'

'Open up!'

He pulled on the light, opened and the door and met a white face.

'They want you downstairs.'

'Yessuh!'

The man stepped to one side and Bigger went past him on down the hall and down the steps into the basement, feeling the eyes of the white man on his back, and hearing as he neared the furnace the muffled breathing of the fire and seeing directly before his eyes Mary's bloody head with its jet-black curly hair, shining and wet with blood on the crumpled newspapers. He saw Britten standing near the furnace with three white men.

'Hello, Bigger.'

'Yessuh,' Bigger said.

'You heard what happened?'

'Yessuh.'

'Listen, boy. You're talking just to me and my men here. Now, tell me, do you think Jan's mixed up in this?'

Bigger's eyes fell. He did not want to answer in a hurry and he did not want to blame Jan definitely, for that would make them question him too closely. He would hint and point in Jan's direction.

'I don't know, suh,' he said.

'Just tell me what you *think*.'

'I don't know, suh,' Bigger said again.

'You *really* saw him here last night, didn't you?'

'Oh, yessuh.'

'You'd swear he told you to take that trunk down and leave the car out in the snow.'

'I – I'd swear to what's true, suh,' said Bigger.

'Did he act like he had anything up his sleeve?'

'I don't know, suh.'

'What time did you say you left?'

'A little before two, suh.'

Britten turned to the other men, one of whom stood near the furnace with his back to the fire, warming his hands behind him. The man's legs were sprawled wide apart and a cigar glowed in a corner of his mouth.

'It must've been that red,' Britten said to him.

'Yeah,' said the man at the furnace. 'What would he have the boy take the trunk down for and leave the car out? It was to throw us off the scent.'

'Listen, Bigger,' said Britten. 'Did you see this guy act in any way out of the ordinary? I mean, sort of nervous, say? Just what *did* he talk about?'

'He talked about Communists . . .'

'Did he ask you to join?'

'He gave me that stuff to read.'

'Come on. Tell us some of the things he said.'

Bigger knew the things that white folks hated to hear Negroes ask for; and he knew that these were the things the reds were always asking for. And he knew that white folks did not like to hear these things asked for even by whites who fought for Negroes.

'Well,' Bigger said, feigning reluctance, 'he told me that some day there wouldn't be no rich folks and no poor folks . . .'

'Yeah?'

'And he said a black man would have a chance . . .'

'Go on.'

'And he said there would be no more lynching . . .'

'And what was the girl saying?'

'She agreed with 'im.'

'How did you feel toward them?'

'I don't know, suh.'

'I mean, did you like 'em?'

He knew that the average white man would not approve of his liking such talk.

'It was my job. I just did what they told me,' he mumbled.

'Did the girl act in any way scared?'

He sensed what kind of a case they were trying to build against Jan and he remembered that Mary had cried last night when he had refused to go into the café with her to eat.

'Well, I don't know, suh. She was crying once . . .'

'*Crying?*'

The men crowded about him.

'Yessuh.'

'Did he hit her?'

'I didn't see that.'

'What did he do then?'

'Well, he put his arms around her and she stopped.'

Bigger had his back to a wall. The crimson luster of the fire gleamed on the white men's faces. The sound of air being sucked upward through the furnace mingled in Bigger's ears with the faint whine of the wind outside in the night. He was tired; he closed his eyes a long second and then opened them, knowing that he had to keep alert and answer questions to save himself.

'Did this fellow Jan say anything to you about white women?'

Bigger tightened with alarm.

'Suh?'

'Did he say he would let you meet some white women if you joined the reds?'

He knew that sex relations between blacks and whites were repulsive to most white men.

'Nawsuh,' he said, simulating abashment.

'Did Jan lay the girl?'

'I don't know, suh.'

'Did you take them to a room or a hotel?'

'Nawsuh. Just to the park.'

'They were in the back seat?'

'Yessuh.'

'How long were you in the park?'

'Well, about two hours, I reckon, suh.'

'Come on, now, boy. Did he lay the girl?'

'I don't know, suh. They was back there kissing and going on.'

'Was she lying down?'

'Well, yessuh. She was,' said Bigger, lowering his eyes because he felt that it would be better to do so. He knew that whites thought that all Negroes yearned for white women, therefore he wanted to show a certain fearful deference even when one's name was mentioned in his presence.

'They were drunk, weren't they?'

'Yessuh. They'd been drinking a lot.'

He heard the sound of autos coming into the driveway. Was this the police?

'Who's that?' Britten asked.

'I don't know,' said one of the men.

'I'd better see,' Britten said.

Bigger saw, after Britten had opened the door, four cars standing in the snow with headlights glowing.

'Who's that?' Britten called.

'The press!'

'There's nothing here for you!' Britten called in an uneasy voice.

'Don't stall us!' a voice answered. 'Some of it's already in the papers. You may as well tell the rest.'

'What's in the papers?' Britten asked as the men entered the basement.

A tall red-faced man shoved his hand into his pocket and brought forth a newspaper and handed it to Britten.

'The reds say you're charging 'em with spiriting away the old man's daughter.'

Bigger darted a glance at the paper from where he was; he saw : RED NABBED AS GIRL VANISHES.

'Goddamn!' said Britten.

'Phew!' said the tall red-faced man. 'What a night! Red arrested! Snowstorm. And this place down here looks like somebody's been murdered.'

'Come on, you,' said Britten. 'You're in Mr Dalton's house now.'

'Oh, I'm sorry.'

'Where's the old man?'

'Upstairs. He doesn't want to be bothered.'

'Is that girl really missing, or is this just a stunt?'

'I can't tell you anything,' Britten said.

'Who's this boy, here?'

'Keep quiet, Bigger,' Britten said.

'Is he the one Erlone said accused him?'

Bigger stood against the wall and looked around vaguely.

'You going to pull the dumb act on us?' asked one of the men.

'Listen, you guys,' said Britten. 'Take it easy. I'll go and see if the old man will see you.'

'That's the time. We're waiting. All the wires are carrying this story.'

Britten went up the steps and left Bigger standing with the crowd of men.

'Your name's Bigger Thomas?' the red-faced man asked.

'Keep quiet, Bigger,' said one of Britten's men.

Bigger said nothing.

'Say, what's all this? This boy can talk if he wants to.'

'This smells like something big to me,' said one of the men.

Bigger had never seen such men before; he did not know how to act toward them or what to expect of them. They were not rich and distant like Mr Dalton, and they were harder than Britten, but in a more impersonal way, a way that maybe was more dangerous than Britten's. Back and forth they walked across the basement floor in the glare of the furnace with their hats on and with cigars and cigarettes in their mouths. Bigger felt in them a coldness that disregarded everybody. They seemed like men out for keen sport. They would be around a long time now that Jan had been arrested and questioned. Just what did they think of what he had told about Jan? Was there any good in Britten's telling him not to talk to them? Bigger's eyes watched the balled newspaper in a white man's gloved hand. If only he would read that paper! The men were silent, waiting for Britten to return. Then one of them came and leaned against the wall, near him. Bigger looked out of the corners of his eyes and said nothing. He saw the man light a cigarette.

'Smoke, kid?'

'Nawsuh,' he mumbled.

He felt something touch the center of his palm. He made a move to look, but a whisper checked him.

'Keep still. It's for you. I want you to give me the dope.'

Bigger's fingers closed over a slender wad of paper; he knew at once that it was money and that he would give it back. He held the money and watched his chance. Things were happening so fast that he felt he was not doing full justice to them. He was tired. Oh, if only he could go to sleep! If only this whole thing could be postponed for a few hours, until he had rested some! He felt that he would have been able to handle it then. Events were like the details of a tortured dream, happening without cause. At times it seemed that he could not quite remember what had gone before and what it was he was expecting to come. At the head of the stairs the door opened and he saw Britten. While the others were looking off, Bigger shoved the money back into the man's hand. The man looked at him, shook his head and flicked his cigarette away and walked to the center of the floor.

'I'm sorry, boys,' Britten said. 'But the old man won't be able to see you till Tuesday.'

Bigger thought quickly; that meant that Mr Dalton was going to pay the money and was not going to call in the police.

'Tuesday?'

'Aw, come on !'

'Where *is* the girl?'

'I'm sorry,' said Britten.

'You're putting us in the position of having to print anything we can get about this case,' said one of the men.

'You all know Mr Dalton,' Britten explained. 'You wouldn't do that. For God's sake, give the man a chance. I can't tell you why now, but it's important. He'd do as much for you some time.'

'Is the girl *missing*?'

'I don't know.'

'Is she *here* in the house?'

Britten hesitated.

'No; I don't think she is.'

'When did she leave?'

'I don't know.'

'When will she be back?'

'I can't say.'

'Is this Erlone fellow telling the truth?' asked one of the men. 'He said that Mr Dalton's trying to slander the Communist Party by having him arrested. And he says it's an attempt to break up his relationship with Miss Dalton.'

'I don't know,' Britten said.

'Erlone was picked up and taken to police headquarters and questioned,' the man continued. 'He claimed that this boy here lied about his being in the home last night. Is *that* true?'

'Really, I can't say anything about that,' Britten said.

'Did Mr Dalton forbid Erlone to see Miss Dalton?'

'I don't know,' Britten said, whipping out a handkerchief and wiping his forehead. 'Honest to God, boys, I can't tell you anything. You'll have to see the old man.'

All eyes lifted at once. Mr Dalton stood at the head of the stairs in the doorway, white-faced, holding a piece of paper in his fingers. Bigger knew at once that it was the kidnap note. What was going to happen now? All of the men talked at once, shouting questions, asking to take pictures.

'Where's Miss Dalton?'

'Did you swear out a warrant for the arrest of Erlone?'

'Were they engaged?'

'Did you forbid her to see him?'

'Did you object to his politics?'

'Don't you want to make a statement, Mr Dalton?'

Bigger saw Mr Dalton lift his hand for silence, then walk slowly down the steps and stand near the men, just a few feet above them. They gathered closer, raising their silver bulbs.

'Do you wish to comment on what Erlone said about your chauffeur?'

'What did he say?' Mr Dalton asked.

'He said the chauffeur had been paid to lie about him.'

'That's not true,' Mr Dalton said firmly.

Bigger blinked as lightning shot past his eyes. He saw the men lowering the silver bulbs.

'Gentlemen,' said Mr Dalton. 'Please! Give me just a moment. I do want to make a statement.' Mr Dalton paused, his lips quivering. Bigger could see that he was very nervous. 'Gentlemen,' Mr Dalton said again, 'I want to make a statement and I want you to take it carefully. The way you men handle this will mean life or death to someone, someone close to this family, to me. Someone...' Mr Dalton's voice trailed off. The basement filled with murmurs of eagerness. Bigger heard the kidnap note crackling faintly in Mr Dalton's fingers. Mr Dalton's face was dead-white and his blood-shot eyes were deep set in his head above patches of dark-colored skin. The fire in the furnace was low and the draft was but a whisper. Bigger

saw Mr Dalton's white hair glisten like molten silver from the
pale sheen of the fire.

Then, suddenly, so suddenly that the men gasped, the door
behind Mr Dalton filled with a flowing white presence. It was
Mrs Dalton, her white eyes held wide and stony, her hands
lifted sensitively upward toward her lips, the fingers long and
white and wide apart. The basement was lit up with the white
flash of a dozen silver bulbs.

Ghostlike, Mrs Dalton movedly noiselessly down the steps
until she came to Mr Dalton's side, the big white cat following
her. She stood with one hand lightly touching the banister and
the other held in mid-air. Mr Dalton did not move or look
round; he placed one of his hands over hers on the banister,
covering it, and faced the men. Meanwhile, the big white cat
bounded down the steps and leaped with one movement upon
Bigger's shoulder and sat perched there. Bigger was still, feeling the cat had given him away, had pointed him out as the
murderer of Mary. He tried to lift the cat down; but its claws
clutched his coat. The silver lightning flashed in his eyes and he
knew that the men had taken pictures of him with the cat
poised upon his shoulder. He tugged at the cat once more and
managed to get it down. It landed on its feet with a long whine,
then began to rub itself against Bigger's leg. Goddamn! Why
can't that cat leave me alone? He heard Mr Dalton speaking.

'Gentlemen, you may take pictures, but wait a moment. I've
just phoned the police and asked that Mr Erlone be released
immediately. I want it known that I do not want to prefer
charges against him. It is important that this be understood. I
hope your papers will carry the story.'

Bigger wondered if this meant that suspicion was now pointing away from Jan? He wondered what would happen if he
tried to leave the house? Were they watching him?

'Further,' Mr Dalton went on, 'I want to announce publicly
that I apologize for his arrest and inconvenience.' Mr Dalton
paused, wet his lips with his tongue, and looked down over the
small knot of men whose hands were busy jotting his words
down upon their white pads of paper. 'And, gentlemen, I

want to announce that Miss Dalton, our daughter ... Miss
Dalton ...' Mr Dalton's voice faltered. Behind him, a little to
one side, stood Mrs Dalton; she placed her white hand upon his
arm. The men lifted their silver bulbs and again lightning
flashed in the red gloom of the basement. 'I – I want to
announce,' Mr Dalton said in a quiet voice that carried
throughout the room, though it was spoken in a tense whisper,
'that Miss Dalton has been kidnaped ...'

'Kidnaped?'

'Oh!'

'When?'

'We think it happened last night,' said Mr Dalton.

'What are they asking?'

'Ten thousand dollars.'

'Have you any idea who it is?'

'We know nothing.'

'Have you had any word from her, Mr Dalton?'

'No; not directly. But we've had a letter from the kidnapers ...'

'Is that it there?'

'Yes. This is the letter.'

'When did you get it?'

'Tonight.'

'Through the mail?'

'No; someone left it under our door.'

'Are you going to pay the ransom?'

'Yes,' said Mr Dalton. 'I'm going to pay. Listen, gentlemen,
you can help me and perhaps save my daughter's life by saying
in your stories that I'll pay as I've been instructed. And, too,
what's most important, tell the kidnapers through your papers
that I shall not call in the police. Tell them I'll do everything
they ask. Tell them to return our daughter. Tell them, for
God's sake, not to kill her, that they will get what they
want ...'

'Have you any idea, Mr Dalton, who they are?'

'I have not.'

'Can we see that letter?'

'I'm sorry, but you can't. The instructions for the delivery of the money are here, and I have been cautioned not to make them public. But say in your papers that these instructions will be followed.'

'When was Miss Dalton last seen?'

'Sunday morning, about two o'clock.'

'Who saw her?'

'My chauffeur and my wife.'

Bigger stared straight before him, not allowing his eyes to move.

'Please don't ask him any questions,' said Mr Dalton. 'I'm speaking for my whole family. I don't want a lot of crazy versions of this story going around. We want our daughter back; that's all that matters now. Tell her in the papers that we're doing all we can to get her back and that everything is forgiven. Tell her that we . . .' Again his voice broke and he could not go on.

'Please, Mr Dalton,' begged one man. 'Just let us take one shot of that note . . .'

'No; no . . . I can't do that.'

'How is it signed?'

Mr Dalton looked straight before him. Bigger wondered if he would tell. He saw Mr Dalton's lips moving silently, debating something.

'Yes; I'll tell you how it's signed,' said the old man, his hands trembling. Mrs Dalton's face turned slightly toward him and her fingers gripped in his coat. Bigger knew that Mrs Dalton was asking him silently if he had not better keep the signature of the note from the papers; and he knew, too, that Mr. Dalton seemed to have reasons of his own for wanting to tell. Maybe it was to let the reds know that he had received their note.

'Yes,' Mr Dalton said. 'It's signed "Red". That's all.'

'*Red?*'

'Yes.'

'Do you know the identity?'

'No.'

'Have you any suspicions?'

243

'Beneath the signature is a scrawled emblem of the Communist Party, the hammer and sickle,' said Mr Dalton.

The men were silent. Bigger saw the astonishment on their faces. Several did not wait to hear more; they rushed out of the basement to telephone their stories in.

'Do you think the Communists did it?'

'I don't know. I'm not positively blaming anybody. I'm only releasing this information to let the public and the kidnapers know that I've received this note. If they'll return my daughter, I'll ask no questions of anyone.'

'Was your daughter mixed up with those people, Mr Dalton?'

'I know nothing about that.'

'Didn't you forbid your daughter to associate with this Erlone?'

'I hope this has nothing to do with that.'

'You think Erlone's mixed in this?'

'I don't know.'

'Why did you have him released?'

'I ordered his arrest before I received this note.'

'Do you feel that maybe he'll return the girl if he's out?'

'I don't know. I don't know if he's got our daughter. I only know that Mrs Dalton and I want our daughter back.'

'Then why did you have Erlone released?'

'Because I have no charges to prefer against him,' said Mr Dalton stubbornly.

'Mr Dalton, hold the letter up, and hold your hand out, like you're making an appeal. Good! Now, put your hand out, too, Mrs Dalton. Like that. O.K., *hold* it!'

Bigger watched the silver bulbs flash again. Mr and Mrs Dalton were standing upon the steps: Mrs Dalton in white and Mr Dalton with the letter in his hand and his eyes looking straight back to the rear wall of the basement. Bigger heard the soft whisper of the fire in the furnace and saw the men adjusting their cameras. Others were standing round, still scribbling nervously upon their pads of paper. The bulbs flashed again and Bigger was startled to see that they were pointed in his direction. He wanted to duck his head, or throw his hands in front of his face, but it was too late. They had enough pictures of him now to know him by sight in a crowd. A few more of the men left and Mr and Mrs Dalton turned and walked slowly up the stairs and disappeared through the kitchen door, the big white cat following close behind them. Bigger still stood with his back to the wall, watching and trying to value every move in relation to himself and his chances of getting the money.

'You suppose we can use Mr Dalton's phone?' one of the men asked Britten.

'Sure.'

Britten led a group of them up the stairs into the kitchen. The three men who had come with Britten sat on the steps and stared gloomily at the floor. Soon the men who had gone to phone their stories in came back. Bigger knew that they wanted to talk to him, Britten also came back and sat upon the steps.

'Say, can't you give us any more dope on this?' one of the reporters asked Britten.

'Mr Dalton's told you everything,' Britten said.

'This is a big story,' said one of the men. 'Say, how did Mrs Dalton take this?'

'She collapsed,' said Britten.

For awhile nobody said anything. Then Bigger saw the men, one by one, turn and stare at him. He lowered his eyes; he knew that they were longing to ask him questions and he did not want that. His eyes roved the room and saw the crumpled copy of the newspaper lying forgotten in a corner. He wanted ever so badly to read it; he would get at it the first opportunity and find out just what Jan had said. Presently, the men began to wander aimlessly about the basement, looking into corners, examining the shovel, the garbage pail, and the trunk. Bigger watched one man stand in front of the furnace. The man's hand reached out and opened the door; a feeble red glare lit the man's face as he stooped and looked inside at the bed of smoldering coals. Suppose he poked deeply into them? Suppose Mary's bones came into view? Bigger held his breath. But the man would not poke into that fire; nobody suspected him. He was just a black clown. He breathed again as the man closed the door. The muscles of Bigger's face jerked violently, making him feel that he wanted to laugh. He turned his head aside and fought to control himself. He was full of hysteria.

'Say, how about a look at the girl's room?' asked one of the men.

'Sure. Why not?' Britten said.

All of the men followed Britten up the stairs and Bigger was left alone. At once his eyes went to the newspaper; he wanted to pick it up, but was afraid. He stepped to the back door and made sure that it was locked; then he went to the top of the stairs and looked hurriedly into the kitchen; he saw no one. He bounded down the steps and snatched up the paper. He opened it and saw a line of heavy black type stretched across the top of the front page: SEEK HYDE PARK HEIRESS MISSING FROM HOME SINCE SATURDAY. GIRL BELIEVED HIDING OUT WITH COMMUNISTS. POLICE NAB LOCAL RED LEADER; GRILLED ON RELATIONSHIP WITH MARY DALTON. AUTHORITIES ACT ON TIP SUPPLIED BY GIRL'S FATHER.

And there was the picture of Jan in the center of page one. It was Jan all right. Just like him. He turned to the story, reading,

Did the foolish dream of solving the problem of human misery and poverty by dividing her father's real estate millions among the lowly force Mary Dalton to leave the palatial Hyde Park home of her parents, Mr and Mrs Henry G. Dalton, 4605 Drexel Boulevard, and take up life under an assumed name with her long-haired friends in the Communist movement?

This was the question that police sought to answer late tonight as they grilled Jan Erlone, executive secretary of the Labor Defenders, a Communist 'front' organization in which it was said that Mary Dalton held a membership in defiance of her father's wishes.

The story went on to say that Jan was being held for investigation at the Eleventh Street Police Station and that Mary had been missing from her home since eight o'clock Saturday night. It also mentioned that Mary had been in the 'company of Erlone until early Sunday morning at a notorious South Side Café in the Black Belt.'

That was all. He had expected more. He looked further. No; here was something else. It was a picture of Mary. It was so lifelike that it reminded him of how she had looked the first time he had seen her; he blinked his eyes. He was looking again in sweaty fear at her head lying upon the sticky newspapers with blood oozing outward toward the edges. Above the picture was a caption: IN DUTCH WITH PA. Bigger lifted his eyes and looked at the furnace; it seemed impossible that she was there in the fire, burning . . . The story in the paper had not been as alarming as he had thought it would be. But as soon as they heard of Mary's being kidnaped, what would happen? He heard footsteps and dropped the paper back in the corner and stood just as he had before, his back against the wall, his eyes vacant and sleepy. The door opened and the men came down the steps, talking in low, excited tones. Again Bigger noticed that they were watching him. Britten also came back.

'Say, why can't we talk to this boy?' one demanded.

'There's nothing he can tell you,' Britten said.

'But he can tell us what he saw. After all, he drove the car last night.'

'O.K. with me,' Britten said. 'But Mr Dalton's told you everything.'

One of the men walked over to Bigger.

'Say, Mike, you think this Erlone fellow did this?'

'My name ain't Mike,' Bigger said, resentfully.

'Oh, I don't mean no harm,' the man said. 'But do you think he did it?'

'Answer his questions, Bigger,' Britten said.

Bigger was sorry he had taken offense. He could not afford to get angry now. And he had no need to be angry. Why should he be angry with a lot of fools? They were looking for the girl and the girl was ten feet from them, burning. He had killed her and they did not know it. He would let them call him 'Mike'.

'I don't know, suh,' he said.

'Come on; tell us what happened.'

'I only work here, suh,' Bigger said.

'Don't be afraid. Nobody's going to hurt you.'

'Mr Britten can tell you,' Bigger said.

The men shook their heads and walked away.

'Good God, Britten!' said one of the men. 'All we've got on this kidnaping is that a letter was found, Erlone's to be released, the letter was signed by 'Red', and there was a hammer and sickle emblem on it. That doesn't make sense. Give us some more details.'

'Listen, you guys,' Britten said. 'Give the old man a chance. He's trying to get his daughter back, alive. He's given you a big story; now wait.'

'Tell us straight now; when was that girl last seen?'

Bigger listened to Britten tell the story all over again. He listened carefully to every word Britten said and to the tone of voice in which the men asked their questions, for he wanted to know if any of them suspected him. But they did not. All of their questions pointed to Jan.

'But Britten,' asked one of the men, 'why did the old man want this Erlone released?'

'Figure it out for yourself,' Britten said.

'Then he thinks Erlone had something to do with the snatching of his daughter and wanted him out so he could give her back?'

'I don't know,' Britten said.

'Aw, come on, Britten.'

'Use your imagination,' Britten said.

Two more of the men buttoned their coats, pulled their hats low over their eyes and left. Bigger knew that they were going to phone in more information to their papers; they were going to tell about Jan's trying to convert him to communism, the Communist literature Jan had given him, the rum, the half-packed trunk being taken down to the station, and lastly, about the kidnap note and the demand for ten thousand dollars. The men looked round the basement with flashlights. Bigger still leaned against the wall. Britten sat on the steps. The fire whispered in the furnace. Bigger knew that soon he would have to clean the ashes out, for the fire was not burning as hotly as it should. He would do that as soon as some of the excitement died down and all of the men left.

'It's pretty bad, hunh, Bigger?' Britten asked.

'Yessuh.'

'I'd bet a million dollars that this is Jan's smart idea.'

Bigger said nothing. He was limp all over; he was standing up here against this wall by some strength not his own. Hours past he had given up trying to exert himself any more; he could no longer call up any energy. So he just forgot it and found himself coasting along.

It was getting a little chilly; the fire was dying. The draft could scarcely be heard. Then the basement door burst open suddenly and one of the men who had gone to telephone came in, his mouth open, his face wet and red from the snow.

'Say!' he called.

'Yeah?'

'What is it?'

'My city editor just told me that that Erlone fellow won't leave jail.'

For a moment the strangeness of the news made them all stare silently. Bigger roused himself and tried to make out just what it meant. Then someone asked the question he longed to ask.

'Won't leave? What you mean?'

'Well, this Erlone refused to go when they told him that Mr Dalton had requested his release. It seems he had got wind of the kidnaping and said that he didn't want to go out.'

'That means he's guilty!' said Britten. 'He doesn't want to leave jail because he knows they'll shadow him and find out where the girl is, see? He's *scared*.'

'What else?'

'Well, this Erlone says he's got a dozen people to swear that he did not come here last night.'

Bigger's body stiffened and he leaned forward slightly.

'That's a lie!' Britten said. 'This boy here saw him.'

'Is that right, boy?'

Bigger hesitated. He suspected a trap. But if Jan really had an alibi, then he had to talk; he had to steer them away from himself.

'Yessuh.'

'Well, somebody's lying. That Erlone fellow says that he can prove it.'

'Prove hell!' Britten said. 'He's just got some of his red friends to lie for him; that's all.'

'But what in hell's the good of his not wanting to leave jail?' asked one of the men.

'He says if he stays in they can't possibly say he's mixed up in this kidnaping business. He said this boy's lying. He claims they told him to say these things in order to blacken his name and reputation. He swears the family knows where the girl is and that this thing is a stunt to raise a cry against the reds.'

The men gathered round Bigger.

'Say, boy, come on with the dope now. Was that guy really here last night?'

'Yessuh; he was here all right.'

'You *saw* 'im?'

'Yessuh.'

'Where?'

'I drove him and Miss Dalton up here in the car. We went upstairs together to get the trunk.'

'And you *left* him here?'

'Yessuh.'

Bigger's heart was pounding, but he tried to keep his face and voice under control. He did not want to seem unduly excited over these new developments. He was wondering if Jan could really prove that he had not been here last night; and he was thinking the question in his own mind when he heard someone ask,

'Who has this Erlone got to prove he was not here last night?'

'He says he met some friend of his when he got on the street car last night. And he says he went to a party after he left Miss Dalton at two-thirty.'

'Where was the party?'

'Somewhere on the North Side.'

'Say, if what he says is true, then there's something fishy here.'

'Naw,' said Britten. 'I'll bet he went to his pals, the ones he planned all of this with. Sure; why wouldn't they alibi for 'im?'

'So *you* really think he did it?'

'Hell yes!' Britten said. 'These reds'll do anything and they stick together. Sure; he's got an alibi. Why shouldn't he have one? He's got enough pals working for 'im. His wanting to stay in jail's nothing but a dodge, but he's not so smart. He thinks that his gag'll work and leave him free of suspicion, but it won't.'

The talk stopped abruptly as the door at the head of the stairs opened. Peggy's head came through.

'You gentlemen want some coffee?' she asked.

'Sure!'

'Atta gal!'

'I'll bring some down in just a minute,' she said, closing the door.

'Who is she?'

'Mrs Dalton's cook and housekeeper,' Britten said.

'She know anything about all this?'

'Naw.'

Again the men turned to Bigger. He felt this time he had to say something more to them. Jan was saying that he was lying and he had to wipe out doubt in their minds. They would think that he knew more than he was telling if he did not talk. After all, their attitude toward him so far made him feel that they did not consider him as being mixed up in the kidnaping. He was just another black ignorant Negro to them. The main thing was to keep their minds turned in another direction, Jan's direction, or that of Jan's friend.

'Say,' one of the men asked, coming close to him and placing a foot upon the edge of the trunk. 'Did this Erlone fellow talk to you about communism?'

'Yessuh.'

'Oh!' Britten exclaimed.

'What?'

'I forgot! Let me show you fellows the stuff he gave the boy to read.'

Britten stood up, his face flushed with eagerness. He ran his hand into his pocket and pulled forth the batch of pamphlets that Jan had given Bigger and held them up for all to see. The men again got their bulbs and flashed their lightning to take pictures of the pamphlets. Bigger could hear their hard breathing; he knew that they were excited. When they finished, they turned to him again.

'Say, boy, was this guy drunk?'

'Yessuh.'

'And the girl, too?'

'Yessuh.'

'He took the girl upstairs when they got here?'

'Yessuh.'

'Say, boy, what do you think of public ownership? Do you think the government ought to build houses for people to live in?'

Bigger blinked.

'Suh?'

'Well, what do you think of private property?'

'I don't own any property. Nawsuh,' Bigger said.

'Aw, he's a dumb cluck. He doesn't know anything,' one of the men whispered in a voice loud enough for Bigger to hear.

There was a silence. Bigger leaned against the wall, hoping that this would satisfy them for a time, at least. The draft could not be heard in the furnace now at all. The door opened again and Peggy came into view carrying a pot of coffee in one hand and a folding card table in the other. One of the men went up the steps and met her, took the table, opened it, and placed it for her. She set the pot upon it. Bigger saw a thin spout of steam jutting from the pot and smelt the good scent of coffee. He wanted some, but he knew that he should not ask with the white men waiting to drink.

'Thank you, sirs,' Peggy mumbled, looking humbly round at the strange faces of the men. 'I'll get the sugar and cream and some cups.'

'Say, boy,' Britten said. 'Tell the men how Jan made you eat with 'im.'

'Yeah; tell us about it.'

'Is it true?'

'Yessuh.'

'You didn't want to eat with 'im, did you?'

'Nawsuh.'

'Did you ever eat with white people before?'

'Nawsuh.'

'Did this guy Erlone say anything to you about white women?'

'Oh, nawsuh.'

'How did you feel, eating with him and Miss Dalton?'

'I don't know, suh. It was my job.'

'You didn't feel just right, did you?'

'Well, suh. They told me to eat and I ate. It was my job.'

'In other words, you felt you had to eat or lose your job?'

'Yessuh,' said Bigger, feeling that this ought to place him in the light of a helpless, bewildered man.

'Good God!' said one of the men. 'What a story! Don't you see it? These Negroes want to be left alone and these reds are forcing 'em to live with 'em, see? Every wire in the country'll carry it!'

'This is better than Loeb and Leopold,' said one.

'Say, I'm slanting this to the primitive Negro who doesn't want to be disturbed by white civilization.'

'A swell idea!'

'Say, is this Erlone really a citizen?'

'That's an angle.'

'Mention his foreign-sounding name.'

'Is he Jewish?'

'I don't know.'

'This is good enough as it is. You can't have everything you want.'

'It's classic!'

'It's a natural!'

Then, before Bigger knew it, the men had their bulbs in their hands again, aiming at him. He hung his head slowly, slowly so as not to let them know that he was trying to dodge them.

'Hold up a little, boy!'

'Stand straight!'

'Look over this way. Now, that's it!'

Yes; the police would certainly have enough pictures of him. He thought it rather bitterly, smiling a smile that did not reach his lips or eyes.

Peggy came back with her arms full of cups, saucers, spoons, a jar of cream and a bowl of sugar.

'Here it is, sirs. Help yourselves.'

She turned to Bigger.

'There's not enough heat upstairs. You'd better clean those ashes out and make a better fire.'

'Yessum.'

Clean the fire out! Good God! Not now, not with the men standing round. He did not move from his place beside the wall; he watched Peggy walk back up the stairs and close the door behind her. Well, he had to do something. Peggy had spoken to him in the presence of these men, and for him not to obey would seem odd. And even if they did not say anything about it, Peggy herself would soon come back and ask about the fire. Yes, he had to do something. He walked to the door of the furnace and opened it. The low bed of fire was red-hot, but he could tell from the weak blast of heat upon his face that it was not as hot as it ought to be, not as hot as it had been when he had shoved Mary in. He was trying to make his tired brain work fast. What could he do to avoid bothering with the ashes? He stooped and opened the lower door; the ashes, white and gray, were piled almost level with the lower grate. No air could get through. Maybe he could sift the ashes down more and make that do until the men left? He would try it. He caught hold of the handle and worked it to and fro, seeing white ashes and red embers falling into the bottom of the furnace. Behind him he could hear the men's talk and the tinkle of their spoons against the cups. Well, there. He had gotten some of the ashes down out of the stove, but they choked the lower bin and still

no air could get through. He would put some coal in. He shut
the doors of the furnace and pulled the lever for coal; there was
the same loud rattle of coal against the tin sides of the chute.
The interior of the furnace grew black with coal. But the draft
did not roar and the coal did not blaze. Goddamn! He stood up
and looked helplessly into the furnace. Ought he to try to slip
out of here and leave this whole foolish thing right now? Naw!
There was no use of being scared; he had a chance to get that
money. Put more coal in; it would burn after a while. He
pulled the lever for still more coal. Inside the furnace he saw the
coal beginning to smoke; there were faint wisps of white smoke
at first, then the smoke drew dark, bulging out. Bigger's eyes
smarted, watered; he coughed.

The smoke was rolling from the furnace now in heavy billowing gray clouds, filling the basement. Bigger backed away,
catching a lungful of smoke. He bent over, coughing. He heard
the men coughing. He had to do something about those ashes,
and quickly. With his hands stretched before him, he groped in
the corner for the shovel, found it, and opened the lower door
of the furnace. The smoke surged out, thick and acrid. Goddamn!

'You'd better do something about those ashes, boy!' one of
the men called.

'That fire can't get any air, Bigger!' It was Britten's voice.

'Yessuh,' Bigger mumbled.

He could scarcely see. He stood still, his eyes closed and stinging, his lungs heaving, trying to expel the smoke. He held onto
the shovel, wanting to move, to do something; but he did not
know what.

'Say, you! Get some of those ashes out of there!'

'What're you trying to do, smother us?'

'I'm getting 'em out,' Bigger mumbled, not moving from
where he stood.

He heard a cup smash on the concrete floor and a man
cursed.

'I can't see! The smoke's got my eyes!'

Bigger heard someone near him; then someone was tugging

at the shovel in his hands. He held onto it desperately, not wanting to let it go, feeling that if he did so he was surrendering his secret, his life.

'Here! Give me that shovel! I'll h-h-help y-you ...' a man coughed.

'Nawsuh. I-I-I can d-do it,' Bigger said.

'C-come on. L-let go!'

His fingers loosened about the shovel.

'Yessuh,' he said, not knowing what else to say.

Through the clouds of smoke he heard the man clanging the shovel round inside the ash bin. He coughed and stepped back, his eyes blazing as though fire had leaped into them. Behind him the other men were coughing. He opened his eyes and strained to see what was happening. He felt that there was suspended just above his head a huge weight that would soon fall and crush him. His body, despite the smoke and his burning eyes and heaving chest, was flexed taut. He wanted to lunge at the man and take the shovel from him, lam him across the head with it and bolt from the basement. But he stood still, hearing the babble of voices and the clanging of the shovel against iron. He knew that the man was digging frantically at the ashes in the bin, trying to clean as much out as possible so that air could pass up through the grates, pipes, chimney and out into the night. He heard the man yell:

'Open that door! I'm choking!'

There was a scuffle of feet. Bigger felt the icy wind of the night sweep over him and he discovered that he was wet with sweat. Somehow something had happened and now things were out of his hands. He was nervously poised, waiting for what the new flow of events would bring. The smoke drifted past him toward the open door. The room was clearing; the smoke thinned to a gray pall. He heard the man grunting and saw him bent over, digging at the ashes in the bin. He wanted to go to him and ask him for the shovel; he wanted to say that he could take care of it now. But he did not move. He felt that he had let things slip through his hands to such an extent that he could not get at them again. Then he heard the draft, this time a long low sucking of air that grew gradually to a drone, then a roar. The air passage was clear.

'There was a hell of a lot of ashes in there, boy,' the man gasped. 'You shouldn't let it get that way.'

'Yessuh,' Bigger whispered.

The draft roared loud now; the air passage was completely clear.

'Shut that door, boy! It's cold in here!' one of the men called.

He wanted to go to the door and keep right on out of it and shut it behind him. But he did not move. One of the men closed it and Bigger felt the cold air fall away from his wet body. He looked round; the men were still standing about the table, red-eyed, sipping coffee.

'What's the matter, boy?' one of them asked.

'Nothing,' Bigger said.

The man with the shovel stood in front of the furnace and looked down into the ashes strewn over the floor. What's he doing? Bigger wondered. He saw the man stoop and poke the shovel into the ashes. *What's he looking at?* Bigger's muscles twitched. He wanted to run to the man's side and see what it was he was looking at; he had in his mind an image of Mary's head lying there bloody and unburnt before the man's eyes. Suddenly, the man straightened, only to stoop again, as though unable to decide if the evidence of his eyes was true. Bigger edged forward, his lungs not taking in or letting out air; he himself was a huge furnace now through which no air could go; and the fear that surged into his stomach, filling him, choking him, was like the fumes of smoke that had belched from the ash bin.

'Say . . .' the man called; his voice sounded tentative, dubious.

'What?' one man at the tabled answered.

'Come here! Look!' The man's voice was low, excited, tense; but what it lacked in volume was more than made up for in the breathless manner in which he spoke. The words had rolled without effort from his lips.

The men set their cups down and ran to the pile of ashes. Bigger, doubtful and uncertain, paused as the men ran past him.

'What is it?'

'What's the matter?'

Bigger tiptoed and looked over their shoulders; he did not know how he got strength enough to go and look; he just found himself standing and peering over the men's shoulders. He saw a pile of scattered ashes, nothing else. But there must be something, or why would the men be looking?

'What is it?'

'See? *This!*'

'What?'

'Look! It's ...'

The man's voice trailed off and he stooped again and poked the shovel deeper. Bigger saw come into full view on the surface of the ashes several small pieces of white bone. Instantly, his whole body was wrapped in a sheet of fear. Yes; he should have cleaned those ashes out; but he had been too excited and scared; he had trapped himself. Now, he must leave; they must not catch him ... With the rush of lightning, these thoughts flashed through his mind, leaving him weak and helpless.

'It's bone ...'

'Aw,' one of the men said. 'That's just some garbage they're burning ...'

'Naw! Wait; let's *see* that!'

'Toorman, come here. You studied medicine once ...'

The man called Toorman reached out his foot and kicked an oblong bone from the ashes; it slid a few inches over the concrete floor.

'My God! It's from a *body* ...'

'And look! Here's something ...'

One of them stooped and picked up a bit of round metal and held it close to his eyes.

'It's an earring ...'

There was silence. Bigger stared without a thought or an image in his mind. There was just the old feeling, the feeling that he had had all his life; he was black and had done wrong; white men were looking at something with which they would soon accuse him. It was the old feeling, hard and constant again

258

now, of wanting to grab something and clutch it in his hands and swing it into someone's face. He knew. They were looking at the bones of Mary's body. Without its making a clear picture in his mind, he understood how it had happened. Some of the bones had not burnt and had fallen into the lower bin when he had worked the handle to sift the ashes. The white man had poked in the shovel to clear the air passage and had raked them out. And now there they lay, tiny, oblong pieces of white bone, cushioned in gray ashes. He could not stay here now. At any moment they would begin to suspect him. They would hold him; they would not let him go even if they were not certain whether he had done it or not. And Jan was still in jail, swearing that he had an alibi. They would know that Mary was dead; they had stumbled upon the white bones of her body. They would be looking for the murderer. The men were silent, bent over, poking into the pile of gray ashes. Bigger saw the hatchet blade come into view. God! The whole world was tumbling down. Quickly, Bigger's eyes looked at their bent backs; they were not watching him. The red glare of the fire lit their faces and the draft of the furnace drummed. Yes; he would go, now! He tiptoed to the rear of the furnace and stopped, listening. The men were whispering in tense tones of horror.

'It's the girl!'

'Good God!'

'Who do you suppose did it?'

Bigger tiptoed up the steps, one at a time, hoping that the roar of the furnace and the men's voices and the scraping of the shovel would drown out the creaking sounds his feet made. He reached the top of the steps and breathed deeply, his lungs aching from holding themselves full of air so long. He stole to the door of his room and opened it and went in and pulled on the light. He turned to the window and put his hands under the upper ledge and lifted; he felt a cold rush of air laden with snow. He heard muffled shouts downstairs and the inside of his stomach glowed white-hot. He ran to the door and locked it and then turned out the light. He groped to the window and climbed into it, feeling again the chilling blast of snowy wind. With his feet upon the bottom ledge, his legs bent under him, his sweaty body shaken by wind, he looked into the snow and tried to see the ground below; but he could not. Then he leaped, headlong, sensing his body twisting in the icy air as he hurtled. His eyes were shut and his hands were clenched as his body turned, sailing through the snow. He was in the air a moment; then he hit. It seemed at first that he hit softly, but the shock of it went through him, up his back to his head and he lay buried in a cold pile of snow, dazed. Snow was in his mouth, eyes, ears; snow was seeping down his back. His hands were wet and cold. Then he felt all of the muscles of his body contract violently, caught in a spasm of reflex action, and at the same time he felt his groin laved with warm water. It was his urine. He had not been able to control the muscles of his hot body against the chilled assault of the wet snow over all his skin. He lifted his head, blinking his eyes, and looked above him. He sneezed. He was himself now; he struggled against the snow, pushing it away from him. He got to his feet, one at a time, and pulled himself out. He walked, then tried to run; but he felt too weak. He went down Drexel Boulevard, not knowing just where he was heading, but knowing that he had to get out of this white neighborhood. He avoided the car line, turned down dark streets, walking more rapidly now, his eyes before him, but turning now and then to look behind.

Yes, he would have to tell Bessie not to go to that house. It was all over. He had to save himself. But it was familiar, this running away. All his life he had been knowing that sooner or later something like this would come to him. And now, here it was. He had always felt outside of this white world, and now it was true. It made things simple. He felt in his shirt. Yes; the gun was still there. He might have to use it. He would shoot before he would let them take him; it meant death either way, and he would die shooting every slug he had.

He came to Cottage Grove Avenue and walked southward. He could not make any plans until he got to Bessie's and got the money. He tried to shut out of his mind the fear of being caught. He lowered his head against the driving snow and tramped through the icy streets with clenched fists. Although his hands were almost frozen, he did not want to put them in his pockets, for that would have made him feel that he would not have been ready to defend himself were the police to accost him suddenly. He went on past street lamps covered with thick coatings of snow, gleaming like huge frosted moons above his head. His face ached from the sub-zero cold and the wind cut into his wet body like a long sharp knife going to the heart of him with pain.

He was in sight of Forty-seventh Street now. He saw, through a gauzelike curtain of snow, a boy standing under an awning selling papers. He pulled his cap visor lower and slipped into a doorway to wait for a car. Back of the newsboy was a stack of papers piled high upon a newsstand. He wanted to see the tall black headline, but the driving snow would not let him. The papers ought to be full of him now. It did not seem strange that they should be, for all his life he had felt that things had been happening to him that should have gone into them. But only after he had acted upon feelings which he had had for years would the papers carry the story, *his* story. He felt that they had not wanted to print it as long as it had remained buried and burning in his own heart. But now that he had thrown it out, thrown it at those who made him live as they wanted, the papers were printing it. He fished two cents out of his pocket; he went over to the boy with averted face.

'*Tribune.*'

He took the paper into a doorway. His eyes swept the streets above the top of it; then he read in tall black type: MILLIONAIRE HEIRESS KIDNAPED. ABDUCTORS DEMAND $10,000 IN RANSOM NOTE. DALTON FAMILY ASK RELEASE OF COMMUNIST SUSPECT. Yes; they had it now. Soon they would have the story of her death, of the reporters' finding her bones in the furnace, of her head being cut off, of his running away during the excitement. He looked up, hearing the approach of a car. When it heaved into sight he saw it was almost empty of passengers. Good! He ran into the street and reached the steps just as the last man got on. He paid his fare, watching to see if the conductor was noticing him; then went through the car, watching to see if any face was turned to him. He stood on the front platform, back of the motorman. If anything happened he could get off quickly here. The car started and he opened the paper again, reading:

A servant's discovery early yesterday evening of a crudely penciled ransom note demanding $10,000 for the return of Mary Dalton, missing Chicago heiress, and the Dalton family's sudden demand for the release of Jan Erlone, Communist leader held in connection with the girl's disappearance, were the startling developments in a case which is baffling local and state police.

The note, bearing the signature of 'Red' and the famed hammer and sickle emblem of the Communist Party, was found sticking under the front door by Peggy O'Flagherty, a cook and housekeeper in the Henry Dalton residence in Hyde Park.

Bigger read a long stretch of type in which was described the 'questioning of a Negro chauffeur', 'the half-packed trunk', 'the Communist pamphlets', 'drunken sexual orgies', 'the frantic parents', and 'the radical's contradictory story'. Bigger's eyes skimmed the words: 'clandestine meetings offered opportunities for abduction', 'police asked not to interfere in case', 'anxious family trying to contact kidnapers'; and:

It was conjectured that perhaps the family had information to the effect that Erlone knew of the whereabouts of Miss Dalton, and certain police officials assigned that as the motive behind the family's request for the radical's release.

Reiterating that police had framed him as part of a drive to oust Communists from Chicago, Erlone demanded that the charges upon which he had been originally held be made public. Failing to obtain a satisfactory answer, he refused to leave jail, whereupon police again remanded him to his cell upon a charge of disorderly conduct.

Bigger lifted his eyes and looked about; no one was watching him. His hand was shaking with excitement. The car moved lumberingly through the snow and he saw that he was near Fiftieth Street. He stepped to the door and said,

'Out.'

The car stopped and he swung off into the driving snow. He was almost in front of Bessie's now. He looked up to her window; it was dark. The thought that she might not be in her room, but out drinking with friends, made him angry. He went into the vestibule. A dim light glowed and his body was thankful for the meager warmth. He could finish reading the paper now. He unfolded it; then, for the first time, he saw his picture. It was down in the lower left-hand corner of page two. Above it he read: REDS TRIED TO SNARE HIM. It was a small picture and his name was under it; he looked solemn and black and his eyes gazed straight and the white cat sat perched upon his right shoulder, its big round black eyes twin pools of secret guilt. And, oh! Here was a picture of Mr and Mrs Dalton standing upon the basement steps. That the image of Mr and Mrs Dalton which he had seen but two hours ago should be seen again so soon made him feel that this whole vague white world which could do things this quickly was more than a match for him, that soon it would track him down and have it out with him. The white-haired old man and the white-haired old woman standing on the steps with their arms stretched forth pleading were a powerful symbol of helpless suffering and would stir up a lot of hate against him when it was found out that a Negro had killed Mary.

Bigger's lips tightened. There was no chance of his getting that money now. They had found Mary and would stop at nothing to get the one who had killed her. There would be a thousand white policeman on the South Side searching for him or any black man who looked like him.

He pressed the bell and waited for the buzzer to ring. Was she there? Again he pressed the bell, holding his finger hard upon it until the door buzzed. He bounded up the steps, sucking his breath in sharply at each lift of his knees. When he reached the second landing he was breathing so hard that he stopped, closed his eyes and let his chest heave itself to stillness. He glanced up and saw Bessie staring sleepily at him through the half-opened door. He went in and stood for a moment in the darkness.

'Turn on the light,' he said.

'Bigger! What's happened?'

'Turn on the light!'

She said nothing and did not move. He groped forward, sweeping the air with his open palm for the cord; he found it and jerked on the light. Then he whirled and looked about him, expecting to see someone lurking in the corners of the room.

'What's happened?' she came forward and touched his clothes. 'You're wet.'

'It's all off,' he said.

'I don't have to do it?' she asked eagerly.

Yes; she was thinking only of herself now. He was alone.

'Bigger, tell me what happened?'

'They know all about it. They'll be after me soon.'

Her eyes were too filled with fear to cry. He walked about aimlessly and his shoes left rings of dirty water on the wooden floor.

'Tell me, Bigger! Please!'

She was wanting the word that would free her of this nightmare; but he would not give it to her. No; let her be with him; let somebody be with him now. She caught hold of his coat and he felt her body trembling.

'Will they come for me, too, Bigger? I didn't want to do it!'

Yes, he would let her know, let her know everything; but let her know it in a way that would bind her to him, at least a little longer. He did not want to be alone now.

'They found the girl,' he said.

'What we going to do, Bigger? Look what you done to me . . .'

She began to cry.

'Aw, come on, kid.'

'You *really* killed her?'

'She's dead,' he said. 'They found her.'

She ran to the bed, fell upon it and sobbed. With her mouth all twisted and her eyes wet, she asked in gasps:

'Y-y-you d-didn't send the l-letter?'

'Yeah.'

'Bigger,' she whimpered.

'There ain't no help for it now.'

'Oh, Lord! They'll come for me. They'll know you did it and they'll go to your home and talk to your ma and brother and everybody. They'll come for me now sure.'

That was true. There was no way for her but to come with him. If she stayed here they would come to her and she would simply lie on the bed and sob out everything. She would not be able to help it. And what she would tell them about him, his habits, his life, would help them to track him down.

'You got the money?'

'It's in my dress pocket.'

'How much is it?'

'Ninety dollars.'

'Well, what you planning to do?' he asked.

'I wish I could kill myself.'

'Ain't no use talking that way.'

'There ain't no way else to talk.'

It was a shot in the dark, but he decided to try it.

'If you don't act better'n this, I'll just leave.'

'Naw; naw . . . Bigger!' she cried, rising and running to him.

'Well, snap out of it,' he said, backing to a chair. He sat down and felt how tired he was. Some strength he did not know he possessed had enabled him to run away, to stand here and talk with her; but now he felt that he would not have strength enough to run even if the police should suddenly burst into the room.

'You h-hurt?' she asked, catching hold of his shoulder.

He leaned forward in the chair and rested his face in the palms of his hands.

'Bigger, what's the matter?'

'I'm tired and awful sleepy,' he sighed.

'Let me fix you something to eat.'

'I need a drink.'

'Naw; no whiskey. You need some hot milk.'

He waited, hearing her move about. It seemed that his body

had turned to a piece of lead that was cold and heavy and wet and aching. Bessie switched on her electric stove, emptied a bottle of milk into a pan and set it upon the glowing red circle. She came back to him and placed her hands upon his shoulders, her eyes wet with fresh tears.

'I'm scared, Bigger.'

'You can't be scared now.'

'You oughtn't've killed her, honey.'

'I didn't mean to, I couldn't help it. I swear!'

'What happened? You never told me.'

'Aw, hell. I was in her room . . .'

'*Her* room?'

'Yeah. She was drunk. She passed out. I . . . I took her there.'

'What she do?'

'She . . . Nothing. She didn't do anything. Her ma came in. She's blind . . .'

'The girl?'

'Naw; her ma. I didn't want her to find me there. Well, the girl was trying to say something and I was scared. I just put the edge of the pillow in her mouth and . . . I didn't mean to kill her. I just pulled the pillow over her face and she died. Her ma came into the room and the girl was trying to say something and her ma had her hands stretched out, like this, see? I was scared she was going to touch me. I just sort of pushed the pillow hard over the girl's face to keep her from yelling. Her ma didn't touch me; I got out of the way. But when she left I went to the bed and the girl . . . She . . . She was dead . . . That was all. She was dead . . . I didn't mean . . .'

'You didn't plan to kill her?'

'Naw; I swear I didn't. But what's the use? Nobody'll believe me.'

'Honey. Don't you see?'

'What?'

'They'll say . . .'

Bessie cried again. He caught her face in his hands. He was concerned; he wanted to see this thing through her eyes at that moment.

'What?'

'They'll . . . They'll say you raped her.'

Bigger stared. He had entirely forgotten the moment when he had carried Mary up the stairs. So deeply had he pushed it all back down into him that it was not until now that its real meaning came back. They would say he had raped her and there would be no way to prove that he had not. That fact had not assumed importance in his eyes until now. He stood up, his jaws hardening. He he raped her? Yes, he had raped her. Every time he felt as he had felt that night, he raped. But rape was not what one did to women. Rape was what one felt when one's back was against a wall and one had to strike out, whether one wanted to or not, to keep the pack from killing one. He committed rape every time he looked into a white face. He was a long, taut piece of rubber which a thousand white hands had stretched to the snapping point, and when he snapped it was rape. But it was rape when he cried out in hate deep in his heart as he felt the strain of living day by day. That, too, was rape.

'They found her?' Bessie asked.

'Hunh?'

'They found her?'

'Yeah. Her bones . . .'

'*Bones?*'

'Aw, Bessie. I didn't know what to do. I put her in the furnace.'

Bessie flung her face to his wet coat and wailed violently.

'Bigger !'

'Hunh?'

'What we going to do?'

'I don't know.'

'They'll be looking for us.'

'They got my picture.'

'Where can we hide?'

'We can stay in some of them old houses for awhile.'

'But they might find us there.'

'There's plenty of 'em. It'll be like hiding in a jungle.'

The milk on the stove boiled over. Bessie rose, her lips still twisted with sobs, and turned off the electric switch. She poured out a glass of milk and brought it to him. He sipped it, slowly, then set the glass aside and leaned over again. They were silent. Bessie gave him the glass once more and he drank it down, then another glass. He stood up, his legs and entire body feeling heavy and sleepy.

'Get your clothes on. And get them blankets and quilts. We got to get out of here.'

She went to the bed and rolled the covers back, rolling the pillows with them; as she worked Bigger went to her and put his hands on her shoulders.

'Where's the bottle?'

She got it from her purse and gave it to him; he drank a long swallow and she put it back.

'Hurry up,' he said.

She sobbed softly as she worked, pausing now and then to wipe tears from her eyes. Bigger stood in the middle of the floor, thinking, Maybe they searching at home now; maybe they talking to Ma and Vera and Buddy. He crossed the floor and twitched back the curtains and looked out. The streets were white and empty. He turned and saw Bessie bent motionless over the pile of bedclothing.

'Come on; we got to get out of here.'

'I don't care what happens.'

'Come on. You can't act like that.'

What could he do with her? She would be a dangerous burden. It would be impossible to take her if she were going to act like this, and yet he could not leave her here. Coldly, he knew that he had to take her with him, and then at some future time settle things with her, settle them in a way that would not leave him in any danger. He thought of it calmly, as if the decision were being handed down to him by some logic not his own, over which he had no control, but which he had to obey.

'You want me to leave you here?'

'Naw; naw ... *Bigger!*'

'Well, come on. Get your hat and coat.'

She was facing him, then she sank to her knees.

'Oh, Lord,' she moaned. 'What's the use of running? They'll catch us anywhere. I should've known this would happen.' She clenched her hands in front of her and rocked to and fro with her eyes closed upon gushing tears. 'All my life's been full of hard trouble. If I wasn't hungry, I was sick. And if I wasn't sick, I was in trouble. I ain't never bothered nobody. I just worked hard every day as long as I can remember, till I was tired enough to drop; then I had to get drunk to forget it. I had to get drunk to sleep. That's all I ever did. And now I'm in this. They looking for me and when they catch me they'll kill me.' She bent her head to the floor. 'God only knows why I ever let you treat me this way. I wish to God I never seen you. I wish one of us had died before we was born. God knows I do! All you ever caused me was trouble, just plain black trouble. All you ever did since we been knowing each other was to get me drunk so's you could have me. That was all! I see it now. I ain't drunk now. I see everything you ever did to me. I didn't want to see it before. I was too busy thinking about how good I felt when I was with you. I thought I was happy, but deep down in me I knew I wasn't. But you got me into this murder and I see it all now. I been a fool, just a blind dumb black drunk fool. Now I got to run away and I know deep down in your heart you really don't care.'

She stopped, choked. He had not listened to what she had said. Her words had made leap to consciousness in him a thousand details of her life which he had long known and they made him see that she was in no condition to be taken along and at the same time in no condition to be left behind. It was not with anger or regret that he thought this, but as a man seeing what he must do to save himself and feeling resolved to do it.

'Come on, Bessie. We can't stay here like this.'

He stooped and with one hand caught hold of her arm and with the other he lifted the bundle of bedclothes. He dragged her across the threshold, and pulled the door after him. He went down the steps; she came stumbling behind, whimpering. When he reached the vestibule, he got his gun from inside his shirt and put it in the pocket of his coat. He might have to use it any minute now. The moment he stepped out of that door he would have his life in his hands. Whatever happened now depended upon him; and when he felt it that way some of his fear left; it was simple again. He opened the door and an icy blast of wind struck his face. He drew back and turned to Bessie.

'Where's the bottle?'

She held out her purse; he got the bottle and took a deep drink.

'Here,' he said. 'You better take one.'

She drank and put the bottle back into the purse. They went into the snow, over the frozen streets, through the sweeping wind. Once she stopped and began to cry. He grabbed her arm.

'Shut up, now! Come on!'

They stopped in front of a tall, snow-covered building whose many windows gaped blackly, like the eye-sockets of empty skulls. He took the purse from her and got the flashlight. He clutched her arm and pulled her up the steps to the front door. It was half-ajar. He put his shoulder to it and gave a stout shove; it yielded grudgingly. It was black inside and the feeble glow of the flashlight did not help much. A sharp scent of rot floated to him and he heard the scurrying of quick, dry feet over the wooden floor. Bessie sucked in her breath deeply, about to scream; but Bigger gripped her arm so hard that she bent halfway over and moaned. As he went up the steps there came frequently to his ears a slight creak, as of a tree bending in wind. With one hand he held her wrist, the bundle of bed-clothes under his arm; with the other he beat off the clinging filmy spider webs that came thick onto his lips and eyes. He walked to the third floor and into a room that had a window opening to a narrow airshaft. It stank of old timber. He circled the spot of the flashlight; the floor was carpeted with black dirt and he saw two bricks lying in corners. He looked at Bessie; her hands covered her face and he could see the damp of tears on her black fingers. He dropped the bundle of bedclothes.

'Unroll 'em and spread 'em out.'

She obeyed. He placed the two pillows near the window, so that when he lay down the window would be just above his head. He was so cold that his teeth chattered. Bessie stood by a wall, leaning against it, crying.

'Take it easy,' he said.

He hoisted the window and looked up the air-shaft; snow flew above the roof of the house. He looked downward and saw nothing but black darkness into which now and then a few flakes of white floated from the sky, falling slowly in the dim glow of the flashlight. He lowered the window and turned back to Bessie; she had not moved. He crossed the floor and took the purse from her and got the half-filled flask and drained it. It was good. It burned in his stomach and took his mind off the cold and the sound of the wind outside. He sat on the edge of the pallet and lit a cigarette. It was the first one he had smoked in a long time; he sucked the hot smoke deep into his lungs and blew it out slowly. The whiskey heated him all over, making his head whirl. Bessie cried, softly, piteously.

'Come on and lay down,' he said.

He took the gun from his coat pocket and put it where he could reach it.

'Come on, Bessie. You'll freeze standing there like that.'

He stood up and pulled off his overcoat and spread it upon the top of the blanket for additional cover; then switched off the flashlight. The whiskey lulled him, numbed his senses. Bessie's soft whimpers came to him through the cold. He took a long last draw from the cigarette and crushed it. Bessie's shoes creaked over the floor. He lay quietly, feeling the warmth of the alcohol spreading through him. He was tense inside; it was as though he had been compelled to hold himself in a certain awkward posture for a long time and then when he had the chance to relax he could not. He was tense with desire, but as long as he knew that Bessie was standing there in the room, he kept it from his mind. Bessie was worried and not to her should his mind turn now in that way. But that part of him which always made him at least outwardly adjusted to what was

expected of him made him now keep what his body wanted out
of full consciousness. He heard Bessie's clothes rustling in the
darkness and he knew that she was pulling off her coat. Soon
she would be lying here beside him. He waited for her. After a
few moments he felt her fingers pass lightly over his face; she
was seeking for the pallet. He reached out, groping, and found
her arm.

'Here; lay down.'

He held the cover for her; she slid down beside him and
stretched out. Now that she was close to him the whiskey made
him whirl faster and the tensity of his body mounted. A gust of
wind rattled the windowpane and made the old building creak.
He felt snug and warm, even though he knew he was in
danger. The building might fall upon him as he slept, but the
police might get him if he were anywhere else. He laid his
fingers upon Bessie's shoulders; slowly he felt the stiffness go
out of her body and as it left the tensity in his own rose and his
blood grew hot.

'Cold?' he asked in a soft whisper.

'Yeah,' she breathed.

'Get close to me.'

'I never thought I'd be like this.'

'It won't be like this always.'

'I'd just as soon die right now.'

'Don't say that.'

'I'm cold all over. I feel like I'll never get warm.'

He drew her closer, till he felt her breath coming full in his
face. The wind swept against the windowpane and the building, whining, then whispered out into silence. He turned from
his back and lay face to face with her, on his side. He kissed
her; her lips were cold. He kept kissing her until her lips grew
warm and soft. A huge warm pole of desire rose in him, insistent and demanding; he let his hand slide from her shoulder
to her breasts, feeling one, then the other; he slipped his other
arm beneath her head, kissing her again, hard and long.

'Please, Bigger . . .'

She tried to turn from him, but his arm held her tightly; she lay still, whimpering. He heard her sigh, a sigh he knew, for he had heard it many times before; but this time he heard in it a sigh deep down beneath the familiar one, a sigh of resignation, a giving up, a surrender of something more than her body. Her head lay limp in the crook of his arm and his hand reached for the hem of her dress, caught it in his fingers and gathered it up slowly. He was swept by a sudden gust of passion and his arms tightened about her. Bessie was still, inert, unresisting, without response. He kissed her again and at once she spoke, not a word, but a resigned and prolonged sound that gave forth a meaning of horror accepted. Her breath went in and out of her lungs in long soft gasps that turned finally into an urgent whisper of pleading.

'Bigger ... *Don't!*'

Her voice came to him now from out of a deep, far-away silence and he paid her no heed. The loud demand of the tensity of his own body was a voice that drowned out hers. In the cold darkness of the room it seemed that he was on some vast turning wheel that made him want to turn faster and faster; that in turning faster he would get warmth and sleep and be rid of his tense fatigue. He was conscious of nothing now but her and what he wanted. He flung the cover back, ignoring the cold, and not knowing that he did it. Bessie's hands were on his chest, her fingers spreading protestingly open, pushing him away. He heard her give a soft moan that seemed not to end even when she breathed in or out; a moan which he heard, too, from far away and without heeding. He had to now. Imperiously driven, he rode roughshod over her whimpering protests, feeling acutely sorry for her as he galloped a frenzied horse down a steep hill in the face of a resisting wind, *don't don't don't Bigger.* And then the wind became so strong that it lifted him high into the dark air, turning him, twisting him, hurling him; faintly, over the wind's howl, he heard: *don't Bigger don't don't* At a moment he could not remember, he had fallen; and now he lay, spent, his lips parted.

He lay still, feeling rid of that hunger and tenseness and hearing the wail of the night wind over and above his and her

273

breathing. He turned from her and lay on his back again, stretching his legs wide apart. He felt the tenseness flow gradually from him. His breathing grew less and less heavy and rapid until he could no longer hear it, then so slow and steady that the consciousness of breathing left him entirely. He was not at all sleepy and he lay, feeling Bessie lying there beside him. He turned his head in the darkness toward her. Her breath came to him slowly. He wondered if she were sleeping; somewhere deep in him he knew that he was lying here waiting for her to go to sleep. Bessie did not figure in what was before him. He remembered that he had seen two bricks lying on the floor of the room as he had entered. He tried to recall just where they were, but could not. But he was sure they were there somewhere; he would have to find them, at least one of them. It would have been much better if he had not said anything to Bessie about the murder. Well, it was her own fault. She had bothered him so much that he had had to tell her. And how on earth could he have known that they would find Mary's bones in the furnace so soon? He felt no regret as the image of the smoking furnace and the white pieces of bone came back to him. He had gazed straight at those bones for almost a full minute and had not been able to realize that they were the bones of Mary's body. He had thought that they might find out some other way and then suddenly confront him with the evidence. Never did he think that he could stand and look at the evidence and not know it.

His thoughts came back to the room. What about Bessie? He listened to her breathing. He could not take her with him and he could not leave her behind. Yes. She was asleep. He reconstructed in his mind the details of the room as he had seen them by the glow of the flashlight when he had first come in. The window was directly behind him, above his head. The flashlight was at his side; the gun was lying beside the flashlight, the handle pointing toward him, so he could get it quickly and be in a position to use it. But he could not use the gun; that would make too much noise. He would have to use a brick. He remembered hoisting the window; it had not been hard. Yes, that was what he could do with it, throw it out of the window, down the narrow air-shaft where nobody would find it until, perhaps, it had begun to smell.

He could not leave her here and he could not take her with him. If he took her along she would be crying all the time; she would be blaming him for all that had happened; she would be wanting whiskey to help her to forget and there would be times when he could not get it for her. The room was black-dark and silent; the city did not exist. He sat up slowly, holding his breath, listening. Bessie's breath was deep, regular. He could not take her and he could not leave her. He stretched out his hand and caught the flashlight. He listened again; her breath came like the sleep of the tired. He was holding the covers off her by sitting up this way and he did not want her to get cold and awaken. He eased the covers back; she still slept. His finger pressed a button on the flashlight and a dim spot of yellow leaped to life on the opposite wall. Quickly, he lowered it to the floor, for fear that it might disturb her; and as he did so there passed before his eyes in a split second of time one of the bricks he had glimpsed when he had first come into the room.

He stiffened; Bessie stirred restlessly. Her deep, regular breathing had stopped. He listened, but could not hear it. He saw her breath as a white thread stretching out over a vast black gulf and felt that he was clinging to it and was waiting to see if the ravel in the white thread which had started would continue and let him drop to the rocks far below. Then he heard her breathing again, in, out; in, out. He, too, breathed again, struggling now with his own breath to control it, to keep it from sounding so loud in his throat that it would awaken her. The fear that had gripped him when she had stirred made him realize that it would have to be quick and sure. Softly, he poked his legs from beneath the blanket, then waited. Bessie breathed, slow, long, heavy, regular. He lifted his arm and the blanket fell away. He stood up and his muscles lifted his body in slow motion. Outside in the cold night the wind moaned and died down, like an idiot in an icy black pit. Turning, he centered the disc of light where he thought Bessie's face must be. Yes. She was asleep. Her black face, stained with tears, was calm. He switched off the light, turned toward the wall and his fingers felt over the cold floor for the brick. He found it, gripped it in his hand and tiptoed back to the pallet. Her breath guided him in the darkness; he stopped where he thought her head must be. He couldn't take her and he couldn't leave her; so he would have to kill her. It was his life against hers. Quickly, to make certain where he must strike, he switched on the light, fearing as he did so that it might awaken her; then switched it off again, retaining as an image before his eyes her black face calm in deep sleep.

He straightened and lifted the brick, but just at that moment the reality of it all slipped from him. His heart beat wildly, trying to force its way out of his chest. No! Not this! His breath swelled deep in his lungs and he flexed his muscles, trying to impose his will over his body. He had to do better than this. Then, as suddenly as the panic had come, it left. But he had to stand here until that picture came back, that motive, that driving desire to escape the law. Yes. It *must* be this way. A sense of the white blur hovering near, of Mary burning, of Britten, of the law tracking him down, came back. Again, he was ready. The brick was in his hand. In his mind his hand traced a quick invisible arc through the cold air of the room; high above his head his hand paused in fancy and imaginatively swooped down to where he thought her head must be. He was rigid; not moving. This was the way it *had* to be. Then he took a deep breath and his hand gripped the brick and shot upward and paused a second and then plunged downward through the darkness to the accompaniment of a deep short grunt from his chest and landed with a thud. *Yes!* There was a dull gasp of surprise, then a moan. No, that must not be! He lifted the brick again and again, until in falling it struck a sodden mass that gave softly but stoutly to each landing blow. Soon he seemed to be striking a wet wad of cotton, of some damp substance whose only life was the jarring of the brick's impact. He stopped, hearing his own breath heaving in and out of his chest. He was wet all over, and cold. How many times he had lifted the brick and brought it down he did not know. All he knew was that the room was quiet and cold and that the job was done.

In his left hand he still held the flashlight, gripping it for sheer life. He wanted to switch it on and see if he had really done it, but could not. His knees were slightly bent, like a runner's poised for a race. Fear was in him again; he strained his ears. Didn't he hear her breathing? He bent and listened. It was his own breathing he heard; he had been breathing so loud that he had not been able to tell if Bessie was still breathing or not.

His fingers on the brick began to ache; he had been gripping it for some minutes with all the strength of his body. He was conscious of something warm and sticky on his hand and his sense of it covered him, all over; it cast a warm glow that enveloped the surface of his skin. He wanted to drop the brick, wanted to be free of this warm blood that crept and grew powerful with each passing moment. Then a dreadful thought rendered him incapable of action. Suppose Bessie was not as she had sounded when the brick hit her? Suppose, when he turned on the flashlight, he would see her lying there staring at him with those round large black eyes, her bloody mouth open in awe and wonder and pain and accusation? A cold chill, colder than the air of the room, closed about his shoulders like a shawl whose strands were woven of ice. It became unbearable and something within him cried out in silent agony; he stooped until the brick touched the floor, then loosened his fingers, bringing his hand to his stomach where he wiped it dry upon his coat. Gradually his breath subsided until he could no longer hear it and then he knew for certain that Bessie was not breathing. The room was filled with quiet and cold and death and blood and the deep moan of the night wind.

But he had to look. He lifted the flashlight to where he thought her head must be and pressed the button. The yellow spot sprang wide and dim on an empty stretch of floor; he moved it over a circle of crumpled bedclothes. There! Blood and lips and hair and face turned to one side and blood running slowly. She seemed limp; he could act now. He turned off the light. Could he leave her here? No. Somebody might find her.

Avoiding her, he stepped to the far side of the pallet, then turned in the dark. He centered the spot of light where he thought the window must be. He walked to the window and stopped, waiting to hear someone challenge his right to do what he was doing. Nothing happened. He caught hold of the window, hoisted it slowly up and the wind blasted his face. He turned to Bessie again and threw the light upon the face of death and blood. He put the flashlight in his pocket and stepped carefully in the dark to her side. He would have to lift her in his arms; his arms hung loose and did not move; he just stood. But he had to move her. He had to get her to the window. He stooped and slid his hands beneath her body, expecting to touch blood, but not touching it. Then he lifted her, feeling the wind screaming a protest against him. He stepped to the window and lifted her into it; he was working fast now that he had started. He pushed her as far out in his arms as possible, then let go. The body hit and bumped against the narrow sides of the air-shaft as it went down into blackness. He heard it strike the bottom.

He turned the light upon the pallet, half-expecting her to still be there; but there was only a pool of warm blood, a faint veil of vapor hovering in the air above it. Blood was on the pillows too. He took them and threw them out of the window, down the air-shaft. It was over.

He eased the window down. He would take the pallet into another room; he wished he could leave it here, but it was cold and he needed it. He rolled the quilts and blanket into a bundle and picked it up and went into the hall. Then he stopped abruptly, his mouth open. *Good God!* Goddamn, yes, it was in her dress pocket! Now, he was in for it. He had thrown Bessie down the air-shaft and the money was in the pocket of her dress! What could he do about it? Should he go down and get it? Anguish gripped him. *Naw!* He did not want to see her again. He felt that if he should ever see her face again he would be overcome with a sense of guilt so deep as to be unbearable. That was a dumb thing to do, he thought. Throwing her away with all that money in her pocket. He sighed and went through the hall and entered another room. Well, he would have to do without money; that was all. He spread the quilts upon the floor and rolled himself into them. He had seven cents between him and starvation and the law and the long days ahead.

He closed his eyes, longing for a sleep that would not come. During the last two days and nights he had lived so fast and hard that it was an effort to keep it all real in his mind. So close had danger and death come that he could not feel that it was he who had undergone it all. And, yet, out of it all, over and above all that had happened, impalpable but real, there remained to him a queer sense of power. *He* had done this. *He* had brought all this about. In all of his life these two murders were the most meaningful things that had ever happened to him. He was living, truly and deeply, no matter what others might think, looking at him with their blind eyes. Never had he had the chance to live out the consequences of his actions; never had his will been so free as in this night and day of fear and murder and flight.

He had killed twice, but in a true sense it was not the first time he had ever killed. He had killed many times before, but only during the last two days had this impulse assumed the form of actual killing. Blind anger had come often and he had either gone behind his curtain or wall, or had quarreled and fought. And yet, whether in running away or in fighting, he had felt the need of the clean satisfaction of facing this thing in all its fulness, of fighting it out in the wind and sunlight, in front of those whose hate for him was so unfathomably deep that, after they had shunted him off into a corner of the city to rot and die, they could turn to him, as Mary had that night in the car, and say: 'I'd like to know how your people live.'

But what was he after? What did he want? What did he love and what did he hate? He did not know. There was something he *knew* and something he *felt*; something the *world* gave him and something he *himself* had; something spread out in *front* of him and something spread out in *back*; and never in all his life, with this black skin of his, had the two worlds, thought and feeling, will and mind, aspiration and satisfaction, been together; never had he felt a sense of wholeness. Sometimes, in his room or on the sidewalk, the world seemed to him a strange labyrinth even when the streets were straight and the walls were square; a chaos which made him feel that something in him should be able to understand it, divide it, focus it. But only under the stress of hate was the conflict resolved. He had been so conditioned in a cramped environment that hard words or kicks alone knocked him upright and made him capable of action – action that was futile because the world was too much for him. It was then that he closed his eyes and struck out blindly, hitting what or whom he could, not looking or caring what or who hit back.

And, under it all, and this made it hard for him, he did not want to make believe that it was solved, make believe that he was happy when he was not. He hated his mother for that way of hers which was like Bessie's. What his mother had was Bessie's whiskey, and Bessie's whiskey was his mother's religion. He did not want to sit on a bench and sing, or lie in a corner and sleep. It was when he read the newspapers or magazines, went to the movies, or walked along the streets with crowds, that he felt what he wanted: to merge himself with others and be a part of this world, to lose himself in it so he could find himself, to be allowed a chance to live like others, even though he was black.

He turned restlessly on his hard pallet and groaned. He had been caught up in a whirl of thought and feeling which had swept him onward and when he opened his eyes he saw that daylight stood outside of a dirty window just above his head. He jumped up and looked out. The snow had stopped falling and the city, white, still, was a vast stretch of roof-tops and sky. He had been thinking about it for hours here in the dark and now there it was, all white, still. But what he had thought about it had made it real with a reality it did not have now in the daylight. When lying in the dark thinking of it, it seemed to have something which left it when it was looked at. Why should not this cold white world rise up as a beautiful dream in which he could walk and be at home, in which it would be easy to tell what to do and what not to do? If only someone had gone before and lived or suffered or died – made it so that it could be understood! It was too stark, not redeemed, not made real with the reality that was the warm blood of life. He felt that there was something missing, some road which, if he had once found it, would have led him to a sure and quiet know-ledge. But why think of that now? A chance for that was gone forever. He had committed murder twice and had created a new world for himself.

*

He left the room and went down to a window on the first floor and looked out. The street was quiet and no cars were running. The tracks were buried under snow. No doubt the blizzard had tied up traffic all over the city.

He saw a little girl pick her way through the snow and stop at a corner newsstand; a man hurried out of a drug store and sold the girl a paper. Could he snatch a paper while the man was inside? The snow was so soft and deep he might get caught trying to get away. Could he find an empty building in which to hide after he had snatched the paper? Yes; that was just the thing. He looked carefully up and down the street; no one was in sight. He went through the door and the wind was like a branding-iron on his face. The sun came out, suddenly, so strong and full that it made him dodge as from a blow; a million bits of sparkle pained his eyes. He went to the news-stand and saw a tall black headline. HUNT BLACK IN GIRL'S DEATH. Yes; they had the story. He walked on and looked for a place to hide after he had snatched the paper. At the corner of an alley he saw an empty building with a gaping window on the first floor. Yes; this was a good place. He mapped out a careful plan of action; he did not want it said that he had done all the things he had and then had got caught stealing a three-cent newspaper.

He went to the drug store and looked inside at the man leaning against a wall, smoking. Yes. Like this! He reached out and grabbed a paper and in the act of grabbing it he turned and looked at the man who was looking at him, a cigarette slanting whitely across his black chin. Even before he moved from his tracks, he ran; he felt his legs turn, start, then slip in snow. Goddamn! The white world tilted at a sharp angle and the icy wind shot past his face. He fell flat and the crumbs of snow ate coldly at his fingers. He got up, on one knee, then on both; when he was on his feet he turned toward the drug store, still clutching the paper, amazed and angry with himself for having been so clumsy. The drug store door opened. He ran.

'Hey!'

As he ducked down the alley he saw the man standing in the snow looking at him and he knew that the man would not follow.

'Hey, you!'

He scrambled to the window, pitched the paper in before him, caught hold and heaved himself upward onto the ledge and then inside. He landed on his feet and stood peering through the window into the alley; all was white and quiet. He picked up the paper and walked down the hallway to the steps and up to the third floor, using the flashlight and hearing his footsteps echo faintly in the empty building. He stopped, clutched his pocket in panic as his mouth flew open. Yes; he had it. He thought that he had dropped the gun when he had fallen in the snow, but it was still there. He sat on the top step of the stairs and opened out the paper, but for quite awhile he did not read. He listened to the creaking of the building caused by the wind sweeping over the city. Yes; he was alone; he looked down and read, REPORTERS FIND DALTON GIRL'S BONES IN FURNACE. NEGRO CHAUFFEUR DISAPPEARS. FIVE THOUSAND POLICE SURROUND BLACK BELT. AUTHORITIES HINT SEX CRIME. COMMUNIST LEADER PROVES ALIBI. GIRL'S MOTHER IN COLLAPSE. He paused and reread the line, AUTHORITIES HINT SEX CRIME. Those words excluded him utterly from the world. To hint that he had committed a sex crime was to pronounce the death sentence; it meant a wiping out of his life even before he was captured; it meant death before death came, for the white men who read those words would at once kill him in their hearts.

The Mary Dalton kidnaping case was dramatically cracked wide open when a group of local newspaper reporters accidentally discovered several bones, later positively established as those of the missing heiress, in the furnace of the Dalton home late today...

*

Search of the Negro's home, 3721 Indiana Avenue, in the heart of the South Side, failed to reveal his whereabouts. Police expressed belief that Miss Dalton met her death at the hands of the Negro, perhaps in a sex crime, and that the white girl's body was burned to destroy evidence.

Bigger looked up. His right hand twitched. He wanted a gun in that hand. He got his gun from his pocket and held it. He read again:

Immediately a cordon of five thousand police, augmented by more than three thousand volunteers, was thrown about the Black Belt. Chief of Police Glenman said this morning that he believed that the Negro was still in the city, since all roads leading in and out of Chicago were blocked by a record-breaking snowfall.

Indignation rose to white heat last night as the news of the Negro's rape and murder of the missing heiress spread through the city.

Police reported that many windows in the Negro sections were smashed.

Every street car, bus, el train and auto leaving the South Side is being stopped and searched. Police and vigilantes, armed with rifles, tear gas, flashlights, and photos of the killer, began at 18th Street this morning and are searching every Negro home under a blanket warrant from the mayor. They are making a careful search of all abandoned buildings, which are said to be hideouts for Negro criminals.

Maintaining that they feared for the lives of their children, a delegation of white parents called upon Superintendent of City Schools Horace Minton, and begged that all schools be closed until the Negro rapist and murderer was captured.

Reports were current that several Negro men were beaten in various North and West Side neighborhoods.

In the Hyde Park and Englewood districts, men organized vigilante groups and sent word to Chief of Police Glenman offering aid.

Glenman said this morning that the aid of such groups would be accepted. He stated that a woefully undermanned police force together with recurring waves of Negro crime made such a procedure necessary.

Several hundred Negroes resembling Bigger Thomas were rounded up from South Side 'hot spots'; they are being held for investigation.

In a radio broadcast last night Mayor Ditz warned of possible mob violence and exhorted the public to maintain order. 'Every effort is being made to apprehend this fiend,' he said.

It was reported that several hundred Negro employees throughout the city had been dismissed from jobs. A well-known banker's wife phoned this paper that she had dismissed her Negro cook, 'for fear that she might poison the children.'

Bigger's eyes were wide and his lips were parted; he scanned the print quickly: 'handwriting experts busy', 'Erlone's fingerprints not found in Dalton home', 'radical still in custody'; and then a sentence leaped at Bigger, like a blow:

Police are not yet satisfied with the account Erlone has given of himself and are of the conviction that he may be linked to the Negro as an accomplice; they feel that the plan of the murder and kidnaping was too elaborate to be the work of a Negro mind.

At that moment he wanted to walk out into the street and up to a policeman and say, 'No! Jan didn't help me! He didn't have a damn thing to do with it! I – I did it!' His lips twisted in a smile that was half-leer and half-defiance.

Holding the paper in taut fingers, he read phrases: 'Negro ordered to clean out ashes ... reluctant to respond ... dreading discovery ... smoke-filled basement ... tragedy of communism and racial mixture ... possibility that kidnap note was work of reds ...'

Bigger looked up. The building was quiet save for the continual creaking caused by the wind. He could not stay here. There was no telling when they were coming into this neighborhood. He could not leave Chicago; all roads were blocked, and all trains, buses and autos were being stopped and searched. It would have been much better if he had tried to leave town at once. He should have gone to some other place, perhaps Gary, Indiana, or Evanston. He looked at the paper and saw a black-and-white map of the South Side, around the borders of which was a shaded portion an inch deep. Under the map ran a line of small print:

Shaded portion shows area already covered by police and vigilantes in search for Negro rapist and murderer. White portion shows area yet to be searched.

He was trapped. He would have to get out of this building. But where could he go? Empty buildings would serve only as long as he stayed within the white portion of the map, and the white portion was shrinking rapidly. He remembered that the paper had been printed last night. That meant that the white portion was now much smaller than was shown here. He closed his eyes, calculating: he was at Fifty-third Street and the hunt had started last night at Eighteenth Street. If they had gone from Eighteenth Street to Twenty-eighth Street last night, then they would have gone from Twenty-eighth Street to Thirty-eighth Street since then. And by midnight tonight they would be at Forty-eighth Street, or right here.

He wondered about empty flats. The paper had not mentioned them. Suppose he found a small, empty kitchenette flat in a building where many people lived? That was by far the safest thing.

He went to the end of the hall and flashed the light on a dirty ceiling and saw a wooden stairway leading to the roof. He climbed and pulled himself up into a narrow passage at the end of which was a door. He kicked at the door several times, each kick making it give slightly until he saw snow, sunshine, and an oblong strip of sky. The wind came stinging into his face and he remembered how weak and cold he was. How long could he keep going this way? He squeezed through and stood in the snow on the roof. Before him was a maze of white, sun-drenched roof-tops.

He crouched behind a chimney and looked down into the street. At the corner he saw the newsstand from which he had stolen the paper; the man who had shouted at him was standing by it. Two black men stopped at the newsstand and bought a paper, then walked into a doorway. One of them leaned eagerly over the other's shoulder. Their lips moved and they pointed their black fingers at the paper and shook their heads as they talked. Two more men joined them and soon there was a small knot of them standing in the doorway, talking and pointing at the paper. They broke up abruptly and went away. Yes; they were talking about him. Maybe all of the black men and women were talking about him this morning; maybe they were hating him for having brought this attack upon them.

He had crouched so long in the snow that when he tried to move he found that his legs had lost all feeling. A fear that he was freezing seized him. He kicked out his legs to restore circulation of his blood, then crawled to the other side of the roof. Directly below him, one floor away, through a window without shades, he saw a room in which were two small iron beds with sheets dirty and crumpled. In one bed sat three naked black children looking across the room to the other bed on which lay a man and woman, both naked and black in the sunlight. There were quick, jerky movements on the bed where the man and woman lay, and the three children were watching. It was familiar; he had seen things like that when he was a little boy sleeping five in a room. Many mornings he had awakened and watched his father and mother. He turned away, thinking: Five of 'em sleeping in one room and here's a great big empty building with just me in it. He crawled back to the chimney, seeing before his eyes an image of the room of five people, all of them blackly naked in the strong sunlight, seen through a sweaty pane: the man and woman moving jerkily in tight embrace, and the three children watching.

Hunger came to his stomach; an icy hand reached down his throat and clutched his intestines and tied them into a cold, tight knot that ached. The memory of the bottle of milk Bessie had heated for him last night came back so strongly that he could almost taste it. If he had that bottle of milk now he would make a fire out of a newspaper and hold the bottle over the flame until it was warm. He saw himself take the top off the white bottle, with some of the warm milk spilling over his black fingers, and then lift the bottle to his mouth and tilt his head and drink. His stomach did a slow flip-flop and he heard it growl. He felt in his hunger a deep sense of duty, as powerful as the urge to breathe, as intimate as the beat of his heart. He felt like dropping to his knees and lifting his face to the sky and saying: 'I'm hungry!' He wanted to pull off his clothes and roll in the snow until something nourishing seeped into his body through the pores of his skin. He wanted to grip something in his hands so hard that it would turn to food. But soon his hunger left; soon he was taking it a little easier; soon his mind rose from the desperate call of his body and concerned itself with the danger that lurked about him. He felt something hard at the corners of his lips and touched it with his fingers; it was frozen saliva.

He crawled back through the door into the narrow passage and lowered himself down the shallow wooden steps into the hallway. He went to the first floor and stood at the window through which he had first climbed. He had to find an empty apartment in some building where he could get warm; he felt that if he did not get warm soon he would simply lie down and close his eyes. Then he had an idea; he wondered why he had not thought of it before. He struck a match and lit the newspaper; as it blazed he held one hand over it awhile, and then the other. The heat came to his skin from far off. When the paper had burned so close that he could no longer hold it, he dropped it to the floor and stamped it out with his shoes. At least he could feel his hands now; at least they ached and let him know that they were his.

He climbed through the window and walked to the street, turned northward, joining the people passing. No one recognized him. He looked for a building with a 'For Rent' sign. He walked two blocks and saw none. He knew that empty flats were scarce in the Black Belt; whenever his mother wanted to move she had to put in requests long months in advance. He remembered that his mother had once made him tramp the streets for two whole months looking for a place to live. The rental agencies had told him that there were not enough houses for Negroes to live in, that the city was condemning houses in which Negroes lived as being too old and too dangerous for habitation. And he remembered the time when the police had come and driven him and his mother and his brother and sister out of a flat in a building which had collapsed two days after they had moved. And he had heard it said that black people, even though they could not get good jobs, paid twice as much rent as whites for the same kind of flats. He walked five more blocks and saw no 'For Rent' sign. Goddamn! Would he freeze trying to find a place in which to get warm? How easy it would be for him to hide if he had the whole city in which to move about! They keep us bottled up here like wild animals, he thought. He knew that black people could not go outside of the Black Belt to rent a flat; they had to live on their side of the 'line'. No white real estate man would rent a flat to a black man other than in the sections where it had been decided that black people might live.

His fists clenched. What was the use of running away? He ought to stop right here in the middle of the sidewalk and shout out what this was. It was so wrong that surely all the black people round him would do something about it; so wrong that all the white people would stop and listen. But he knew that they would simply grab him and say that he was crazy. He reeled through the streets, his bloodshot eyes looking for a place to hide. He paused at a corner and saw a big black rat leaping over the snow. It shot past him into a doorway where it slid out of sight through a hole. He looked wistfully at that gaping black hole through which the rat had darted to safety.

He passed a bakery and wanted to go in and buy some rolls with the seven cents he had. But the bakery was empty of customers and he was afraid that the white proprietor would recognize him. He would wait until he came to a Negro business establishment, but he knew that there were not many of them. Almost all businesses in the Black Belt were owned by Jews, Italians, and Greeks. Most Negro businesses were funeral parlors; white undertakers refused to bother with dead black bodies. He came to a chain grocery store. Bread sold here for five cents a loaf, but across the 'line' where white folks lived, it sold for four. And now, of all times, he could not cross that 'line'. He stood looking through the plate glass at the people inside. Ought he to go in? He had to. He was starving. They trick us every breath we draw! he thought. They gouge our eyes out! He opened the door and walked to the counter. The warm air made him dizzy; he caught hold of a counter in front of him and steadied himself. His eyes blurred and there swam before him a vast array of red and blue and green and yellow cans stacked high upon shelves. All about him he heard the soft voices of men and women.

'You waited on, sir?'

'A loaf of bread,' he whispered.

'Anything else, sir?'

'Naw.'

The man's face went away and came again; he heard paper rustling.

'Cold out, isn't it?'

'Hunh? Oh, yessuh.'

He laid the nickel on the counter; he saw the blurred loaf being handed to him.

'Thank you. Call again.'

He walked unsteadily to the door with the loaf under his arm. Oh, Lord! If only he could get into the street! In the doorway he met people coming in; he stood to one side to let them pass, then went into the cold wind, looking for an empty flat. At any moment he expected to hear his name shouted; expected to feel his arms being grabbed. He walked five blocks before he saw a two-story flat building with a 'For Rent' sign in a window. Smoke bulged out of chimneys and he knew that it was warm inside. He went to the front door and read the little vacancy notice pasted on the glass and saw that the flat was a rear one. He went down the alley to the rear steps and mounted to the second floor. He tried a window and it slid up easily. He was in luck. He hoisted himself through and dropped into a warm room, a kitchen. He was suddenly tense, listening. He heard voices, they seemed to be coming from the room in front of him. Had he made a mistake? No. The kitchen was not furnished; no one, it seemed, lived in here. He tiptoed to the next room and found it empty; but he heard the voices even more clearly now. He saw still another room leading farther; he tiptoed and looked. That room, too, was empty, but the sound of the voices was coming so loud that he could make out the words. An argument was going on in the front flat. He stood with the loaf of bread in his hands, his legs wide apart, listening.

'Jack, yuh mean t' stan' there 'n' say yuh'd give tha' nigger up t' the white folks?'

'Damn right Ah would!'

'But, Jack, s'pose he ain' guilty?'

'Whut in hell he run off fer then?'

'Mabbe he thought they wuz gonna blame the murder on *him*!'

'Lissen, Jim. Ef he wuzn't guilty, then he oughta stayed 'n' faced it. Ef Ah knowed where tha' nigger wuz Ah'd turn 'im up 'n' git these white folks off me.'

'But, Jack, *ever'* nigger looks guilty t' white folks when somebody's done a crime.'

'Yeah; tha's 'cause so many of us ack like Bigger Thomas; tha's all. When yuh ack like Bigger Thomas yuh stir up trouble.'

'But, Jack, who's stirring up trouble now? The papers say they beatin' us up all over the city. They don' care whut black man they git. We's all dogs in they sight! Yuh gotta stan' up 'n' fight these folks.'

' 'N' git killed? Hell, naw! Ah gotta family. Ah gotta wife 'n' baby. Ah ain't startin' no fool fight. Yuh can't git no justice pertectin' men who kill . . .'

'We's *all* murderers t' them, Ah tell yuh!'

'Lissen, Jim. Ah'm a hard-workin' man. Ah fixes the streets

wid a pick an' shovel ever' day, when Ah git a chance. But the boss tol' me he didn't wan' me in them streets wid this mob feelin' among the white folks ... He says Ah'll git killed. So he lays me off. Yuh see, tha' goddamn nigger Bigger Thomas made me lose mah job ... He made the white folks think we's *all* jus' like him!'

'But, Jack, Ah tell yuh they think it awready. Yuh's a good man, but tha' ain' gonna keep 'em from comin' t' yo' home, is it? Hell, naw! We's all black 'n' we jus' as waal *ack* black, don' yuh see?'

'Aw, Jim, it's awright t' git mad, but yuh gotta look at things straight. Tha' guy made me lose mah job. Tha' ain' fair! How is Ah gonna eat? Ef Ah knowed where the black sonofabitch wuz Ah'd call the cops 'n' let 'em come 'n' git 'im!'

'Waal, Ah wouldn't. Ah'd die firs'!'

'Man, yuh crazy! Don' yuh wan' a home 'n' wife 'n' chillun? Whut's fightin' gonna git yuh? There's *mo'* of them than us. They could kill us all. Yuh gotto learn t' live 'n' git erlong wid people.'

'When folks hate me, Ah don' wanna git erlong.'

'But we gotta *eat*! We gotta *live*!'

'Ah don' care! Ah'd die firs'!'

'Aw, hell! Yuh crazy!'

'Ah don' care whut yuh say. Ah'd die 'fo' Ah'd let 'em scare me inter tellin' on tha' man. Ah tell yuh, Ah'd die firs'!'

He tiptoed back into the kitchen and took out his gun. He would stay here and if his own people bothered him he would use it. He turned on the water faucet and put his mouth under the stream and the water exploded in his stomach. He sank to his knees and rolled in agony. Soon the pain ceased and he drank again. Then, slowly, so that the paper would not rustle, he unwrapped the loaf of bread and chewed a piece. It tasted good, like cake, with a sweetish and smooth flavor he had never thought bread could have. As he ate his hunger returned in full force and he sat on the floor and held a fistful of bread in each hand, his cheeks bulging and his jaws working and his Adam's apple going up and down with each swallow. He could not stop until his mouth became so dry that the bread balled on his tongue; he held it there, savoring the taste.

He stretched out on the floor and sighed. He was drowsy, but when he was on the verge of sleep he jerked abruptly to a dull wakefulness. Finally, he slept, then sat up, half-awake, following an unconscious prompting of fear. He groaned and his hands flayed the air to ward off an invisible danger. Once he got up completely and walked a few steps with outstretched hands and then lay down in a spot almost ten feet from where he had originally slept. There were two Biggers: one was determined to get rest and sleep at any cost; and the other shrank from images charged with terror. There came a long space of time in which he did not move; he lay on his back, his hands folded upon his chest, his mouth and eyes open. His chest rose and fell so slowly and gently that it seemed that during the intervals when it did not move he would never breathe again. A wan sun came onto his face, making the black skin shine like dull metal; the sun left and the quiet room filled with deep shadows.

As he slept there stole into his consciousness a disturbing, rhythmic throbbing which he tried to fight off to keep from waking up. His mind, protecting him, wove the throb into patterns of innocent images. He thought he was in the Paris Grill listening to the automatic phonograph playing; but that was not satisfying. Next, his mind told him that he was at home in bed and his mother was singing and shaking the mattress, wanting him to get up. But this image, like the others, failed to quiet him. The throb pulsed on, insistent, and he saw hundreds of black men and women beating drums with their fingers. But that, too, did not answer the question. He tossed restlessly on the floor, then sprang to his feet, his heart pounding, his ears filled with the sound of singing and shouting.

He went to the window and looked out; in front of him, down a few feet, through a window, was a dim-lit church. In it a crowd of black men and women stood between long rows of wooden benches, singing, clapping hands, and rolling their heads. Aw, them folks go to church every day in the week, he thought. He licked his lips and got another drink of water. How near were the police? What time was it? He looked at his watch and found that it had stopped running; he had forgotten to wind it. The singing from the church vibrated through him, suffusing him with a mood of sensitive sorrow. He tried not to listen, but it seeped into his feelings, whispering of another way of life and death, coaxing him to lie down and sleep and let them come and get him, urging him to believe that all life was a sorrow that had to be accepted. He shook his head, trying to rid himself of the music. How long had he slept? What were the papers saying now? He had two cents left; that would buy a *Times*. He picked up what remained of the loaf of bread and the music sang of surrender, resignation. *Steal away, Steal away, Steal away to Jesus* ... He stuffed the bread into his pockets; he would eat it some time later. He made sure that his gun was still intact, hearing, *Steal away, Steal away home, I ain't got long to stay here* ... It was dangerous to stay here, but it was also dangerous to go out. The singing filled his ears; it was complete, self-contained, and it mocked his fear and loneliness, his deep yearning for a sense of wholeness. Its fulness contrasted so sharply with his hunger, its richness with his emptiness, that he recoiled from it while answering it. Would it not have been better for him had he lived in that world the music sang of? It would have been easy to have lived in it, for it was his mother's world, humble, contrite, believing. It had a center, a core, an axis, a heart which he needed but could never have unless he laid his head upon a pillow of humility and gave up his hope of living in the world. And he would never do that.

He heard a streetcar passing in the street; they were running again. A wild thought surged through him. Suppose the police had already searched this neighborhood and had overlooked him? But sober judgment told him that that was impossible. He patted his pocket to make sure the gun was there, then climbed through the window. Cold wind smote his face. It must be below zero, he thought. At both ends of the alley the street lamps glowed through the murky air, refracted into mammoth

balls of light. The sky was dark blue and far away. He walked
to the end of the alley and turned onto the sidewalk, joining the
passing stream of people. He waited for someone to challenge
his right to walk there, but no one did.

At the end of the block he saw a crowd of people and fear
clutched hard at his stomach. What were they doing? He
slowed and saw that they were gathered about a newsstand.
They were black people and they were buying papers to read
about how the white folks were trying to track him to earth. He
lowered his head and went forward and slipped into the crowd.
The people were talking excitedly. Cautiously, he held out two
cents in his cold fingers. When he was close enough, he saw the
front page; his picture was in the center of it. He bent his head
lower, hoping that no one would see him closely enough to see
that it was he who was pictured there.

'*Times,*' he said.

He tucked the paper under his arm, edged out of the crowd
and walked southward, looking for an empty flat. At the next
corner he saw a 'For Rent' sign in a building which he knew
was cut up into small kitchenette flats. This was what he
wanted. He went to the door and read the sign; there was an
empty flat on the fourth floor. He walked to the alley and began
to mount the outside rear stairs, his feet softly crunching in
snow. He heard a door open; he stopped, got his gun, and
waited, kneeling in the snow.

'Who's that?'

It was a woman's voice. Then a man's voice sounded.

'What's the matter, Ellen?'

'I thought I heard someone out here on the porch.'

'Ah, you're simply nervous. You're scared of all this stuff
you've been reading in the papers.'

'But I'm sure I heard somebody.'

'Aw, empty the garbage and shut the door. It's cold.'

Bigger flattened against the building, in the dark. He saw a
woman come out of a door, pause, look round; she went to the
far end of the porch and dumped something into a garbage pail
and went back inside. I would've had to kill 'em both if she saw

me, he thought. He tiptoed up to the fourth floor and found
two windows, both of them dark. He tried to lift the screen in
one of them and found it frozen. Gently, he shook it to and fro
until it loosened; then he lifted it out and laid it on the porch in
the snow. Inch by inch, he raised the window, breathing so
loud that he thought surely people must hear him even in the
streets. He climbed through into a dark room and struck a
match. An electric light was on the other side of the room and
he went to it and pulled the chain. He put his cap over the bulb
so that no light would seep through to the outside, then opened
the paper. Yes; here was a large picture of him. At the top of
the picture ran a tall line of black type: 24-HOUR SEARCH
FAILS TO UNEARTH RAPIST. In another column he saw:
RAID 1,000 NEGRO HOMES. INCIPIENT RIOT QUELLED AT
47TH AND HALSTED. There was another map of the South
Side. This time the shaded area had deepened from both the
north and south, leaving a small square of white in the middle
of the oblong Black Belt. He stood looking at that tiny square
of white as though gazing down into the barrel of a gun. He
was there on that map, in that white spot, standing in a room
waiting for them to come. Dead-set, his eyes stared above the
top of the paper. There was nothing left for him but to shoot it
out. He examined the map again; the police had come from the
north as far south as Fortieth Street; and they had come from
the south as far north as Fiftieth Street. That meant that he was
somewhere in between, and they were minutes away. He read:

Today and last night eight thousand armed men combed cellars,
old buildings and more than one thousand Negro homes in the
Black Belt in a vain effort to apprehend Bigger Thomas, 20-year-old
Negro rapist and killer of Mary Dalton, whose bones were found last
Sunday night in a furnace.

Bigger's eyes went down the page, snatching at what he
thought most important: 'word spread that the slayer had been
captured, but was immediately denied', 'before night police and
vigilantes will have covered the entire Black Belt', 'raiding
numerous Communist headquarters throughout the city', 'the

arrest of hundreds of reds failed, however, to uncover any clues', 'public warned by mayor against "boring from within", ...' Then:

A curious sidelight was revealed today when it become known that the apartment building in which the Negro killer lived is owned and managed by a sub-firm of the Dalton Real Estate Company.

He lowered the paper; he could read no more. The one fact to remember was that eight thousand men, white men, with guns and gas, were out there in the night looking for him. According to this paper, they were but a few blocks away. Could he get to the roof of this building? If so, maybe he could crouch there until they passed. He thought of burying himself deep in the snow of the roof, but he knew that that was impossible. He pulled the chain again and plunged the room in darkness. Using the flashlight, he went to the door and opened it and looked into the hall. It was empty and a dim light burned at the far end. He put out the flashlight and tiptoed, looking at the ceiling, searching for a trapdoor leading to the roof. Finally, he saw a pair of wooden steps leading upward. Suddenly, his muscles stiffened as though a wire strung through his body had jerked him. A siren shriek entered the hallway. And immediately he heard voices, excited, low, tense. From somewhere down below a man called,

'They's comin'!'

There was nothing to do now but go up; he clutched the wooden steps above him and climbed, wanting to get out of sight before anyone came into the hall. He reached the trapdoor and pushed against it with his head; it opened. He grabbed something solid in the darkness above him and hoisted himself upward, hoping as he did so that it would hold him and not let him go crashing down upon the hall floor. He rested on his knees, his chest heaving. Then he eased the door shut, peering just in time to see a door in the hall opening. That was close! The siren sounded again; it was outside in the street. It seemed to sound a warning that no one could hide from it; that action to escape was futile; that soon the men with guns and gas would come and penetrate where the siren sound had penetrated.

He listened; there were throbs of motors; shouts rose from the streets; there were screams of women and curses of men. He heard footsteps on the stairs. The siren died and began again, on a high, shrill note this time. It made him want to clutch at his throat; as long as it sounded it seemed that he could not breathe. He had to get to the roof! He switched on the flashlight and crawled through a narrow loft till he came to an opening. He put his shoulder to it and heaved; it gave so suddenly and easily that he drew back in fear. He thought that someone had snatched it open from above and in the same instant of its opening he saw an expanse of gleaming white snow against the dark smudge of night and a stretch of luminous sky. A medley of crashing sounds came, louder than he had thought that sound could be: horns, sirens, screams. There was hunger in those sounds as they crashed over the roof-tops and chimneys; but under it, low and distinct, he heard voices of fear: curses of men and cries of children.

Yes; they were looking for him in every building and on every floor and in every room. They wanted him. His eyes jerked upward as a huge, sharp beam of yellow light shot into the sky. Another came, crossing it like a knife. Then another. Soon the sky was full of them. They circled slowly, hemming him in; bars of light forming a prison, a wall between him and the rest of the world; bars weaving a shifting wall of light into which he dared not go. He was in the midst of it now; this was what he had been running from ever since that night Mrs Dalton had come into the room and had charged him with such fear that his hands had gripped the pillow with fingers of steel and had cut off the air from Mary's lungs.

Below him was a loud, heavy pounding, like a far-away rumble of thunder. He had to get to the roof; he struggled upward, then fell flat, in deep soft snow, his eyes riveted upon a white man across the street upon another roof. Bigger watched the man whirl the beam of a flashlight. Would the man look in his direction? Could the beam of a flashlight make him visible from where the man was? He watched the man walk round awhile and then disappear.

Quickly, he rose and shut the trapdoor. To leave it open would create suspicion. Then he fell flat again, listening. There was the sound of many running feet below him. It seemed that an army was thundering up the stairs. There was nowhere he could run to now; either they caught him or they did not. The thundering grew louder and he knew that the men were nearing the top floor. He lifted his eyes and looked in all directions, watching roofs to the left and right of him. He did not want to be surprised by someone creeping up on him from behind. He saw that the roof to his right was not joined to the one upon which he lay; that meant that no one could steal up on him from that direction. The one to his left was joined to the roof of the building upon which he lay, making it one long icy runway. He lifted his head and looked; there were other roofs joined, too. He could run over those roofs, over the snow and round those chimneys until he came to the building that dropped to the ground. Then that would be all. Would he jump off and kill himself? He did not know. He had an almost mystic feeling that if he were ever cornered something in him would prompt him to act the right way, the right way being the way that would enable him to die without shame.

He heard a noise close by; he looked round just in time to see a white face, a head, then shoulders pull into view upon the roof to the right of him. A man stood up, cut sharply against the background of roving yellow lights. He watched the man twirl a pencil of light over the snow. Bigger raised his gun and trained it upon the man and waited; if the light reached him, he would shoot. What would he do afterwards? He did not know. But the yellow spot never reached him. He watched the man go down, feet first, then shoulders and head; he was gone.

He relaxed a bit; at least the roof to his right was safe now. He waited to hear sounds that would tell him that someone was climbing up through the trapdoor. The rumbling below him rose in volume with the passing seconds, but he could not tell if the men were coming closer or receding. He waited and held his gun. Above his head the sky stretched in a cold, dark-blue oval, cupping the city like an iron palm covered with silk. The wind blew, hard, icy, without ceasing. It seemed to him that he had already frozen, that pieces could be broken off him, as one chips bits from a cake of ice. In order to know that he still had the gun in his hand he had to look at it, for his hand no longer had any feeling.

Then he was stiff with fear. There were pounding feet right below him. They were on the top floor now. Ought he to run to the roof to his left? But he had seen no one search that roof; if he ran he might come face to face with someone coming up out of another trapdoor. He looked round, thinking that maybe someone was creeping upon him; but there was nobody. The sound of feet came louder. He put his ear to the naked ice and listened. Yes; they were walking about in the hallway; there were several of them directly under him, near the trapdoor. He looked again to the roof on his left, wanting to run to it and hide; but was afraid. Were they coming up? He listened; but there were so many voices he could not make out the words. He did not want them to surprise him. Whatever happened, he wanted to go down looking into the faces of those that would kill him. Finally, under the terror-song of the siren, the voices came so close that he could hear words clearly.

'God, but I'm tired!'

'I'm cold!'

'I believe we're just wasting time.'

'Say, Jerry! You going to the roof this time?'

'Yeah; I'll go.'

'That nigger might be in New York by now.'

'Yeah. But we better look.'

'Say, did you see that brown gal in there?'

'The one that didn't have much on?'

'Yeah.'

'Boy, she was a peach, wasn't she?'

'Yeah; I wonder what on earth a nigger wants to kill a white woman for when he has such good-looking women in his own race . . .'

'Boy, if she'd let me stay here I'd give up this goddamn hunt.'

'Come on. Give a lift. You'd better hold this ladder. It seems rickety.'

'O.K.'

'Hurry up. Here comes the captain.'

Bigger was set. Then he was not set. He clung to a chimney that stood a foot from the trapdoor. Ought he to stay flat or stand up? He stood up, pushing against the chimney, trying to merge with it. He held the gun and waited. Was the man coming up? He looked to the roof to his left; it was still empty. But if he ran to it he might meet someone. He heard footsteps in the passage of the loft. Yes; the man was coming. He waited for the trapdoor to open. He held the gun tightly; he wondered if he was holding it too tightly, so tightly that it would go off before he wanted it to. His fingers were so cold that he could not tell how much pressure he was putting behind the trigger. Then, like a shooting star streaking across a black sky, the fearful thought came to him that maybe his fingers were frozen so stiff that he could not pull the trigger. Quickly, he felt his right hand with his left: but even that did not tell him anything. His right hand was so cold that all he felt was one cold piece of flesh touching another. He had to wait and see. He had to have faith. He had to trust himself; that was all.

The trapdoor opened, slightly at first, then wide. He watched it, his mouth open, staring through the blur of tears which the cold wind had whipped into his eyes. The door came all the way open, cutting off his view for a moment, then it fell back softly upon the snow. He saw the bare head of a white man – the back of the head – framed in the narrow opening, stenciled against the yellow glare of the restless bars of light. Then the head turned slightly and Bigger saw the side of a white face. He watched the man, moving like a figure on the screen in close-up slow motion, come out of the hole and stand with his back to him, flashlight in hand. The idea took hold swiftly. Hit him. Hit him! In the head. Whether it would help or not, he did not know and it did not matter. He had to hit this man before he turned that spot of yellow on him and then yelled for the others. In the split second that he saw the man's head, it seemed that an hour passed, an hour filled with pain and doubt and anguish and suspense, filled with the sharp throb of life lived upon a needle-point. He lifted his left hand, caught the gun which he held in his right, took it into the fingers of his left hand, turned it round, caught it again in his right and held it by the barrel: all one motion, swift, silent; done in one breath with eyes staring unblinkingly. *Hit him!* He lifted it, high, by the barrel. Yes. *Hit him!* His lips formed the words as he let it come down with a grunt which was a blending of a curse, a prayer, and a groan.

He felt the impact of the blow throughout the length of his arm, jarring his flesh slightly. His hand stopped in mid-air, at the point where the metal of the gun had met the bone of the skull; stopped, frozen, still, as though again about to lift and descend. In the instant, almost of the blow being struck, the white man emitted something like a soft cough; his flashlight fell into the snow, a fast flick of vanishing light. The man fell away from Bigger, on his face, full length in the cushion of snow, like a man falling soundlessly in a deep dream. Bigger was aware of the clicking sound of the metal against the bone of the skull; it stayed on in his ears, faint but distinct, like a sharp bright point lingering on in front of the eyes when a light has gone out suddenly and darkness is everywhere – so the click of the gun handle against the man's head stayed on in his ears. He had not moved from his tracks; his right hand was still extended, upward, in mid-air; he lowered it, looking at the man, the sound of the metal against bone fading in his ears like a dying whisper.

The sound of the siren had stopped at some time which he did not remember; then it started again, and the interval in which he had not heard it seemed to hold for him some preciously hidden danger, as though for a dreadful moment he had gone to sleep at his post with an enemy near. He looked through the whirling spokes of light and saw a trapdoor open upon the roof to his left. He stood rigid, holding the gun, watching, waiting. If only the man did not see him when he came up! A head came into view; a white man climbed out of the trapdoor and stood in the snow.

He flinched; someone was crawling in the loft below him. Would he be trapped? A voice, a little afraid, called from the open hole through which the man whom he had struck had climbed.

'Jerry!'

The voice sounded clearly in spite of the siren and the clang of the fire wagons.

'Jerry!'

The voice was a little louder now. It was the man's partner. Bigger looked back to the roof to his left; the man was still standing there, flashing a light round. If he would only leave! He had to get away from this trapdoor here. If that man came up to see about his partner and found him sprawled in the snow he would yell before he got a chance to hit him. He squeezed against the chimney, looking at the man on the roof to his left, holding his breath. The man turned, walked toward the trapdoor and climbed through. He waited to hear the door shut; it did. Now, that roof was clear! He breathed a silent prayer.

'Jeeerry!'

With gun in hand, Bigger crept across the roof. He came to a small mound of brick, where the upjutting ridge of the building's flat top joined that of the other. He paused and looked back. The hole was still empty. If he tried to climb over, would the man come out of the hole just in time to see him? He had to take the chance. He grabbed the ledge, hoisted himself upon it, and lay flat for a moment on the ice, then slid to the other side, rolling over. He felt snow in his face and eyes; his chest heaved. He crawled to another chimney and waited; it was so cold that he had a wild wish to merge into the icy bricks of the chimney and have it all over. He heard the voice again, this time loud, insistent:

'Jerry!'

He looked out from behind the chimney. The hole was still empty. But the next time the voice came he knew that the man was coming out, for he could feel the tremor of the voice, as though it were next to him.

'Jerry!'

Then he saw the man's face come through; it was stuck like a piece of white pasteboard above the top of the hole and when the man's voice sounded again Bigger knew that he had seen his partner in the snow.

'Jerry! *Say!*'

Bigger lifted his gun and waited.

'Jerry...'

The man came out of the hole and stood over his partner, then scrambled in again, screaming:

'Say! Say!'

Yes; the man would spread the word. Ought he to run? Suppose he went down into the trapdoor of another roof? Naw! There would be people standing in the hallways and they would be afraid; they would scream at the sight of him and he would be caught. They would be glad to give him up and put an end to this terror. It would be better to run farther over the roofs. He rose; then, just as he was about to run, he saw a head bob up in the hole. Another man came through and stood over Jerry. He was tall and he stooped over Jerry's form and seemed to be putting his hand upon his face. Then another came through. One of the men centered his flashlight on Jerry's body and Bigger saw one bend and roll the body over. The spotlight lit Jerry's face. One of the men ran to the sheer edge of the roof, overlooking the street; his hand went to his mouth and Bigger heard the sound of a whistle, sharp, thin. The roar in the street died; the siren stopped; but the circling columns of yellow continued to whirl. In the peace and quiet of the sudden calm, the man yelled,

'Surround the block!'

Bigger heard an answering shout.

'You got a line on 'im?'

'I think he's round here!'

A wild yell went up. Yes; they felt that they were near him now. He heard the man's shrill whistle sounding again. It got quiet, but not so quiet as before. There were shouts of wild joy floating up.

'Send up a stretcher and a detail of men!'

'O.K.!'

The man turned and went back to Jerry lying in the snow. Bigger heard snatches of talk.

'... how do you suppose it happened?'

'Looks like he was hit ...'

'... maybe he's about ...'

'Quick! Take a look over the roof!'

He saw one of the men rise and flash a light. The circling beams lit the roof to a daylight brightness and he could see that one man held a gun. He would have to cross to other roofs before this man or others came upon him. They were suspicious and would comb every inch of space on top of these houses. On all fours, he scrambled to the next ledge and then turned and looked back; the man was still standing, throwing the spot of yellow about over the snow. Bigger grabbed the icy ledge, hoisted himself flat upon it, and slid over. He did not think now of how much strength was needed to climb and run; the fear of capture made him forget even the cold, forget even that he had no strength left. From somewhere in him, out of the depths of flesh and blood and bone, he called up energy to run and dodge with but one impulse: he had to elude these men. He was crawling to the other ledge, over the snow, on his hands and knees, when he heard the man yell,

'There he is!'

The three words made him stop; he had been listening for them all night and when they came he seemed to feel the sky crashing soundlessly about him. What was the use of running? Would it not be better to stop, stand up, and lift his hands high above his head in surrender? Hell, naw! He continued to crawl.

'Stop, *you*!'

A shot rang out, whining past his head. He rose and ran to the ledge, leaped over; ran to the next ledge, leaped over it. He darted among the chimneys so that no one could see him long enough to shoot. He looked ahead and saw something huge and round and white looming up in the dark: a bulk rising up sheer from the snow of the roof and swelling in the night, glittering in the glare of the searching knives of light. Soon he would not be able to go much farther, for he would reach that point where the roof ended and dropped to the street below. He wove among the chimneys, his feet slipping and sliding over snow, keeping in mind that white looming bulk which he had glimpsed ahead of him. Was it something that would help him? Could he get upon it, or behind it, and hold them off? He was listening and expecting more shots as he ran, but none came.

He stopped at a ledge and looked back; he saw in the lurid glare of the slashing lances of light a man stumbling over the snow. Ought he to stop and shoot? Naw! More would be coming in a moment and he would only waste time. He had to find some place to hide, some ambush from which he could fight. He ran to another ledge, past the white looming bulk which now towered directly above him, then stopped, blinking: deep down below was a sea of white faces and he saw himself falling, spinning straight down into that ocean of boiling hate. He gripped the icy ledge with his fingers, thinking that if he had been running any faster he would have gone right off the roof, hurtling four floors.

Dizzily, he drew back. This was the end. There were no more roofs over which to run and dodge. He looked; the man was still coming. Bigger stood up. The siren was louder than before and there were more shouts and screams. Yes; those in the streets knew now that the police and vigilantes had trapped him upon the roofs. He remembered the quick glimpse he had had of the white looming bulk; he looked up. Directly above him, white with snow, was a high water tank with a round, flat top. There was a ladder made of iron whose slick rungs were coated with ice that gleamed like neon in the circling blades of yellow. He caught hold and climbed. He did not know where he was going; he knew only that he had to hide.

He reached the top of the tank and three shots sang past his head. He lay flat, on his stomach, in snow. He was high above the roof-tops and chimneys now and he had a wide view. A man was climbing over a near-by ledge, and beyond him was a small knot of men, their faces lit to a distinct whiteness by the swinging pencils of light. Men were coming up out of the trap-door far in front of him and were moving toward him, dodging behind chimneys. He raised the gun, leveled it, aimed, and shot; the men stopped but no one fell. He had missed. He shot again. No one fell. The knot of men broke up and disappeared behind ledges and chimneys. The noise in the street rose in a flood of strange joy. No doubt the sound of the pistol shots made them think that he was shot, captured, or dead.

He saw a man running toward the water tank in the open; he shot again. The man ducked behind a chimney. He had missed. Perhaps his hands were too cold to shoot straight? Maybe he ought to wait until they were closer? He turned his head just in time to see a man climbing over the edge of the roof, from the street side. The man was mounting a ladder which had been hoisted up the side of the building from the ground. He leveled the gun to shoot, but the man got over and left his line of vision, disappearing under the tank.

Why could he not shoot straight and fast enough? He looked in front of him and saw two men running under the tank. There were three men beneath the tank now. They were surrounding him, but they could not come for him without exposing themselves.

A small black object fell near his head in the snow, hissing, shooting forth a white vapor, like a blowing plume, which was carried away from him by the wind. Tear gas! With a movement of his hand he knocked it off the tank. Another came and he knocked it off. Two more came and he shoved them off. The wind blew strong, from the lake. It carried the gas away from his eyes and nose. He heard a man yell,

'Stop it! The wind's blowing it away! He's throwing 'em back!'

The bedlam in the street rose higher; more men climbed through trapdoors to the roof. He wanted to shoot, but remembered that he had but three bullets left. He would shoot when they were closer and he would save one bullet for himself. They would not take him alive.

'Come on down, boy!'

He did not move; he lay with gun in hand, waiting. Then, directly under his eyes, four white fingers caught hold of the icy edge of the water tank. He gritted his teeth and struck the white fingers with the butt of the gun. They vanished and he heard a thud as a body landed on the snow-covered roof. He lay waiting for more attempts to climb up, but none came.

'It's no use fighting, boy! You're caught! Come on down!!'

He knew that they were afraid, and yet he knew that it would soon be over, one way or another: they would either capture or kill him. He was surprised that he was not afraid. Under it all some part of his mind was beginning to stand aside; he was going behind his curtain, his wall, looking out with sullen stares of contempt. He was outside of himself now, looking on; he lay under a winter sky lit with tall gleams of whirling light, hearing thirsty screams and hungry shouts. He clutched his gun, defiant, unafraid.

'Tell 'em to hurry with the hose! The nigger's armed!'

What did that mean? His eyes roved, watching for a moving object to shoot at; but none appeared. He was not conscious of his body now; he could not feel himself at all. He knew only that he was lying here with a gun in his hand, surrounded by men who wanted to kill him. Then he heard a hammering noise near by; he looked. Behind the edge of a chimney he saw a trapdoor open.

'All right, boy!' a hoarse voice called. 'We're giving you your last chance. Come on down!'

He lay still. What was coming? He knew that they were not going to shoot, for they could not see him. Then what? And while wondering, he knew: a furious whisper of water, gleaming like silver in the bright lights, streaked above his head with vicious force, passing him high in the air and hitting the roof beyond with a thudding drone. They had turned on the water hose; the fire department had done that. They were trying to drive him into the open. The stream of water was coming from behind the chimney where the trapdoor had opened, but as yet the water had not touched him. Above him the rushing stream jerked this way and that; they were trying to reach him with it. Then the water hit him, in the side; it was like the blow of a pile driver. His breath left and he felt a dull pain in his side that spread, engulfing him. The water was trying to push him off the tank; he gripped the edges hard, feeling his strength ebbing. His chest heaved and he knew from the pain that throbbed in him that he would not be able to hold on much longer with water pounding at his body like this. He felt cold, freezing; his blood turned to ice, it seemed. He gasped, his mouth open. Then the gun loosened in his fingers; he tried to grip it again and found that he could not. The water left him; he lay gasping, spent.

'Throw that gun down, boy!'

He gritted his teeth. The icy water clutched again at his body like a giant hand; the chill of it squeezed him like the circling coils of a monstrous boa constrictor. His arms ached. He was behind his curtain now, looking down at himself freezing under the impact of water in sub-zero winds. Then the stream of water veered from his body.

'Throw that gun down, boy!'

He began to shake all over; he let go of the gun completely. Well, this was all. Why didn't they come for him? He gripped the edges of the tank again, digging his fingers into the snow and ice. His strength left. He gave up. He turned over on his back and looked weakly up into the sky through the high shifting lattices of light. This was all. They could shoot him now. Why didn't they shoot? Why didn't they come for him?

'Throw that gun down, boy!'

They wanted the gun. He did not have it. He was not afraid any more. He did not have strength enough to be.

'Throw that gun down, boy!'

Yes; take the gun and shoot it at them, shoot it empty. Slowly, he stretched out his hand and tried to pick up the gun, but his fingers were too stiff. Something laughed in him, cold and hard; he was laughing at himself. Why didn't they come

for him? They were afraid. He rolled his eyes, looking long-
ingly at the gun. Then, while he was looking at it, the stream of
hissing silver struck it and whirled it off the tank, out of
sight . . .

'There it is!'
'Come on down, boy! You're through!'
'Don't go up there! He might have another gun!'
'Come on down, boy!'

He was outside of it all now. He was too weak and cold to
hold onto the edges of the tank any longer; he simply lay atop
the tank, his mouth and eyes open, listening to the stream of
water whir above him. Then the water hit him again, in the
side; he felt his body sliding over the slick ice and snow. He
wanted to hold on, but could not. His body teetered on the
edge; his legs dangled in air. Then he was falling. He landed
on the roof, on his face, in snow, dazed.

He opened his eyes and saw a circle of white faces; but he was
outside of them, behind his curtain, his wall, looking on. He
heard men talking and their voices came to him from far away.

'That's him, all right!'
'Get 'im down to the street!'
'The water did it!'
'He seems half-frozen!'
'All right, get 'im down to the street!'

He felt his body being dragged across the snow of the roof.
Then he was lifted and put, feet first, into a trapdoor.

'You got 'im?'
'Yeah! Let 'im drop on!'
'O.K.!'

He dropped into rough hands inside of the dark loft. They
were dragging him by his feet. He closed his eyes and his head
slid along over rough planking. They struggled him through
the last trapdoor and he knew that he was inside of a building,
for warm air was on his face. They had him by his legs again
and were dragging him down a hall, over smooth carpet.

There was a short stop, then they started down the stairs with
him, his head bumping along the steps. He folded his wet arms

about his head to save himself, but soon the steps had pounded his elbows and arms so hard that all of his strength left. He relaxed, feeling his head bounding painfully down the steps. He shut his eyes and tried to lose consciousness. But he still felt it, drumming like a hammer in his brain. Then it stopped. He was near the street; he could hear shouts and screams coming to him like the roar of water. He was in the street now, being dragged over snow. His feet were up in the air, grasped by strong hands.

'Kill 'im!'

'Lynch 'im!'

'That black sonofabitch!'

They let go of his feet; he was in the snow, lying flat on his back. Round him surged a sea of noise. He opened his eyes a little and saw an array of faces, white and looming.

'Kill that black ape!'

Two men stretched his arms out, as though about to crucify him; they placed a foot on each of his wrists, making them sink deep down in the snow. His eyes closed, slowly, and he was swallowed in darkness.

BOOK THREE

Fate

THERE was no day for him now, and there was no night; there was but a long stretch of time, a long stretch of time that was very short; and then – the end. Toward no one in the world did he feel any fear now, for he knew that fear was useless; and toward no one in the world did he feel any hate now, for he knew that hate would not help him.

Though they carried him from one police station to another, though they threatened him, persuaded him, bullied him, and stormed at him, he steadfastly refused to speak. Most of the time he sat with bowed head, staring at the floor; or he lay full length upon his stomach, his face buried in the crook of an elbow, just as he lay now upon a cot with the pale yellow sunshine of a February sky falling obliquely upon him through the cold steel bars of the Eleventh Street Police Station.

Food was brought to him upon trays and an hour later the trays were taken away, untouched. They gave him packages of cigarettes, but they lay on the floor, unopened. He would not even drink water. He simply lay or sat, saying nothing, not noticing when anyone entered or left his cell. When they wanted him to go from one place to another, they caught him by the wrist and led him; he went without resistance, walking always with dragging feet, head down. Even when they snatched him up by the collar, his weak body easily lending itself to be manhandled, he looked without hope or resentment, his eyes like two still pools of black ink in his flaccid face. No one had seen him save the officials and he had asked to see no one. Not once during the three days following his capture had an image of what he had done come into his mind. He had thrust the whole thing back of him, and there it lay, monstrous

311

and horrible. He was not so much in a stupor, as in the grip of a deep physiological resolution not to react to anything.

Having been thrown by an accidental murder into a position where he had sensed a possible order and meaning in his relations with the people about him; having accepted the moral guilt and responsibility for that murder because it had made him feel free for the first time in his life; having felt in his heart some obscure need to be at home with people and having demanded ransom money to enable him to do it – having done all this and failed, he chose not to struggle any more. With a supreme act of will springing from the essence of his being, he turned away from his life and the long train of disastrous consequences that had flowed from it and looked wistfully upon the dark face of ancient waters upon which some spirit had breathed and created him, the dark face of the waters from which he had been first made in the image of a man with a man's obscure need and urge; feeling that he wanted to sink back into those waters and rest eternally.

And yet his desire to crush all faith in him was in itself built upon a sense of faith. The feelings of his body reasoned that if there could be no merging with the men and women about him, there should be a merging with some other part of the natural world in which he lived. Out of the mood of renunciation there sprang up in him again the will to kill. But this time it was not directed outward toward people, but inward, upon himself. Why not kill that wayward yearning within him that had led him to this end? He had reached out and killed and had not solved anything, so why not reach inward and kill that which had duped him? This feeling sprang up of itself, organically, automatically; like the rotted hull of a seed forming the soil in which it should grow again.

And, under and above it all, there was the fear of death before which he was naked and without defense; he had to go forward and meet his end like any other living thing upon the earth. And regulating his attitude toward death was the fact that he was black, unequal, and despised. Passively, he hungered for another orbit between two poles that would let him live again; for a new mode of life that would catch him up with the tension of hate and love. There would have to hover above him, like the stars in a full sky, a vast configuration of images and symbols whose magic and power could lift him up and make him live so intensely that the dread of being black and unequal would be forgotten; that even death would not matter, that it would be a victory. This would have to happen before he could look them in the face again: a new pride and a new humility would have to be born in him, a humility springing from a new identification with some part of the world in which he lived, and this identification forming the basis for a new hope that would function in him as pride and dignity.

But maybe it would never come; maybe there was no such thing for him; maybe he would have to go to his end just as he was, dumb, driven, with the shadow of emptiness in his eyes. Maybe this was all. Maybe the confused promptings, the excitement, the tingling, the elation – maybe they were false lights that led nowhere. Maybe they were right when they said that a black skin was bad, the covering of an apelike animal. Maybe he was just unlucky, a man born for dark doom, an obscene joke happening amid a colossal din of siren screams and white faces and circling lances of light under a cold and silken sky. But he could not feel that for long; just as soon as his feelings reached such a conclusion, the conviction that there was some way out surged back into him, strong and powerful, and, in his present state, condemning and paralyzing.

And then one morning a group of men came and caught him by the wrists and led him into a large room in the Cook County Morgue, in which there were many people. He blinked from the bright lights and heard loud and excited talking. The compact array of white faces and the constant flashing of bulbs for pictures made him stare in mounting amazement. His defense of indifference could protect him no longer. At first he thought that it was the trial that had begun, and he was prepared to sink back into his dream of nothingness. But it was not a court room. It was too informal for that. He felt crossing his feelings a sensation akin to the same one he had had when the reporters had first come into Mr Dalton's basement with their hats on, smoking cigars and cigarettes, asking questions; only now it was much stronger. There was in the air a silent mockery that challenged him. It was not their hate he felt; it was something deeper than that. He sensed that in their attitude toward him they had gone beyond hate. He heard in the sound of their voices a patient certainty; he saw their eyes gazing at him with calm conviction. Though he could not have put it into words, he felt that not only had they resolved to put him to death, but that they were determined to make his death mean more than a mere punishment; that they regarded him as a figment of that black world which they feared and were anxious to keep under control. The atmosphere of the crowd told him that they were going to use his death as a bloody symbol of fear to wave before the eyes of that black world. And as he felt it, rebellion rose in him. He had sunk to the lowest point this side of death, but when he felt his life again threatened in a way that meant that he was to go down the dark road a helpless spectacle of sport for others, he sprang back into action, alive, contending.

He tried to move his hands and found that they were shackled by strong bands of cold steel to white wrists of policemen sitting to either side of him. He looked round; a policeman stood in front of him and one in back. He heard a sharp, metallic click and his hands were free. There was a rising murmur of voices and he sensed that it was caused by his movements. Then his eyes became riveted on a white face, tilted slightly upward. The skin had a quality of taut anxiety and around the oval of white face was a framework of whiter hair. It was Mrs Dalton, sitting quietly, her frail, waxen hands folded in her lap. Bigger remembered as he looked at her that moment of stark terror when he had stood at the side of the bed in the dark blue room hearing his heart pound against his ribs with his fingers upon the pillow pressing down upon Mary's face to keep her from mumbling.

Sitting beside Mrs Dalton was Mr Dalton, looking straight before him with wide-open, unblinking eyes. Mr Dalton turned slowly and looked at Bigger and Bigger's eyes fell.

He saw Jan: blond hair; blue eyes; a sturdy, kind face looking squarely into his own. Hot shame flooded him as the scene in the car came back; he felt again the pressure of Jan's fingers upon his hand. And then shame was replaced by guilty anger as he recalled Jan's confronting him upon the sidewalk in the snow.

He was getting tired; the more he came to himself, the more a sense of fatigue seeped into him. He looked down at his clothes; they were damp and crumpled and the sleeves of his coat were drawn halfway up his arms. His shirt was open and he could see the black skin of his chest. Suddenly, he felt the fingers of his right hand throb with pain. Two fingernails were torn off. He could not remember how it had happened. He tried to move his tongue and found it swollen. His lips were dry and cracked and he wanted water. He felt giddy. The lights and faces whirled slowly, like a merry-go-round. He was falling swiftly through space...

When he opened his eyes he was stretched out upon a cot. A white face loomed above him. He tried to lift his body and was pushed back.

'Take it easy, boy. Here; drink this.'

A glass touched his lips. Ought he to drink? But what difference did it make? He swallowed something warm; it was milk. When the glass was empty he lay upon his back and stared at the white ceiling; the memory of Bessie and the milk she had warmed for him came back strongly. Then the image of her death came and he closed his eyes, trying to forget. His stomach growled; he was feeling better. He heard a low drone of voices. He gripped the edge of the cot and sat up.

'Hey! How're you feeling, boy?'

'Hunh?' he grunted. It was the first time he had spoken since they had caught him.

'How're you feeling?'

He closed his eyes and turned his head away, sensing that they were white and he was black, ·that they were the captors and he the captive.

'He's coming out of it.'

'Yeah. That crowd must've got 'im.'

'Say, boy! You want something to eat?'

He did not answer.

'Get 'im something. He doesn't know what he wants.'

'You better lie down, boy. You'll have to go back to the inquest this afternoon.'

He felt their hands pushing him back onto the cot. The door closed; he looked round. He was alone. The room was quiet. He had come out into the world again. He had not tried to; it had just happened. He was being turned here and there by a surge of strange forces he could not understand. It was not to save his life that he had come out; he did not care what they did to him. They could place him in the electric chair right now, for all he cared. It was to save his pride that he had come. He did not want them to make sport of him. If they had killed him that night when they were dragging him down the steps, that would have been a deed born of their strength over him. But he felt they had no right to sit and watch him, to use him for whatever they wanted.

The door opened and a policeman brought in a tray of food, set it on a chair next to him, and left. There was steak and fried potatoes and coffee. Gingerly, he cut a piece of steak and put it into his mouth. It tasted so good that he tried to swallow it before he chewed it. He sat on the edge of the cot and drew the chair forward so that he could reach the food. He ate so fast that his jaws ached. He stopped and held the food in his mouth, feeling the juices of his glands flowing round it. When he was through, he lit a cigarette, stretched out upon the cot and closed his eyes. He dozed off to an uneasy sleep.

Then suddenly he sat upright. He had not seen a newspaper in a long time. What were they saying now? He got up; he swayed and the room lurched. He was still weak and giddy. He leaned against the wall and walked slowly to the door. Cautiously, he turned the knob. The door swung in and he looked into the face of a policeman.

'What's the matter, boy?'

He saw a heavy gun sagging at the man's hip. The policeman caught him by the wrist and led him back to the cot.

'Here; take it easy.'

'I want a paper,' he said.

'Hunh? A paper?'

'I want to read the paper.'

'Wait a minute. I'll see.'

The policeman went out and presently returned with an armful of papers.

'Here you are, boy. You're in 'em all.'

He did not turn to the papers until after the man had left the room. Then he spread out the *Tribune* and saw: NEGRO RAPIST FAINTS AT INQUEST. He understood now; it was the inquest he had been taken to. He had fainted and they had brought him here. He read:

Overwhelmed by the sight of his accusers, Bigger Thomas, Negro sex-slayer, fainted dramatically this morning at the inquest of Mary Dalton, millionaire Chicago heiress.

Emerging from a stupor for the first time since his capture last Monday night, the black killer sat cowed and fearful as hundreds sought to get a glimpse of him.

'He looks exactly like an ape!' exclaimed a terrified young white girl who watched the black slayer being loaded onto a stretcher after he had fainted.

Though the Negro killer's body does not seem compactly built, he gives the impression of possessing abnormal physical strength. He is about five feet, nine inches tall and his skin is exceedingly black. His lower jaw protrudes obnoxiously, reminding one of a jungle beast.

His arms are long, hanging in a dangling fashion to his knees. It is easy to imagine how this man, in the grip of a brain-numbing sex passion, overpowered little Mary Dalton, raped her, murdered her, beheaded her, then stuffed her body into a roaring furnace to destroy the evidence of his crime.

His shoulders are huge, muscular, and he keeps them hunched, as if about to spring upon you at any moment. He looks at the world with a strange, sullen, fixed-from-under stare, as though defying all efforts of compassion.

All in all, he seems a beast utterly untouched by the softening influences of modern civilization. In speech and manner he lacks the charm of the average, harmless, genial, grinning southern darky so beloved by the American people.

The moment the killer made his appearance at the inquest, there were shouts of 'Lynch 'im! Kill 'im!'

But the brutish Negro seemed indifferent to his fate, as though inquests, trials, and even the looming certainty of the electric chair held no terror for him. He acted like an earlier missing link in the human species. He seemed out of place in a white man's civilization.

An Irish police captain remarked with deep conviction: 'I'm convinced that death is the only cure for the likes of him.'

For three days the Negro has refused all nourishment. Police believe that he is either trying to starve himself to death and cheat the chair, or that he is trying to excite sympathy for himself.

From Jackson, Mississippi, came a report yesterday from Edward Robertson, editor of the *Jackson Daily Star*, regarding Bigger Thomas' boyhood there. The editor wired:

'Thomas comes of a poor darky family of a shiftless and immoral variety. He was raised here and is known to local residents as an irreformable sneak thief and liar. We were unable to send him to the chain gang because of his extreme youth.

'Our experience here in Dixie with such depraved types of Negroes has shown that only the death penalty, inflicted in a public and dramatic manner, has any influence upon their peculiar mentality. Had that nigger Thomas lived in Mississippi and committed such a crime, no power under Heaven could have saved him from death at the hands of indignant citizens.

'I think it but proper to inform you that in many quarters it is believed that Thomas, despite his dead-black complexion, may have a minor portion of white blood in his veins, a mixture which generally makes for a criminal and intractable nature.

'Down here in Dixie we keep Negroes firmly in their places and we make them know that if they so much as touch a white woman, good or bad, they cannot live.

'When Negroes become resentful over imagined wrongs, nothing brings them to their senses so quickly as when citizens take the law into their hands and make an example out of a trouble-making nigger.

'Crimes such as the Bigger Thomas murders could be lessened by segregating all Negroes in parks, playgrounds, cafés, theatres, and street cars. Residential segregation is imperative. Such measures tend to keep them as much as possible out of direct contact with white women and lessen their attacks against them.

'We of the South believe that the North encourages Negroes to get more education than they are organically capable of absorbing, with the result that northern Negroes are generally more unhappy and restless than those of the South. If separate schools were maintained, it would be fairly easy to limit the Negroes' education by regulating the appropriation of moneys through city, county, and state legislative bodies.

'Still another psychological deterrent can be attained by conditioning Negroes so that they have to pay deference to the white person with whom they come in contact. This is done by regulating their speech and actions. We have found that the injection of an element of constant fear has aided us greatly in handling the problem.'

He lowered the paper; he could not read any more. Yes, of course; they were going to kill him; but they were having this sport with him before they did it. He held very still; he was trying to make a decision; not thinking, but feeling it out. Ought he to go back behind his wall? *Could* he go back now? He felt that he could not. But would not any effort he made not turn out like the others? Why go forward and meet more hate? He lay on the cot, feeling as he had felt that night when his fingers had gripped the icy edges of the water tank under the roving flares of light, knowing that men crouched below him with guns and tear gas, hearing the screams of sirens and shouts rising thirstily from ten thousand throats...

Overcome with drowsiness, he closed his eyes; then opened them abruptly. The door swung in and he saw a black face. Who was this? A tall, well-dressed black man came forward and paused. Bigger pulled up and leaned on his elbow. The man came all the way to the cot and stretched forth a dingy palm, touching Bigger's hand.

'Mah po' boy! May the good Lawd have mercy on yuh.'

He stared at the man's jet-black suit and remembered who he was: Reverend Hammond, the pastor of his mother's church. And at once he was on guard against the man. He shut his heart and tried to stifle all feeling in him. He feared that the preacher would make him feel remorseful. He wanted to tell him to go; but so closely associated in his mind was the man with his mother and what she stood for that he could not speak.

In his feelings he could not tell the difference between what this man evoked in him and what he had read in the papers; the love of his own kind and the hate of others made him feel equally guilty now.

'How yuh feel, son?' the man asked; he did not answer and the man's voice hurried on: 'Yo' ma ast me t' come 'n' see yuh. She wants t' come too.'

The preacher knelt upon the concrete floor and closed his eyes. Bigger clamped his teeth and flexed his muscles; he knew what was coming.

'Lawd Jesus, turn Yo' eyes 'n' look inter the heart of this po' sinner! Yuh said mercy wuz awways Yo's 'n' ef we ast fer it on bended knee Yuh'd po' it out inter our hearts 'n' make our cups run over! We's astin' Yuh t' po' out Yo' mercy now, Lawd! Po' it out fer this po' sinner boy who stan's in deep need of it! Ef his sins be as scarlet, Lawd, wash 'em white as snow! Fergive 'im fer whutever he's done, Lawd! Let the light of Yo' love guide 'im th'u these dark days! 'N' he'p them who's a-tryin' to he'p 'im, Lawd! Enter inter they hearts 'n' breathe compassion on they sperits! We ast this in the nama Yo' Son Jesus who died on the cross 'n' gave us the mercy of Yo' love! Ahmen...'

Bigger stared unblinkingly at the white wall before him as the preacher's words registered themselves in his consciousness. He knew without listening what they meant; it was the old voice of his mother telling of suffering, of hope, of love beyond this world. And he loathed it because it made him feel as condemned and guilty as the voice of those who hated him.

'Son...'

Bigger glanced at the preacher, and then away.

'Fergit ever'thing but yo' soul, son. Take yo' mind off ever'thing but eternal life. Fergit whut the newspaper say. Fergit yuh's black. Gawd looks past yo' skin 'n' inter yo' soul, son. He's lookin' at the only parta yuh that's *His*. He wants yuh 'n' He loves yuh. Give yo'se'f t' 'Im, son. Lissen, lemme tell yeh why yuh's here; lemme tell yuh a story tha'll make yo' heart glad...'

Bigger sat very still, listening and not listening. If someone had afterwards asked him to repeat the preacher's words, he would not have been able to do so. But he felt and sensed their meaning. As the preacher talked there appeared before him a vast black silent void and the images of the preacher swam in that void, grew large and powerful; familiar images which his mother had given him when he was a child at her knee; images which in turn aroused impulses long dormant, impulses that he had suppressed and sought to shunt from his life. They were images which had once given him a reason for living, had explained the world. Now they sprawled before his eyes and seized his emotions in a spell of awe and wonder.

... an endless reach of deep murmuring waters upon whose face was darkness and there was no form no shape no sun no stars and no land and a voice came out of the darkness and the waters moved to obey and there emerged slowly a huge spinning ball and the voice said *let there be light* and there was light and it was good light and the voice said *let there be a firmament* and the waters parted and there was a vast space over the waters which formed into clouds stretching above the waters and like an echo the voice came from far away saying *let dry land appear* and with thundering rustling the waters drained off and mountain peaks reared into view and there were valleys and rivers and the voice called the dry land *earth* and the waters *seas* and the earth grew grass and trees and flowers that gave off seed that fell to the earth to grow again and the earth was lit by the light of a million stars and for the day there was a sun and for the night there was a moon and there were days and weeks and months and years and the voice called out of the twilight and moving creatures came forth out of the great waters whales and all kinds of living creeping things and on the land there were beasts and cattle and the voice said *let us make man in our own image* and from the dusty earth a man rose up and loomed against the day and the sun and after him a woman rose up and loomed against the night and the moon and they lived as one flesh and there was no Pain no Longing no Time no Death and Life was like the flowers that bloomed round them in the garden of earth and out of the clouds came a voice saying *eat not of the fruit of the tree in the midst of the garden, neither touch it, lest ye die* . . .

The preacher's words ceased droning. Bigger looked at him out of the corners of his eyes. The preacher's face was black and sad and earnest and made him feel a sense of guilt deeper than that which even his murder of Mary had made him feel. He had killed within himself the preacher's haunting picture of life even before he had killed Mary; that had been his first murder. And now the preacher made it walk before his eyes like a ghost in the night, creating within him a sense of exclusion that was as cold as a block of ice. Why should this thing rise now to plague him after he had pressed a pillow of fear and hate over its face to smother it to death? To those who wanted to kill him he was not human, not included in that picture of Creation; and that was why he had killed it. To live, he had created a new world for himself, and for that he was to die.

Again the preacher's words seeped into his feelings:

'Son, yuh know whut tha' tree wuz? It wuz the tree of knowledge. It wuzn't enuff fer man t' be like Gawd, he wanted t' know *why*. 'N' all Gawd wanted 'im t' do wuz bloom like the flowers in the fiel's, live as chillun. Man wanted t' know why 'n' he fell from light t' darkness, from love t' damnation, from blessedness t' shame. 'N' Gawd cast 'em outa the garden 'n' tol' the man he had t' git his bread by the sweat of his brow 'n' tol' the woman she had t' bring fo'th her chillun in pain 'n' sorrow. The worl' turned ergin 'em 'n' they had t' fight the worl' fer life . . .'

. . . the man and the woman walked fearfully among trees their hands covering their nakedness and back of them high in the twilight against the clouds an angel waved a flaming sword driving them out of the garden into the wild night of cold wind and tears and pain and death and the man and woman took their food and burnt it to send smoke to the sky begging forgiveness . . .

'Son, fer thousan's of years we been prayin' for Gawd t' take th' cuss off us. Gawd heard our prayers 'n' said He'd show us a way back t' 'Im. His Son Jesus came down t' earth 'n' put on human flesh 'n' lived 'n' died t' show us the way. Jesus let men crucify 'Im; but His death wuz a victory. He showed us tha' t' live in this worl' wuz t' be crucified by it. This worl' ain' our home. Life ever' day is a crucifixion. There ain' but one way out, son, 'n' tha's Jesus' way, the way of love 'n' fergiveness. Be like Jesus. Don't resist. Thank Gawd tha' He done chose this way fer yuh t' come t' 'Im. It's love tha's gotta save yuh, son. Yuh gotta b'lieve tha' Gawd gives eternal life th'u the love of Jesus. Son, look at me . . .'

Bigger's black face rested in his hands and he did not move.

'Son, promise me yuh'll stop hatin' long enuff fer Gawd's love t' come inter yo' heart.'

Bigger said nothing.

'Won't yuh promise, son?'

Bigger covered his eyes with his hands.

'Jus' say yuh'll *try*, son.'

Bigger felt that if the preacher kept asking he would leap up and strike him. How could he believe in that which he had killed? He was guilty. The preacher rose, sighed, and drew from his pocket a small wooden cross with a chain upon it.

'Look, son. Ah'm holdin' in mah hands a wooden cross taken from a tree. A tree is the worl', son. 'N' nailed t' this tree is a sufferin' man. Tha's whut life is, son. Sufferin'. How kin yuh keep from b'lievin' the word of Gawd when Ah'm holdin' befo' yo' eyes the only thing tha' gives a meanin' t' yo' life? Here, lemme put it roun' yo' neck. When yuh git alone, look at this cross, son, 'n' b'lieve . . .'

They were silent. The wooden cross hung next to the skin of Bigger's chest. He was feeling the words of the preacher, feeling that life was flesh nailed to the world, a longing spirit imprisoned in the days of the earth.

He glanced up, hearing the doorknob turn. The door opened and Jan stood framed in it, hesitating. Bigger sprang to his feet, galvanized by fear. The preacher also stood, took a step backward, bowed, and said,

'Good mawnin', suh.'

Bigger wondered what Jan could want of him now. Was he not caught and ready for trial? Would not Jan get his revenge? Bigger stiffened as Jan walked to the middle of the floor and stood facing him. Then it suddenly occurred to Bigger that he need not be standing, that he had no reason to fear bodily harm from Jan here in jail. He sat and bowed his head; the room was quiet, so quiet that Bigger heard the preacher and Jan breathing. The white man upon whom he had tried to blame his crime stood before him and he sat waiting to hear angry words. Well, why didn't he speak? He lifted his eyes; Jan was looking straight at him and he looked away. But Jan's face was not angry. If he were not angry, then what did he want? He looked again and saw Jan's lips move to speak, but no words came. And when Jan did speak his voice was low and there were long pauses between the words; it seemed to Bigger that he was listening to a man talk to himself.

'Bigger, maybe I haven't the words to say what I want to say, but I'm going to try ... This thing hit me like a bomb. It t-t-took me all week to get myself together. They had me in jail and I couldn't for the life of me figure out what was happening ... I – I don't want to worry you, Bigger. I know you're in trouble. But there's something I just got to say ... You needn't talk to me unless you want to, Bigger. I think I know something of what you're feeling now. I'm not dumb, Bigger; I can understand, even if I didn't seem to understand that night...' Jan paused, swallowed, and lit a cigarette. 'Well, you jarred me ... I see now. I was kind of blind. I – I just wanted to come here and tell you that I'm not angry ... I'm not angry and I want you to let me help you. I don't hate you for trying to blame this thing on me ... Maybe you had good reasons ... I don't know. And maybe in a certain sense, I'm the one who's really guilty...' Jan paused again and sucked long and hard at his cigarette, blew the smoke out slowly and nervously bit his lips. 'Bigger, I've never done anything against you and your people in my life. But I'm a white man and it would be asking too much to ask you not to hate me, when every white man you see hates you. I – I know my ... my face looks like theirs to

you, even though I don't feel like they do. But I didn't know
we were so far apart until that night ... I can understand now
why you pulled that gun on me when I waited outside that
house to talk to you. It was the only thing you could have done;
but I didn't know my white face was making you feel guilty,
condemning you ...' Jan's lips hung open, but no words came
from them; his eyes searched the corners of the room.

Bigger sat silently, bewildered, feeling that he was on a vast
blind wheel being turned by stray gusts of wind. The preacher
came forward.

'Is yuh Mistah Erlone?'

'Yes,' said Jan, turning.

'Tha' wuz a mighty fine thing you jus' said, suh. Ef anybody
needs he'p, this po' boy sho does. Ah'm Reveren' Hammon'.'

Bigger saw Jan and the preacher shake hands.

'Though this thing hurt me, I got something out of it,' Jan
said, sitting down and turning to Bigger. 'It made me see
deeper into men. It made me see things I knew, but had forgotten. I – I lost something, but I got something, too ...' Jan
tugged at his tie and the room was silent, waiting for him to
speak. 'It taught me that it's your right to hate me, Bigger. I see
now that you couldn't do anything else but that; it was all you
had. But, Bigger, if I say you got the right to hate me, then that
ought to make things a little different, oughtn't it? Ever since I
got out of jail I've been thinking this thing over and I felt that
I'm the one who ought to be in jail for murder instead of you.
But that can't be, Bigger. I can't take upon myself the blame for
what one hundred million people have done.' Jan leaned forward and stared at the floor. 'I'm not trying to make up to you,
Bigger. I didn't come here to feel sorry for you. I don't suppose
you're so much worse off than the rest of us who get tangled up
in this world. I'm here because I'm trying to live up to this
thing as I see it. And it isn't easy, Bigger. I – I loved that girl
you killed. I – I loved ...' His voice broke and Bigger saw his
lips tremble. 'I was in jail grieving for Mary and then I thought
of all the black men who've been killed, the black men who had
to grieve when their people were snatched from them in slavery

and since slavery. I thought that if they could stand it, then I ought to.' Jan crushed the cigarette with his shoe. 'At first, I thought old man Dalton was trying to frame me, and I wanted to kill him. And when I heard that you'd done it, I wanted to kill you. And then I got to thinking. I saw if I killed, this thing would go on and on and never stop. I said, "I'm going to help that guy, if he lets me."'

'May Gawd in heaven bless yuh, son,' the preacher said.

Jan lit another cigarette and offered one to Bigger; but Bigger refused by keeping his hands folded in front of him and staring stonily at the floor. Jan's words were strange; he had never heard such talk before. The meaning of what Jan had said was so new that he could not react to it; he simply sat, staring, wondering, afraid even to look at Jan.

'Let me be on your side, Bigger,' Jan said. 'I can fight this thing with you, just like you've started it. I can come from all of those white people and stand here with you. Listen, I got a friend, a lawyer. His name is Max. He understands this thing and wants to help you. Won't you talk to him?'

Bigger understood that Jan was not holding him guilty for what he had done. Was this a trap? He looked at Jan and saw a white face, but an honest face. This white man believed in him, and the moment he felt that belief he felt guilty again; but in a different sense now. Suddenly, this white man had come up to him, flung aside the curtain and walked into the room of his life. Jan had spoken a declaration of friendship that would make other white men hate him: a particle of white rock had detached itself from that looming mountain of white hate and had rolled down the slope, stopping still at his feet. The word had become flesh. For the first time in his life a white man became a human being to him; and the reality of Jan's humanity came in a stab of remorse: he had killed what this man loved and had hurt him. He saw Jan as though someone had performed an operation upon his eyes, or as though someone had snatched a deforming mask from Jan's face.

Bigger started nervously; the preacher's hand came to his shoulder.

'Ah don't wanna break in 'n' meddle where Ah ain' got no bisness, suh,' the preacher said in a tone that was militant, but deferring. 'But there ain' no usa draggin' no communism in this thing, Mistah. Ah respecks yo' feelin's powerfully, suh; but whut yuh's astin' jus' stirs up mo' hate. Whut this po' boy needs is understandin' . . .'

'But he's got to fight for it,' Jan said.

'Ah'm wid yuh when yuh wanna change men's hearts,' the preacher said. 'But Ah can't go wid yuh when yuh wanna stir up mo' hate . . .'

Bigger sat looking from one to the other, bewildered.

'How on earth are you going to change men's hearts when the newspapers are fanning hate into them every day?' Jan asked.

'Gawd kin change 'em!' the preacher said fervently.

Jan turned to Bigger.

'Won't you let my friend help you, Bigger?'

Bigger's eyes looked round the room, as if seeking a means of escape. What could he say? He was guilty.

'Forget me,' he mumbled.

'I can't,' Jan said.

'It's over for me,' Bigger said.

'Don't you believe in yourself?'

'Naw,' Bigger whispered tensely.

'You believed enough to kill. You thought you were settling something, or you wouldn't've killed,' Jan said.

Bigger stared and did not answer. Did this man believe in him *that* much?

'I want you to talk to Max,' Jan said.

Jan went to the door. A policeman opened it from the outside. Bigger sat, open-mouthed, trying to feel where all this was bearing him. He saw a man's head come into the door, a head strange and white, with silver hair and a lean white face that he had never seen before.

'Come on in,' Jan said.

'Thanks.'

The voice was quiet, firm, but kind; there was about the

man's thin lips a faint smile that seemed to have always been there. The man stepped inside; he was tall.

'How are you, Bigger?'

Bigger did not answer. He was doubtful again. Was this a trap of some kind?

'This is Reverend Hammond, Max,' Jan said.

Max shook hands with the preacher, then turned to Bigger.

'I want to talk with you,' Max said. 'I'm from the Labor Defenders. I want to help you.'

'I ain't got no money,' Bigger said.

'I know that. Listen, Bigger, don't be afraid of me. And don't be afraid of Jan. We're not angry with you. I want to represent you in court. Have you spoken to any other lawyer?'

Bigger looked at Jan and Max again. They seemed all right. But how on earth could they help him? He wanted help, but dared not think that anybody would want to do anything for him now.

'Nawsuh,' he whispered.

'How have they treated you? Did they beat you?'

'I been sick,' Bigger said, knowing that he had to explain why he had not spoken or eaten in three days. 'I been sick and I don't know.'

'Are you willing to let us handle your case?'

'I ain't got no money.'

'Forget about that. Listen, they're taking you back to the inquest this afternoon. But you don't have to answer any questions, see? Just sit and say nothing. I'll be there and you won't have to be scared. After the inquest they'll take you to the Cook County Jail and I'll be over to talk with you.'

'Yessuh.'

'Here; take these cigarettes.'

'Thank you, suh.'

The door swung in and a tall, big-faced man with gray eyes came forward hurriedly. Max and Jan and the preacher stood to one side. Bigger stared at the man's face; it teased him. Then he remembered: it was Buckley, the man whose face he had seen the workmen pasting upon a billboard a few mornings ago. Bigger listened to the men talk, feeling in the tones of their voices a deep hostility toward one another.

'So, you're horning in again, hunh, Max?'

'This boy's my client and he's signing no confessions,' Max said.

'What the hell do I want with his confession?' Buckley asked. 'We've got enough evidence on him to put him in a dozen electric chairs.'

'I'll see that his rights are protected,' Max said.

'Hell, man! You can't do him any good.'

Max turned to Bigger.

'Don't let these people scare you, Bigger.'

Bigger heard, but did not answer.

'What in hell you reds can get out of bothering with a black thing like that, God only knows,' Buckley said, rubbing his hands across his eyes.

'You're afraid that you won't be able to kill this boy before the April elections, if we handle his case, aren't you, Buckley?' Jan asked.

Buckley whirled.

'Why in God's name can't you pick out somebody decent to defend sometimes? Somebody who'll appreciate it. Why do you reds take up with scum like this...?'

'You and your tactics have forced us to defend this boy,' Max said.

'What do you mean?' Buckley asked.

'If you had not dragged the name of the Communist Party into this murder, I'd not be here,' Max said.

'Hell, this boy signed the name of the Communist Party to the kidnap note...'

'I realize that,' Max said. 'The boy got the idea from the newspapers. I'm defending this boy because I'm convinced that men like you made him what he is. His trying to blame the Communists for his crime was a natural reaction for him. He had heard men like you lie about the Communists so much that he believed them. If I can make the people of this country understand why this boy acted like he did, I'll be doing more than defending him.'

Buckley laughed, bit off the tip of a fresh cigar, lit it and stood puffing. He advanced to the center of the room, cocked his head to one side, took the cigar out of his mouth and squinted at Bigger.

'Boy, did you ever think you'd be as important a man as you are right now?'

Bigger had been on the verge of accepting the friendship of Jan and Max, and now this man stood before him. What did the puny friendship of Jan and Max mean in the face of a million men like Buckley?

'I'm the State's Attorney,' Buckley said, walking from one end of the room to the other. His hat was on the back of his head. A white silk handkerchief peeped from the breast pocket of his black coat. He paused by the cot, towering over Bigger. How soon were they going to kill him, Bigger wondered. The breath of warm hope which Jan and Max had blown so softly upon him turned to frost under Buckley's cold gaze.

'Boy, I'd like to give you a piece of good advice. I'm going to be honest with you and tell you that you don't have to talk to me unless you want to, and I'll tell you that whatever you say to me might be used against you in court, see? But, boy, you're *caught*! That's the first thing you want to understand. We know what you've done. We got the evidence. So you might as well talk.'

'He'll decide that with me,' Max said.

Buckley and Max faced each other.

'Listen, Max. You're wasting your time. You'll never get this boy off in a million years. Nobody can commit a crime against a family like the Daltons and sneak out of it. Those poor old parents are going to be in that court room to see that this boy *burns*! This boy killed the *only* thing they had. If you want to save your face, you and your buddy can leave now and the papers won't know you were in here . . .'

'I reserve the right to determine whether I should defend him or not,' Max said.

'Listen, Max. You think I'm trying to hoodwink you, don't you?' Buckley asked, turning and going to the door. 'Let me show you something.'

A policeman opened the door and Buckley said,

'Tell 'em to come in.'

'O.K.'

The room was silent. Bigger sat on the cot, looking at the floor. He hated this; if anything could be done in his behalf, he himself wanted to do it; not others. The more he saw others exerting themselves, the emptier he felt. He saw the policeman fling the door wide open. Mr and Mrs Dalton walked in slowly and stood; Mr Dalton was looking at him, his face white. Bigger half-rose in dread, then sat again, his eyes lifted, but unseeing. He sank back to the cot.

Swiftly, Buckley crossed the room and shook hands with Mr Dalton, and, turning to Mrs Dalton, said:

'I'm dreadfully sorry, madam.'

Bigger saw Mr Dalton look at him, then at Buckley.

'Did he say who was in this thing with him?' Mr Dalton asked.

'He's just come out of it,' Buckley said. 'And he's got a lawyer now.'

'I have charge of his defense,' Max said.

Bigger saw Mr Dalton look briefly at Jan.

'Bigger, you're a foolish boy if you don't tell who was in this thing with you,' Mr Dalton said.

Bigger tightened and did not answer. Max walked over to Bigger and placed a hand on his shoulder.

'I will talk to him, Mr Dalton,' Max said.

'I'm not here to bully this boy,' Mr Dalton said. 'But it'll go easier with him if he tells all he knows.'

There was silence. The preacher came forward slowly, hat in hand, and stood in front of Mr Dalton.

'Ah'm a preacher of the gospel, suh,' he said. ' 'N' Ah'm mighty sorry er'bout whut's done happened t' yo' daughter. Ah knows of yo' good work, suh. 'N' the likes of this should'na come t' yuh.'

Mr Dalton sighed and said wearily,

'Thank you.'

'The best thing you can do is help us,' Buckley said, turning to Max. 'A grave wrong has been done to two people who've helped Negroes more than anybody I know.'

'I sympathize with you, Mr Dalton,' Max said. 'But killing this boy isn't going to help you or any of us.'

'I tried to help him,' Mr Dalton said.

'We wanted to send him to school,' said Mrs Dalton faintly.

'I know,' Max said. 'But those things don't touch the fundamental problem involved here. This boy comes from an oppressed people. Even if he's done wrong, we must take that into consideration.'

'I want you to know that my heart is not bitter,' Mr Dalton said. 'What this boy has done will not influence my relations with the Negro people. Why, only today I sent a dozen ping-pong tables to the South Side Boys' Club...'

'Mr Dalton!' Max exclaimed, coming forward suddenly. 'My God, man! Will ping-pong keep men from murdering? Can't you *see*? Even after losing your daughter, you're going to keep going in the *same* direction? Don't you grant as much life-feeling to other men as you have? Could *ping-pong* have kept you from making your millions? This boy and millions like him want a meaningful life, not ping-pong...'

'What do you want me to do?' Mr Dalton asked coldly. 'Do you want me to die and atone for a suffering I never caused? I'm not responsible for the state of this world. I'm doing all one man can. I suppose you want me to take my money and fling it out to the millions who have nothing?'

'No; no; no... Not that,' Max said. 'If you felt that millions of others experienced life as deeply as you, but differently, you'd see that what you're doing doesn't help. Something of a more fundamental nature...'

'Communism!' Buckley boomed, pulling down the corners of his lips. 'Gentlemen, let's don't be childish! This boy's going on trial for his life. My job is to enforce the laws of this state...'

Buckley's voice stopped as the door opened and the policeman looked inside.

'What is it?' Buckley asked.

'The boy's folks are here.'

Bigger cringed. Not this! Not here; not *now*! He did not want his mother to come in here now, with these people standing round. He looked about with a wild, pleading expression. Buckley watched him, then turned back to the policeman.

'They have a right to see 'im,' Buckley said. 'Let 'em come in.'

Though he sat, Bigger felt his legs trembling. He was so tense in body and mind that when the door swung in he bounded up and stood in the middle of the room. He saw his mother's face; he wanted to run to her and push her back through the door. She was standing still, one hand upon the doorknob; the other hand clutched a frayed pocketbook, which she dropped and ran to him, throwing her arms around him, crying,

'My baby . . .'

Bigger's body was stiff with dread and indecision. He felt his mother's arms tight about him and he looked over her shoulder and saw Vera and Buddy come slowly inside and stand, looking about timidly. Beyond them he saw Gus and G.H. and Jack, their mouths open in awe and fear. Vera's lips were trembling and Buddy's hands were clenched. Buckley, the preacher, Jan, Max, Mr and Mrs Dalton stood along the wall, behind him, looking on silently. Bigger wanted to whirl and blot them from sight. The kind words of Jan and Max were forgotten now. He felt that all of the white people in the room were measuring every inch of his weakness. He identified himself with his family and felt their naked shame under the eyes of white folks. While looking at his brother and sister and feeling his mother's arms about him; while knowing that Jack and G.H. and Gus were standing awkwardly in the doorway staring at him in curious disbelief – while being conscious of all this, Bigger felt a wild and outlandish conviction surge in him: *They ought to be glad!* It was a strange but strong feeling, springing from the very depths of his life. Had he not taken fully upon himself the crime of being black? Had he not done the thing which they dreaded above all others? Then they ought not stand here and pity him, cry over him; but look at him and go home, contented, feeling that their shame was washed away.

'Oh, Bigger, son!' his mother wailed. 'We been so worried ... We ain't slept a single night! The police is there all the time ... They stand outside our door ... They watch and follow us everywhere! Son, son ...'

Bigger heard her sobs; but what could he do? She ought not to have come here. Buddy came over to him, fumbling with his cap.

'Listen, Bigger, if you didn't do it, just tell me and I'll fix 'em. I'll get a gun and kill four or five of 'em ...'

The room gasped. Bigger turned his head quickly and saw that the white faces along the wall were shocked and startled.

'Don't talk that way, Buddy,' the mother sobbed. 'You want me to die right now? I can't stand no more of this. You mustn't talk that way ... We in enough trouble now ...'

'Don't let 'em treat you bad, Bigger,' Buddy said stoutly.

Bigger wanted to comfort them in the presence of the white folks, but did not know how. Desperately, he cast about for something to say. Hate and shame boiled in him against the people behind his back; he tried to think of words that would defy them, words that would let them know that he had a world and life of his own in spite of them. And at the same time he wanted those words to stop the tears of his mother and sister, to quiet and soothe the anger of his brother; he longed to stop those tears and that anger because he knew that they were futile, that the people who stood along the wall back of him had the destiny of him and his family in their heads.

'Aw, Ma, don't you-all worry none,' he said, amazed at his own words; he was possessed by a queer, imperious nervous energy. 'I'll be out of this in no time.'

His mother gave him an incredulous stare. Bigger turned his head again and looked feverishly and defiantly at the white faces along the wall. They were staring at him in surprise. Buckley's lips were twisted in a faint smile. Jan and Max looked dismayed. Mrs Dalton, white as the wall behind her, listened, open-mouthed. The preacher and Mr Dalton were shaking their heads sadly. Bigger knew that no one in the room, except Buddy, believed him. His mother turned her face away and cried. Vera knelt upon the floor and covered her face with her hands.

'Bigger,' his mother's voice came low and quiet; she caught his face between the palms of her trembling hands. 'Bigger,' she said, 'tell me. Is there anything, *any*thing we can do?'

He knew that his mother's question had been prompted by his telling her that he would get out of all this. He knew that they had nothing; they were so poor that they were depending upon public charity to eat. He was ashamed of what he had done; he should have been honest with them. It had been a wild and foolish impulse that had made him try to appear strong and innocent before them. Maybe they would remember him only by those foolish words after they had killed him. His mother's eyes were sad, skeptical; but kind, patient, waiting for his answer. Yes; he had to wipe out that lie, not only so that they might know the truth, but to redeem himself in the eyes of those white faces behind his back along the white wall. He was lost; but he would not cringe; he would not lie, not in the presence of that white mountain looming behind him.

'There ain't nothing, Ma. But I'm all right,' he mumbled.

There was silence. Buddy lowered his eyes. Vera sobbed louder. She seemed so little and helpless. She should not have come here. Her sorrow accused him. If he could only make her go home. It was precisely to keep from feeling this hate and shame and despair that he had always acted hard and tough toward them; and now he was without defense. His eyes roved the room, seeing Gus and G.H. and Jack. They saw him looking at them and came forward.

'I'm sorry, Bigger,' Jack said, his eyes on the floor.

'They picked us up, too,' G.H. said, as though trying to comfort Bigger with the fact. 'But Mr Erlone and Mr Max got us out. They tried to make us tell about a lot of things we didn't do, but we wouldn't tell.'

'Anything we can do, Bigger?' Gus asked.

'I'm all right,' Bigger said. 'Say, when you go, take Ma home, will you?'

'Sure; sure,' they said.

Again there was silence and Bigger's taut nerves ached to fill it up.

'How you l-l-like them sewing classes at the Y, Vera?' he asked.

Vera tightened her hands over her face.

'Bigger,' his mother sobbed, trying to talk through her tears. 'Bigger, honey, she won't go to school no more. She says the other girls look at her and make her 'shamed . . .'

He had lived and acted on the assumption that he was alone, and now he saw that he had not been. What he had done made others suffer. No matter how much he would long for them to forget him, they would not be able to. His family was a part of him, not only in bood, but in spirit. He sat on the cot and his mother knelt at his feet. Her face was lifted to his; her eyes were empty, eyes that looked upward when the last hope of earth had failed.

'I'm praying for you, son. That's all I can do now,' she said. 'The Lord knows I did all I could for you and your sister and brother. I scrubbed and washed and ironed from morning till night, day in and day out, as long as I had strength in my old body. I did all I know how, son, and if I left anything undone, it's just 'cause I didn't know. It's just 'cause your poor old ma couldn't see, son. When I heard the news of what happened, I got on my knees and turned my eyes to God and asked Him if I had raised you wrong. I asked Him to let me bear your burden if I did wrong by you. Honey, your poor old ma can't do nothing now. I'm old and this is too much for me. I'm at the end of my rope. Listen, son, your poor old ma wants you to promise her one thing . . . Honey, when ain't nobody round you, when you alone, get on your knees and tell God everything. Ask Him to guide you. That's all you can do now. Son, *promise* me you'll go to Him.'

'Ahmen!' the preacher intoned fervently.

'Forget me, Ma,' Bigger said.

'Son, I can't forget you. You're my boy. I brought you into this world.'

'Forget me, Ma.'

'Son, I'm worried about you. I can't help it. You got your soul to save. I won't be able to rest as long as I'm on this earth if I thought you had gone away from us without asking God for help. Bigger, we had a hard time in this world, but through it all, we been together, ain't we?'

'Yessum,' he whispered.

'Son, there's a place where we can be together again in the great bye and bye. God's done fixed it so we can. He's fixed a meeting place for us, a place where we can live without fear. No matter what happens to us here, we can be together in God's heaven. Bigger, your old ma's a-begging you to promise her you'll pray.'

'She's tellin' yuh right, son,' the preacher said.

'Forget me, Ma,' Bigger said.

'Don't you want to see your old ma again, son?'

Slowly, he stood up and lifted his hands and tried to touch his mother's face and tell her yes; and as he did so something screamed deep down in him that it was a lie, that seeing her after they killed him would never be. But his mother believed; it was her last hope; it was what had kept her going through the long years. And she was now believing it all the harder because of the trouble he had brought upon her. His hands finally touched her face and he said with a sigh (knowing that it would never be, knowing that his heart did not believe, knowing that when he died, it would be over, forever):

'I'll pray, Ma.'

Vera ran to him and embraced him. Buddy looked grateful. His mother was so happy that all she could do was cry. Jack and G.H. and Gus smiled. Then his mother stood up and encircled him with her arms.

'Come here, Vera,' she whimpered.

Vera came.

'Come here, Buddy.'

Buddy came.

'Now, put your arms around your brother,' she said.

They stood in the middle of the floor, crying, with their arms locked about Bigger. Bigger held his face stiff, hating them and himself, feeling the white people along the wall watching. His mother mumbled a prayer, to which the preacher chanted.

'Lord, here we is, maybe for the last time. You gave me these children, Lord, and told me to raise 'em. If I failed, Lord, I did the best I could (*Ahmen!*) These poor children's been with me a long time and they's all I got. Lord, please let me see 'em again after the sorrow and suffering of this world! (*Hear her, Lawd!*) Lord, please let me see 'em where I can love 'em in peace. Let me see 'em again beyond the grave!' (*Have mercy, Jesus!*) You said You'd heed prayer, Lord, and I'm asking this in the name of Your son.'

'Ahmen 'n' Gawd bless yuh, Sistah Thomas,' the preacher said.

They took their arms from round Bigger, silently, slowly; then turned their faces away, as though their weakness made them ashamed in the presence of powers greater than themselves.

'We leaving you now with God, Bigger,' his mother said. 'Be sure and pray, son.'

They kissed him.

Buckley came forward.

'You'll have to go now, Mrs Thomas,' he said. He turned to Mr and Mrs Dalton. 'I'm sorry, Mrs Dalton. I didn't mean to keep you standing there so long. But you see how things are . . .'

Bigger saw his mother straighten suddenly and stare at the blind white woman.

'Is you Mrs Dalton?' she asked.

Mrs Dalton moved nervously, lifted her thin, white hands and tilted her head. Her mouth came open and Mr Dalton placed an arm about her.

'Yes,' Mrs Dalton whispered.

'Oh, Mrs Dalton, come right this way,' Buckley said hurriedly.

'No; please,' Mrs Dalton said. 'What is it, Mrs Thomas?'

Bigger's mother ran and knelt on the floor at Mrs Dalton's feet.

'Please, mam!' she wailed. 'Please, don't let 'em kill my boy! You know how a mother feels! Please, mam ... We live in your house ... They done asked us to move ... We ain't got nothing...'

Bigger was paralyzed with shame; he felt violated.

'*Ma!*' he shouted, more in shame than anger.

Max and Jan ran to the black woman and tried to lift her up.

'That's all right, Mrs Thomas,' Max said. 'Come with me.'

'Wait,' Mrs Dalton said.

'Please, mam! Don't let 'em kill my boy! He ain't never had a chance! He's just a poor boy! Don't let 'em kill 'im! I'll work for you for the rest of my life! I'll do anything you say, mam!' the mother sobbed.

Mrs Dalton stooped slowly, her hands trembling in the air. She touched the mother's head.

'There's nothing I can do now,' Mrs Dalton said calmly. 'It's out of my hands. I did all I could, when I wanted to give your boy a chance at life. You're not to blame for this. You must be brave. Maybe it's better...'

'If you speak to 'em, they'll listen to you, mam,' the mother sobbed. 'Tell 'em to have mercy on my boy...'

'Mrs Thomas, it's too late for me to do anything now,' Mrs Dalton said. 'You must not feel like this. You have your other children to think of...'

'I know you hate us, mam! You lost your daughter...'

'No; no ... I don't hate you,' Mrs Dalton said.

The mother crawled from Mrs Dalton to Mr Dalton.

'You's rich and powerful,' she sobbed. 'Spare me my boy...'

Max struggled with the black woman and got her to her feet. Bigger's shame for his mother amounted to hate. He stood with clenched fists, his eyes burning. He felt that in another moment he would have leaped at her.

'That's all right, Mrs Thomas,' Max said.

Mr Dalton came forward.

'Mrs Thomas, there's nothing we can do,' he said. 'This thing is out of our hands. Up to a certain point we can help you, but beyond that ... People must protect themselves. But you won't have to move. I'll tell them not to make you move.'

The black woman sobbed. Finally, she quieted enough to speak.

'Thank you, sir. God knows I thank you ...'

She turned again toward Bigger, but Max led her from the room. Jan caught hold of Vera's arm and led her forward, then stopped in the doorway, looking at Jack and G.H. and Gus.

'You boys going to the South Side?'

'Yessuh,' they said.

'Come on. I got a car downstairs. I'll take you.'

'Yessuh.'

Buddy lingered, looking wistfully at Bigger.

'Good-bye, Bigger,' he said.

'Good-bye, Buddy,' Bigger mumbled.

The preacher passed Bigger and pressed his arm.

'Gawd bless you, son.'

They all left except Buckley. Bigger sat again upon the cot, weak and exhausted. Buckley stood over him.

'Now, Bigger, you see all the trouble you've caused? Now, I'd like to get this case out of the way as soon as possible. The longer you stay in jail, the more agitation there'll be for and against you. And that doesn't help you any, no matter who tells you it does. Boy, there's not but one thing for you to do, and that's to come clean. I know those reds, Max and Erlone, have told you a lot of things about what they're going to do for you. But, don't believe 'em. They're just after publicity, boy; just after building themselves up at your expense, see? They can't do a *damn* thing for you! You're dealing with the *law* now! And if you let those reds put a lot of fool ideas into your head, then you're gambling with your own life.'

Buckley stopped and relit his cigar. He cocked his head to one side, listening.

'You hear that?' he asked softly.

Bigger looked at him, puzzled. He listened, hearing a faint din.

'Come here, boy. I want to show you something,' he said, rising and catching hold of Bigger's arm.

Bigger was reluctant to follow him.

'Come on. Nobody's going to hurt you.'

Bigger followed him out of the door; there were several policemen standing on guard in the hallway. Buckley led Bigger to a window through which he looked and saw the streets below crowded with masses of people in all directions.

'See that, boy? Those people would like to lynch you. That's why I'm asking you to trust me and talk to me. The quicker we get this thing over, the better for you. We're going to try to keep 'em from bothering you. But can't you see the longer they stay around here, the harder it'll be for us to handle them?'

Buckley let go of Bigger's arm and hoisted the window; a cold wind swept in and Bigger heard a roar of voices. Involuntarily, he stepped backward. Would they break into the jail? Buckley shut the window and led him back to the room. He sat upon the cot and Buckley sat opposite him.

'You look like an intelligent boy. You see what you're in. Tell me about this thing. Don't let those reds fool you into saying you're not guilty. I'm talking to you as straight as I'd talk to a son of mine. Sign a confession and get this over with.'

Bigger said nothing; he sat looking at the floor.

'Was Jan mixed up in this?'

Bigger heard the faint excited sound of mob voices coming through the concrete walls of the building.

'He proved an alibi and he's free. Tell me, did he leave you holding the bag?'

Bigger heard the far-away clang of a streetcar.

'If he made you do it, then sign a complaint against him.'

Bigger saw the shining tip of the man's black shoes; the sharp creases in his striped trousers; the clear, icy glinting of the eye-glasses upon his high, long nose.

'Boy,' said Buckley in a voice so loud that Bigger flinched, 'where's Bessie?'

Bigger's eyes widened. He had not thought of Bessie but once since his capture. Her death was unimportant beside that of Mary's; he knew that when they killed him it would be for Mary's death, not Bessie's.

'Well, boy, we found her. You hit her with a brick, but she didn't die right away . . .'

Bigger's muscles jerked him to his feet. Bessie *alive*. But the voice droned on and he sat down.

'She tried to get out of that air-shaft, but she couldn't. She froze to death. We got the brick you hit her with. We got the blanket and the quilt and the pillows you took from her room. We got a letter from her purse she had written to you and hadn't mailed, a letter telling you she didn't want to go through with trying to collect the ransom money. You see, boy, we got you. Come on, now, tell me all about it.'

Bigger said nothing. He buried his face in his hands.

'You raped her, didn't you? Well, if you won't tell about Bessie, then tell me about that woman you raped and choked to death over on University Avenue last fall.'

Was the man trying to scare him, or did he really think he had done other killings?

'Boy, you might just as well tell me. We've got a line on all you ever did. And how about the girl you attacked in Jackson Park last summer? Listen, boy, when you were in your cell sleeping and wouldn't talk, we brought women in to identify you. Two women swore complaints against you. One was the sister of the woman you killed last fall, Mrs Clinton. The other woman, Miss Ashton, says you attacked her last summer by climbing through the window of her bedroom.'

'I ain't bothered no woman last summer or last fall either,' Bigger said.

'Miss Ashton identified you. She swears you're the one.'

'I don't know nothing about it.'

342

'But Mrs Clinton, the sister of the woman you killed last fall, came to your cell and pointed you out. Who'll believe you when you say you didn't do it? You killed and raped two women in two days; who'll believe you when you say you didn't rape and kill the others? Come on, boy. You haven't a chance of holding out.'

'I don't know nothing about other women,' Bigger repeated stubbornly.

Bigger wondered how much did the man really know. Was he lying about the other women in order to get him to tell about Mary and Bessie? Or were they really trying to pin other crimes upon him?

'Boy, when the newspapers get hold of what we've got on you, you're cooked. I'm not the one who's doing this. The Police Department is digging up the dirt and bringing it to me. Why don't you talk? Did you kill the other women? Or did somebody make you do it? Was Jan in this business? Were the reds helping you? You're a fool if Jan was mixed up in this and you won't tell.'

Bigger shifted his feet and listened to the faint clang of another streetcar passing. The man leaned forward, caught hold of Bigger's arm and spoke while shaking him.

'You're hurting nobody but yourself holding out like this, boy! Tell me, were Mary, Bessie, Mrs Clinton's sister, and Miss Ashton the only women you raped or killed?'

The words burst out of Bigger:

'I never heard of no Miss Clinton or Miss Ashton before!'

'Didn't you attack a girl in Jackson Park last summer?'

'Naw!'

'Didn't you choke and rape a woman on University Avenue last fall?'

'Naw!'

'Didn't you climb through a window out in Englewood last fall and rape a woman?'

'Naw; naw! I tell you I didn't!'

'You're not telling the truth, boy. Lying won't get you anywhere.'

'I *am* telling the truth!'

'Whose idea was the kidnap note? Jan's?'

'He didn't have nothing to do with it,' said Bigger, feeling a keen desire on the man's part to have him implicate Jan.

'What's the use of your holding out, boy? Make it easy for yourself.'

Why not talk and get it over with? They knew he was guilty. They could prove it. If he did not talk, then they would say he had committed every crime they could think of.

'Boy, why didn't you and your pals rob Blum's store like you'd planned to last Saturday?'

Bigger looked at him in surprise. They had found that out, too!

'You didn't think I knew about that, did you? I know a lot more, boy. I know about that dirty trick you and your friend Jack pulled off in the Regal Theatre, too. You wonder how I know it? The manager told us when we were checking up. I know what boys like you do, Bigger. Now, come on. You wrote that kidnap note, didn't you?'

'Yeah,' he sighed. 'I wrote it.'

'Who helped you?'

'Nobody.'

'Who was going to help you to collect the ransom money?'

'Bessie.'

'Come on. Was it Jan?'

'Naw.'

'Bessie?'

'Yeah.'

'Then why did you kill her?'

Nervously, Bigger's fingers fumbled with a pack of cigarettes and got one out. The man struck a match and held a light for him, but he struck his own match and ignored the offered flame.

'When I saw I couldn't get the money, I killed her to keep her from talking,' he said.

'And you killed Mary, too?'

'I didn't mean to kill her, but it don't matter now,' he said.

'Did you lay her?'

'Naw.'

'You laid Bessie before you killed her. The doctors said so. And now you expect me to believe you didn't lay Mary.'

'I *didn't*!'

'Did Jan?'

'Naw.'

'Didn't Jan lay her first and then you? . . .'

'Naw; naw . . .'

'But Jan wrote the kidnap note, didn't he?'

'I never saw Jan before that night.'

'But didn't he write the note?'

'Naw; I tell you he didn't.'

'*You* wrote the note?'

'Yeah.'

'Didn't Jan tell you to write it?'

'Naw.'

'Why did you kill Mary?'

He did not answer.

'See here, boy. What you say doesn't make sense. You were never in the Dalton home until Saturday night. Yet, in one night a girl is raped, killed, burnt, and the next night a kidnap note is sent. Come on. Tell me everything that happened and about everybody who helped you.'

'There wasn't nobody but me. I don't care what happens to me, but you can't make me say things about other people.'

'But you told Mr Dalton that Jan was in this thing, too.'

'I was trying to blame it on him.'

'Well, come on. Tell me everything that happened.'

Bigger rose and went to the window. His hands caught the cold steel bars in a hard grip. He knew as he stood there that he could never tell why he had killed. It was not that he did not really want to tell, but the telling of it would have involved an explanation of his entire life. The actual killing of Mary and Bessie was not what concerned him most; it was knowing and feeling that he could never make anybody know what had driven him to it. His crimes were known, but what he had felt before he committed them would never be known. He would have gladly admitted his guilt if he had thought that in doing so he could have also given in the same breath a sense of the deep, choking hate that had been his life, a hate that he had not wanted to have, but could not help having. How could he do that? The impulsion to try to tell was as deep as had been the urge to kill.

He felt a hand touch his shoulder; he did not turn round; his eyes looked downward and saw the man's gleaming black shoes.

'I know how you feel, boy. You're colored and you feel that you haven't had a square deal, don't you?' the man's voice came low and soft; and Bigger, listening, hated him for telling him what he knew was true. He rested his tired head against the steel bars and wondered how was it possible for this man to know so much about him and yet be so bitterly against him. 'Maybe you've been brooding about this color question a long time, hunh, boy?' the man's voice continued low and soft. 'Maybe you think I don't understand? But I do. I know how it feels to walk along the streets like other people, dressed like them, talking like them, and yet excluded for no reason except that you're black. I know your people. Why, they give me votes out there on the South Side every election. I once talked to a colored boy who raped and killed a woman, just like you raped and killed Mrs Clinton's sister . . .'

'I didn't do it!' Bigger screamed.

'Why keep saying that? If you talk, maybe the judge'll help you. Confess it all and get it over with. You'll feel better. Say, listen, if you tell me everything, I'll see that you're sent to the hospital for an examination, see? If they say you're not responsible, then maybe you won't have to die . . .'

Bigger's anger rose. He was not crazy and he did not want to be called crazy.

'I don't want to go to no hospital.'

'It's a way out for you, boy.'

'I don't want no way out.'

'Listen, start at the beginning. Who was the first woman you ever killed?'

He said nothing. He wanted to talk, but he did not like the note of intense eagerness in the man's voice. He heard the door behind him open; he turned his head just in time to see another white man look in questioningly.

'I thought you wanted me,' the man said.

'Yes; come on in,' Buckley said.

The man came in and took a seat, holding a pencil and paper on his knee.

'Here, Bigger,' Buckley said, taking Bigger by the arm. 'Sit down here and tell me all about it. Get it *over* with.'

Bigger wanted to tell how he had felt when Jan had held his hand; how Mary had made him feel when she asked him about how Negroes lived; the tremendous excitement that had hold of him during the day and night he had been in the Dalton home – but there were no words for him.

'You went to Mr Dalton's home at five-thirty that Saturday, didn't you?'

'Yessuh,' he mumbled.

Listlessly, he talked. He traced his every action. He paused at each question Buckley asked and wondered how he could link up his bare actions with what he had felt; but his words came out flat and dull. White men were looking at him, waiting for his words, and all the feelings of his body vanished, just as they had when he was in the car between Jan and Mary. When he was through, he felt more lost and undone than when he was captured. Buckley stood up; the other white man rose and held out the papers for him to sign. He took the pen in hand. Well, why shouldn't he sign? He was guilty. He was lost. They were going to kill him. Nobody could help him. They were standing in front of him, bending over him, looking at him, waiting. His hand shook. He signed.

Buckley slowly folded the papers and put them into his pocket. Bigger looked up at the two men, helplessly, wonderingly. Buckley looked at the other white man and smiled.

'That was not as hard as I thought it would be,' Buckley said.

'He came through like a clock,' the other man said.

Buckley looked down at Bigger and said,

'Just a scared colored boy from Mississippi.'

There was a short silence. Bigger felt that they had forgotten him already. Then he heard them speaking.

'Anything else, chief?'

'Naw. I'll be at my club. Let me know how the inquest turns out.'

'O.K., chief.'

'So long.'

'I'll be seeing you, chief.'

Bigger felt so empty and beaten that he slid to the floor. He heard the feet of the men walking away softly. The door opened and shut. He was alone, profoundly, inescapably. He rolled on the floor and sobbed, wondering what it was that had hold of him, why he was here.

*

He lay on the cold floor sobbing; but really he was standing up strongly with contrite heart; holding his life in his hands, staring at it with a wondering question. He lay on the cold floor sobbing; but really he was pushing forward with his puny strength against a world too big and too strong for him. He lay on the cold floor sobbing; but really he was groping forward with fierce zeal into a welter of circumstances which he felt contained a water of mercy for the thirst of his heart and brain.

He wept because he had once again trusted his feelings and they had betrayed him. Why should he have felt the need to try to make his feelings known? And why did not he hear resounding echoes of his feelings in the hearts of others? There were times when he did hear echoes, but always they were couched in tones which, living as a Negro, he could not answer or accept without losing face with the world which had first evoked in him the song of manhood. He feared and hated the preacher because the preacher had told him to bow down and ask for a mercy he knew he needed; but his pride would never let him do that, not this side of the grave, not while the sun shone. And Jan? And Max? They were telling him to believe in himself. Once before he had accepted completely what his life had made him feel, even unto murder. He had emptied the vessel which life had filled for him and found the emptying meaningless. Yet the vessel was full again, waiting to be poured out. But no! Not blindly this time! He felt that he could not move again unless he swung out from the base of his own feelings; he felt that he would have to have light in order to act now.

Gradually, more from a lessening of strength than from peace of soul, his sobs ceased and he lay on his back, staring at the ceiling. He had confessed and death loomed now for certain in a public future. How could he go to his death with white faces looking on and saying that only death would cure him for having flung into their faces his feeling of being black? How could death be victory now?

He sighed, pulled up off the floor and lay on the cot, half-awake, half-asleep. The door opened and four policemen came and stood above him; one touched his shoulder.

'Come on, boy.'

He rose and looked at them questioningly.

'You're going back to the inquest.'

They clicked the handcuffs upon his wrists and led him into the hall, to a waiting elevator. The doors closed and he dropped downward through space, standing between four tall, silent men in blue. The elevator stopped; the doors opened and he saw a restless crowd of people and heard a babble of voices. They led him through a narrow aisle.

'That sonofa*bitch*!'

'Gee, isn't he *black*!'

'Kill 'im!'

A hard blow came to his temple and he slumped to the floor. The faces and voices left him. Pain throbbed in his head and the right side of his face numbed. He held up an elbow to protect himself; they yanked him back upon his feet. When his sight cleared he saw policemen struggling with a slender white man. Shouts rose in a mighty roar. To the front of him a white man pounded with a hammerlike piece of wood upon a table.

'Quiet! Or the room'll be cleared of everybody except witnesses!'

The clamor ceased. The policemen pushed Bigger into a chair. Stretching to the four walls of the room was a solid sheet of white faces. Standing with squared shoulders all around were policemen with clubs in hand, silver metal on their chests, faces red and stern, gray and blue eyes alert. To the right of the man at the table, in rows of three each, six men sat still and silent, their hats and overcoats on their knees. Bigger looked about and saw the pile of white bones lying atop a table; beside them lay the kidnap note, held in place by a bottle of ink. In the center of the table were white sheets of paper fastened together by a metal clasp; it was his signed confession. And there was Mr Dalton, white-faced, white-haired; and beside him was Mrs Dalton, still and straight, her face, as always, tilted trustingly upward, to one side. Then he saw the trunk into which he had stuffed Mary's body, the trunk which he had lugged down the stairs and had carried to the station. And, yes, there was the blackened hatchet blade and a tiny round piece of metal. Bigger felt a tap on his shoulder and looked around; Max was smiling at him.

'Take it easy, Bigger. You won't have to say anything here. It won't be long.'

The man at the front table rapped again.

'Is there a member of the deceased's family here, one who can give us the family history?'

A murmur swept the room. A woman rose hurriedly and went to the blind Mrs Dalton, caught hold of her arm, led her forward to a seat to the extreme right of the man at the table, facing the six men in the rows of chairs. That must be Mrs Patterson, Bigger thought, remembering the woman Peggy had mentioned as Mrs Dalton's maid.

'Will you please raise your right hand?'

Mrs Dalton's frail, waxen hand went up timidly. The man asked Mrs Dalton if the testimony she was about to give was the truth, the whole truth and nothing but the truth, so help you God, and Mrs Dalton answered,

'Yes, sir; I do.'

Bigger sat stolidly, trying not to let the crowd detect any fear in him. His nerves were painfully taut as he hung onto the old woman's words. Under the man's questioning, Mrs Dalton said that her age was fifty-three, that she lived at 4605 Drexel Boulevard, that she was a retired school teacher, that she was the mother of Mary Dalton and the wife of Henry Dalton. When the man began asking questions relating to Mary, the crowd leaned forward in their seats. Mrs Dalton said that Mary was twenty-three years of age, single; that she carried about thirty thousand dollars' worth of insurance, that she owned real estate amounting to approximately a quarter of a million dollars, and that she was active right up to the date of her death. Mrs Dalton's voice came tense and faint and Bigger wondered how much more of this he could stand. Would it not have been much better to have stood up in the full glare of those roving knives of light and let them shoot him down? He could have cheated them out of this show, this hunt, this eager sport.

'Mrs Dalton,' the man said, 'I'm the Deputy Coroner and it is with considerable anxiety that I ask you these questions. But it is necessary for me to trouble you in order to establish the identity of the deceased . . .'

'Yes, sir,' Mrs Dalton whispered.

Carefully, the coroner lifted from the table at his side a tiny piece of blackened metal; he turned, fronted Mrs Dalton, then paused. The room was so quiet that Bigger could hear the coroner's footsteps on the wooden floor as he walked to Mrs Dalton's chair. Tenderly, he caught her hand in his and said,

'I'm placing in your hand a metal object which the police retrieved from the ashes of the furnace in the basement of your home. Mrs Dalton, I want you to feel this metal carefully and tell me if you remember ever having felt it before.'

Bigger wanted to turn his eyes away, but he could not. He watched Mrs Dalton's face; he saw the hand tremble that held the blackened bit of metal. Bigger jerked his head round. A woman began to sob without restraint. A wave of murmurs rose through the room. The coroner took a quick step back to the table and rapped sharply with his knuckles. The room was instantly quiet, save for the sobbing woman, Bigger looked back to Mrs Dalton. Both of her hands were now fumbling nervously with the piece of metal; then her shoulders shook. She was crying.

'Do you recognize it?'

'Y-y-yes ...'

'What is it?'

'A-a-an earring ...'

'When did you first come in contact with it?'

Mrs Dalton composed her face, and, with tears on her cheeks, answered,

'When I was a girl, years ago ...'

'Do you remember precisely when?'

'Thirty-five years ago.'

'You once owned it?'

'Yes; it was one of a pair.'

'Yes, Mrs Dalton. No doubt the other earring was destroyed in the fire. This one dropped through the grates into the bin under the furnace. Now, Mrs Dalton, how long did you own this pair of earrings?'

'For thirty-three years.'

'How did they come into your possession?'

'Well, my mother gave them to me when I was of age. My grandmother gave them to my mother when she was of age, and I in turn gave them to my daughter when she was of age ...'

'What do you mean, of age?'

'At eighteen.'

'And when did you give them to your daughter?'

'About five years ago.'

'She wore them all the time?'

'Yes.'

'Are you positive that this is one of the same earrings?'

'Yes. There can be no mistake. They were a family heirloom. There are no two others like them. My grandmother had them designed and made to order.

'Mrs Dalton, when were you last in the company of the deceased?'

'Last Saturday night, or I should say, early Sunday morning.'

'At what time?'

'It was nearly two o'clock, I think.'

'Where was she?'

'In her room, in bed.'

'Were you in the habit of seeing, I mean, in the habit of meeting your daughter at such an hour?'

'No. I knew that she'd planned to go to Detroit Sunday morning. When I heard her come in I wanted to find out why she'd stayed out so late . . .'

'Did you speak with her?'

'No. I called her several times, but she did not answer.'

'Did you touch her?'

'Yes; slightly.'

'But she did not speak to you?'

'Well, I heard some mumbling . . .'

'Do you know who it was?'

'No.'

'Mrs Dalton, could your daughter by any means, in your judgment, have been dead then, and you not have known or suspected it?'

'I don't know.'

'Do you know if your daughter was alive when you spoke to her?'

'I don't know. I assumed she was.'

'Was there anyone else in the room at the time?'

'I don't know. But I felt strange there.'

'Strange? What do you mean, strange?'

'I – I don't know. I wasn't satisfied, for some reason. It seemed to me that there was something I should have done, or said. But I kept saying to myself, "She's asleep; that's all." '

'If you felt so dissatisfied, why did you leave the room without trying to awaken her?'

Mrs Dalton paused before answering; her thin mouth was wide open and her face tilted far to one side.

'I smelt alcohol in the room,' she whispered.

'Yes?'

'I thought Mary was intoxicated.'

'Had you ever encountered your daughter intoxicated before?'

'Yes; and that was why I thought she was intoxicated then. It was the same odor.'

'Mrs Dalton, if someone had possessed your daughter sexually while she lay on that bed, could you in any way have detected it?'

The room buzzed. The coroner rapped for order.

'I don't know,' she whispered.

'Just a few more questions, please, Mrs Dalton. What aroused your suspicions that something had befallen your daughter?'

'When I went to her room the next morning I felt her bed and found that she had not slept in it. Next I felt in her clothes rack and found that she had not taken the new clothes she had bought.'

'Mrs Dalton, you and your husband have given large sums of money to Negro educational institutions, haven't you?'

'Yes.'

'Could you tell us roughly how much?'

'Over five million dollars.'

'You bear no ill will toward the Negro people?'

'No; none whatever.'

'Mrs Dalton, please, tell us what was the last thing you did when you stood above your daughter's bed that Sunday morning?'

'I – I ...' She paused, lowered her head and dabbed at her eyes. 'I knelt at the bedside and prayed ...' she said, her words coming in a sharp breath of despair.

'That is all. Thank you, Mrs Dalton.'

The room heaved a sigh. Bigger saw the woman lead Mrs Dalton back to her seat. Many eyes in the room were fastened upon Bigger now, cold gray and blue eyes, eyes whose tense hate was worse than a shout or a curse. To get rid of that concentrated gaze, he stopped looking, even though his eyes remained open.

The coroner turned to the men sitting in rows to his right and said,

354

'You gentlemen, the jurors, are any of you acquainted with the deceased or are any of you members of the family?'

One of the men rose and said,

'No, sir.'

'Would there be any reason why you could not render a fair and impartial verdict in this?'

'No, sir.'

'Is there any objection to these men serving as jurors in this case?' the coroner asked of the entire room.

There was no answer.

'In the name of the coroner, I will ask the jurors to rise, pass by this table, and view the remains of the deceased, one Mary Dalton.'

In silence the six men rose and filed past the table, each looking at the pile of white bones. When they were seated again, the coroner called,

'We will now hear Mr Jan Erlone!'

Jan rose, came forward briskly, and was asked to swear to tell the truth, the whole truth, and nothing but the truth, so help him God. Bigger wondered if Jan would turn on him now. He wondered if he could really trust any white man, even this white man who had come and offered him his friendship. He leaned forward to hear. Jan was asked several times if he was a foreigner and Jan said no. The coroner walked close to Jan's chair and leaned the upper part of his body forward and asked in a loud voice,

'Do you believe in social equality for Negroes?'

The room stirred.

'I believe all races are equal ...' Jan began.

'Answer *yes* or *no*, Mr Erlone! You're not on a soap box. *Do* you believe in social equality for Negroes?'

'Yes.'

'Are you a member of the Communist Party?'

'Yes.'

'In what condition was Miss Dalton when you left her last Sunday morning?'

'What do you mean?'

'Was she drunk?'

'I would not say she was drunk. She had had a few drinks.'

'What time did you leave her?'

'It was about one-thirty, I think.'

'Was she in the front seat of the car?'

'Yes; she was in the front seat.'

'Had she been in the front seat all along?'

'No.'

'Was she in the front seat when you left the café?'

'No.'

'Did you put her in the front seat when you left the car?'

'No; she said she wanted to sit up front.'

'You didn't *ask* her to?'

'No.'

'When you left her, was she able to get out of the car alone?'

'I think so.'

'Had you had any relations with her while in the back seat that would have tended to make her, let us say, stunned, too weak to have gotten out alone?'

'No!'

'Is it not true, Mr Erlone, that Miss Dalton was in no condition to protect herself and you lifted her into that front seat?'

'No! I didn't lift her into the front seat!'

Jan's voice sounded throughout the room. There was a quick buzzing of conversation.

'Why did you leave an unprotected white girl alone in a car with a drunken Negro?'

'I was not aware that Bigger was drunk and I did not consider Mary as being unprotected.'

'Had you at any time in the past left Miss Dalton alone in the company of Negroes?'

'No.'

'You had never used Miss Dalton as bait before, had you?'

Bigger was startled by a noise behind him. He turned his head; Max was on his feet.

'Mr Coroner, I realize that this is not a trial. But the questions being asked now have no earthly relation to the cause and manner of the death of the deceased.'

'Mr Max, we are allowing plenty of latitude here. The grand jury will determine whether the testimony offered here has any relation or not.'

'But questions of this sort inflame the public mind . . .'

'Now, listen, Mr Max. No question asked in this room will inflame the public mind any more than has the death of Mary Dalton, and you know it. You have the right to question any of these witnesses, but I will not tolerate any publicity-seeking by your kind here!'

'But Mr Erlone is not on trial here, Mr Coroner!'

'He is suspected of being implicated in this murder! And we're after the one who killed this girl and the reasons for it! If you think these questions have the wrong construction, you may question the witness when we're through. But you cannot regulate the questions asked here!'

Max sat down. The room was quiet. The coroner paced to and fro a few seconds before he spoke again; his face was red and his lips were pressed tight.

'Mr Erlone, didn't you give that Negro material relating to the Communist Party?'

'Yes.'

'What was the nature of that material?'

'I gave him some pamphlets on the Negro question.'

'Material advocating the equality of whites and blacks?'

'It was material which explained . . .'

'Did that material contain a plea for "unity of whites and blacks"?'

'Why, yes.'

'Did you, in your agitation of that drunken Negro, tell him that it was all right for him to have sexual relations with white women?'

'No!'

'Did you advise Miss Dalton to have sexual relations with him?'

'No!'

'Did you *shake hands* with that Negro?'

'Yes.'

'Did you *offer* to shake hands with him?'

'Yes. It is what any decent person...'

'Confine yourself to answering the questions, please, Mr Erlone. We want none of your Communist explanations here. Tell me, did you *eat* with that Negro?'

'Why, yes.'

'You *invited* him to eat?'

'Yes.'

'Miss Dalton was at the table when you *invited* him to sit down?'

'Yes.'

'How many times have you eaten with Negroes before?'

'I don't know. Many times.'

'You *like* Negroes?'

'I make no distinctions...'

'Do you *like* Negroes, Mr Erlone?'

'I object!' Max shouted. 'How on earth is that related to this case!'

'You cannot regulate these questions!' the coroner shouted. 'I've told you that before! A woman has been foully murdered. This witness brought the deceased into contact with the last person who saw her alive. We have the right to determine what this witness' attitude was toward that girl and that Negro!' The coroner turned back to Jan. 'Now, Mr Erlone, didn't you ask that Negro to sit in the front seat of the car, *between* you and Miss Dalton?'

'No; he was already in the front seat.'

'But you *didn't* ask him to get into the *back* seat, did you?'

'No.'

'Why *didn't* you?'

'My God! The man is human! Why don't you ask me...?'

'I'm asking these questions and you're answering them. Now, tell me, Mr Erlone, would you have invited that Negro to sleep with you?'

'I refuse to answer that question!'

'But you didn't refuse that drunken Negro the right to sleep with that girl, did you?'

'His right to associate with her or anybody else was not in question . . .'

'Did you try to keep that Negro *from* Miss Dalton?'

'I didn't . . .'

'Answer yes or no!'

'No!'

'Have you a sister?'

'Why, yes.'

'Where is she?'

'In New York.'

'Is she married?'

'No.'

'Would you consent for her to marry a Negro?'

'I have nothing to do with whom she marries.'

'Didn't you tell that drunken Negro to call you Jan instead of Mr Erlone?'

'Yes; but . . .'

'Confine yourself to answering the questions!'

'But, Mr Coroner, you imply . . .'

'I'm trying to establish a motive for the murder of that innocent girl!'

'No; you're not! You're trying to indict a race of people and a political party!'

'We want no statements! Tell me, was Miss Dalton in a condition to say good-bye to you when you left her in that car with the drunken Negro?'

'Yes. She said good-bye.'

'Tell me, how much liquor did you give Miss Dalton that night?'

'I don't know.'

'What kind of liquor was it?'

'Rum.'

'Why did you prefer rum?'

'I don't know. I just bought rum.'

'Was it to stimulate the body to a great extent?'

'No.'

'How much was bought?'

'A fifth of a gallon.'

'Who paid for it?'

'I did.'

'Did that money come from the treasury of the Communist Party?'

'No!'

'Don't they allow you a budget for recruiting expenses?'

'No!'

'How much was drunk before you bought the fifth of rum?'

'We had a few beers.'

'How many?'

'I don't know.'

'You don't remember much about what happened that night, do you?'

'I'm telling you all I remember.'

'*All* you remember?'

'Yes.'

'Is it possible that you don't remember some things?'

'I'm telling you all I remember.'

'Were you too drunk to remember everything that happened?'

'No.'

'You knew what you were doing?'

'Yes.'

'You deliberately left the girl in that condition?'

'She was in no *condition*!'

'Just how drunk was she after the beers and rum?'

'She seemed to know what she was doing.'

'Did you have any fears about her being able to defend herself?'

'No.'

'Did you care?'

'Of course, I did.'

'You thought that whatever would happen would be all right?'

'I thought she was all right.'

'Just tell me, Mr Erlone, how drunk was Miss Dalton?'

'Well, she was a little high, if you know what I mean.'

'Feeling good?'

'Yes; you could say that.'

'Receptive?'

'I don't know what you mean.'

'Were you satisfied when you left her?'

'What do you mean?'

'You had enjoyed her company?'

'Why, yes.'

'And after enjoying a woman like that, isn't there a let-down?'

'I don't know what you mean.'

'It was late, wasn't it, Mr Erlone? You wanted to go home?'

'Yes.'

'You did not want to remain with her any longer?'

'No; I was tired.'

'So you left her to the Negro?'

'I left her in the car. I didn't leave her to anybody.'

'But the Negro was in the car?'

'Yes.'

'And she got in the front seat with him?'

'Yes.'

'And you did not try to stop her?'

'No.'

'And all three of you had been drinking?'

'Yes.'

'And you were satisfied to leave her like that, with a drunken Negro?'

'What do you *mean*?'

'You had no fear for her?'

'Why, no.'

'You felt that she, being drunk, would be as satisfied with anyone else as she had been with you?'

'No; no ... Not that way. You're leading ...'

'Just answer the questions. Had Miss Dalton, to your knowledge, ever had sex relations with a Negro before?'

'No.'

'Did you think that that would be as good a time as any for her to learn?'

'No; no ...'

'Didn't you promise to contact the Negro to see if he was grateful enough to join the Communist Party?'

'I didn't say I'd contact him.'

'Didn't you tell him you'd contact him within two or three days?'

'No.'

'Mr Erlone, are you sure you didn't say that?'

'Oh, yes! But it was not with the construction you are putting upon it ...'

'Mr Erlone, were you surprised when you heard of the death of Miss Dalton?'

'Yes. At first I was too stunned to believe it. I thought surely there was some mistake.'

'You hadn't expected that drunken Negro to go that far, had you?'

'I hadn't expected anything.'

'But you told that Negro to read those Communist pamphlets, didn't you?'

'I gave them to him.'

'You told him to *read* them?'

'Yes.'

'But you didn't expect him to go so far as to rape and kill the girl?'

'I didn't expect anything in that direction at all.'

'That's all, Mr Erlone.'

Bigger watched Jan go back to his seat. He knew how Jan felt. He knew what the man had been trying to do in asking the questions. He was not the only object of hate here. What did the reds want that made the coroner hate Jan so?'

'Will Mr Henry Dalton please come forward?' the coroner asked.

Bigger listened as Mr Dalton told how the Dalton family always hired Negro boys as chauffeurs, especially when those

Negro boys were handicapped by poverty, lack of education, misfortune, or bodily injury. Mr Dalton said that this was to give them a chance to support their families and go to school. He told how Bigger had come to the house, how timid and frightened he had acted, and how moved and touched the family had been for him. He told how he had not thought that Bigger had had anything to do with the disappearance of Mary, and how he had told Britten not to question him. He then told of receiving the kidnap note, and of how shocked he had been when he was informed that Bigger had fled his home, thereby indicating his guilt.

When the coroner's questioning was over, Bigger heard Max ask,

'May I direct a few questions?'

'Certainly. Go right ahead,' the coroner said.

Max went forward and stood directly in front of Mr Dalton.

'You are the president of the Dalton Real Estate Company, are you not?'

'Yes.'

'Your company owns the building in which the Thomas family has lived for the past three years, does it not?'

'Well, no. My company owns the stock in a company that owns the house.'

'I see. What is the name of *that* company?'

'The South Side Real Estate Company.'

'Now, Mr Dalton, the Thomas family paid you . . .'

'Not to *me*! They pay rent to the South Side Real Estate Company.'

'You own the controlling stock in the Dalton Real Estate Company, don't you?'

'Why, yes.'

'And that company in turn owns the stock that controls the South Side Real Estate Company, doesn't it?'

'Why, yes.'

'I think I can say that the Thomas family pays rent to *you*?'

'Indirectly, yes.'

'Who formulates the policies of these two companies?'

'Why, I do.'

'Why is it that you charge the Thomas family and other Negro families more rent for the same kind of houses than you charge white?'

'I don't fix the rent scales,' Mr Dalton said.

'Who does?'

'Why, the law of supply and demand regulates the price of houses.'

'Now, Mr Dalton, it has been said that you donate millions of dollars to educate Negroes. Why is it that you exact an exorbitant rent of eight dollars per week from the Thomas family for one unventilated, rat-infested room in which four people eat and sleep?'

The coroner leaped to his feet.

'I'll not tolerate your brow-beating this witness! Have you no sense of decency? This man is one of the most respected men in this city! And your questions have no bearing ...'

'They *do* have a bearing!' Max shouted. 'You said we could question with latitude here! I'm trying to find the guilty person, too! Jan Erlone is not the only man who's influenced Bigger Thomas! There were many others *before* him. I have as much right to determine what effect their attitude has had upon his conduct as you had to determine what Jan Erlone's had!'

'I'm willing to answer his questions if it will clear things up,' Mr Dalton said quietly.

'Thank you, Mr Dalton. Now, tell me, why is it that you charged the Thomas family eight dollars per week for one room in a tenement?'

'Well, there's a housing shortage.'

'All over Chicago?'

'No. Just here on the South Side.'

'You own houses in other sections of the city?'

'Yes.'

'They why don't you rent those houses to Negroes?'

'Well ... Er ... I – I – I don't think they'd like to live any other place.'

'Who told you that?'

'Nobody.'

'You came to that conclusion yourself?'

'Why, yes.'

'Isn't it true you *refuse* to rent houses to Negroes if those houses are in other sections of the city?'

'Why, yes.'

'Why?'

'Well, it's an old custom.'

'Do you think that custom is right?'

'I didn't make the custom,' Mr Dalton said.

'Do you think that custom is right?' Max asked again.

'Well, I think Negroes are happier when they're together.'

'Who told you *that*?'

'Why, nobody.'

'Aren't they more profitable when they're together?'

'I don't know what you mean.'

'Mr Dalton, doesn't this policy of your company tend to keep Negroes on the South Side, in one area?'

'Well, it works that way. But I didn't originate . . .'

'Mr Dalton, you give millions to help Negroes. May I ask why you don't charge them less rent for fire-traps and check that against your charity budget?'

'Well, to charge them less rent would be unethical.'

'*Unethical!*'

'Why, yes. I would be underselling my competitors.'

'Is there an agreement among realtors as to what Negroes should be charged for rent?'

'No. But there's a code of ethics in business.'

'So, the profits you take from the Thomas family in rents, you give back to them to ease the pain of their gouged lives and to salve the ache of your own conscience?'

'That's a distortion of fact, sir !'

'Mr Dalton, why do you contribute money to Negro education?'

'I want to see them have a chance.'

'Have you ever employed any of the Negroes you helped to educate?'

'Why, no.'

'Mr Dalton, do you think that the terrible conditions under which the Thomas family lived in one of your houses may in some way be related to the death of your daughter?'

'I don't know what you mean.'

'That's all,' said Max.

After Mr Dalton left the stand, Peggy came, then Britten, a host of doctors, reporters, and many policemen.

'We will now hear from Bigger Thomas!' the coroner called.

A wave of excited voices swept over the room. Bigger's fingers gripped the arms of the chair. Max's hand touched his shoulder. Bigger turned and Max whispered,

'Sit still.'

Max rose.

'Mr Coroner?'

'Yes?'

'In the capacity of Bigger Thomas' lawyer, I'd like to state that he does not wish to testify here.'

'His testimony would help to clear up any doubt as to the cause of the death of the deceased,' the coroner said.

'My client is already in police custody and it is his right to refuse . . .'

'All right. All right,' the coroner said.

Max sat down.

'Stay in your seat. It's all right,' Max whispered to Bigger.

Bigger relaxed and felt his heart pounding. He longed for something to happen so that the white faces would stop staring at him. Finally, the faces turned away. The coroner strode to the table and lifted the kidnap note with a slow, long, delicate, and deliberate gesture.

'Gentlemen,' he said, facing the six men in the rows of chairs, 'you have heard the testimony of the witnesses. I think, however, that you should have the opportunity to examine the evidence gathered by the Police Department.'

The coroner gave the kidnap note to one of the jurors who read it and passed it on to the others. All of the jurors examined the purse, the blood-stained knife, the blackened hatchet blade, the Communist pamphlets, the rum bottle, the trunk, and the signed confession.

'Owing to the peculiar nature of this crime, and owing to the fact that the deceased's body was all but destroyed, I deem it imperative that you examine one additional piece of evidence. It will help shed light upon the actual manner of the death of the deceased,' the coroner said.

He turned and nodded in the direction of two white-coated attendants who stood at the rear door. The room was quiet. Bigger wondered how much longer it would last; he felt that he could not stand much more. Now and then the room blurred and a slight giddiness came over him; but his muscles would flex taut and it would pass. The hum of voices grew suddenly loud and the coroner rapped for order. Then a commotion broke out. Bigger heard a man's voice saying,

'Move aside, please!'

He looked and saw the two white-coated attendants pushing an oblong, sheet-covered table through the crowd and down the aisle. What's this? Bigger wondered. He felt Max's hand come onto his shoulder.

'Take it easy, Bigger. This'll soon be over.'

'What they doing?' Bigger asked in a tense whisper.

For a long moment Max did not answer. Then he said uncertainly,

'I don't know.'

The oblong table was pushed to the front of the room. The coroner spoke in a deep, slow voice that was charged with passionate meaning:

'As Deputy Coroner, I have decided, in the interests of justice, to offer in evidence the raped and mutilated body of one Bessie Mears, and the testimony of police officers and doctors relating to the cause and manner of her death . . .'

The coroner's voice was drowned out. The room was in an uproar. For two minutes the police had to pound their clubs against the walls to restore quiet. Bigger sat still as stone as Max rushed past him and stopped a few feet from the sheet-covered table.

'Mr Coroner,' Max said. 'This is outrageous! Your indecent exhibition of that girl's dead body serves no purpose but that of an incitement to mob violence . . .'

'It will enable the jury to determine the exact manner of the death of Mary Dalton, who was slain by the man who slew Bessie Mears!' the coroner said in a scream that was compounded of rage and vindictiveness.

'The confession of Bigger Thomas covers all the evidence necessary for this jury!' Max said. 'You are criminally appealing to mob emotion . . .'

'That's for the grand jury to determine!' the coroner said. 'And you cannot interrupt these proceedings any longer! If you persist in this attitude, you'll be removed from this room! I have the legal right to determine what evidence is necessary . . .'

Slowly, Max turned and walked back to his seat, his lips a thin line, his face white, his head down.

Bigger was crushed, helpless. His lips dropped wide apart. He felt frozen, numb. He had completely forgotten Bessie during the inquest of Mary. He understood what was being done. To offer the dead body of Bessie as evidence and proof that he had murdered Mary would make him appear a monster; it would stir up more hate against him. Bessie's death had not been mentioned during the inquest and all of the white faces in the room were utterly surprised. It was not because he had thought any the less of Bessie that he had forgotten her, but Mary's death had caused him the most fear; not her death in itself, but what it meant to him as a Negro. They were bringing Bessie's body in now to make the white men and women feel that nothing short of a quick blotting out of his life would make the city safe again. They were using his having killed Bessie to kill him for his having killed Mary, to cast him in a light that would sanction any action taken to destroy him. Though he had killed a black girl and a white girl, he knew that it would be for the death of the white girl that he would be punished. The black girl was merely 'evidence'. And under it all he knew that the white people did not really care about Bessie's being killed. White people never searched for Negroes who kill other Negroes. He had even heard it said that white people felt it was good when one Negro killed another; it meant that they had one Negro less to contend with. Crime for a Negro was only when he harmed whites, took white lives, or injured white property. As time passed he could not help looking and listening to what was going on in the room. His eyes rested wistfully on the still oblong white draped form under the sheet on the table and he felt a deeper sympathy for Bessie than at any time when she was alive. He knew that Bessie, too, though dead, though killed by him, would resent her dead body being used in this way. Anger quickened in him: an old feeling that Bessie had often described to him when she had come from long hours of hot toil in the white folks' kitchens, a feeling of being forever commanded by others so much that thinking and feeling for one's self was impossible. Not only had he lived where they told him to live, not only had he done what they told him to do, not only had he done these things until he had killed to be quit of them; but even after obeying, after killing, they still ruled him. He was their property, heart and soul, body and blood; what they did claimed every atom of him, sleeping and waking; it colored life and dictated the terms of death.

The coroner rapped for order, then rose and stepped to the table and with one sweep of his arm flung the sheet back from Bessie's body. The sight, bloody and black, made Bigger flinch involuntarily and lift his hands to his eyes and at the same instant he saw blinding flashes of the silver bulbs flicking through the air. His eyes looked with painful effort to the back of the room, for he felt that if he saw Bessie again he would rise from his chair and sweep his arm in an attempt to blot out this room and the people in it. Every nerve of his body helped him to stare without seeing and to sit amid the noise without hearing.

A pain came to the front of his head, right above the eyes. As the slow minutes dragged, his body was drenched in cold sweat. His blood throbbed in his ears; his lips were parched and dry; he wanted to wet them with his tongue, but could not. The tense effort to keep out of his consciousness the terrible sight of

Bessie and the drone of the voices would not allow him to move a single muscle. He sat still, surrounded by an invisible cast of concrete. Then he could hold out no longer. He bent forward and buried his face in his hands. He heard a far-away voice speaking from a great height . . .

'The jury will retire to the next room.'

Bigger lifted his head and saw the six men rise and file out through a rear door. The sheet had been pulled over Bessie's body and he could not see her. The voices in the room grew loud and the coroner rapped for order. The six men filed slowly back to their chairs. One of them gave the coroner a slip of paper. The coroner rose, lifted his hand for silence and read a long string of words that Bigger could not understand. But he caught phrases:

'. . . the said Mary Dalton came to her death in the bedroom of her home, located at 4605 Drexel Boulevard, from suffocation and strangulation due to external violence, said violence received when the deceased was choked by the hands of one, Bigger Thomas, during the course of criminal rape . . .

'. . . we, the jury, believe that the said occurrence was murder and recommend that the said Bigger Thomas be held to the grand jury on a charge of murder, until released by due process of law . . .'

The voice droned on, but Bigger did not listen. This meant that he was going to jail to stay there until tried and executed. Finally, the coroner's voice stopped. The room was full of noise. Bigger heard men and women walking past him. He looked about like a man waking from a deep sleep. Max had hold of his arm.

'Bigger?'

He turned his head slightly.

'I'll see you tonight. They're taking you to the Cook County Jail. I'll come there and talk things over with you. We'll see what can be done. Meanwhile, take it easy. As soon as you can, lie down and get some sleep, hear?'

Max left him. He saw two policemen wheeling Bessie's body back through the door. The two policemen who sat to either

side of him took his arms and locked his wrists to theirs. Two
more policemen stood in front of him and two more stood in
back.

'Come on, boy.'

Two policemen walked ahead, making a path for him in the
dense crowd. As he passed white men and women they were
silent, but as soon as he was some few feet away, he heard their
voices rise. They took him out of the front door, into the hall.
He thought that they were going to take him back upstairs and
he made a motion to go in the direction of the elevator, but they
jerked him back roughly.

'This way!'

They led him out of the front door of the building, to the
street. Yellow sunshine splashed the sidewalks and buildings. A
huge throng of people covered the pavement. The wind blew
hard. Out of the shrill pitch of shouts and screams he caught a
few distinct words:

'... turn 'im loose ...'

'... give 'im what he gave that girl ...'

'... let us take care of 'im ...'

'... burn that black ape ...'

A narrow aisle was cleared for him across the width of the
pavement to a waiting car. As far as he could see there were
blue-coated white men with bright silver stars shining on their
chests. They wedged him tightly into the back seat of the car,
between the two policemen to whom he was handcuffed. The
motor throbbed. Ahead, he saw a car swing out from the curb
and roll with screaming siren down the street through the sunshine. Another followed it. Then four more. At last the car in
which he sat fell in line behind them. Back of him he heard
other cars pulling out from the curb, with throbbing motors and
shrieking sirens. He looked at the passing buildings out of the
side window, but could not recognize any familiar landmarks.
To each side of him were peering white faces with open
mouths. Soon, however, he knew that he was heading southward. The sirens screamed so loud that he seemed to be riding a
wave of sound. The cars swerved onto State Street. At Thirty-

fifth Street the neighborhood became familiar. At Thirty-seventh Street he knew that two blocks to his left was his home. What were his mother and brother and sister doing now? And where were Jack and G.H. and Gus? The rubber tires sang over the flat asphalt. There was a policeman at every corner, waving the cars on. Where were they taking him? Maybe they were going to keep him in a jail on the South Side? Maybe they were taking him to the Hyde Park Police Station? They reached Forty-seventh Street and rolled eastward, toward Cottage Grove Avenue. They came to Drexel Boulevard and swung north again. He stiffened and leaned forward. Mr Dalton lived on this street. What were they going to do with him? The cars slowed and stopped directly in front of the Dalton gate. What were they bringing him here for? He looked at the big brick house, drenched in sunshine, still, quiet. He looked into the faces of the two policemen who sat to either side of him; they were staring silently ahead. Upon the sidewalks, to the front and rear of him, were long lines of policemen with drawn guns. White faces filled the apartment windows all round him. People were pouring out of doors, running toward the Dalton home. A policeman with a golden star upon his chest came to the door of the car, opened it, glanced at him briefly, then turned to the driver.

'O.K., boys; take 'im out.'

They led him to the curb. Already a solidly packed crowd stood all over the sidewalks, the streets, on lawns, and behind the lines of the policemen. He heard a white boy yell,

'There's the nigger that killed Miss Mary!'

They led him through the gate, down the walk, up the steps; he stood a second facing the front door of the Dalton home, the same door before which he had stood so humbly with his cap in his hand a little less than a week ago. The door opened and he was led down the hall to the rear stairs and up to the second floor, to the door of Mary's room. It seemed that he could not breathe. What did they bring him here for? His body was once more wet with sweat. How long could he stand this without collapsing again? They led him into the room. It was crowded with armed policemen and newspapermen ready with their bulbs. He looked round; the room was just as he had seen it *that* night. There was the bed upon which he had smothered Mary. The clock with the glowing dial stood on the small dresser. The same curtains were at the windows and the shades were still far up, as far up as they had been that night when he had stood near them and had seen Mrs Dalton in flowing white grope her way slowly into the dark blue room with her hands lifted before her. He felt the eyes of the men upon him and his body stiffened, flushing hot with shame and anger. The man with the golden star on his chest came to him and spoke in a soft low tone.

'Now, Bigger, be a good boy. Just relax and take it easy. We want you to take your time and show us just what happened that night, see? And don't mind the boys' taking pictures. Just go through the motions you went through that night . . .'

Bigger glared; his whole body tightened and he felt that he was going to rise another foot in height.

'Come on,' the man said. 'Nobody's going to hurt you. Don't be afraid.'

Outrage burned in Bigger.

'Come on. Show us what you did.'

He stood without moving. The man caught his arm and tried to lead him to the bed. He jerked back violently, his muscles flexed taut. A hot band of fire encircled his throat. His teeth clamped so hard that he could not have spoken had he tried. He backed against a wall, his eyes lowered in a baleful glare.

'What's the matter, boy?'

Bigger's lips pulled back, showing his white teeth. Then he blinked his eyes; the flashlights went off and he knew in the instant of their flashing that they had taken his picture showing him with his back against a wall, his teeth bared in a snarl.

'Scared, boy? You weren't scared that night you were in here with that girl, were you?'

Bigger wanted to take enough air into his lungs to scream, 'Yes! I was scared!' But who would believe him? He would go to his death without ever trying to tell men like these what he had felt that night. When the man spoke again, his tone had changed.

'Come on, now, boy. We've treated you pretty nice, but we can get tough if we have to, see? It's up to *you*! Get over there by that bed and show us how you raped and murdered that girl!'

'I didn't rape her,' Bigger said through stiff lips.

'Aw, come on. What you got to lose now? Show us what you did.'

'I don't want to.'

'You *have* to!'

'I *don't* have to.'

'Well, we'll *make* you!'

'You can't make me do nothing but die!'

And as he said it, he wished that they would shoot him so that he could be free of them forever. Another white man with a golden star upon his chest walked over.

'Drop it. We got our case.'

'You think we ought to?'

'Sure. What's the use?'

'O.K., boys. Take 'im back to the car.'

They clamped the steel handcuffs on his wrists and led him down the hall. Even before the front door was opened, he heard the faint roar of voices. As far as he could see through the glass panels, up and down the street, were white people standing in the cold wind and sunshine. They took him through the door and the roar grew louder; as soon as he was visible the roar reached a deafening pitch and continued to rise each second. Surrounded by policemen, he was half-dragged and half-lifted along the narrow lane of people, through the gate, toward the waiting car.

'You black ape!'

'Shoot that bastard!'

He felt hot spittle splashing against his face. Somebody tried to leap at him, but was caught by the policemen and held back. As he stumbled along a high bright object caught his eyes; he looked up. Atop a building across the street, above the heads of the people, loomed a flaming cross. At once he knew that it had

374

something to do with him. But why should they burn a cross?
As he gazed at it he remembered the sweating face of the black
preacher in his cell that morning talking intensely and solemnly
of Jesus, of there being a cross for him, a cross for everyone, and
of how the lowly Jesus had carried the cross, paving the way,
showing how to die, how to love and live the life eternal. But
he had never seen a cross burning like that one upon the roof.
Were white people wanting him to love Jesus, too? He heard
the wind whipping the flames. No! That was not right; they
ought not burn a cross. He stood in front of the car, waiting for
them to push him in, his eyes wide with astonishment, his impulses deadlocked, trying to remember something.

'He's looking at it!'

'He sees it!'

The eyes and faces about him were not at all the way the
black preacher's had been when he had prayed about Jesus and
His love, about His dying upon the cross. The cross the
preacher had told him about was bloody, not flaming; meek,
not militant. It had made him feel awe and wonder, not fear
and panic. It had made him want to kneel and cry, but this
cross made him want to curse and kill. Then he became conscious of the cross that the preacher had hung round his throat;
he felt it nestling against the skin of his chest, an image of the
same cross lay blazed in front of his eyes high upon the roof
against the cold blue sky, its darting tongues of fire lashed to a
hissing fury by the icy wind.

'Burn 'im!'

'Kill 'im!'

It gripped him: that cross was not the cross of Christ, but the
cross of the Ku Klux Klan. He had a cross of salvation round
his throat and they were burning one to tell him that they hated
him! No! He did not want that! Had the preacher trapped
him? He felt betrayed. He wanted to tear the cross from his
throat and throw it away. They lifted him into the waiting car
and he sat between two policemen, still looking fearfully at the
fiery cross. The sirens screamed and the cars rolled slowly
through the crowded streets and he was feeling the cross that

touched his chest, like a knife pointed at his heart. His fingers ached to rip it off; it was an evil and black charm which would surely bring him death now. The cars screamed up State Street, then westward on Twenty-sixth Street, one behind the other. People paused on the sidewalks to look. Ten minutes later they stopped in front of a huge white building; he was led up steps, down hallways and then halted in front of a cell door. He was pushed inside; the handcuffs were unlocked and the door clanged shut. The men lingered, looking at him curiously.

With bated breath he tore his shirt open, not caring who saw him. He gripped the cross and snatched it from his throat. He threw it away, cursing a curse that was almost a scream.

'I don't want it!'

The men gasped and looked at him, amazed.

'Don't throw that away, boy. That's your *cross*!'

'I can die without a cross!'

'Only God can help you now, boy. You'd better get your soul right!'

'I ain't got no soul!'

One of the men picked up the cross and brought it back.

'Here, boy; keep this. This is *God*'s cross!'

'I don't care!'

'Aw, leave 'im alone!' one of the men said.

They left, dropping the cross just inside the cell door. He picked it up and threw it away again. He leaned weakly against the bars, spent. What were they trying to do to him? He lifted his head, hearing footsteps. He saw a white man coming toward him, then a black man. He straightened and stiffened. It was the old preacher who had prayed over him that morning.

The white man began to unlock the door.

'I don't want you!' Bigger shouted.

'Son!' the preacher admonished.

'I don't want you!'

'What's the matter, son?'

'Take your Jesus and go!'

'But, son! Yuh don't know whut yuh's sayin'! Lemme pray fer yuh!'

'Pray for yourself!'

The white guard caught the preacher by the arm and, pointing to the cross on the floor, said,

'Look, Reverend, he threw his cross away.'

The preacher looked and said:

'Son, don't spit in Gawd's face!'

'I'll spit in your face if you don't leave me alone!' Bigger said.

'The reds've been talking to 'im,' the guard said, piously touching his fingers to his forehead, his chest, his left shoulder, and then his right; making the sign of the cross.

'That's a goddamn lie!' Bigger shouted. His body seemed a flaming cross as words boiled hysterically out of him. 'I told you I don't want you! If you come in here, I'll kill you! Leave me alone!'

Quietly, the old black preacher stooped and picked up the cross. The guard inserted the key in the lock and the door swung in. Bigger ran to it and caught the steel bars in his hands and swept the door forward, slamming it shut. It smashed the old black preacher squarely in the face, sending him reeling backward upon the concrete. The echo of steel crashing against steel resounded throughout the long quiet corridor, wave upon wave, dying somewhere far away.

'You'd better leave 'im alone now,' the guard said. 'He seems pretty wild.'

The preacher rose slowly and gathered his hat, Bible, and the cross from the floor. He stood a moment with his hand nursing his bruised face.

'Waal, son. Ah'll leave yuh t' yo' Gawd,' he sighed, dropping the cross back inside the cell.

The preacher walked away. The guard followed. Bigger was alone. His emotions were so intense that he really saw and heard nothing. Finally, his hot and taut body relaxed. He saw the cross, snatched it up and held it for a long moment in fingers of steel. Then he flung it again through the bars of the cell. It hit the wall beyond with a lone clatter.

*

Never again did he want to feel anything like hope. That was what was wrong; he had let that preacher talk to him until somewhere in him he had begun to feel that maybe something could happen. Well, something *had* happened: the cross the preacher had hung round his throat had been burned in front of his eyes.

When his hysteria had passed, he got up from the floor. Through blurred eyes he saw men peering at him from the bars of other cells. He heard a low murmur of voices and in the same instant his consciousness recorded without bitterness – like a man stepping out of his house to go to work and noticing that the sun is shining – the fact that even here in the Cook County Jail Negro and white were segregated into different cell-blocks. He lay on the cot with closed eyes and the darkness soothed him some. Occasionally his muscles twitched from the hard storm of passion that had swept him. A small hard core in him resolved never again to trust anybody or anything. Not even Jan. Or Max. They were all right, maybe; but whatever he thought or did from now on would have to come from him and him alone, or not at all. He wanted no more crosses that might turn to fire while still on his chest.

His inflamed senses cooled slowly. He opened his eyes. He heard a soft tapping on a near-by wall. Then a sharp whisper:

'Say, you new guy!'

He sat up, wondering what they wanted.

'Ain't you the guy they got for that Dalton job?'

His hands clenched. He lay down again. He did not want to talk to them. They were not his kind. He felt that they were not here for crimes such as his. He did not want to talk to the whites because they were white and he did not want to talk to Negroes because he felt ashamed. His own kind would be too curious about him. He lay a long while, empty of mind, and then he heard the steel door open. He looked and saw a white man with a tray of food. He sat up and the man brought the tray to the cot and placed it beside him.

'Your lawyer sent this, kid. You got a good lawyer,' the man said.

'Say, can I see a paper?' Bigger asked.

'Well, now,' the man said, scratching his head. 'Oh, what the hell. Yeah; sure. Here, take mine. I'm through with it. And say, your lawyer's bringing some clothes for you. He told me to tell you.'

Bigger did not hear him; he ignored the tray of food and opened out the paper. He paused, waiting to hear the door shut. When it clanged, he bent forward to read, then paused again, wondering about the man who had just left, amazed at how friendly he had acted. For a fleeting moment, while the man had been in his cell he had not felt apprehensive, cornered. The man had acted straight, matter-of-fact. It was something he could not understand. He lifted the paper close and read: NEGRO KILLER SIGNS CONFESSIONS FOR TWO MURDERS. SHRINKS AT INQUEST WHEN CONFRONTED WITH BODY OF SLAIN GIRL. ARRAIGNED TOMORROW. REDS TAKE CHARGE OF KILLER'S DEFENSE. NOT GUILTY PLEA LIKELY. His eyes ran over the paper, looking for some clue that would tell him something of his fate.

... slayer will undoubtedly pay supreme penalty for his crimes ... there is no doubt of his guilt ... what is doubtful is how many other crimes he has committed ... killer attacked at inquest ...

Then:

Expressing opinions about Communists' defending the Negro rapist and killer, Mr David A. Buckley, State's Attorney, said: 'What else can you expect from a gang like that? I'm in favor of cleaning them out lock, stock, and barrel. I'm of the conviction that if you got to the bottom of red activity in this country, you'd find the root of many an unsolved crime.'

When questioned as to what effect the Thomas trial would have upon the forthcoming April elections, in which he is a candidate to succeed himself, Mr Buckley took his pink carnation from the lapel of his morning coat and waved the reporters away with a laugh.

A long scream sounded and Bigger dropped the paper, jumped to his feet, and ran to the barred door to see what was happening. Down the corridor he saw six white men struggling with a brown-skinned Negro. They dragged him over the floor by his feet and stopped directly in front of Bigger's cell door. As the door swung in, Bigger backed to his cot, his mouth open in astonishment. The man was turning and twisting in the white men's hands, trying desperately to free himself.

'Turn me loose! Turn me loose!' the man screamed over and over.

The men lifted him and threw him inside, locked the door, and left. The man lay on the floor for a moment, then scrambled to his feet and ran to the door.

'Give me my papers!' he screamed.

Bigger saw that the man's eyes were blood-red; the corners of his lips were white with foam. Sweat glistened on his brown face. He clutched the bars with such frenzy that when he yelled his entire body vibrated. He seemed so agonized that Bigger wondered why the men did not give him his belongings. Emotionally, Bigger sided with the man.

'You can't get away with it!' the man yelled.

Bigger went to him and placed a hand on his shoulder.

'Say, what they got of yours?' he asked.

The man ignored him, shouting,

'I'll report you to the President, you hear? Bring me my papers or let me out of here, you white bastards! You want to destroy all my evidence! You can't cover up your crimes! I'll publish them to the whole world! I know why you're putting me in jail! The Professor told you to! But he's not going to get away with it . . .'

Bigger watched, fascinated, fearful. He had the sensation that the man was too emotionally wrought up over whatever it was that he had lost. Yet the man's emotions seemed real; they affected him, compelling sympathy.

'Come back here!' the man screamed. 'Bring me my papers or I'll tell the President and have you dismissed from office . . .'

What papers did they have of his? Bigger wondered. Who was the president the man yelled about? And who was the professor? Over the man's screams Bigger heard a voice calling from another cell,

'Say, you new guy!'

Bigger avoided the frenzied man and went to the door.

'He's balmy!' a white man said. 'Make 'em take 'im outta your cell. He'll kill you. He went off his nut from studying too much at the University. He was writing a book on how colored people live and he says somebody stole all the facts he'd found. He says he's got to the bottom of why colored folks are treated bad and he's going to tell the President and have things changed, see? He's *nuts*! He swears that his university professor had him locked up. The cops picked him up this morning in his underwear; he was in the lobby of the Post Office building, waiting to speak to the President . . .'

Bigger ran from the door to the cot. All of his fear of death, all his hate and shame vanished in face of his dread of this insane man turning suddenly upon him. The man still clutched the bars, screaming. He was about Bigger's size. Bigger had the queer feeling that his own exhaustion formed a hairline upon which his feelings were poised, and that the man's driving frenzy would suck him into its hot whirlpool. He lay on the cot and wrapped his arms about his head, torn with a nameless anxiety, hearing the man's screams in spite of his need to escape them.

'You're afraid of me!' the man shouted. 'That's why you put me in here! But I'll tell the President anyhow! I'll tell 'im you make us live in such crowded conditions on the South Side that one out of every ten of us is insane! I'll tell 'im that you dump all the stale foods into the Black Belt and sell them for more than you can get anywhere else! I'll tell 'im you tax us, but you won't build hospitals! I'll tell 'im the schools are so crowded that they breed perverts! I'll tell 'im you hire us last and fire us first! I'll tell the President and the League of Nations . . .'

Then men in other cells began to holler.

'Pipe down, you nut!'

'Take 'im away!'

'Throw 'im out!'

'The hell with you!'

381

'You can't scare me!' the man yelled. 'I know you! They put you in here to watch me!'

The men set up a clamor. But soon a group of men dressed in white came running with a stretcher. They unlocked the cell and grabbed the yelling man, laced him in a strait-jacket, flung him onto the stretcher and carted him away. Bigger sat up and stared before him, hopelessly. He heard voices calling from cell to cell.

'Say, what they got of his?'

'Nothing! He's nuts!'

Finally, things quieted. For the first time since his capture, Bigger felt that he wanted someone near him, something physical to cling to. He was glad when he heard the lock in his door click. He sat up; a guard loomed over him.

'Come on, boy. Your lawyer's here.'

He was handcuffed and led down the hall to a small room where Max stood. He was freed of the steel links on his wrists and pushed inside; he heard the door shut behind him.

'Sit down, Bigger. Say, how do you feel?'

Bigger sat down on the edge of the chair and did not answer. The room was small. A single yellow electric globe dropped from the ceiling. There was one barred window. All about them was profound silence. Max sat opposite Bigger, and Bigger's eyes met his and fell. Bigger felt that he was sitting and holding his life helplessly in his hands, waiting for Max to tell him what to do with it; and it made him hate himself. An organic wish to cease to be, to stop living, seized him. Either he was too weak, or the world was too strong; he did not know which. Over and over he had tried to create a world to live in, and over and over he had failed. Now, once again, he was waiting for someone to tell him something; once more he was poised on the verge of action and commitment. Was he letting himself in for more hate and fear? What could Max do for him now? Even if Max tried hard and honestly, were there not thousands of white hands to stop Max? Why not tell him to go home? His lips trembled to speak, to tell Max to leave; but no words came. He felt that even in speaking in that way he would be indicating how hopeless he felt, thereby disrobing his soul to more shame.

'I bought some clothes for you,' Max said. 'When they give 'em to you in the morning, put 'em on. You want to look your best when you come up for arraignment.'

Bigger was silent; he glanced at Max again, and then away.

'What's on your mind, Bigger?'

'Nothing,' he mumbled.

'Now, listen, Bigger. I want you to tell me all about yourself . . .'

'Mr Max, it ain't no use in you doing nothing!' Bigger blurted.

Max eyed him sharply.

'Do you really feel that way, Bigger?'

'There ain't no way else to feel.'

'I want to talk to you honestly, Bigger. I see no way out of this but a plea of guilty. We can ask for mercy, for life in prison . . .'

'I'd rather die!'

'Nonsense. You want to live.'

'For what?'

'Don't you want to fight this thing?'

'What can I do? They got me.'

'You don't want to die that way, Bigger.'

'It don't matter which way I die,' he said; but his voice choked.

'Listen, Bigger, you're facing a sea of hate now that's no different from what you've faced all your life. And because it's that way, you've *got* to fight. If they can wipe you out, then they can wipe others out, too.'

'Yeah,' Bigger mumbled, resting his hands upon his knees and staring at the black floor. 'But I can't win.'

'First of all, Bigger. Do you trust me?'

Bigger grew angry.

'You can't help me, Mr Max,' he said, looking straight into Max's eyes.

'But do you trust me, Bigger?' Max asked again.

Bigger looked away. He felt that Max was making it very difficult for him to tell him to leave.

'I don't know, Mr Max.'

'Bigger, I know my face is white,' Max said. 'And I know that almost every white face you've met in your life had it in for you, even when that white face didn't know it. Every white man considers it his duty to make a black man keep his distance. He doesn't know why most of the time, but he acts that way. It's the way things are, Bigger. But I want you to know that you can trust me.'

'It ain't no use, Mr Max.'

'You want me to handle your case?'

'You can't help me none. They got me.'

Bigger knew that Max was trying to make him feel that he accepted the way he looked at things and it made him as self-conscious as when Jan had taken his hand and shaken it that night in the car. It made him live again in that hard and sharp consciousness of his color and feel that shame and fear that went with it, and at the same time it made him hate himself for feeling it. He trusted Max. Was Max not taking upon himself a thing that would make other whites hate him? But he doubted if Max could make him see things in a way that would enable him to go to his death. He doubted that God Himself could give him a picture for that now. As he felt at present, they would have to drag him to the chair, as they had dragged him down the steps the night they captured him. He did not want his feelings tampered with; he feared that he might walk into another trap. If he expressed belief in Max, if he acted on that belief, would it not end just as all other commitments of faith had ended? He wanted to believe; but was afraid. He felt that he should have been able to meet Max halfway; but, as always, when a white man talked to him, he was caught out in No Man's Land. He sat slumped in his chair with his head down and he looked at Max only when Max's eyes were not watching him.

'Here; take a cigarette, Bigger.' Max lit Bigger's and then lit his own; they smoked awhile. 'Bigger, I'm your lawyer. I want to talk to you honestly. What you say is in strictest confidence...'

Bigger stared at Max. He felt sorry for the white man. He saw that Max was afraid that he would not talk at all. And he had no desire to hurt Max. Max leaned forward determinedly. Well, tell him. Talk. Get it over with and let Max go.

'Aw, I don't care what I say or do now...'

'Oh, yes, you *do*!' Max said quickly.

In a fleeting second an impulse to laugh rose up in Bigger, and left. Max was anxious to help him and he had to die.

'Maybe I do care,' Bigger drawled.

'If you don't care about what you say or do, then why didn't you re-enact that crime out at the Dalton home today?'

'I wouldn't do nothing for *them*.'

'Why?'

'They hate black folks,' he said.

'*Why*, Bigger?'

'I don't know, Mr Max.'

'Bigger, don't you know they hate others, too?'

'Who they hate?'

'They hate trade unions. They hate folks who try to organize. They hate Jan.'

'But they hate black folks more than they hate unions,' Bigger said. 'They don't treat union folks like they do me.'

'Oh, yes, they do. You think that because your color makes it easy for them to point you out, segregate you, exploit you. But they do that to others, too. They hate me because I'm trying to help you. They're writing me letters, calling me a "dirty Jew".'

'All I know is that they hate me,' Bigger said grimly.

'Bigger, the State's Attorney gave me a copy of your confession. Now, tell me, did you tell him the truth?'

'Yeah. There wasn't nothing else to do.'

'Now, tell me this, Bigger. Why did you do it?'

Bigger sighed, shrugged his shoulders and sucked his lungs full of smoke.

'I don't know,' he said; smoke eddied slowly from his nostrils.

'Did you plan it?'

'Naw.'

'Did anybody help you?'

'Naw.'

'Had you been thinking about doing something like that for a long time?'

'Naw.'

'How did it happen?'

'It just happened, Mr Max.'

'Are you sorry?'

'What's the use of being sorry? That won't help me none.'

'You can't think of any reason why you did it?'

Bigger was staring straight before him, his eyes wide and shining. His talking to Max had evoked again in him that urge to talk, to tell, to try to make his feelings known. A wave of excitement flooded him. He felt that he ought to be able to reach out with his bare hands and carve from naked space the concrete, solid reasons why he had murdered. He felt them that strongly. If he could do that, he would relax; he would sit and wait until they told him to walk to the chair; and he would walk.

'Mr Max, I don't know. I was all mixed up. I was feeling so many things at once.'

'Did you rape her, Bigger?'

'Naw, Mr Max. I didn't. But nobody'll believe me.'

'Had you planned to before Mrs Dalton came into the room?'

Bigger shook his head and rubbed his hands nervously across his eyes. In a sense he had forgotten Max was in the room. He was trying to feel the texture of his own feelings, trying to tell what they meant.

'Oh, I don't know. I was feeling a little that way. Yeah, I reckon I was. I was drunk and she was drunk and I was feeling that way.'

'But, did you rape her?'

'Naw. But everybody'll say I did. What's the use? I'm black. They say black men do that. So it don't matter if I did or if I didn't.'

'How long had you known her?'

'A few hours.'

'Did you like her?'

'*Like* her?'

Bigger's voice boomed so suddenly from his throat that Max started. Bigger leaped to his feet; his eyes widened and his hands lifted midway to his face, trembling.

'No! No! Bigger ...' Max said.

'*Like* her? I *hated* her! So help me God, I hated her!' he shouted,

'Sit down, Bigger!'

'I hate her now, even though she's dead! God knows, I hate her right now ...'

Max grabbed him and pushed him back into the chair.

'Don't get excited, Bigger. Here; take it easy!'

Bigger quieted, but his eyes roved the room. Finally, he lowered his head and knotted his fingers. His lips were slightly parted.

'You say you hated her?'

'Yeah; and I ain't sorry she's dead.'

'But what had she done to you? You say you had just met her.'

'I don't know. She didn't do nothing to me.' He paused and ran his hand nervously across his forehead. 'She ... It was ... Hell, I don't know. She asked me a lot of questions. She acted and talked in a way that made me hate her. She made me feel like a dog. I was so mad I wanted to cry ...' His voice trailed off in a plaintive whimper. He licked his lips. He was caught in a net of vague, associative memory: he saw an image of his little sister, Vera, sitting on the edge of a chair crying because he had shamed her by 'looking' at her; he saw her rise and fling her shoe at him. He shook his head, confused. 'Aw, Mr Max, she wanted me to tell her how Negroes live. She got into the front seat of the car where I was ...'

'But, Bigger, you don't hate people for that. She was being kind to you ...'

'Kind, hell! She wasn't kind to me!'

'What do you mean? She accepted you as another human being.'

'Mr Max, we're all split up. What you say is kind ain't kind at all. I didn't know nothing about that woman. All I knew was that they kill us for women like her. We live apart. And then she comes and acts like that to me.'

'Bigger, you should have tried to understand. She was acting toward you only as she knew how.'

Bigger glared about the small room, searching for an answer. He knew that his actions did not seem logical and he gave up trying to explain them logically. He reverted to his feelings as a guide in answering Max.

'Well, I acted toward her only as I know how. She was rich. She and her kind own the earth. She and her kind say black folks are dogs. They don't let you do nothing but what they want . . .'

'But, Bigger, *this* woman was trying to help you!'

'She didn't act like it.'

'How *should* she have acted?'

'Aw, I don't know, Mr Max. White folks and black folks is strangers. We don't know what each other is thinking. Maybe she was trying to be kind; but she didn't act like it. To me she looked and acted like all other white folks . . .'

'But she's not to be blamed for that, Bigger.'

'She's the same color as the rest of 'em,' he said defensively.

'I don't understand, Bigger. You say you hated her and yet you say you felt like having her when you were in the room and she was drunk and you were drunk . . .'

'Yeah,' Bigger said, wagging his head and wiping his mouth with the black of his hand. 'Yeah; that's funny, ain't it?' He sucked at his cigarette. 'Yeah; I reckon it was because I knew I oughtn't've wanted to. I reckon it was because they say we black men do that anyhow. Mr Max, you know what some white men say we black men do? They say we rape white women when we got the clap and they say we do that because we believe that if we rape white women then we'll get rid of the clap. That's what some white men *say*. They *believe* that. Jesus,

Mr Max, when folks says things like that about you, you whipped before you born. What's the use? Yeah; I reckon I was feeling that way when I was in the room with her. They say we do things like that and they say it to kill us. They draw a line and say for you to stay on your side of the line. They don't care if there's no bread over on your side. They don't care if you die. And then they say things like that about you and when you try to come from behind your line they kill you. They feel they ought to kill you then. Everybody wants to kill you then. Yeah; I reckon I was feeling that way and maybe the reason was because they say it. Maybe that was the reason.'

'You mean you wanted to defy them? You wanted to show them that you dared, that you didn't care?'

'I don't know, Mr Max. But what I got to care about? I knew that some time or other they was going to get me for something. I'm black. I don't have to do nothing for 'em to get me. The first white finger they point at me, I'm a goner, see?'

'But, Bigger, when Mrs Dalton came into that room, why didn't you stop right there and tell her what was wrong? You wouldn't've been in all this trouble then . . .

'Mr Max, so help me God, I couldn't do nothing when I turned around and saw that woman coming to that bed. Honest to God, I didn't know what I was doing . . .'

'You mean you went blank?'

'Naw; naw . . . I knew what I was doing, all right. But I couldn't help it. That's what I mean. It was like another man stepped inside of my skin and started acting for me . . .'

'Bigger, tell me, did you feel more attraction for Mary than for the women of your own race?'

'Naw. But they say that. It ain't true. I hated her then and I hate her now.'

'But why did you kill Bessie?'

'To keep her from talking. Mr Max, after killing that white woman, it wasn't hard to kill somebody else. I didn't have to think much about killing Bessie. I knew I had to kill her and I did. I had to get away . . .'

'Did you hate Bessie?'

'Naw.'

'Did you love her?'

'Naw. I was just scared. I wasn't in love with Bessie. She was just my girl. I don't reckon I was ever in love with nobody. I killed Bessie to save myself. You have to have a girl, so I had Bessie. And I killed her.'

'Bigger, tell me, when did you start hating Mary?'

'I hated her as soon as she spoke to me, as soon as I saw her. I reckon I hated her before I saw her ...'

'But, *why*?'

'I told you. What her kind ever let us do?'

'What, exactly, Bigger, did you want to do?'

Bigger sighed and sucked at his cigarette.

'Nothing, I reckon. Nothing. But I reckon I wanted to do what other people do.'

'And because you couldn't, you hated her?'

Again Bigger felt that his actions were not logical, and again he fell back upon his feelings for a guide in answering Max's questions.

'Mr Max, a guy gets tired of being told what he can do and can't do. You get a little job here and a little job there. You shine shoes, sweep streets; anything ... You don't make enough to live on. You don't know when you going to get fired. Pretty soon you get so you can't hope for nothing. You just keep moving all the time, doing what other folks say. You ain't a man no more. You just work day in and day out so the world can roll on and other people can live. You know, Mr Max, I always think of white folks ...'

He paused. Max leaned forward and touched him.

'Go on, Bigger.'

'Well, they own everything. They choke you off the face of the earth. They like God ...' He swallowed, closed his eyes and sighed. 'They don't even let you feel what you want to feel. They after you so hot and hard you can only feel what they doing to you. They kill you before you die.'

'But, Bigger, I asked you what it was that you wanted to do so badly that you had to hate them?'

'Nothing. I reckon I didn't want to do nothing.'

'But you said that people like Mary and her kind never let you do anything.'

'Why should I want to do anything? I ain't got a chance. I don't know nothing. I'm just black and they make the laws.'

'What would you like to have been?'

Bigger was silent for a long time. Then he laughed without sound, without moving his lips; it was three short expulsions of breath forced upward through his nostrils by the heaving of his chest.

'I wanted to be an aviator once. But they wouldn't let me go to the school where I was suppose' to learn it. They built a big school and then drew a line around it and said that nobody could go to it but those who lived within the line. That kept all the colored boys out.'

'And what else?'

'Well, I wanted to be in the army once.'

'Why didn't you join?'

'Hell, it's a Jim Crow army. All they want a black man for is to dig ditches. And in the navy, all I can do is wash dishes and scrub floors.'

'And was there anything else you wanted to do?'

'Oh, I don't know. What's the use now? I'm through, washed up. They got me. I'll die.'

'Tell me the things you *thought* you'd have liked to do?'

'I'd like to be in business. But what chance has a black guy got in business? We ain't got no money. We don't own no mines, no railroads, no nothing. They don't want us to. They made us stay in one little spot . . .'

'And you didn't want to stay there?'

Bigger glanced up; his lips tightened. There was a feverish pride in his bloodshot eyes.

'I *didn't*,' he said.

Max stared and sighed.

'Look, Bigger. You've told me the things you could not do. But you did something. You committed these crimes. You killed two women. What on earth did you think you could get out of it?'

Bigger rose and rammed his hands into his pockets. He leaned against the wall, looking vacantly. Again he forgot that Max was in the room.

'I don't know. Maybe this sounds crazy. Maybe they going to burn me in the electric chair for feeling this way. But I ain't worried none about them women I killed. For a little while I was free. I was doing something. It was wrong, but I was feeling all right. Maybe God'll get me for it. If He do, all right. But I ain't worried. I killed 'em 'cause I was scared and mad. But I been scared and mad all my life and after I killed that first woman, I wasn't scared no more for a little while.'

'What were you afraid of?'

'Everything,' he breathed and buried his face in his hands.

'Did you ever hope for anything, Bigger?'

'What for? I couldn't get it. I'm black,' he mumbled.

'Didn't you ever want to be happy?'

'Yeah; I guess so,' he said, straightening.

'How did you think you could be happy?'

'I don't know. I wanted to do things. But everything I wanted to do I couldn't. I wanted to do what the white boys in school did. Some of 'em went to college. Some of 'em went to the army. But I couldn't go.'

'But still, you wanted to be happy?'

'Yeah; sure. Everybody wants to be happy, I reckon.'

'Did you think you ever would be?'

'I don't know. I just went to bed at night and got up in the morning. I just lived from day to day. I thought maybe I would be.'

'How?'

'I don't know,' he said in a voice that was almost a moan.

'What did you think happiness would be like?'

'I don't know. It wouldn't be like this.'

'You ought to have some idea of what you wanted, Bigger.'

'Well, Mr Max, if I was happy I wouldn't always be wanting to do something I know I couldn't do.'

'And why did you always want to?'

'I couldn't help it. Everybody feels that way, I reckon. And I did, too. Maybe I would've been all right if I could've done something I wanted to do. I wouldn't be scared then. Or mad, maybe. I wouldn't be always hating folks; and maybe I'd feel at home, sort of.'

'Did you ever go to the South Side Boys' Club, the place where Mr Dalton sent those ping-pong tables?'

'Yeah; but what the hell can a guy do with ping-pong?'

'Do you feel that the club kept you out of trouble?'

Bigger cocked his head.

'Kept me out of trouble?' he repeated Max's words. 'Naw; that's where we planned most of our jobs.'

'Did you ever go to church, Bigger?'

'Yeah; when I was little. But that was a long time ago.'

'Your folks were religious?'

'Yeah; they went to church all the time.'

'Why did you stop going?'

'I didn't like it. There was nothing in it. Aw, all they did was sing and shout and pray all the time. And it didn't get 'em nothing. All the colored folks do that, but it don't get 'em nothing. The white folks got everything.'

'Did you ever feel happy in church?'

'Naw. I didn't want to. Nobody but poor folks get happy in church.'

'But you are poor, Bigger.'

Again Bigger's eyes lit with a bitter and feverish pride.

'I ain't that poor,' he said.

'But Bigger, you said that if you were where people did not hate you and you did not hate them, you could be happy. Nobody hated you in church. Couldn't you feel at home there?'

'I wanted to be happy in this world, not out of it. I didn't want that kind of happiness. The white folks like for us to be religious, then they can do what they want to with us.'

'A little while ago you spoke of God "getting you" for killing those women. Does that mean you believe in Him?'

'I don't know.'

'Aren't you afraid of what'll happen to you after you die?'

'Naw. But I don't want to die.'

'Didn't you know that the penalty for killing that white woman would be death?'

'Yeah; I knew it. But I felt like she was killing me, so I didn't care.'

'If you could be happy in religion now, would you want to be?'

'Naw. I'll be dead soon enough. If I was religious, I'd be dead now.'

'But the church promises eternal life?'

'That's for whipped folks.'

'You don't feel like you've had a chance, do you?'

'Naw; but I ain't asking nobody to be sorry for me. Naw; I ain't asking that at all. I'm black. They don't give black people a chance, so I took a chance and lost. But I don't care none now. They got me and it's all over.'

'Do you feel, Bigger, that somehow, somewhere, or sometime or other you'll have a chance to make up for what you didn't get here on earth?'

'Hell, naw! When they strap me in that chair and turn on the heat, I'm through, for always.'

'Bigger, I want to ask you something about your race. Do you love your people?'

'I don't know, Mr Max. We all black and the white folks treat us the same.'

'But Bigger, your race is doing things for you. There are Negroes leading your people.'

'Yeah; I know. I heard about 'em. They all right, I guess.'

'Don't you know any of 'em?'

'Naw.'

'Bigger, are there many Negro boys like you?'

'I reckon so. All of 'em I know ain't got nothing and ain't going nowhere.'

'Why didn't you go to some of the leaders of your race and tell them how you and other boys felt?'

'Aw, hell, Mr Max. They wouldn't listen to me. They rich,

even though the white folks treat them almost like they do me. They almost like white people, when it comes to guys like me. They say guys like me make it hard for them to get along with white folks.'

'Did you ever hear any of your leaders make speeches?'

'Yeah, sure. At election time.'

'What did you think of them?'

'Aw, I don't know. They all the same. They wanted to get elected to office. They wanted money, like everybody else. Mr Max, it's a game and they play it.'

'Why didn't you play it?'

'Hell, what do I know? I ain't got nothing. Nobody'll pay any attention to me. I'm just a black guy with nothing. I just went to grammar school. And politics is full of big shots, guys from colleges.'

'Didn't you trust them?'

'I don't reckon they wanted anybody to trust 'em. They wanted to get elected to office. They paid you to vote.'

'Did you ever vote?'

'Yeah; I voted twice. I wasn't old enough, so I put my age up so I could vote and get the five dollars.'

'You didn't mind selling your vote?'

'Naw; why should I?'

'You didn't think politics could get you anything?'

'It got me five dollars on election day.'

'Bigger, did any white people ever talk to you about labor unions?'

'Naw; nobody but Jan and Mary. But she oughtn't done it ... But I couldn't help what I did. And Jan. I reckon I did him wrong by signing "Red" to that ransom note.'

'Do you believe he's your friend now?'

'Well, he ain't against me. He didn't turn against me today when they was questioning him. I don't think he hates me like the others. I suppose he's kind of hurt about Miss Dalton, though.'

'Bigger, did you think you'd ever come to this?'

'Well, to tell the truth, Mr Max, it seems sort of natural-like,

395

me being here facing that death chair. Now I come to think of it, it seems like something like this just had to be.'

They were silent. Max stood up and sighed. Bigger watched to see what Max was thinking, but Max's face was white and blank.

'Well, Bigger,' Max said. 'We'll enter a plea of not guilty at the arraignment tomorrow. But when the trial comes up we'll change it to a plea of guilty and ask for mercy. They're rushing the trial; it may be held in two or three days. I'll tell the judge all I can of how you feel and why. I'll try to get him to make it life in prison. That's all I can see under the circumstances. I don't have to tell you how they feel toward you, Bigger. You're a Negro; you know. Don't hope for too much. There's an ocean of hot hate out there against you and I'm going to try to sweep some of it back. They want your life; they want revenge. They felt they had you fenced off so that you could not do what you did. Now they're mad because deep down in them they believe that they made you do it. When people feel that way, you can't reason with 'em. Then, too, a lot depends upon what judge we have. Any twelve white men in this state will have already condemned you; we can't trust a jury. Well, Bigger, I'll do the best I can.'

They were silent. Max gave him another cigarette and took one for himself. Bigger watched Max's head of white hair, his long face, the deep-gray, soft, sad eyes. He felt that Max was kind, and he felt sorry for him.

'Mr Max, if I was you I wouldn't worry none. If all folks was like you, then maybe I wouldn't be here. But you can't help that now. They going to hate you for trying to help me. I'm gone. They got me.'

'Oh, they'll hate me, yes,' said Max. 'But I can take it. That's the difference. I'm a Jew and they hate me, but I know why and I can fight. But sometimes you can't win no matter how you fight; that is, you can't win if you haven't got time. And they're pressing us now. But you need not worry about their hating me for defending you. The fear of hate keeps many whites from trying to help you and your kind. Before I can fight your battle,

I've got to fight a battle with them.' Max snuffed out his cigarette. 'I got to go now,' Max said. He turned and faced Bigger. 'Bigger, how do you feel?'

'I don't know. I'm just setting here waiting for 'em to come and tell me to walk to that chair. And I don't know if I'll be able to walk or not.'

Max averted his face and opened the door. A guard came and caught Bigger by the wrist.

'I'll see you in the morning, Bigger,' Max called.

Back in his cell, Bigger stood in the middle of the floor, not moving. He was not stoop-shouldered now, nor were his muscles taut. He breathed softly, wondering about the cool breath of peace that hovered in his body. It was as though he were trying to listen to the beat of his own heart. All round him was darkness and there were no sounds. He could not remember when he had felt as relaxed as this before. He had not thought of it or felt it while Max was speaking to him; it was not until after Max had gone that he discovered that he had spoken to Max as he had never spoken to anyone in his life; not even to himself. And his talking had eased from his shoulders a heavy burden. Then he was suddenly and violently angry. Max had tricked him! But no. Max had not compelled him to talk; he had talked of his own accord, prodded by excitement, by a curiosity about his own feelings. Max had only sat and listened, had only asked questions. His anger passed and fear took its place. If he were as confused as this when his time came, they really *would* have to drag him to the chair. He had to make a decision: in order to walk to that chair he had to weave his feelings into a hard shield of either hope or hate. To fall between them would mean living and dying in a fog of fear.

He was balanced on a hairline now, but there was no one to push him forward or backward, no one to make him feel that he had any value or worth – no one but himself. He brushed his hands across his eyes, hoping to untangle the sensations fluttering in his body. He lived in a thin, hard core of consciousness; he felt time slipping by; the darkness round him lived, breathed. And he was in the midst of it, wanting again to let his body taste of that short respite of rest he had felt after talking with Max. He sat down on the cot; he had to grasp this thing.

Why had Max asked him all those questions? He knew that Max was seeking facts to tell the judge; but in Max's asking of those questions he had felt a recognition of his life, of his feelings, of his person that he had never encountered before. What was this? Had he done wrong? Had he let himself in for another betrayal? He felt as though he had been caught off his guard. But this, this – confidence? He had no right to be proud; yet he had spoken to Max as a man who *had* something. He had told Max that he did not want religion, that he had not stayed in his place. He had no right to feel that, no right to forget that he was to die, that he was black, a murderer; he had no right to forget that, not even for a second. Yet he had.

He wondered if it were possible that after all everybody in the world felt alike? Did those who hated him have in them the same thing Max had seen in him, the thing that had made Max ask him those questions? And what motive could Max have in helping? Why would Max risk that white tide of hate to help him? For the first time in his life he had gained a pinnacle of feeling upon which he could stand and see vague relations that he had never dreamed of. If that white looming mountain of hate were not a mountain at all, but people, people like himself, and like Jan – then he was faced with a high hope the like of which he had never thought could be, and a despair the full depths of which he knew he could not stand to feel. A strong counter-emotion waxed in him, urging him, warning him to leave this newly seen and newly felt thing alone, that it would lead him to but another blind alley, to deeper hate and shame.

Yet he saw and felt but one life, and that one life was more than a sleep, a dream; life was all life had. He knew that he would not wake up some time later, after death, and sigh at how simple and foolish his dream had been. The life he saw was short and his sense of it goaded him. He was seized with a nervous eagerness. He stood up in the middle of the cell floor and tried to see himself in relation to other men, a thing he had always feared to try to do, so deeply stained was his own mind with the hate of others for him. With this new sense of the value of himself gained from Max's talk, a sense fleeting and obscure, he tried to feel that if Max had been able to see the man in him beneath those wild and cruel acts of his, acts of fear and hate and murder and flight and despair, then he *too* would hate, if *he* were *they*, just as now *he* was hating *them* and *they* were hating *him*. For the first time in his life he felt ground beneath his feet, and he wanted it to stay there.

He was tired, sleepy, and feverish; but he did not want to lie down with this war raging in him. Blind impulses welled up in his body, and his intelligence sought to make them plain to his understanding by supplying images that would explain them. Why was all this hate and fear? Standing trembling in his cell, he saw a dark vast fluid image rise and float; he saw a black sprawling prison full of tiny black cells in which people lived; each cell had its stone jar of water and a crust of bread and no one could go from cell to cell and there were screams and curses and yells of suffering and nobody heard them, for the walls were thick and darkness was everywhere. Why were there so many cells in the world? But was this true? He wanted to believe, but was afraid. Dare he flatter himself that much? Would he be struck dead if he made himself the equal of others, even in fancy?

He was too weak to stand any longer. He sat again on the edge of the cot. How could he find out if this feeling of his was true, if others had it? How could one find out about life when one was about to die? Slowly he lifted his hands in the darkness and held them in mid-air, the fingers spread weakly open. If he reached out with his hands, and if his hands were electric wires, and if his heart were a battery giving life and fire to those hands, and if he reached out with his hands and touched other people, reached out through these stone walls and felt other hands connected with other hearts – if he did that, would there be a reply, a shock? Not that he wanted those hearts to turn their warmth to him; he was not wanting that much. But just to know that they were there and warm! Just that, and no more; and it would have been enough, more than enough. And in that touch, response of recognition, there would be union, identity; there would be a supporting oneness, a wholeness which had been denied him all his life.

Another impulse rose in him, born of desperate need, and his mind clothed it in an image of a strong blinding sun sending hot rays down and he was standing in the midst of a vast crowd of men, white men and black men and all men, and the sun's rays melted away the many differences, the colors, the clothes, and drew what was common and good upward toward the sun ...

He stretched out full length upon the cot and groaned. Was he foolish in feeling this? Was it fear and weakness that made this desire come to him now that death was near? How could a notion that went so deep and caught up so much of him in one swoop of emotion be wrong? Could he trust bare, naked feeling this way? But he had; all his life he had hated on the basis of bare sensation. Why should he not accept this? Had he killed Mary and Bessie and brought sorrow to his mother and brother and sister and put himself in the shadow of the electric chair only to find out this? Had he been blind all along? But there was no way to tell now. It was too late ...

He would not mind dying now if he could only find out what this meant, what he was in relation to all the others that lived, and the earth upon which he stood. Was there some battle everybody was fighting, and he had missed it? And if he had missed it, were not the whites to blame for it? Were they not the ones to hate even now? Maybe. But he was not interested in hating them now. He had to die. It was more important to him to find out what this new tingling, this new elation, this new excitement meant.

He felt he wanted to live now – not escape paying for his crime – but live in order to find out, to see if it were true, and to feel it more deeply; and, if he had to die, to die within it. He felt that he would have lost all if he had to die without fully feeling it, without knowing for certain. But there was no way now. It was too late ...

He lifted his hands to his face and touched his trembling lips.

Naw ... Naw ... He ran to the door and caught the cold steel bars in his hot hands and gripped them tightly, holding himself erect. His face rested against the bars and he felt tears roll down his cheeks. His wet lips tasted salt. He sank to his knees and sobbed: 'I don't want to die ... I don't want to die ...'

*

Having been bound over to the grand jury and indicted by it, having been arraigned and having pled not guilty to the charge of murder and been ordered to trial – all in less than a week, Bigger lay one sunless gray morning on his cot, staring vacantly at the black steel bars of the Cook County Jail.

Within an hour he would be taken to court where they would tell him if he was to live or die, and when. And with but a few minutes between him and the beginning of judgment, the obscure longing to possess the thing which Max had dimly evoked in him was still a motive. He felt he *had* to have it now. How could he face that court of white men without something to sustain him? Since that night when he had stood alone in his cell, feeling the high magic which Max's talk had given him, he was more than ever naked to the hot blasts of hate.

There were moments when he wished bitterly that he had not felt those possibilities, when he wished that he could go again behind his curtain. But that was impossible. He had been lured into the open, and trapped, twice trapped; trapped by being in jail for murder, and again trapped by being stripped of emotional resources to go his death.

In an effort to recapture that high moment, he had tried to talk with Max, but Max was preoccupied, busy preparing his plea to the court to save his life. But Bigger wanted to save his *own* life. Yet he knew that the moment he tried to put his feelings into words, his tongue would not move. Many times, when alone after Max had left him, he wondered wistfully if there was not a set of words which he had in common with others, words which would evoke in others a sense of the same fire that smoldered in him.

He looked out upon the world and the people about him with

a double vision: one vision pictured death, an image of him, alone, sitting strapped in the electric chair and waiting for the hot current to leap through his body; and the other vision pictured life, an image of himself standing amid throngs of men, lost in the welter of their lives with the hope of emerging again, different, unafraid. But so far only the certainty of death was his; only the unabating hate of the white faces could be seen; only the same dark cell, the long lonely hours, only the cold bars remained.

Had his will to believe in a new picture of the world made him act a fool and thoughtlessly pile horror upon horror? Was not his old hate a better defense than this agonized uncertainty? Was not an impossible hope betraying him to this end? On how many fronts could a man fight at once? Could he fight a battle within as well as without? Yet he felt that he could not fight the battle for his life without first winning the one raging within him.

His mother and Vera and Buddy had come to visit him and again he had lied to them, telling them that he was praying, that he was at peace with the world and men. But that lie had only made him feel more shame for himself and more hate for them; it had hurt because he really yearned for that certainty of which his mother spoke and prayed, but he could not get it on the terms on which he felt he had to have it. After they had left, he told Max not to let them come again.

A few moments before the trial, a guard came to his cell and left a paper.

'Your lawyer sent this,' he said and left.

He unfolded the *Tribune* and his eyes caught a headline: TROOPS GUARD NEGRO KILLER'S TRIAL. Troops? He bent forward and read: PROTECT RAPIST FROM MOB ACTION. He went down the column:

Fearing outbreaks of mob violence, Gov. H. M. O'Dorsey ordered out two regiments of the Illinois National Guard to keep public peace during the trial of Bigger Thomas, Negro rapist and killer, it was announced from Springfield, the capital, this morning.

His eyes caught phrases: 'sentiment against killer still rising', 'public opinion demands death penalty', 'fear uprising in Negro sector', and 'city tense'.

Bigger sighed and stared into space. His lips hung open and he shook his head slowly. Was he not foolish in even listening when Max talked of saving his life? Was he not heightening the horror of his own end by straining after a flickering hope? Had not this voice of hate been sounding long before he was born; and would it not still sound long after he was dead?

He read again, catching phrases: 'the black killer is fully aware that he is in danger of going to the electric chair', 'spends most of his time reading newspaper accounts of his crime and eating luxurious meals sent to him by Communist friends', 'killer not sociable or talkative', 'Mayor lauds police for bravery', and 'a vast mass of evidence assembled against killer'. Then:

In relation to the Negro's mental condition, Dr Calvin H. Robinson, a psychiatric attaché of the police department, declared: 'There is no question but that Thomas is more alert mentally and more cagy than we suspect. His attempt to blame the Communists for the murder and kidnap note and his staunch denial of having raped the white girl indicate that he may be hiding many other crimes.'

Professional psychologists at the University of Chicago pointed out this morning that white women have an unusual fascination for Negro men. 'They think,' said one of the professors who requested that his name not be mentioned in connection with the case, 'that white women are more attractive than the women of their own race. They just can't help themselves.'

It was said that Boris A. Max, the Negro's communistic lawyer, will enter a plea of not guilty and try to free his client through a long drawn-out jury trial.

Bigger dropped the paper, stretched out upon the cot and closed his eyes. It was the same thing over and over again. What was the use of reading it?

'Bigger!'

Max was standing outside of the cell. The guard opened the door and Max walked in.

'Well, Bigger, how do you feel?'

'All right, I reckon,' he mumbled.

'We're on our way to court.'

Bigger rose and looked vacantly round the cell.

'Are you ready?'

'Yeah,' Bigger sighed. 'I reckon I am.'

'Listen, son. Don't be nervous. Just take it easy.'

'Will I be setting near you?'

'Sure. Right at the same table. I'll be there throughout the entire trial. So don't be scared.'

A guard led him outside the door. The corridor was lined with policemen. It was silent. He was placed between two policemen and his wrists were shackled to theirs. Black and white faces peered at him from behind steel bars. He walked stiffly between the two policemen; ahead of him walked six more; and he heard many more walking in back. They led him to an elevator that took him to an underground passage. They walked through a long stretch of narrow tunnel; the sound of their feet echoed loudly in the stillness. They reached another elevator and rode up and walked along a hallway crowded with excited people and policemen. They passed a window and. Bigger caught a quick glimpse of a vast crowd of people standing behind closely formed lines of khaki-clad troops. Yes, those were the troops and the mob the paper had spoken of.

He was taken into a room. Max led the way to a table. After the handcuffs were unlocked, Bigger sat, flanked by policemen. Softly, Max laid his right hand upon Bigger's knee.

'We've got just a few minutes,' Max said.

'Yeah,' Bigger mumbled. His eyes were half-closed; his head. leaned slightly to one side and his eyes looked beyond Max at some point in space.

'Here,' Max said. 'Straighten your tie.'

Bigger tugged listlessly at the knot.

'Now, maybe you'll have to say something just once, see...'

'You mean in the courtroom?'

'Yes; but I'll...'

Bigger's eyes widened with fear.

'Naw!'

'Now, listen, son ...'

'But I don't want to say nothing.'

'I'm trying to save your life ...'

Bigger's nerves gave way and he spoke hysterically:

'They going to *kill* me! You *know* they going to kill me ...'

'But you'll *have* to, Bigger. Now, listen ...'

'Can't you fix it so I won't have to say nothing?'

'It's only a word or two. When the judge asks how you want to plead, say guilty.'

'Will I have to stand up?'

'Yes.'

'I don't want to.'

'Don't you realize I'm trying to save your life? Help me just this little bit ...'

'I reckon I don't care. I reckon you can't save it.'

'You mustn't feel that way ...'

'I can't help it.'

'Here's another thing. The court'll be full, see? Just go in and sit down. You'll be right by me. And let the judge see that you notice what's going on.'

'I hope Ma won't be there.'

'I asked her to come. I want the judge to see her,' Max said.

'She'll feel bad.'

'All of this is for you, Bigger.'

'I reckon I ain't worth it.'

'Well, this thing's bigger than you, son. In a certain sense, every Negro in America's on trial out there today.'

'They going to kill me anyhow.'

'Not if we fight. Not if I tell them how you've had to live.'

A policeman walked over to Max, tapped him lightly on the shoulder, and said,

'The judge's waiting.'

'All right,' Max said. 'Come on, Bigger. Let's go. Keep your chin up.'

*

They stood and were surrounded by policemen. Bigger walked beside Max down a hallway and then through a door. He saw a huge room crowded with men and women. Then he saw a small knot of black faces, over to one side of the room, behind a railing. A deep buzzing of voices came to him. Two policemen pushed the people to one side, making a path for Max and Bigger. Bigger moved forward slowly, feeling Max's hand tugging at the sleeve of his coat. They reached the front of the room.

'Sit down,' Max whispered.

As Bigger sat the lightning of silver bulbs flashed in his eyes; they were taking more pictures of him. He was so tense in mind and body that his lips trembled. He did not know what to do with his hands; he wanted to put them into his coat pockets; but that would take too much effort and would attract attention. He kept them lying on his knees, palms up. There was a long and painful wait. The voices behind him still buzzed. Pale yellow sunshine fell through high windows and slashed the air.

He looked about. Yes; there were his mother and brother and sister; they were staring at him. There were many of his old school mates. There was his teacher, two of them. And there were G.H. and Jack and Gus and Doc. Bigger lowered his eyes. These were the people to whom he had once boasted, acted tough; people whom he had once defied. Now they were watching him as he sat here. They would feel that they were right and he was wrong. The old, hot choking sensation came back to his stomach and throat. Why could they not just shoot him and get it over with? They were going to kill him anyhow, so why make him go through with this? He was startled by the sound of a deep, hollow voice booming and a banging on a wooden table.

'Everybody rise, please . . .'

Everybody stood up. Bigger felt Max's hand touch his arm and he rose and stood with Max. A man, draped in long black robes and with a dead-white face, came through a rear door and sat behind a high pulpit-like railing. That's the judge, Bigger thought, easing back into his seat.

'Hear ye, hear ye...' Bigger heard the hollow voice booming again. He caught snatches of phrases: '... this Honorable Branch of the Cook County Criminal Court ... now in session ... pursuant to adjournment ... the Honorable Chief Justice Alvin C. Hanley, presiding...'

Bigger saw the judge look toward Buckley and then toward him and Max. Buckley rose and went to the foot of the railing; Max also rose and went forward. They talked a moment to the judge in low voices and then each went back to his seat. A man sitting just below the judge rose and began reading a long paper in a voice so thick and low that Bigger could only hear some of the words.

'... indictment number 666-983 ... the People of the State of Illinois vs. Bigger Thomas ... The Grand Jurors chosen, selected and sworn in and for the said County of Cook, present that Bigger Thomas did rape and inflict sexual injury upon the body ... strangulation by hand ... smother to death and dispose of body by burning same in furnace ... did with knife and hatchet sever head from body ... said acts committed upon one Mary Dalton, and contrary to the form of the statute in such case made and provided, against the peace and dignity of the People of the State of Illinois...'

The man pronounced Bigger's name over and over again, and Bigger felt that he was caught up in a vast but delicate machine whose wheels would whir no matter what was pitted against them. Over and over the man said that he had killed Mary and Bessie; that he had beheaded Mary; that he had battered Bessie with a brick; that he had raped both Mary and Bessie; that he had shoved Mary in the furnace; that he had thrown Bessie down the air-shaft and left her to freeze to death; and that he had stayed on in the Dalton home when Mary's body was burning and had sent a kidnap note. When the man finished, a gasp of astonishment came from the court-room and Bigger saw faces turning and looking in his direction. The judge rapped for order and asked,

'Is the defendant ready to enter a plea to this indictment?'

Max rose.

'Yes, Your Honor. The defendant, Bigger Thomas, pleads guilty.'

Immediately Bigger heard a loud commotion. He turned his head and saw several men pushing through the crowd toward the door. He knew that they were newspapermen. The judge rapped again for order. Max tried to continue speaking, but the judge stopped him.

'Just a minute, Mr Max. We must have order!'

The room grew quiet.

'Your Honor,' Max said, 'after long and honest deliberation, I have determined to make a motion in this court to withdraw our plea of not guilty and enter a plea of guilty.

'The laws of this state allow the offering of evidence in mitigation of punishment, and I shall request, at such time as the Court deems best, that I be given the opportunity to offer evidence as to the mental and emotional attitude of this boy, to show the degree of responsibility he had in these crimes. Also, I want to offer evidence as to the youth of this boy. Further, I want to prevail upon this Court to consider this boy's plea of guilty as evidence mitigating his punishment...'

'Your Honor!' Buckley shouted.

'Allow me to finish,' Max said.

Buckley came to the front of the room, his face red.

'You cannot plead that boy both guilty and insane,' Buckley said. 'If you claim Bigger Thomas is insane, the State will demand a jury trial...'

'Your Honor,' Max said, 'I do not claim that this boy is legally insane. I shall endeavor to show, through the discussion of evidence, the mental and emotional attitude of this boy and the degree of responsibility he had in these crimes.'

'That's a defense of insanity!' Buckley shouted.

'I'm making no such defense,' Max said.

'A man is either sane or insane,' Buckley said.

'There are degrees of insanity,' Max said. 'The laws of this state permit the hearing of evidence to ascertain the degree of responsibility. And, also, the law permits the offering of evidence toward the mitigation of punishment.'

'The State will submit witnesses and evidence to establish the legal sanity of the defendant,' Buckley said.

There was a long argument which Bigger did not understand. The judge called both lawyers forward to the railing and they talked for over an hour. Finally, they went back to their seats and the judge looked toward Bigger and said,

'Bigger Thomas, will you rise?'

His body flushed hot. As he had felt when he stood over the bed with the white blur floating toward him; as he had felt when he had sat in the car between Jan and Mary; as he had felt when he had seen Gus coming through the door of Doc's poolroom – so he felt now: constricted, taut, in the grip of a powerful, impelling fear. At that moment it seemed that any action under heaven would have been preferable to standing. He wanted to leap from his chair and swing some heavy weapon and end this unequal fight. Max caught his arm.

'Stand up, Bigger.'

He rose, holding on to the edge of the table, his knees trembling so that he thought that they would buckle under him. The judge looked at him a long time before speaking. Behind him Bigger heard the room buzzing with the sound of voices. The judge rapped for order.

'How far did you get in school?' the judge asked.

'Eighth grade,' Bigger whispered, surprised at the question.

'If your plea is guilty, and the plea is entered in this case,' the judge said and paused, 'the Court may sentence you to death,' the judge said and paused again, 'or the Court may sentence you to the penitentiary for the term of your natural life,' the judge said and paused yet again, 'or the Court may sentence you to the penitentiary for a term of not less than fourteen years.

'Now, do you understand what I have said?'

Bigger looked at Max; Max nodded to him.

'Speak up,' the judge said. 'If you do not understand what I have said, then say so.'

'Y-y-yessuh; I understand,' he whispered.

'Then, realizing the consequences of your plea, do you still plead guilty?'

'Y-y-yessuh,' he whispered again feeling that it was all a wild and intense dream that must end soon, somehow.

'That's all. You may sit down,' the judge said.

He sat.

'Is the State prepared to present its evidence and witnesses?' the judge asked.

'We are, Your Honor,' said Buckley, rising and half-facing the judge and the crowd.

'Your Honor, my statement at this time will be very brief. There is no need for me to picture to this Court the horrible details of these dastardly crimes. The array of witnesses for the State, the confession made and signed by the defendant himself, and the concrete evidence will reveal the unnatural aspect of this vile offense against God and man more eloquently than I could ever dare. In more than one respect, I am thankful that this is the case, for some of the facts of this evil crime are so fantastic and unbelievable, so utterly beast-like and foreign to our whole concept of life, that I feel incapable of communicating them to this Court.

'Never in my long career as an officer of the people have I been placed in a position where I've felt more unalterably certain of my duty. There is no room here for evasive, theoretical, or fanciful interpretations of the law.' Buckley paused, surveyed the courtroom, then stepped to the table and lifted from it the knife with which Bigger had severed Mary's head from her body. 'This case is as clean-cut as this murderer's knife, the knife that dismembered an innocent girl!' Buckley shouted. He paused again and lifted from the table the brick with which Bigger had battered Bessie in the abandoned building. 'Your Honor, this case is as solid as this brick, the brick that battered a poor girl's brains out!' Buckley again looked at the crowd in the courtroom. 'It is not often,' Buckley continued, 'that a representative of the people finds the masses of the citizens who elected him to office standing literally at his back, waiting for him to enforce the law...' The room was quiet as a tomb. Buckley strode to the window and with one motion of his hand hoisted it up. The rumbling mutter of the vast mob swept in. The courtroom stirred.

'Kill 'im now!'

'Lynch 'im!'

The judge rapped for order.

'If this is not stopped, I'll order the room cleared!' the judge said.

Max was on his feet.

'I object!' Max said. 'This is highly irregular. In effect, it is an attempt to intimidate this Court.'

'Objection sustained,' the judge said. 'Proceed in a fashion more in keeping with the dignity of your office and this Court, Mr State's Attorney.'

'I'm very sorry, Your Honor,' Buckley said, going toward the railing and wiping his face with a handkerchief. 'I was laboring under too much emotion, I merely wanted to impress the Court with the urgency of this situation . . .'

'The Court is waiting to hear you plea,' the judge said.

'Yes; of course, Your Honor,' Buckley said. 'Now, what are the issues here? The indictment fully states the crime to which the defendant has entered a plea of guilty. The counsel for the defense claims, and would have this Court believe, that the mere act of entering a plea of guilty to this indictment should be accepted as evidence mitigating punishment.

'Speaking for the grief-stricken families of Mary Dalton and Bessie Mears, and for the People of the State of Illinois, thousands of whom are massed out beyond that window waiting for the law to take its course, I say that no such quibbling, no such trickery shall pervert this Court and cheat the law!

'A man commits two of the most horrible murders in the history of American civilization; he confesses; and his counsel would have us believe that because he pleads guilty after dodging the law, after attempting to murder the officers of the law, that his plea should be looked upon as evidence mitigating his punishment!

'I say, Your Honor, this is an insult to the Court and to the intelligent people of this state! If such crimes admit of such defense, if this fiend's life is spared because of such a defense, I shall resign my office and tell those people out there in the streets that I can no longer protect their lives and property! I

shall tell them that our courts, swamped with mawkish senti-
mentality, are no longer fit instruments to safeguard the public
peace! I shall tell them that we have abandoned the fight for
civilization!

'After entering such a plea, the counsel for the defense
indicates that he shall ask this Court to believe that the mental
and emotional life of the defendant are such that he does not
bear full responsibility for these cowardly rapes and murders.
He asks this Court to imagine a legendary No Man's Land of
human thought and feeling. He tells us that a man is sane
enough to commit a crime, but is not sane enough to be tried
for it! Never in my life have I heard such sheer legal cynicism,
such a cold-blooded and calculated attempt to bedevil and evade
the law in my life! I say that this shall *not* be!

'The State shall insist that this man be tried by jury, if the
defense continues to say that he is insane. If his plea is simply
guilty, then the State demands the death penalty for these black
crimes.

'At such time as the Court may indicate, I shall offer evidence
and put witnesses upon the stand to testify that this defendant is
sane and is responsible for these bloody crimes . . .'

'Your Honor!' Max called.

'You shall have time to plead for your client!' Buckley
shouted. 'Let me finish!'

'Do you have an objection?' the judge asked, turning to Max.

'I do!' Max said. 'I hesitate to interrupt the State's Attorney,
but the impression he is trying to make is that I claim that this
boy is insane. That is *not* true. Your Honor, let me state once
again that this poor boy, Bigger, enters a plea of guilty . . .'

'I object!' Buckley shouted. 'I object to the counsel for the
defendant speaking of this defendant before this Court by any
name other than that written in the indictment. Such names as
"Bigger" and "this poor boy" are used to arouse sympathy . . .'

'Sustained,' the judge said. 'In the future, the defendant
should be designated by the name under which the indictment
was drawn. Mr Max, I think you should allow the State's
Attorney to continue.'

'There's nothing further I have to say, Your Honor,' Buckley said. 'If it pleases the Court, I am ready to call my witnesses.'

'How many witnesses have you?' Max asked.

'Sixty,' Buckley said.

'Your Honor,' Max said. 'Bigger Thomas has entered a plea of guilty. It seems to me that sixty witnesses are not needed.'

'I intend to prove that this defendant is sane, that he was and is responsible for these frightful crimes,' Buckley said.

'The Court will hear them,' the judge said.

'Your Honor,' Max said. 'Let me clear this thing up. As you know, the time granted me to prepare a defense for Bigger Thomas is pitifully brief, so brief as to be without example. This hearing was rushed to the top of the calendar so that this boy might be tried while the temper of the people is white-hot.

'A change of venue is of no value now. The same condition of hysteria exists all over this state. These circumstances have placed me in a position of not doing what I think wisest, but of doing what I must. If anybody but a Negro boy were charged with murder, the State's Attorney would not have rushed this case to trial and demanded the death penalty.

'The State has sought to create the impression that I am going to say that this boy is insane. That is *not* true. I shall put no witnesses upon this stand. *I* shall witness for Bigger Thomas. I shall present argument to show that his extreme youth, his mental and emotional life, and the reason why he has pleaded guilty, should and must mitigate his punishment.

'The State's Attorney has sought to create the belief that I'm trying to spring some surprise upon this Court by having my client enter a plea of guilty; he has sought to foster the notion that some legal trick is involved in the offering of evidence to mitigate this boy's punishment. But we have had many, many such cases to come before the courts of Illinois. The Loeb and Leopold case, for example. This is a regular procedure provided for by the enlightened and progressive laws of our state. Shall we deny this boy, because he is poor and black, the same protection, the same chance to be heard and understood that we have so readily granted to others?

'Your Honor, I am not a coward, but I could not ask that this boy be freed and given a chance at life while that mob howls beyond that window. I ask what I *must*. I ask, over the shrill cries of the mob, that you spare his life!

'The law of Illinois, regarding a plea of guilty to murder before a court, is as follows: the Court may impose the death penalty, imprison that defendant for life, or for a term of not less than fourteen years. Under this law the Court is able to hear evidence as to the aggravation or mitigation of the offense. The object of this law is to caution the Court to seek to find out *why* a man killed and to allow that *why* to be the measure of the mitigation of the punishment.

'I noticed that the State's Attorney did not dwell upon why Bigger Thomas killed those two women. There is a mob waiting, he says, so let us kill. His only plea is that if we do not kill, then the mob will kill.

'He did not discuss the motive for Bigger Thomas' crime because he *could* not. It is to his advantage to act quickly, before men have had time to think, before the full facts are known. For he knows that if the full facts were known, if men had time to reflect, he could not stand there and shout for death!

'What motive actuated Bigger Thomas? There was no motive as motive is understood under our laws today, Your Honor. I shall go deeper into this when I sum up. It is because of the almost instinctive nature of these crimes that I say that the mental and emotional life of this boy is important in deciding his punishment. But, as the State whets the appetite of the mob by needlessly parading witness after witness before this Court, as the State inflames the public mind further with the ghastly details of this boy's crime, I shall listen for the State's Attorney to tell the Court *why* Bigger Thomas killed.

'This boy is young, not only in years, but in his attitude toward life. He is not old enough to vote. Living in a Black Belt district, he is younger than most boys of his age, for he has not come in contact with the wide variety and depths of life. He has had but two outlets for his emotions: work and sex – and he knew these in their most vicious and degrading forms.

'I shall ask this Court to spare this boy's life and I have faith enough in this Court to believe that it will consent.'

Max sat down. The courtroom was filled with murmurs.

'The Court will adjourn for one hour and reconvene at one o'clock,' the judge said.

Flanked by policemen, Bigger was led back into the crowded hall. Again he passed a window and he saw a sprawling mob held at bay by troops. He was taken to a room where a tray of food rested on a table. Max was there, waiting for him.

'Come on and sit down, Bigger. Eat something.'

'I don't want nothing.'

'Come on. You've got to hold up.'

'I ain't hungry.'

'Here; take a smoke.'

'Naw.'

'You want a drink of water?'

'Naw.'

Bigger sat in a chair, leaned forward, rested his arms on the table, and buried his face in the crooks of his elbows. He was tired. Now that he was out of the courtroom, he felt the awful strain under which he had been while the men had argued about his life. All of the vague thoughts and excitement about finding a way to live and die were far from him now. Fear and dread were the only possible feelings he could have in that courtroom. When the hour was up, he was led back into court. He rose with the rest when the judge came, and then sat again.

'The State may call its witnesses,' the judge said.

'Yes, Your Honor,' Buckley said.

The first witness was an old woman whom Bigger had not seen before. During the questioning, he heard Buckley call her Mrs Rawlson. Then he heard the old woman say that she was the mother of Mrs Dalton. Bigger saw Buckley give her the earring he had seen at the inquest, and the old woman told of how the pair of earrings had been handed down through the years from mother to daughter. When Mrs Rawlson was through, Max said that he had no desire to examine her or any of the State's witnesses. Mrs Dalton was led to the stand and she told the same story she had told at the inquest. Mr Dalton told again why he had hired Bigger and pointed him out as 'the Negro boy who came to my home to work'. Peggy also pointed him out, saying through her sobs, 'Yes; he's the boy.' All of them said that he had acted like a very quiet and sane boy.

Britten told how he had suspected that Bigger knew something of the disappearance of Mary; and said that 'that black boy is as sane as I am.' A newspaperman told of how the smoke in the furnace had caused the discovery of Mary's bones. Bigger heard Max rise when the newspaperman had finished.

'Your Honor,' Max said. 'I'd like to know how many more newspapermen are to testify?'

'I have just fourteen more,' Buckley said.

'Your Honor,' Max said. 'This is totally unnecessary. There is a plea of guilty here . . .'

'I'm going to prove that that killer is sane!' Buckley shouted.

'The Court will hear them,' the judge said. 'Proceed, Mr Buckley.'

Fourteen more newspapermen told about the smoke and the bones and said that Bigger acted 'just like all other colored boys'. At five o'clock the court recessed and a tray of food was placed before Bigger in a small room, with six policemen standing guard. The nerves of his stomach were so taut that he could only drink the coffee. Six o'clock found him back in court. The room grew dark and the lights were turned on. The parade of witnesses ceased to be real to Bigger. Five white men came to the stand and said that the handwriting on the kidnap note was his; that it was the same writing which they had found on his 'homework papers taken from the files of the school he used to attend'. Another white man said that the fingerprints of Bigger Thomas were found on the door of 'Miss Dalton's room'. Then six doctors said Bessie had been raped. Four colored waitresses from Ernie's Kitchen Shack pointed him out as the 'colored boy who was at the table that night with the white man and the white woman'. And they said he had acted 'quiet and sane'. Next came two white women, school teachers, who said that Bigger was 'a dull boy, but thoroughly sane'. One witness

melted into another. Bigger ceased to care. He stared listlessly.
At times he could hear the faint sound of the winter wind
blowing outdoors. He was too tired to be glad when the session
ended. Before they took him back to his cell, he asked Max,

'How long will it last?'

'I don't know, Bigger. You'll have to be brave and hold up.'

'I wish it was over.'

'This is your life, Bigger. You got to fight.'

'I don't care what they do to me. I wish it was over.'

The next morning they woke him, fed him, and took him
back to court. Jan came to the stand and said what he had said
at the inquest. Buckley made no attempt to link Jan with the
murder of Mary. G.H. and Gus and Jack told of how they used
to steal from stores and newsstands, of the fight they had had
the morning they planned to rob Blum's. Doc told of how
Bigger had cut the cloth of his pool table and said that Bigger
was 'mean and bad, but sane'. Sixteen policemen pointed him
out as 'the man we captured, Bigger Thomas'. They said that a
man who could elude the law as skillfully as Bigger had was
'sane and responsible'. A man from the juvenile court said that
Bigger had served three months in a reform school for stealing
auto tires.

There was a recess and in the afternoon five doctors said that
they thought Bigger was 'sane, but sullen and contrary'. Buckley brought forth the knife and purse Bigger had hidden in the
garbage pail and informed the Court that the city's dump had
been combed for four days to find them. The brick he had used
to strike Bessie with was shown; then came the flashlight, the
Communist pamphlets, the gun, the blackened earring, the
hatchet blade, the signed confession, the kidnap note, Bessie's
bloody clothes, the stained pillows and quilts, the trunk, and
the empty rum bottle which had been found in the snow near a
curb. Mary's bones were brought in and women in the courtroom began to sob. Then a group of twelve workmen brought
in the furnace, piece by piece, from the Dalton basement and
mounted it upon a giant wooden platform. People in the room
stood to look and the judge ordered them to sit down.

Buckley had a white girl, the size of Mary, crawl inside of the furnace 'to prove beyond doubt that it could and did hold and burn the ravished body of innocent Mary Dalton; and to show that the poor girl's head could not go in and the sadistic Negro cut it off'. Using an iron shovel from the Dalton basement, Buckley showed how the bones had been raked out; explained how Bigger had 'craftily crept up the stairs during the excitement and taken flight'. Mopping sweat from his face, Buckley said,

'The State rests, Your Honor!'

'Mr Max,' the judge said. 'You may proceed to call your witnesses.'

'The defense does not contest the evidence introduced here,' Max said. 'I therefore waive the right to call witnesses. As I stated before, at the proper time I shall present a plea in Bigger Thomas' behalf.'

The judge informed Buckley that he could sum up. For an hour Buckley commented upon the testimony of the State's witnesses and interpreted the evidence, concluding with the words,

'The intellectual and moral faculties of mankind may as well be declared impotent, if the evidence and testimony submitted by the State are not enough to compel this Court to impose the death sentence upon Bigger Thomas, this despoiler of women!'

'Mr Max, will you be prepared to present your plea tomorrow?' the judge asked.

'I will, Your Honor.'

Back in his cell, Bigger tumbled lifelessly onto his cot. Soon it'll all be over, he thought. Tomorrow might be the last day; he hoped so. His sense of time was gone; night and day were merged now.

The next morning he was awake in his cell when Max came. On his way to court he wondered what Max would say about him. Could Max really save his life? In the act of thinking the thought, he thrust it from him. If he kept hope from his mind, then whatever happened would seem natural. As he was led down the hall, past windows, he saw that the mob and the troops still surrounded the court house. The building was still jammed with muttering people. Policemen had to make an aisle for him in the crowd.

A pang of fear shot through him when he saw that he had been the first to get to the table. Max was somewhere behind him, lost in the crowd. It was then that he felt more deeply than ever what Max had grown to mean to him. He was defenseless now. What was there to prevent those people from coming across those railings and dragging him into the street, now that Max was not here? He sat, not daring to look round, conscious that every eye was upon him. Max's presence during the trial had made him feel that somewhere in that crowd that stared at him so steadily and resentfully was something he could cling to, if only he could get at it. There smoldered in him the hope that Max had made him feel in the first long talk they had had. But he did not want to risk trying to make it flare into flame now, not with this trial and the words of hate from Buckley. But neither did he snuff it out; he nursed it, kept it as his last refuge.

When Max came Bigger saw that his face was pale and drawn. There were dark rings beneath the eyes. Max laid a hand on Bigger's knee and whispered,

'I'm going to do all I can, son.'

Court opened and the judge said,

'Are you ready to proceed, Mr Max?'

'Yes, Your Honor.'

Max rose, ran his hand through his white hair and went to the front of the room. He turned and half-faced the judge and Buckley, looking out over Bigger's head to the crowd. He cleared his throat.

'Your Honor, never in my life have I risen in court to make a plea with a firmer conviction in my heart. I know that what I have to say here today touches the destiny of an entire nation. My plea is for more than one man and one people. Perhaps it is in a manner fortunate that the defendant has committed one of the darkest crimes in our memory; for if we can encompass the life of this man and find out what has happened to him, if we can understand how subtly and yet strongly his life and fate are linked to ours – if we can do this, perhaps we shall find the key to our future, that rare vantage point upon which every man and woman in this nation can stand and view how inextricably our hopes and fears of today create the exultation and doom of tomorrow.

'Your Honor, I have no desire to be disrespectful to this Court, but I must be honest. A man's life is at stake. And not only is this man a criminal, but he is a black criminal. And as such, he comes into this court under a handicap, notwithstanding our pretensions that all are equal before the law.

'This man is *different*, even though his crime differs from similar crimes only in degree. The complex forces of society have isolated here for us a symbol, a test symbol. The prejudices of men have stained this symbol, like a germ stained for examination under the microscope. The unremitting hate of men has given us a psychological distance that will enable us to see this tiny social symbol in relation to our whole sick social organism.

'I say, Your Honor, that the mere act of understanding Bigger Thomas will be a thawing out of icebound impulses, a dragging of the sprawling forms of dread out of the night of fear into the light of reason, an unveiling of the unconscious ritual of death in which we, like sleep-walkers, have participated so dreamlike and thoughtlessly.

'But I make no excessive claims, Your Honor. I do not deal in magic. I do not say that if we understand this man's life we shall solve all our problems, or that when we have all the facts at our disposal we shall automatically know how to act. Life is not that simple. But I do say that, if, after I have finished, you feel that death is necessary, then you are making an open choice. What I want to do is inject the consciousness of this Court, through the discussion of evidence, the two possible courses of action open to us and the inevitable consequences flowing from each. And then, if we say death, let us mean it; and if we say life, let us mean that too; but whatever we say, let us know upon what ground we are putting our feet, what the consequences are for us and those whom we judge.

'Your Honor, I would have you believe that I am not insensible to the deep burden of responsibility I am throwing upon your shoulders by the manner in which I have insisted upon conducting the defense of this boy's life, and in my resolve to place before you the entire degree of his guilt for judgment. But, under the circumstances, what else could I have done? Night after night, I have lain without sleep, trying to think of a way to picture to you and to the world the causes and reasons why this Negro boy sits here a self-confessed murderer. How can I, I asked myself, make the picture of what has happened to this boy show plain and powerful upon a screen of sober reason, when a thousand newspaper and magazine artists have already drawn it in lurid ink upon a million sheets of public print? Dare I, deeply mindful of this boy's background and race, put his fate in the hands of a jury (not of his peers, but of an alien and hostile race!) whose minds are already conditioned by the press of the nation; a press which has already reached a decision as to his guilt, and in countless editorials suggested the measure of his punishment?

'No! I could not! So today I come to face this Court, rejecting a trial by jury, willingly entering a plea of guilty, asking in the light of the laws of this state that this boy's life be spared for reasons which I believe affect the foundations of our civilization.

'The most habitual thing for this Court to do is to take the line of least resistance and follow the suggestion of the State's Attorney and say, "Death!" And that would be the end of this case. But that would not be the end of this crime! That is why this Court must do otherwise.

'There are times, Your Honor, when reality bears features of such an impellingly moral complexion that it is impossible to follow the hewn path of expediency. There are times when life's ends are so raveled that reason and sense cry out that we stop and gather them together again before we can proceed.

'What atmosphere surrounds this trial? Are the citizens soberly intent upon seeing that the law is executed? That retribution is dealt out in measure with the offense? That the guilty and only the guilty is caught and punished?

'No! Every conceivable prejudice has been dragged into this case. The authorities of the city and state deliberately inflamed the public mind to the point where they could not keep the peace without martial law. Responsible to nothing but their own corrupt conscience, the newspapers and the prosecution launched the ridiculous claim that the Communist Party was in some way linked to these two murders. Only here in court yesterday morning did the State's Attorney cease implying that Bigger Thomas was guilty of other crimes, crimes which he could not prove.

'The hunt for Bigger Thomas served as an excuse to terrorize the entire Negro population, to arrest hundreds of Communists, to raid labor union headquarters and workers' organizations. Indeed, the tone of the press, the silence of the church, the attitude of the prosecution, and the stimulated temper of the people are of such a nature as to indicate that *more* than revenge is being sought upon a man who has committed a crime.

'What is the cause of all this high feeling and excitement? Is it the crime of Bigger Thomas? Were Negroes liked yesterday and hated today because of what he has done? Were labor unions and workers' halls raided solely because a Negro committed a crime? Did those white bones lying on that table evoke the gasp of horror that went up from the nation?

'Your Honor, you know that that is *not* the case! All of the factors in the present hysteria existed before Bigger Thomas was ever heard of. Negroes, workers, and labor unions were hated as much yesterday as they are today.

'Crimes of even greater brutality and horror have been committed in this city. Gangsters have killed and have gone free to kill again. But none of that brought forth an indignation to equal this.

'Your Honor, that mob did not come here of its own accord! It was *incited*! Until a week ago those people lived their lives as quietly as always.

'Who, then, fanned this latent hate into fury? Whose interest is that thoughtless and misguided mob serving?

'The State's Attorney knows, for he promised the Loop

bankers that if he were re-elected demonstrations for relief would be stopped! The Governor of the State knows, for he has pledged the Manufacturers' Association that he would use troops against workers who went out on strike! The Mayor knows, for he told the merchants of the city that the budget would be cut down, that no new taxes would be imposed to satisfy the clamor of the masses of the needy!

'There is guilt in the rage that demands that this man's life be snuffed out quickly! There is fear in the hate and impatience which impels the action of the mob congregated upon the streets beyond that window! All of them – the mob and the mob-masters; the wire-pullers and the frightened; the leaders and their pet vassals – know and feel that their lives are built upon a historical deed of wrong against many people, people from whose lives they have bled their leisure and their luxury! Their feeling of guilt is as deep as that of the boy who sits here on trial today. Fear and hate and guilt are the keynotes of this drama!

'Your Honor, for the sake of this boy and myself, I wish I could bring to this Court evidence of a morally worthier nature. I wish I could say that love, ambition, jealousy, the quest for adventure, or any of the more romantic feelings were back of these two murders. If I could honestly invest the hapless actor in this fateful drama with feelings of a loftier cast, my task would be easier and I would feel confident of the outcome. The odds would be with me, for I would be appealing to men bound by common ideals to judge with pity and understanding one of their brothers who erred and fell in struggle. But I have no choice in this matter. Life has cut this cloth; not I.

'We must deal here with the raw stuff of life, emotions and impulses and attitudes as yet unconditioned by the strivings of science and civilization. We must deal here with a first wrong which, when committed by us, was understandable and inevitable; and then we must deal with the long trailing black sense of guilt stemming from that wrong, a sense of guilt which self-interest and fear would not let us atone. And we must deal here with the hot blasts of hate engendered in others by that first wrong, and then the monstrous and horrible crimes flowing from that hate, a hate which has seeped down into the hearts and molded the deepest and most delicate sensibilities of multitudes.

'We must deal here with a dislocation of life involving millions of people, a dislocation so vast as to stagger the imagination; so fraught with tragic consequences as to make us rather not want to look at it or think of it; so old that we would rather try to view it as an order of nature and strive with uneasy conscience and false moral fervor to keep it so.

'We must deal here, on both sides of the fence, among whites as well as blacks, among workers as well as employers, with men and women in whose minds there loom good and bad of such height and weight that they assume proportions of abnormal aspect and construction. When situations like this arise, instead of men feeling that they are facing other men, they feel that they are facing mountains, floods, seas: forces of nature whose size and strength focus the minds and emotions to a degree of tension unusual in the quiet routine of urban life. Yet this tension exists within the limits of urban life, undermining it and supporting it in the same gesture of being.

'Allow me, Your Honor, before I proceed to cast blame and ask for mercy, to state emphatically that I do *not* claim that this boy is a victim of injustice, nor do I ask that this Court be sympathetic with him. That is not my object in embracing his character and his cause. It is not to tell you only of suffering that I stand here today, even though there are frequent lynchings and floggings of Negroes throughout the country. If you react only to that part of what I say, then you, too, are caught as much as he in the mire of blind emotion, and this vicious game will roll on, like a bloody river to a bloodier sea. Let us banish from our minds the thought that this is an unfortunate victim of injustice. The very concept of injustice rests upon a premise of equal claims, and this boy here today makes no claim upon you. If you think or feel that he does, then you, too, are blinded by a feeling as terrible as that which you condemn in him, and without as much justification. The feeling of guilt which has

424

caused all of the mob-fear and mob-hysteria is the counterpart of his own hate.

'Rather, I plead with you to see a mode of *life* in our midst, a mode of life stunted and distorted, but possessing its own laws and claims, an existence of men growing out of the soil prepared by the collective but blind will of a hundred million people. I beg you to recognize human life draped in a form and guise alien to ours, but springing from a soil plowed and sown by all our hands. I ask you to recognize the laws and processes flowing from such a condition, understand them, seek to change them. If we do none of these, then we should not pretend horror or surprise when thwarted life expresses itself in fear and hate and crime.

'This is life, new and strange; strange, because we fear it; new, because we have kept our eyes turned from it. This is life lived in cramped limits and expressing itself not in terms of our good and bad, but in terms of its own fulfillment. Men are men and life is life, and we must deal with them as they are: and if we want to change them, we must deal with them in the form in which they exist and have their being.

'Your Honor, I must still speak in general terms, for the background of this boy must be shown, a background which has acted powerfully and importantly upon his conduct. Our forefathers came to these shores and faced a harsh and wild country. They came here with a stifled dream in their hearts, from lands where their personalities had been denied, as even we have denied the personality of this boy. They came from cities of the old world where the means to sustain life were hard to get or own. They were colonists and they were faced with a difficult choice: they had either to subdue this wild land or be subdued by it. We need but turn our eyes upon the imposing sweep of streets and factories and buildings to see how completely they have conquered. But in conquering they *used* others, used their lives. Like a miner using a pick or a carpenter using a saw, they bent the will of others to their own. Lives to them were tools and weapons to be wielded against a hostile land and climate.

'I do not say this in terms of moral condemnation. I do not say it to rouse pity in you for the black men who were slaves for two and one-half centuries. It would be foolish now to look back upon that in the light of injustice. Let us not be naïve: men do what they must, even when they feel that they are being driven by God, even when they feel they are fulfilling the will of God. Those men were engaged in a struggle for life and their choice in the matter was small indeed. It was the imperial dream of a feudal age that made men enslave others. Exalted by the will to rule, they could not have built nations on so vast a scale had they not shut their eyes to the humanity of other men, men whose lives were necessary for their building. But the invention and widespread use of machines made the further direct enslavement of men economically impossible, and so slavery ended.

'Let me, Your Honor, dwell a moment longer upon the danger of looking upon this boy in the light of injustice. If I should say that he is a victim of injustice, then I would be asking by implication for sympathy; and if one insists upon looking at this boy in the light of sympathy, he will be swamped by a feeling of guilt so strong as to be indistinguishable from hate.

'Of all things, men do not like to feel that they are guilty of wrong, and if you make them feel guilt, they will try desperately to justify it on any grounds; but, failing that, and seeing no immediate solution that will set things right without too much cost to their lives and property, they will kill that which evoked in them the condemning sense of guilt. And this is true of all men, whether they be white or black; it is a peculiar and powerful, but common, need.

'This guilt-fear is the basic tone of the prosecution and of the people in this case. In their hearts they feel that a wrong has been done and when a Negro commits a crime against them, they fancy they see the ghastly evidence of that wrong. So the men of wealth and property, the victims of attack who are eager to protect their profits, say to their guilty hirelings, "Stamp out this ghost!" Or, like Mr Dalton, they say, "Let's do something for this man so he won't feel that way." But then it is too late.

'If only ten or twenty Negroes had been put into slavery, we could call it injustice, but there were hundreds of thousands of them throughout the country. If this state of affairs had lasted for two or three years, we could say that it was unjust; but it lasted for more than two hundred years. Injustice which lasts for three long centuries and which exists among millions of people over thousands of square miles of territory, is injustice no longer; it is an accomplished fact of life. Men adjust themselves to their land; they create their own laws of being; their notions of right and wrong. A common way of earning a living gives them a common attitude toward life. Even their speech is colored and shaped by what they must undergo. Your Honor, injustice blots out one form of life, but another grows up in its place with its own rights, needs, and aspirations. What is happening* here today is not injustice, but *oppression*, an attempt to throttle or stamp out a new form of life. And it is this new form of life that has grown up here in our midst that puzzles us, that expresses itself, like a weed growing from under a stone, in terms we call crime. Unless we grasp this problem in the light of this new reality, we cannot do more than salve our feelings of guilt and rage with more murder when a man, living under such conditions, commits an act which we call a crime.

'This boy represents but a tiny aspect of a problem whose reality sprawls over a third of this nation. Kill him! Burn the life out of him! And still when the delicate and unconscious machinery of race relations slips, there will be murder again. How can law contradict the lives of millions of people and hope to be administered successfully? Do we believe in magic? Do you believe that by burning a cross you can frighten a multitude, paralyze their will and impulses? Do you think that the white daughters in the homes of America will be any safer if you kill this boy? No! I tell you in all solemnity that they won't! The surest way to make certain that there will be more such murders is to kill this boy. In your rage and guilt, make thousands of other black men and women feel that the barriers are tighter and higher! Kill him and swell the tide of pent-up lava that will some day break loose, not in a single, blundering, accidental, individual crime, but in a wild cataract of emotion that will brook no control. The all-important thing for this Court to remember in deciding this boy's fate is that, though his crime was accidental, the emotions that broke loose were *already* there; the thing to remember is that this boy's way of life was a way of guilt; that his crime existed long before the murder of Mary Dalton; that the accidental nature of his crime took the guise of a sudden and violent rent in the veil behind which he lived, a rent which allowed his feelings of resentment and estrangement to leap forth and find objective and concrete form.

'Obsessed with guilt, we have sought to thrust a corpse from before our eyes. We have marked off a little plot of ground and buried it. We tell our souls in the deep of the black night that it is dead and that we have no reason for fear or uneasiness.

'But the corpse returns and raids our homes! We find our daughters murdered and burnt! And we say, "Kill! Kill!"

'But, Your Honor, I say: "Stop! Let us look at what we are doing!" For the corpse is not dead! It still lives! It has made itself a home in the wild forest of our great cities, amid the rank and choking vegetation of slums! It has forgotten our language! In order to live it has sharpened its claws! It has grown hard and calloused! It has developed a capacity for hate and fury which we cannot understand! Its movements are unpredictable! By night it creeps from its lair and steals toward the settlements of civilization! And at the sight of a kind face it does not lie down upon its back and kick up its heels playfully to be tickled and stroked. No; it leaps to kill!

'Yes, Mary Dalton, a well-intentioned white girl with a smile upon her face, came to Bigger Thomas to help him. Mr Dalton, feeling vaguely that a social wrong existed, wanted to give him a job so that his family could eat and his sister and brother could go to school. Mrs Dalton, trying to grope her way toward a sense of decency, wanted him to go to school and learn a trade. But when they stretched forth their helping hands, death struck! Today they mourn and wait for revenge. The wheel of blood continues to turn!

'I have only sympathy for those kind-hearted, white-haired parents. But to Mr Dalton, who is a real estate operator, I say now: "You rent houses to Negroes in the Black Belt and you refuse to rent to them elsewhere. You kept Bigger Thomas in that forest. You kept the man who murdered your daughter a stranger to her and you kept your daughter a stranger to him."

'The relationship between the Thomas family and the Dalton family was that of renter to landlord, customer to merchant, employee to employer. The Thomas family got poor and the Dalton family got rich. And Mr Dalton, a decent man, tried to salve his feelings by giving money. But, my friend, gold was not enough! Corpses cannot be bribed! Say to yourself, Mr Dalton, "I offered my daughter as a burnt sacrifice and it was not enough to push back into its grave this thing that haunts me."

'And to Mrs Dalton, I say: "Your philanthropy was as tragically blind as your sightless eyes!"

'And to Mary Dalton, if she can hear me, I say: "I stand here today trying to make your death *mean* something!"

'Let me, Your Honor, explain further the meaning of Bigger Thomas' life. In him and men like him is what was in our forefathers when they first came to these strange shores hundreds of years ago. We were lucky. They are not. We found a land whose tasks called forth the deepest and best we had; and we built a nation, mighty and feared. We poured and are still pouring our soul into it. But we have told them: "This is a white man's country!" They are yet looking for a land whose tasks can call forth their deepest and best.

'Your Honor, consider the mere physical aspect of our civilization. How alluring, how dazzling it is! How it excites the senses! How it seems to dangle within easy reach of everyone the fulfillment of happiness! How constantly and overwhelmingly the advertisements, radios, newspapers, and movies play upon us! But in thinking of them remember that to many they are tokens of mockery. These bright colors may fill our hearts with elation, but to many they are daily taunts. Imagine a man walking amid such a scene, a part of it, and yet knowing that it is *not* for him!

'We planned the murder of Mary Dalton, and today we come to court and say: "We had nothing to do with it!" But every school teacher knows that this is not so, for every school teacher knows the restrictions which have been placed upon Negro education. The authorities know that it is not so, for they have made it plain in their every act that they mean to keep Bigger Thomas and his kind within rigid limits. All real estate operators know that it is not so, for they have agreed among themselves to keep Negroes within the ghetto-areas of cities. Your Honor, we who sit here today in this courtroom are witnesses. We know this evidence, for we helped to create it.

'But the question may be asked, "If this boy thought that he was somehow wronged, why did he not go into a court of law and seek a redress of his grievances? Why should he take the law into his own hands?" Your Honor, this boy had no notion before he murdered, and he has none now, of having been wronged by any specific individuals. And, to be honest with you, the very life he has led has created in him a frame of mind which makes him expect much less of this Court than you will ever know.

'This boy's crime was not an act of retaliation by an injured man against a person who he thought had injured him. If it were, then this case would be simple indeed. This is the case of a man's mistaking a whole race of men as a part of the natural structure of the universe and of his acting toward them accordingly. He murdered Mary Dalton accidentally, without thinking, without plan, without conscious motive. But, after he murdered, he accepted the crime. And that's the important thing. It was the first full act of his life; it was the most meaningful, exciting, and stirring thing that had ever happened to him. He accepted it because it made him free, gave him the possibility of choice, of action, the opportunity to act and to feel that his actions carried weight.

'We are dealing here with an impulse stemming from deep down. We are dealing here not with how man acts toward man, but with how a man acts when he feels that he must defend himself against, or adapt himself to, the total natural world in which he lives. The central fact to be understood here is not who wronged this boy, but what kind of a vision of the world did he have before his eyes, and where did he get such a vision as to make him, without premeditation, snatch the life of another person so quickly and instinctively that even though there was an element of accident in it, he was willing after the crime to say: "Yes; I did it. I had to."

'I know that it is the fashion these days for a defendant to say: "Everything went blank to me." But this boy does not say that. He says the opposite. He says he knew what he was doing but felt he *had* to do it. And he says he feels no sorrow for having done it.

'Do men regret when they kill in war? Does the personality of a soldier coming at you over the top of a trench matter?

'No! You kill to keep from being killed! And after a victorious war you return to a free country, just as this boy, with his hands stained with the blood of Mary Dalton, felt that he was free for the first time in his life.

'Multiply Bigger Thomas twelve million times, allowing for environmental and temperamental variations, and for those Negroes who are completely under the influence of the church, and you have the psychology of the Negro people. But once you see them as a whole, once your eyes leave the individual and encompass the mass, a new quality comes into the picture. Taken collectively, they are not simply twelve million people; in reality they constitute a separate nation, stunted, stripped, and held captive *within* this nation, devoid of political, social, economic, and property rights.

'Do you think that you can kill one of them – even if you killed one every day in the year – and make the others so full of fear that they would not kill? No! Such a foolish policy has never worked and never will. The more you kill, the more you deny and separate, the more will they seek another form and way of life, however blindly and unconsciously. And out of what can they weave a different life, out of what can they mold a new existence, living organically in the same towns and cities, the same neighborhoods with us? I ask, out of what – but what we *are* and *own*?

'Your Honor, there are four times as many Negroes in America today as there were people in the original Thirteen Colonies when they struck for their freedom. These twelve million Negroes, conditioned broadly by our own notions as we were by European ones when we first came here, are struggling within unbelievably narrow limits to achieve that feeling of at-home-ness for which we once strove so ardently. And, compared with our own struggle, they are striving under conditions far more difficult. If anybody can, surely we ought to be able to understand what these people are after. This vast stream of life, dammed and muddied, is trying to sweep toward the fulfillment which all of us seek so fondly, but find so impossible to put into words. When we said that men are "endowed with certain inalienable rights, among these are life, liberty, and the pursuit of happiness", we did not pause to define "happiness". That is the unexpected quality in our quest, and we have never tried to put it into words. That is why we say, "Let each man serve God in his own fashion."

'But there are some broad features of the kind of happiness we are seeking which are known. We know that happiness comes to men when they are caught up, absorbed in a meaning-ful task or duty to be done, a task or duty which in turn sheds justification and sanction back down upon their humble labors. We know that this may take many forms: in religion it is the story of the creation of man, of his fall, and of his redemption; compelling men to order their lives in certain ways, all cast in terms of cosmic images and symbols which swallow the soul in fulness and wholeness. In art, science, industry, politics, and social action it may take other forms. But these twelve million Negroes have access to none of these highly crystallized modes of expression, save that of religion. And many of them know religion only in its more primitive form. The environment of tense urban centers has all but paralyzed the impulse for religion as a way of life for them today, just as it has for us.

'Feeling the capacity to be, to live, to act, to pour out the spirit of their souls into concrete and objective form with a high fervor born of their racial characteristics, they glide through our complex civilization like wailing ghosts; they spin like fiery planets lost from their orbits; they wither and die like trees ripped from native soil.

'Your Honor, remember that men can starve from a lack of self-realization as much as they can from a lack of bread! And they can *murder* for it, too! Did we not build a nation, did we not wage war and conquer in the name of a dream to realize our personalities and to make those realized personalities secure!

'But did Bigger Thomas really *murder*? At the risk of offending the sensibilities of this Court, I ask the question in the light of the ideals by which *we* live! Looked at from the outside, maybe it was murder; yes. But to him it was *not* murder. If it was murder, then what was the motive? The prosecution has shouted, stormed, and threatened, but he has not said *why* Bigger Thomas killed! He has not said why because he does not know. The truth is, Your Honor, there was no motive as you and I understand motives within the scope of our laws today. The truth is, this boy did *not* kill! Oh, yes; Mary Dalton is dead. Bigger Thomas smothered her to death. Bessie Mears is dead. Bigger Thomas battered her with a brick in an abandoned building. But did he murder? Did he kill? Listen: what Bigger Thomas did early that Sunday morning in the Dalton home and what he did that Sunday night in that empty building was but a tiny aspect of what he had been doing all his life long! He was *living*, only as he knew how, and as we have forced him to live. The actions that resulted in the death of those two women were as instinctive and inevitable as breathing or blinking one's eyes. It was an act of *creation*!

'Let me tell you more. Before this trial the newspapers and the prosecution said that this boy had committed other crimes. It is true. He is guilty of numerous crimes. But search until the day of judgment, and you will find not one shred of evidence of them. He has murdered many times, but there are no corpses. Let me explain. This Negro boy's entire attitude toward life is a *crime*! The hate and fear which we have inspired in him, woven by our civilization into the very structure of his consciousness, into his blood and bones, into the hourly functioning of his personality, have become the justification of his existence.

'Every time he comes in contact with us, he kills! It is a physiological and psychological reaction, embedded in his being. Every thought he thinks is potential murder. Excluded from, and unassimilated in our society, yet longing to gratify impulses akin to our own but denied the objects and channels evolved through long centuries for their socialized expression, every sunrise and sunset make him guilty of subversive actions. Every movement of his body is an unconscious protest. Every desire, every dream, no matter how intimate or personal, is a plot or a conspiracy. Every hope is a plan for insurrection. Every glance of the eye is a threat. *His very existence is a crime against the state!*

'It so happened that that night a white girl was present in a bed and a Negro boy was standing over her, fascinated with fear, hating her; a blind woman walked into the room and that Negro boy killed that girl to keep from being discovered in a position which he knew *we* claimed warrants the death penalty. But that is only *one* side of it! He was impelled toward murder as much through the thirst for excitement, exultation, and elation as he was through fear! It was his way of *living*!

'Your Honor, in our blindness we have so contrived and ordered the lives of men that the moths in their hearts flutter toward ghoulish and incomprehensible flames!

'I have not explained the relationship of Bessie Mears to this boy. I have not forgotten her. I omitted to mention her until now because she was largely omitted from the consciousness of Bigger Thomas. His relationship to this poor black girl also reveals his relationship to the world. But Bigger Thomas is not here on trial for having murdered Bessie Mears. And he knows that. What does this mean? Does not the life of a Negro girl

mean as much in the eyes of the law as the life of a white girl?
Yes, perhaps, in the abstract. But under the stress of fear and
flight, Bigger Thomas did not think of Bessie. He could not.
The attitude of America toward this boy regulated his most
intimate dealings with his own kind. After he had killed Mary
Dalton he killed Bessie Mears to silence her, to save himself.
After he had killed Mary Dalton the fear of having killed a
white woman filled him to the exclusion of everything else. He
could not react to Bessie's death; his consciousness was determined by the fear that hung above him.

'But, one might ask, did he not love Bessie? Was she not his
girl? Yes; she was his girl. He had to have a girl, so he had
Bessie. But he did not love her. Is love possible to the life of a
man I've described to this Court? Let us see. Love is not based
upon sex alone, and that is all he had with Bessie. He wanted
more, but the circumstances of his life and her life would not
allow it. And the temperament of both Bigger and Bessie kept
it out. Love grows from stable relationships, shared experience,
loyalty, devotion, trust. Neither Bigger nor Bessie had any of
these. What was there they could hope for? There was no
common vision binding their hearts together; there was no
common hope steering their feet in a common path. Even
though they were intimately together, they were confoundingly
alone. They were physically dependent upon each other and
they hated that dependence. Their brief moments together were
for purposes of sex. They loved each other as much as they
hated each other; perhaps they hated each other more than they
loved. Sex warms the deep roots of life; it is the soil out of
which the tree of love grows. But these were trees without
roots, trees that lived by the light of the sun and what chance
rain that fell upon stony ground. Can disembodied spirits love?
There existed between them fitful splurges of physical elation;
that's all.

'Your Honor, is this boy alone in feeling deprived and
baffled? Is he an exception? Or are there others? There are
others, Your Honor, millions of others, Negro and white, and
that is what makes our future seem a looming image of

violence. The feeling of resentment and the balked longing for some kind of fulfillment and exultation – in degrees more or less intense and in actions more or less conscious – stalk day by day through this land. The consciousness of Bigger Thomas, and millions of others more or less like him, white and black, according to the weight of the pressure we have put upon them, forms the quicksands upon which the foundations of our civilization rest. Who knows when some slight shock, disturbing the delicate balance between social order and thirsty aspiration, shall send the skyscrapers in our cities toppling? Does that sound fantastic? I assure you that it is no more fantastic than those troops and that waiting mob whose presence and guilty anger portend something which we dare not even *think*!

'Your Honor, Bigger Thomas was willing to vote for and follow any man who would have led him out of his morass of pain and hate and fear. If that mob outdoors is afraid of *one* man, what will it feel if *millions* rise? How soon will someone speak the word that resentful millions will understand: the word to be, to act, to live? Is this Court so naïve as to think that they will not take a chance that is even less risky than that Bigger Thomas took? Let us not concern ourselves with that part of Bigger Thomas' confession that says he murdered accidentally, that he did not rape the girl. It really does not matter. What does matter is that he was guilty *before* he killed! That was why his whole life became so quickly and naturally organized, pointed, charged with a new meaning when this thing occurred. Who knows when another "accident" involving millions of men will happen, an "accident" that will be the dreadful day of our doom?

'Lodged in the heart of this moment is the question of power which time will unfold!

'Your Honor, another civil war in these states is not impossible; and if the misunderstanding of what this boy's life means is an indication of how men of wealth and property are misreading the consciousness of the submerged millions today, one may truly come.

'I do not propose that we try to solve this entire problem here in this courtroom today. That is not within the province of our duty, nor even, I think, within the scope of our ability. But our decision as to whether this black boy is to live or die can be made in accordance with what actually exists. It will at least indicate that we *see* and *know*! And our seeing and knowing will comprise a consciousness of how inescapably this one man's life will confront us ten million fold in the days to come.

'I ask that you spare this boy, send him to prison for life. What would prison mean to Bigger Thomas? It holds advantages for him that a life of freedom never had. To send him to prison would be more than an act of mercy. You would be for the first time conferring *life* upon him. He would be brought for the first time within the orbit of our civilization. He would have an identity, even though it be but a number. He would have for the first time an openly designated relationship with the world. The very building in which he would spend the rest of his natural life would be the best he has ever known. Sending him to prison would be the first recognition of his personality he has ever had. The long black empty years ahead would constitute for his mind and feelings the only certain and durable object around which he could build a meaning for his life. The other inmates would be the first men with whom he could associate on a basis of equality. Steel bars between him and the society he offended would provide a refuge from hate and fear.

'I say, Your Honor, give this boy his life. And in making this concession we uphold those two fundamental concepts of our civilization, those two basic concepts upon which we have built the mightiest nation in history – personality and security – the conviction that the person is inviolate and that which sustains him is equally so.

'Let us not forget that the magnitude of our modern life, our railroads, power plants, ocean liners, airplanes, and steel mills flowered from these two concepts, grew from our dream of creating an invulnerable base upon which man and his soul can stand secure.

'Your Honor, this Court and those troops are not the real

agencies that keep the public peace. Their mere presence is proof that we are letting peace slip through our fingers. Public peace is the act of public trust; it is the faith that *all* are secure and will *remain* secure.

'When men of wealth urge the use and show of force, quick death, swift revenge, then it is to protect a little spot of private security against the resentful millions from whom they have filched it, the resentful millions in whose militant hearts the dream and hope of security still lives.

'Your Honor, I ask in the name of all we are and believe, that you spare this boy's life! With every atom of my being, I beg this in order that not only may this black boy live, but that we ourselves may not die!'

Bigger heard Max's last words ring out in the courtroom. When Max sat down he saw that his eyes were tired and sunken. He could hear his breath coming and going heavily. He had not understood the speech, but he had felt the meaning of some of it from the tone of Max's voice. Suddenly he felt that his life was not worth the effort that Max had made to save it. The judge rapped with the gavel, calling a recess. The court was full of noise as Bigger rose. The policemen marched him to a small room and stood waiting, on guard. Max came and sat beside him, silent, his head bowed. A policeman brought a tray of food and set it on the table.

'Eat, son,' Max said.

'I ain't hungry.'

'I did the best I could,' Max said.

'I'm all right,' Bigger said.

Bigger was not at that moment really bothered about whether Max's speech had saved his life or not. He was hugging the proud thought that Max had made the speech all for him, to save his life. It was not the meaning of the speech that gave him pride, but the mere act of it. That in itself was something. The food on the tray grew cold. Through a partly opened window Bigger heard the rumbling voice of the mob. Soon he would go back and hear what Buckley would say. Then it would all be over, save for what the judge would say. And when the judge spoke he would know if he was to live or die. He leaned his head on his hands and closed his eyes. He heard Max stand up, strike a match, and light a cigarette.

'Here; take a smoke, Bigger.'

He took one and Max held the flame; he sucked the smoke deep into his lungs and discovered that he did not want it. He held the cigarette in his fingers and the smoke curled up past his bloodshot eyes. He jerked his head when the door opened; a policeman looked in.

'Court's opening in two minutes!'

'All right,' Max said.

Flanked again by policemen, Bigger went back to court. He rose when the judge came and then sat again.

'The Court will hear the State,' the judge said.

Bigger turned his head and saw Buckley rise. He was dressed in a black suit and there was a tiny pink flower in the lapel of his coat. The man's very look and bearing, so grimly assured, made Bigger feel that he was already lost. What chance had he against a man like that? Buckley licked his lips and looked out over the crowd; then he turned to the judge.

'Your Honor, we all dwell in a land of living law. Law embodies the will of the people. As an agent and servant of the law, as a representative of the organized will of the people, I am here to see that the will of the people is executed firmly and without delay. I intend to stand here and see that that is done, and if it is not done, then it will be only over my most solemn and emphatic protest.

'As a prosecuting officer of the State of Illinois, I come before this honorable Court to urge that the full extent of the law, the death penalty – the only penalty of the law that is feared by murderers! – be allowed to take its course in this most important case.

'I urge this for the protection of our society, our homes, and our loved ones. I urge this in the performance of my sworn duty to see, in so far as I am humanly capable, that the administration of law is just, that the safety and sacredness of human life are maintained, that the social order is kept intact, and that crime is prevented and punished. I have no interest or feeling in this case beyond the performance of this sworn duty.

'I represent the families of Mary Dalton and Bessie Mears and a hundred million law-abiding men and women of this nation who are laboring in duty or industry. I represent the forces which allow the arts and sciences to flourish in freedom and peace, thereby enriching the lives of us all.

'I shall not lower the dignity of this Court, nor the righteousness of the people's cause, by attempting to answer the silly, alien, communistic, and dangerous ideas advanced by the defense. And I know of no better way to discourage such thinking than the imposition of the death penalty upon this miserable human fiend, Bigger Thomas!

'My voice may sound harsh when I say: *Impose the death penalty and let the law take its course in spite of the specious call for sympathy!* But I am really merciful and sympathetic, because the enforcement of this law in its most drastic form will enable millions of honest men and women to sleep in peace tonight, to know that tomorrow will not bring the black shadow of death over their homes and lives!

'My voice may sound vindictive when I say: *Make the defendant pay the highest penalty for his crimes!* But what I am really saying is that the law is sweet when it is enforced and protects a million worthy careers, when it shields the infant, the aged, the helpless, the blind, and the sensitive from the ravishing of men who know no law, no self-control, and no sense of reason.

'My voice may sound cruel when I say: *The defendant merits the death penalty for his self-confessed crimes!* But what I am really saying is that the law is strong and gracious enough to allow all of us to sit here in this courtroom today and try this case with dispassionate interest, and not tremble with fear that at this very moment some half-human black ape may be climbing through the windows of our homes to rape, murder, and burn our daughters!

'Your Honor, I say that the law is holy; that it is the foundation of all our cherished values. It permits us to take for granted

440

the sense of the worth of our persons and turn our energies to higher and nobler ends.

'Man stepped forward from the kingdom of the beast the moment he felt that he could think and feel in security, knowing that sacred law had taken the place of his gun and knife.

'I say that the law is holy because it makes us human! And woe to the men – and the civilization of those men! – who, in misguided sympathy or fear, weaken the stout structure of the law which insures the harmonious working of our lives on this earth.

'Your Honor, I regret that the defense has raised the viperous issue of race and class hate in this trial. I sympathize with those whose hearts were pained, as mine was pained, when Mr Max so cynically assailed our sacred customs. I pity this man's deluded and diseased mind. It is a sad day for American civilization when a white man will try to stay the hand of justice from a bestial monstrosity who has ravished and struck down one of the finest and most delicate flowers of our womanhood.

'Every decent white man in America ought to swoon with joy for the opportunity to crush with his heel the woolly head of this black lizard, to keep him from scuttling on his belly farther over the earth and spitting forth his venom of death!

'Your Honor, literally I shrink from the mere recital of this dastardly crime. I cannot speak of it without feeling somehow contaminated by the mere telling of it. A bloody crime has that power! It is that steeped and dyed with repellent contagion!

'A wealthy, kindly disposed white man, a resident of Chicago for more than forty years, sends to the relief agency for a Negro boy to act as chauffeur to his family. The man specifies in his request that he wants a boy who is handicapped either by race, poverty, or family responsibility. The relief authorities search through their records and select the Negro family which they think merits such aid: that family was the Thomas family, living then as now at 3721 Indiana Avenue. A social worker visits the family and informs the mother that the family is to be taken off the relief rolls and her son placed in private employment. The mother, a hard-working Christian woman, consents.

In due time the relief authorities send a notification to the oldest son of the family, Bigger Thomas, this black mad dog who sits here today, telling him that he must report for work.

'What was the reaction of this sly thug when he learned that he had an opportunity to support himself, his mother, his little sister, and his little brother? Was he grateful? Was he glad that he was having something offered to him that ten million men in America would have fallen on their knees and thanked God for?

'No! He cursed his mother! He said that he did not want to work! He wanted to loaf about the streets, steal from newsstands, rob stores, meddle with women, frequent dives, attend cheap movies, and chase prostitutes! That was the reaction of this sub-human killer when he was confronted with the Christian kindness of a man he had never seen!

'His mother prevailed upon him, pled with him; but the plight of his mother, worn out from a life of toil, had no effect upon this hardened black thing. The future of his sister, an adolescent school girl, meant nothing to him. The fact that the job would have enabled his brother to return to school was not enticing to Bigger Thomas.

'But, suddenly, after three days of persuasion by his mother, he consented. Had any of her arguments reached him at long last? Had he begun to feel his duty toward himself and his family? No! Those were not the considerations that drove this rapacious beast from his den into the open! He consented only when his mother informed him that the relief would cut off their supply of food if he did not accept. He agreed to go to work, but forbade his mother to speak to him within the confines of the home, so outraged was he that he had to earn his bread by the sweat of his brow. It was hunger that drove him out, sullen, angry, still longing to stay upon the streets and steal as he had done before, and for which he had once landed in a reform school.

'After seeing a movie that Saturday morning, he went to the Dalton home. He was welcomed there with lavish kindness. He was given a room; he was told that he would receive extra money for himself, over and above his weekly wages. He was fed. He was asked if he wanted to go back to school and learn a trade. But he refused. His mind and heart – if this beast can be said to have a mind and a heart! – were not set upon any such goals.

'Less than an hour after he had been in that house, he met Mary Dalton, who asked him if he wanted to join a union. Mr Max, whose heart bleeds for labor, did not tell us why his client should have resented that.

'What black thoughts passed through that Negro's scheming brain the first few moments after he saw that trusting white girl standing before him? We have no way of knowing, and perhaps this piece of human scum, who sits here today begging for mercy, is wise in not telling us. But we can use our imagination; we can look upon what he subsequently did and surmise.

'Two hours later he was driving Miss Dalton to the Loop. Here occurs the first misunderstanding in this case. The general notion is that Miss Dalton, by having this Negro drive her to the Loop instead of to school, was committing an act of disobedience against her family. But that is not for us to judge. That is for Mary Dalton and her God to settle. It was admitted by her family that she went contrary to a wish of theirs; but Mary Dalton was of age and went where she pleased.

'This Negro drove Miss Dalton to the Loop where she was joined by a young white man, a friend of hers. From there they went to a South Side café and ate and drank. Being in a Negro neighborhood, they invited this Negro to eat with them. When they talked, they included him in their conversation. When liquor was ordered, enough was bought so that he, too, could drink.

'Afterwards he drove the couple through Washington Park for some two hours. Around two o'clock in the morning this friend of Miss Dalton's left the car and went to visit some friends of his. Mary Dalton was left alone in that car with this Negro, who had received nothing from her but kindness. From that point onward, we have no exact knowledge of what really happened, for we have only this black cur's bare word for it, and I am convinced that he is not telling us all.

'We don't know just when Mary Dalton was killed. But we do know this: her head was completely severed from her body! We know that both the head and the body were stuffed into the furnace and burned!

'My God, what bloody scenes must have taken place! How swift and unexpected must have been that lustful and murderous attack! How that poor child must have struggled to escape that maddened ape! How she must have pled on bended knee, with tears in her eyes, to be spared the vile touch of his horrible person! Your Honor, must not this infernal monster have burned her body to destroy evidence of offenses *worse* than rape? That treacherous beast must have known that if the marks of his teeth were ever seen on the innocent white flesh of her breasts, he would not have been accorded the high honor of sitting here in this court of law! O suffering Christ, there are no words to tell of a deed so black and awful!

'And the defense would have us believe that this was an act of *creation*! It is a wonder that God in heaven did not drown out his lying voice with a thunderous "NO!" It is enough to make the blood stop flowing in one's veins to hear a man excuse this cowardly and beastly crime on the ground that it was "instinctive"!

'The next morning Bigger Thomas took Miss Dalton's trunk, half-packed, to the La Salle Street Station and prepared to send it off as though nothing had happened, as though Miss Dalton were still alive. But the bones of Miss Dalton's body were found in the furnace that evening.

'The burning of the body and the taking of the half-packed trunk to the station mean just one thing, Your Honor. It shows that the rape and murder were *planned*, that an attempt was made to destroy evidence so that the crime could be carried on to the point of ransom. If Miss Dalton were accidentally killed, as this Negro so pathetically tried to make us believe when he first "confessed", then why did he burn her body? Why did he take her trunk to the station when he knew that she was dead?

'There is but one answer! He planned to rape, to kill, to collect! He burned the body to get rid of evidences of *rape*! He took the trunk to the station to gain time in which to burn the body and prepare the kidnap note. He killed her because he *raped* her! Mind you, Your Honor, the central crime here is *rape*! Every action points toward that!

'Knowing that the family had called in private investigators, the Negro tried to throw the suspicion elsewhere. In other words, he was not above seeing an innocent man die for his crime. When he could not kill any more, he did the next best thing. He lied! He sought to blame the crime upon one of Miss Dalton's friends, whose political beliefs, he thought, would damn him. He told wild lies of taking the two of them, Miss Dalton and her friend, to her room. He said that he had been told to go home and leave the car out in the snow in the driveway all night. Knowing that his lies were being found out, he tried yet another scheme. He tried to collect money!

'Did he flee the scene when the investigators were at work? No! Coldly, without feeling, he stayed on in the Dalton home, ate, slept, basking in the misguided kindness of Mr Dalton, who refused to allow him to be questioned upon the theory that he was a poor boy who needed *protection*!

'He needed as much protection as you would give a coiled rattler!

'While the family was searching heaven and earth for their daughter, this ghoul writes a kidnap note demanding ten thousand dollars for the *safe return* of Miss Dalton! But the discovery of the bones in the furnace put that foul dream to an end!

'And the defense would have us believe that this man acted in fear! Has fear, since the beginning of time, driven men to such lengths of calculation?

'Again, we have but the bare word of this worthless ape to go on. He fled the scene and went to the home of a girl, Bessie Mears, with whom he had long been intimate. There something occurred that only a cunning beast could have done. This girl had been frightened into helping him collect the ransom money, and he had placed in her keeping the money he had stolen from the corpse of Mary Dalton. He killed that poor girl, and even yet it staggers my mind to think that such a plan for murder could have been hatched in a human brain. He persuaded this girl, who loved him deeply – despite the assertions of Mr Max, that godless Communist, who tried to make you believe otherwise! – as I said, he persuaded this girl who loved him deeply to run away with him. They hid in an abandoned building. And there, with a blizzard raging outside, in the sub-zero cold and darkness, he committed rape and murder again, *twice* in twenty-four hours!

'I repeat, Your Honor, I cannot understand it! I have dealt with many a murderer in my long service to the state, but never have I encountered the equal of this. So eager was this demented savage to rape and kill that he forgot the only thing that might have helped him to escape; that is, the money he had stolen from the dead body of Mary Dalton, which was in the pocket of Bessie Mears' dress. He took the ravished body of that poor working girl – the money was in her dress, I say – and dumped it four floors down an air-shaft. The doctors told us that that girl was not dead when she hit the bottom of that shaft; she froze to death later, trying to climb out!

'Your Honor, I spare you the ghastly details of these murders. The witnesses have told all.

'But I demand, in the name of the people of this state, that this man die for these crimes!

'I demand this so that others may be deterred from similar crimes, so that peaceful and industrious people may be safe. Your Honor, millions are waiting for your word! They are waiting for you to tell them that jungle law does not prevail in this city! They want you to tell them that they need not sharpen their knives and load their guns to protect themselves. They are waiting, Your Honor, beyond that window! Give them your word so that they can, with calm hearts, plan for the future! Slay the dragon of doubt that causes a million hearts to pause tonight, a million hands to tremble as they lock their doors!

'When men are pursuing their normal rounds of duty and a crime as black and bloody as this is committed, they become paralyzed. The more horrible the crime, the more stunned, shocked, and dismayed is the tranquil city in which it happens; the more helpless are the citizens before it.

'Restore confidence to those of us who still survive, so that we may go on and reap the rich harvests of life. Your Honor, in the name of Almighty God, I plead with you to be merciful to us!'

Buckley's voice boomed in Bigger's ears and he knew what the loud commotion meant when the speech had ended. In the back of the room several newspapermen were scrambling for the door. Buckley wiped his red face and sat down. The judge rapped for order, and said:

'Court will adjourn for one hour.'

Max was on his feet.

'Your Honor, you cannot do this ... Is it your intention ... More time is needed ... You ...'

'The Court will give its decision then,' the judge said.

There were shouts. Bigger saw Max's lips moving, but he could not make out what he was saying. Slowly, the room quieted. Bigger saw that the expressions on the faces of the men and women were different now. He felt that the thing had been decided. He knew that he was to die.

'Your Honor,' Max said, his voice breaking from an intensity of emotion. 'It seems that for careful consideration of the evidence and discussion submitted, more time is ...'

'The Court reserves the right to determine how much time is needed, Mr Max,' the judge said.

Bigger knew that he was lost. It was but a matter of time, of formality.

He did not know how he got back into the little room; but when he was brought in he saw the tray of food still there, uneaten. He sat down and looked at the six policemen who stood silently by. Guns hung from their hips. Ought he to try to snatch one and shoot himself? But he did not have enough spirit to respond positively to the idea of self-destruction. He was paralyzed with dread.

Max came in, sat, and lit a cigarette.

'Well, son. We'll have to wait. We've got an hour.'

There was a banging on the door.

'Don't let any of those reporters in here,' Max told a police-man.

'O.K.'

Minutes passed. Bigger's head began to ache with the sus-pense of it. He knew that Max had nothing to say to him and he had nothing to say to Max. He had to wait; that was all; wait for something he knew was coming. His throat tightened. He felt cheated. Why did they have to have a trial if it had to end this way?

'Well, I reckon it's all over for me now,' Bigger sighed, speaking as much for himself as for Max.

'I don't know,' Max said.

'I know,' Bigger said.

'Well, let's wait.'

'He's making up his mind too quick. I know I'm going to die.'

'I'm sorry, Bigger. Listen, why don't you eat?'

'I ain't hungry.'

'This thing isn't over yet. I can ask the Governor ...'

'It ain't no use. They got me.'

'You don't know.'

'I know.'

Max said nothing. Bigger leaned his head upon the table and closed his eyes. He wished Max would leave him now. Max had done all he could. He should go home and forget him.

The door opened.

'The judge'll be ready in five minutes!'

Max stood up. Bigger looked at his tired face.

'All right, son. Come on.'

Walking between policemen, Bigger followed Max back into the courtroom. He did not have time to sit down before the judge came. He remained standing until the judge was seated, then he slid weakly into his chair. Max rose to speak, but the judge lifted his hand for silence.

'Will Bigger Thomas rise and face the Court?'

The room was full of noise and the judge rapped for quiet.

With trembling legs, Bigger rose, feeling in the grip of a nightmare.

'Is there any statement you wish to make before sentence is passed upon you?'

He tried to open his mouth to answer, but could not. Even if he had had the power of speech, he did not know what he could have said. He shook his head, his eyes blurring. The courtroom was profoundly quiet now. The judge wet his lips with his tongue and lifted a piece of paper that crackled loudly in the silence.

'In view of the unprecedented disturbance of the public mind, the duty of this Court is clear,' the judge said and paused.

Bigger groped for the edge of the table with his hand and clung to it.

'In Number 666-983, indictment for murder, the sentence of the Court is that you, Bigger Thomas, shall die on or before midnight of Friday, March third, in a manner prescribed by the laws of this State.

'This Court finds your age to be twenty.

'The Sheriff may retire with the prisoner.'

Bigger understood every word; and he seemed not to react to the words, but to the judge's face. He did not move; he stood looking up into the judge's white face, his eyes not blinking. Then he felt a hand upon his sleeve; Max was pulling him back into his seat. The room was in an uproar. The judge rapped with his gavel. Max was on his feet, trying to say something; there was too much noise and Bigger could not tell what it was. The handcuffs were clicked upon him and he was led through the underground passage back to his cell. He lay on the cot and something deep down in him said, It's over now ... It's all over ...

Later on the door opened and Max came in and sat softly beside him on the cot. Bigger turned his face to the wall.

'I'll see the Governor, Bigger. It's not over yet ...'

'Go 'way,' Bigger whispered.

'You've got to ...'

'Naw. Go 'way ...'

He felt Max's hand on his arm; then it left. He heard the steel door clang shut and he knew that he was alone. He did not stir; he lay still, feeling that by being still he would stave off feeling and thinking, and that was what he wanted above all right now. Slowly, his body relaxed. In the darkness and silence he turned over on his back and crossed his hands upon his chest. His lips moved in a whimper of despair.

*

In self-defense he shut out the night and day from his mind, for if he had thought of the sun's rising and setting, of the moon or the stars, of clouds or rain, he would have died a thousand deaths before they took him to the chair. To accustom his mind to death as much as possible, he made all the world beyond his cell a vast gray land where neither night nor day was, peopled by strange men and women whom he could not understand, but with those lives he longed to mingle once before he went.

He did not eat now; he simply forced food down his throat without tasting it, to keep the gnawing pain of hunger away, to keep from feeling dizzy. And he did not sleep; at intervals he closed his eyes for awhile, no matter what the hour, then opened them at some later time to resume his brooding. He wanted to be free of everything that stood between him and his end, him and the full and terrible realization that life was over without meaning, without anything being settled, without con- flicting impulses being resolved.

His mother and brother and sister had come to see him and he had told them to stay home, not to come again, to forget him. The Negro preacher who had given him the cross had come and he had driven him away. A white priest had tried to persuade him to pray and he had thrown a cup of hot coffee into his face. The priest had come to see other prisoners since then, but had not stopped to talk with him. That had evoked in Bigger a sense of his worth almost as keen as that which Max had roused in him during the long talk that night. He felt that his making the priest stand away from him and wonder about his motives for refusing to accept the consolations of religion was a sort of recognition of his personality on a plane other than that which the priest was ordinarily willing to make.

Max had told him that he was going to see the Governor, but he had heard no more from him. He did not hope that anything would come of it; he referred to it in his thoughts and feelings as something happening outside of his life, which could not in any way alter or influence the course of it.

But he did want to see Max and talk with him again. He recalled the speech Max had made in court and remembered with gratitude the kind, impassioned tone. But the meaning of the words escaped him. He believed that Max knew how he felt, and once more before he died he wanted to talk with him and feel with as much keenness as possible what his living and dying meant. That was all the hope he had now. If there were any sure and firm knowledge for him, it would have to come from himself.

He was allowed to write three letters a week, but he had written to no one. There was no one to whom he had anything to say, for he had never given himself whole-heartedly to any-one or anything, except murder. What could he say to his mother and brother and sister? Of the old gang, only Jack had been his friend, and he had never been so close to Jack as he would have liked. And Bessie was dead; he had killed her.

When tired of mulling over his feelings, he would say to himself that it was he who was wrong, that he was no good. If he could have really made himself believe that, it would have been a solution. But he could not convince himself. His feelings clamored for an answer his mind could not give.

All his life he had been most alive, most himself when he had felt things hard enough to fight for them; and now here in this cell he felt more than ever the hard central core of what he had lived. As the white mountain had once loomed over him, so now the black wall of death loomed closer with each fleeting hour. But he could not strike out blindly now; death was a different and bigger adversary.

Though he lay on his cot, his hands were groping fumblingly

through the city of men for something to match the feelings smoldering in him; his groping was a yearning to know. Frantically, his mind sought to fuse his feelings with the world about him, but he was no nearer to knowing than ever. Only his black body lay here on the cot, wet with the sweat of agony.

If he were nothing, if this were all, then why could not he die without hesitancy? Who and what was he to feel the agony of a wonder so intensely that it amounted to fear? Why was this strange impulse always throbbing in him when there was nothing outside of him to meet it and explain it? Who or what had traced this restless design in him? Why this eternal reaching for something that was not there? Why this black gulf between him and the world: warm red blood here and cold blue sky there, and never a wholeness, a oneness, a meeting of the two?

Was *that* it? Was it simply fever, feeling without knowing, seeking without finding? Was this the all, the meaning, the end? With these feelings and questions the minutes passed. He grew thin and his eyes held the red blood of his body.

The eve of his last day came. He longed to talk to Max more than ever. But what could he say to him? Yes; that was the joke of it. He could not talk about this thing, so elusive it was; and yet he acted upon it every living second.

The next day at noon a guard came to his cell and poked a telegram through the bars. He sat up and opened it.

BE BRAVE GOVERNOR FAILED DONE ALL POSSIBLE SEE YOU SOON

MAX

He balled the telegram into a tight knot and threw it into a corner.

He had from now until midnight. He had heard that six hours before his time came they would give him some more clothes, take him to the barber shop, and then take him to the death cell. He had been told by one of the guards not to worry, that 'eight seconds after they take you out of your cell and put that black cap over your eyes, you'll be dead, boy'. Well, he could stand that. He had in his mind a plan: he would flex his muscles and shut his eyes and hold his breath and think of absolutely nothing while they were handling him. And when the current struck him, it would all be over.

He lay down again on the cot, on his back, and stared at the tiny bright yellow electric bulb glowing on the ceiling above his head. It contained the fire of death. If only those tiny spirals of heat inside that glass globe would wrap round him now – if only someone would attach the wires to his iron cot while he dozed off – if only when he was in a deep dream they would kill him ...

He was in an uneasy sleep when he heard the voice of a guard.

'Thomas! Here's your lawyer!'

He swung his feet to the floor and sat up. Max was standing at the bars. The guard unlocked the door and Max walked in.

Bigger had an impulse to rise, but he remained seated. Max came to the center of the floor and stopped. They looked at each other for a moment.

'Hello, Bigger.'

Silently, Bigger shook hands with him. Max was before him, quiet, white, solid, real. His tangible presence seemed to belie all the vague thoughts and hopes that Bigger had woven round him in his broodings. He was glad that Max had come, but he was bewildered.

'How're you feeling?'

For an answer, Bigger sighed heavily.

'You get my wire?' Max asked, sitting on the cot.

Bigger nodded.

'I'm sorry, son.'

There was silence. Max was at his side. The man who had lured him on a quest toward a dim hope was there. Well, why didn't he speak now? Here was his chance, his last chance. He lifted his eyes shyly to Max's; Max was looking at him. Bigger looked off. What he wanted to say was stronger in him when he was alone; and though he imputed to Max the feelings he wanted to grasp, he could not talk of them to Max until he had forgotten Max's presence. Then fear that he would not be able to talk about this consuming fever made him panicky. He struggled for self-control; he did not want to lose this driving impulse; it was all he had. And in the next second he felt that it was all foolish, useless, vain. He stopped trying, and in the very moment he stopped, he heard himself talking with tight throat, in tense, involuntary whispers; he was trusting the sound of his voice rather than the sense of his words to carry his meaning.

'I'm all right, Mr Max. You ain't to blame for what's happening to me ... I know you did all you could ...' Under the pressure of a feeling of futility his voice trailed off. After a short silence he blurted, 'I just r-r-reckon I h-had it coming ...' He stood up, full now, wanting to talk. His lips moved, but no words came.

'Is there anything I can do for you, Bigger?' Max asked softly.

Bigger looked at Max's gray eyes. How could he get into that man a sense of what he wanted? If he could only tell him! Before he was aware of what he was doing, he ran to the door and clutched the cold steel bars in his hands.

'I – I ...'

'Yes, Bigger?'

Slowly, Bigger turned and came back to the cot. He stood before Max again, about to speak, his right hand raised. Then he sat down and bowed his head.

'What is it, Bigger? Is there anything you want me to do on the outside? Any message you want to send?'

'Naw,' he breathed.

'What's on your mind?'

'I don't know.'

He could not talk. Max reached over and placed a hand on his shoulder, and Bigger could tell by its touch that Max did not know, had no suspicion of what he wanted, of what he was trying to say. Max was upon another planet, far off in space. Was there any way to break down this wall of isolation? Distractedly, he gazed about the cell, trying to remember where he had heard words that would help him. He could recall none. He had lived outside of the lives of men. Their modes of communication, their symbols and images, had been denied him. Yet Max had given him the faith that at bottom all men lived as he lived and felt as he felt. And of all the men he had met, surely Max knew what he was trying to say. Had Max left him? Had Max, knowing that he was to die, thrust him from his thoughts and feelings, assigned him to the grave? Was he already numbered among the dead? His lips quivered and his eyes grew misty. Yes; Max had left him. Max was not a friend. Anger welled in him. But he knew that anger was useless.

Max rose and went to a small window; a pale bar of sunshine fell across his white head. And Bigger, looking at him, saw that sunshine for the first time in many days; and as he saw it, the entire cell, with its four close walls, became crushingly real. He glanced down at himself; the shaft of yellow sun cut across his chest with as much weight as a beam forged of lead. With a convulsive gasp, he bent forward and shut his eyes. It was not a white mountain looming over him now; Gus was not whistling 'The Merry-Go-Round Broke Down' as he came into Doc's poolroom to make him go and rob Blum's; he was not standing over Mary's bed with the white blur hovering near; – this new adversary did not make him taut; it sapped strength and left him weak. He summoned his energies and lifted his head and struck out desperately, determined to rise from the grave, resolved to force upon Max the reality of his living.

'I'm glad I got to know you before I go!' he said with almost a shout; then was silent, for that was not what he had wanted to say.

Max turned and looked at him; it was a casual look, devoid of the deeper awareness that Bigger sought so hungrily.

'I'm glad I got to know you, too, Bigger. I'm sorry we have to part this way. But I'm old, son. I'll be going soon myself . . .'

'I remembered all them questions you asked me . . .'

'What questions?' Max asked, coming and sitting again on the cot.

'That night . . .'

'What night, son?'

Max did not even *know*! Bigger felt that he had been slapped. Oh, what a fool he had been to build hope upon such shifting sand! But he had to *make* him know!

'That night you asked me to tell all about myself,' he whimpered despairingly.

'Oh.'

He saw Max look at the floor and frown. He knew that Max was puzzled.

'You asked me questions nobody ever asked me before. You knew that I was a murderer two times over, but you treated me like a man...'

Max looked at him sharply and rose from his cot. He stood in front of Bigger for a moment and Bigger was on the verge of believing that Max knew, understood; but Max's next words showed him that the white man was still trying to comfort him in the face of death.

'You're human, Bigger,' Max said wearily. 'It's hell to talk about things like this to one about to die...' Max paused; Bigger knew that he was searching for words that would soothe him, and he did not want them. 'Bigger,' Max said, 'in the work I'm doing, I look at the world in a way that shows no whites and no blacks, no civilized and no savages ... When men are trying to change human life on earth, those little things don't matter. You don't notice 'em. They're just not there. You forget them. The reason I spoke to you as I did, Bigger, is because you made me feel how badly men want to live...'

'But sometimes I wish you hadn't asked me them questions,' Bigger said in a voice that had as much reproach in it for Max as it had for himself.

'What do you mean, Bigger?'

'They made me think and thinking's made me scared a little...'

Max caught Bigger's shoulders in a tight grip; then his fingers loosened and Bigger sank back to the cot; but his eyes were still fastened upon Bigger's face. Yes; Max knew now. Under the shadow of death, he wanted Max to tell him about life.

'Mr Max, how can I die!' Bigger asked; knowing as the

words boomed from his lips that a knowledge of how to live was a knowledge of how to die.

Max turned his face from him, and mumbled,

'Men die alone, Bigger.'

But Bigger had not heard him. In him again, imperiously, was the desire to talk, to tell; his hands were lifted in mid-air and when he spoke he tried to charge into the tone of his words what he *himself* wanted to hear, what *he* needed.

'Mr Max, I sort of saw myself after that night. And I sort of saw other people, too.' Bigger's voice died; he was listening to the echoes of his words in his own mind. He saw amazement and horror on Max's face. Bigger knew that Max would rather not have him talk like this; but he could not help it. He had to die and he had to talk. 'Well, it's sort of funny, Mr Max. I ain't trying to dodge what's coming to me.' Bigger was growing hysterical. 'I know I'm going to get it. I'm going to die. Well, that's all right now. But really I never wanted to hurt nobody. That's the truth, Mr Max. I hurt folk 'cause I felt I had to; that's all. They was crowding me too close; they wouldn't give me no room. Lots of times I tried to forget 'em, but I couldn't. They wouldn't let me...' Bigger's eyes were wide and unseeing; his voice rushed on; 'Mr Max, I didn't mean to do what I did. I was trying to do something else. But it seems like I never could. I was always wanting something and I was feeling that nobody would let me have it. So I fought 'em. I thought they was hard and I acted hard.' He paused, then whimpered in confession, 'But I ain't hard, Mr Max. I ain't hard even a little bit ...' He rose to his feet. 'But ... I – I won't be crying none when they take me to that chair. But I'll b-b-be feeling inside of me like I was crying ... I'll be feeling and thinking that they didn't see me and I didn't see them...' He ran to the steel door and caught the bars in his hands and shook them, as though trying to tear the steel from its concrete moorings. Max went to him and grabbed his shoulders.

'Bigger,' Max said helplessly.

Bigger grew still and leaned weakly against the door.

'Mr Max, I know the folks who sent me here to die hated me;

I know that. B-b-but you reckon th-they was like m-me, trying to g-get something like I was, and when I'm dead and gone they'll be saying like I'm saying now that they didn't mean to hurt nobody ... th-that they were t-trying to get something, too ...?'

Max did not answer. Bigger saw a look of indecision and wonder come into the old man's eyes.

'Tell me, Mr Max. You think they was?'

'Bigger,' Max pleaded.

'*Tell* me, Mr Max!'

Max shook his head and mumbled,

'You're asking me to say things I don't want to say ...'

'But I want to *know*!'

'You're going to die, Bigger ...'

Max's voice faded. Bigger knew that the old man had not wanted to say that; he had said it because he had pushed him, had made him say it. They were silent for a moment longer, then Bigger whispered,

'That's why I want to know ... I reckon it's 'cause I know I'm going to die that makes me want to know ...'

Max's face was ashy. Bigger feared that he was going to leave. Across a gulf of silence, they looked at each other. Max sighed.

'Come here, Bigger,' he said.

He followed Max to the window and saw in the distance the tips of sun-drenched buildings in the Loop.

'See all those buildings, Bigger?' Max asked, placing an arm about Bigger's shoulders. He spoke hurriedly, as though trying to mold a substance which was warm and pliable, but which might soon cool.

'Yeah. I see 'em ...'

'You lived in one of them once, Bigger. They're made out of steel and stone. But the steel and stone don't hold 'em together. You know what holds those buildings up, Bigger? You know what keeps them in their place, keeps them from tumbling down?'

Bigger looked at him, bewildered.

'It's the belief of men. If men stopped believing, stopped having faith, they'd come tumbling down. Those buildings sprang up out of the hearts of men, Bigger. Men like you. Men kept hungry, kept needing, and those buildings kept growing and unfolding. You once told me you wanted to do a lot of things. Well, that's the feeling that keeps those buildings in their places...'

'You mean ... You talking about what I said that night, when I said I wanted to do a lot of things?' Bigger's voice came quiet, childlike in its tone of hungry wonder.

'Yes. What you felt, what you wanted, is what keeps those buildings standing there. When millions of men are desiring and longing, those buildings grow and unfold. But, Bigger, those buildings aren't growing any more. A few men are squeezing those buildings tightly in their hands. The buildings can't unfold, can't feed the dreams men have, men like you ... The men on the inside of those buildings have begun to doubt, just as you did. They don't believe any more. They don't feel it's their world. They're restless, like you, Bigger. They have nothing. There's nothing through which they can grow and unfold. They go in the streets and they stand outside of those buildings and look and wonder...'

'B-b-but what they hate me for?' Bigger asked.

'The men who own those buildings are afraid. They want to keep what they own, even if it makes others suffer. In order to keep it, they push men down in the mud and tell them that they are beasts. But men, men like you, get angry and fight to re-enter those buildings, to live again. Bigger, you killed. That was wrong. That was not the way to do it. It's too late now for you to ... work with ... others who are t-trying to ... believe and make the world live again ... But it's not too late to believe what you felt, to understand what you felt...'

Bigger was gazing in the direction of the buildings; but he did not see them. He was trying to react to the picture Max was drawing, trying to compare that picture with what he had felt all his life.

'I always wanted to do something,' he mumbled.

They were silent and Max did not speak again until Bigger looked at him. Max closed his eyes.

'Bigger, you're going to die. And if you die, die free. You're trying to believe in yourself. And every time you try to find a way to live, your own mind stands in the way. You know why that is? It's because others have said you were bad and they made you live in bad conditions. When a man hears that over and over and looks about him and sees that his life *is* bad, he begins to doubt his own mind. His feelings drag him forward and his mind, full of what others say about him, tells him to go back. The job in getting people to fight and have faith is in making them believe in what life has made them feel, making, them feel that their feelings are as good as those of others.

'Bigger, the people who hate you feel just as you feel, only they're on the other side of the fence. You're black, but that's only a part of it. Your being black, as I told you before, makes it easy for them to single you out. Why do they do that? They want the things of life, just as you did, and they're not particular about how they get them. They hire people and they don't pay them enough; they take what people own and build up power. They rule and regulate life. They have things arranged so that they can do those things and the people can't fight back. They do that to black people more than others because they say that black people are inferior. But, Bigger, they say that *all* people who work are inferior. And the rich people don't want to change things; they'll lose too much. But deep down in them they feel like you feel, Bigger, and in order to keep what they've got, they make themselves believe that men who work are not quite human. They do like you did, Bigger, when you refused to feel sorry for Mary. But on both sides men want to live; men are fighting for life. Who will win? Well, the side that feels life most, the side with the most humanity and the most men. That's why ... y-you've got to b-believe in yourself, Bigger ...'

Max's head jerked up in surprise when Bigger laughed.

'Ah, I reckon I believe in myself ... I ain't got nothing else ... I got to die ...'

He stepped over to Max. Max was leaning against the window.

'Mr Max, you go home. I'm all right ... Sounds funny, Mr Max, but when I think about what you say I kind of feel what I wanted. It makes me feel I was kind of right ...' Max opened his mouth to say something and Bigger drowned out his voice. 'I ain't trying to forgive nobody and I ain't asking for nobody to forgive me. I ain't going to cry. They wouldn't let me live and I killed. Maybe it ain't fair to kill, and I reckon I really didn't want to kill. But when I think of why all the killing was, I begin to feel what I wanted, what I am ...'

Bigger saw Max back away from him with compressed lips. But he felt he had to make Max understand how he saw things now.

'I didn't want to kill!' Bigger shouted. 'But what I killed for, I *am*! It must've been pretty deep in me to make me kill! I must have felt it awful hard to murder ...'

Max lifted his hand to touch Bigger, but did not.

'No; no; no ... Bigger, not that ...' Max pleaded despairingly.

'What I killed for must've been good!' Bigger's voice was full of frenzied anguish. 'It must have been good! When a man kills, it's for something ... I didn't know I was really alive in this world until I felt things hard enough to kill for 'em ... It's the truth, Mr Max. I can say it now, 'cause I'm going to die. I know what I'm saying real good and I know how it sounds. But I'm all right. I feel all right when I look at it that way ...'

Max's eyes were full of terror. Several times his body moved nervously, as though he were about to go to Bigger; but he stood still.

'I'm all right, Mr Max. Just go and tell Ma I was all right and not to worry none, see? Tell her I was all right and wasn't crying none ...'

Max's eyes were wet. Slowly, he extended his hand. Bigger shook it.

'Good-bye, Bigger,' he said quietly.

'Good-bye, Mr Max.'

Max groped for his hat like a blind man; he found it and

jammed it on his head. He felt for the door, keeping his face averted. He poked his arm through and signaled for the guard. When he was let out he stood for a moment, his back to the steel door. Bigger grasped the bars with both hands.

'Mr Max . . .'

'Yes, Bigger.' He did not turn around.

'I'm all right. For real, I am.'

'Good-bye, Bigger.'

'Good-bye, Mr Max.'

Max walked down the corridor.

'Mr Max !'

Max paused, but did not look.

'Tell . . . Tell Mister . . . Tell Jan hello . . .'

'All right, Bigger.'

'Good-bye !'

'Good-bye !'

He still held on to the bars. Then he smiled a faint, wry, bitter smile. He heard the ring of steel against steel as a far door clanged shut.

All Pan books are available at your local bookshop or newsagent, or can be ordered direct from the publisher. Indicate the number of copies required and fill in the form below.

Send to: **CS Department, Pan Books Ltd., P.O. Box 40, Basingstoke, Hants. RG21 2YT.**

or phone: 0256 469551 (Ansaphone), quoting title, author and Credit Card number.

Please enclose a remittance* to the value of the cover price plus: 60p for the first book plus 30p per copy for each additional book ordered to a maximum charge of £2.40 to cover postage and packing.

*Payment may be made in sterling by UK personal cheque, postal order, sterling draft or international money order, made payable to Pan Books Ltd.

Alternatively by Barclaycard/Access:

Card No.

Signature:

Applicable only in the UK and Republic of Ireland.

While every effort is made to keep prices low, it is sometimes necessary to increase prices at short notice. Pan Books reserve the right to show on covers and charge new retail prices which may differ from those advertised in the text or elsewhere.

NAME AND ADDRESS IN BLOCK LETTERS PLEASE:

....

Name————————————————————————————

Address————————————————————————————

3/87